walking

on

trampolines

walking on trampolines

FRANCES WHITING

GALLERY BOOKS

New York   London   Toronto   Sydney   New Delhi

G

Gallery Books
A Division of Simon & Schuster, Inc.
230 Avenue of the Americas
New York, NY 10020

Originally published in 2013 in Australia by Pan Macmillan Australia Pty Limited.

First Gallery Books trade paperback edition February 2015

GALLERY BOOKS and colophon are registered trademarks of Simon & Schuster, Inc.

For information about special discounts for bulk purchases, please contact Simon & Schuster Special Sales at 1-866-506-1949 or business@simonandschuster.com.

The Simon & Schuster Speakers Bureau can bring authors to your live event. For more information or to book an event, contact the Simon & Schuster Speakers Bureau at 1-866-248-3049 or visit our website at www.simonspeakers.com.

Interior design by Robert E. Ettlin

Manufactured in the United States of America

10 9 8 7 6 5 4 3 2 1

Library of Congress Cataloging-in-Publication Data is available.

ISBN 978-1-4767-8001-6
ISBN 978-1-4767-8002-3 (ebook)

walking
on
trampolines

prologue

His skin.

My fingers could trace the path it has traveled.

Comma-shaped scar on left knee—bike crash, "Red Demon" dragster, 1974; stitches above right eyebrow—surfboard fin chop, Cabarita, 1982; faint outline of navy blue, homemade tattoo on left wrist—high school, my initials.

I know this skin; I know how it feels, I know how it smells, I know every single inch of him.

Joshua Keaton.

He rolls toward me in the ocean of a bed we are lying in at the Hotel du Laurent, restless and hot beneath its cool sheets.

Little waves of nausea tumble through my stomach, and my head aches at each throbbing temple—precursors, I know, to a hangover that could, as Simone would say, fell a buffalo.

I slip out of bed and go to the bathroom to stare raccoon-eyed into the mirror and consider the girl who has done this thing.

There is something caught in my hair, small and rosy and round.

Confetti.

From the church yesterday, where we stood on the cobblestones, surrounded by women in bright dresses and children squeezing through pin-striped legs.

My father had put his hand on my cheek just before we went in. "It will be all right, you know, Lulu," he had said—and it was.

When I entered the church, Josh had turned to look at me, and in that moment it all faded away—the sandalwood candles, the clutches of tiny pink rosebuds tied to the pews—and I was back at the counter of Snow's corner store, where Josh and I stood staring at each other with dumbstruck smiles on our sixteen-year-old faces.

I had walked up the church's aisle on the strength of that look, walked toward Josh determined, from this day forth, for better or worse, to think only about where we were heading, instead of always tugging at every detail of where we had been.

I slide back into the bed and Josh moves toward me, resting his head on my chest, where it rises and falls with my breath, his dark curls caught beneath my fingers, his arms reaching out for me in the half-light, his eyes sleepily opening to widen in horror.

"Lulu," he says, "what the hell?"

He sits bolt upright in the bed and a torrent of swear words fall from his lips, raining down on us like yesterday's confetti.

Because, while I may have woken up in a tangle of just-married sheets beside Joshua Keaton and his all-too-familiar skin, I was not his bride.

chapter one

There is a moment in panic when time stills, suspended like Chinese lanterns across a street, and in that instant you can fool yourself that everything will be all right if you just *stay calm*.

There was a polite knock at the door, a short, sharp rap, like a cough, followed by a series of much louder ones, fists hammering against the wood.

I took Josh, who was flailing around the hotel room and tripping over the white sheet he was holding to his chest as if it could somehow cover what he had done—what we had done—into the bathroom.

"Josh," I said, holding his shoulders and trying to keep him still long enough to look him in the eye, "we've got to stay calm. I'm fairly sure that's Annabelle out there, and we've got to try to explain why you're here before she comes in and rips both our heads off."

Josh's eyes opened wide as the reality of the situation dawned on him.

"Oh, fuck," he said, helpfully.

But it was too late—we both heard the hotel-room door open, and with it, the arrival of Cyclone Annabelle.

I peeped out to see her standing beside a terrified-looking duty manager, clutching a set of master keys in his hand, then shut the bathroom door as quietly as I could.

"Joshua," Annabelle's voice cut across the room, dripping icy courtesy. "Come out of that bathroom now, and Tallulah, could you come out too, please?"

It was the *please* that did it.

I had known Annabelle Andrews since we were just girls. I had seen her angry; I had heard her hiss and steam and yell like a banshee when things had not gone her way; I had seen her weep, knock to the ground a man in a nightclub who had been rude to her, reduce several others to tears. But I had never, ever seen her be polite.

Truly petrified now, I pushed Josh out the door to face her and locked myself in.

In a matter of seconds, after a few muffled shouts and one big bang that must have been the door slamming, it fell silent.

I lay down on the tiled floor, letting its coolness embrace me, and as the hotel room's air-conditioning system buzzed quietly in the background, I closed my eyes and remembered.

Everything.

I was twelve years old when Annabelle Andrews sashayed into my life via my seventh-grade classroom, straight past Sister Scholastica, who was attempting to beam out her usual introduction.

"All right, girls, please meet the latest addition to the Saint Rita's family, Annabelle Andrews, who has come to our lovely Juniper Bay from Sydney, where she— Annabelle, we haven't chosen a seat for you yet."

"That's all right, Sister," Annabelle replied. "I'll just sit here."

Not "May I sit here?" Not "Is there anybody else sitting here?" But "I'll just sit here."

Dropping her books on the desk next to mine, Annabelle grinned from ear to ear, sat down, and claimed me as her own.

"What's your name?" she whispered as Sister Scholastica

flapped around us, clearly upset by this diversion from the usual proceedings.

"Tallulah," I whispered back.

"Tallulah who?"

"De Longland," I answered. "But nobody calls me Tallulah—everyone calls me Lulu."

She never from that moment on called me Lulu; it was always Tallulah. "Tallulah de Longland," she said slowly, ignoring me and letting all the *L*s in my name loll about lazily in her mouth before passing judgment.

"That," she announced, "is a seriously glamorgeous name."

Annabelle liked to hitch parts of words together, hooking them up to form new ones, making her own language. She would eventually allow me to share in this language, and if I came up with a word she particularly liked, she'd exclaim in a mock-English accent, "Tallulah, that's brilltaking!"

Annabelle's language quickly became a way for us to speak to each other that pretty much excluded everybody else—which suited Annabelle just fine.

"After all," as she would tell me again and again as she dragged me away from Stella Kelly and Simone Wilson, who up until Annabelle's arrival had been my closest friends, "why should we waste time with people who are—let's be honest, Tallulah—bordinary?"

At the end of that first morning, during which Annabelle had stood—or rather sat—her ground and refused to budge from her position next to me, it was a done deal, and we were, for better or worse, best friends.

God, I loved her.

She was hilariocious.

I sometimes wonder if Annabelle chose me purely because of my name. Stuffed to its nylon seams with Tracey Stewarts and Lorraine O'Neills, Tallulah de Longland was about as glamorgeous as it was going to get at Saint Rita's School for Young Ladies, or, as Annabelle called it, Saint Rita's School for Young Lesbians.

But choose me, for reasons I could never really understand, she did, and when I first started going to Annabelle's house, in all its glorious mayhem, with her mother Annie's dramatic announcements and her father, Frank, absentmindedly wandering about, I used to worry that it would all be taken away from me.

I thought that Annabelle would open those green cat eyes of hers and see that I didn't belong there.

She would wake up one morning, realize that I was an intruder, and toss me back to the Traceys and Lorraines, where I really belonged. "Oh my God, Tallulah," I imagined she would cry, "I never realized you were so tediocre!"

But she never did, and eventually, somewhere along the journey of our daily walks home, arguing about whose house we would go to, I stopped expecting her to.

Annabelle's house, known throughout the Bay as "the River House," sat guarded by twin gargoyles at its gates, its roof lines slowly disappearing beneath a cloak of intertwining branches, and its garden tumbling all the way down to the river.

"I live in a jungle," Annabelle would sigh dramatically every time we got to her front gate. She was right, but this ignored the fact there was a beautiful, if crumbling, house underneath it, and somewhere within its beehive walls were Annabelle's parents, Frank and Annie.

Everyone knew who they were, of course, the arrival of the Andrews in our small coastal town akin to someone letting out a flock of peacocks on our front lawns. Both well-known artists "from Sydney," everyone kept repeating, as if it were another country, which, I suppose, it may as well have been.

My first visit to the River House was on a Friday afternoon after school, beginning with Frank opening the front door with a flourish and holding out a tray of cakes: "You must be Tallulah," he said. "Come in, come in, I have made you some round lamingtons! What do you think of that?"

What did I think of that?

Lamingtons had always been my favorite cakes, but everyone knew they were square, not round.

Covered in chocolate and coconut and shaped like dice, Frank's version was more like misshapen marbles. My mother, Rose, I thought, would have a fit if she saw them.

I also thought that Frank Andrews was the most wonderful man I had ever met. He was old-school-Hollywood handsome; his face, like all the Andrews men—was a beaten-up road map of deep ruts and jagged edges, crossed tracks and lines like cliff drops falling from cheekbones.

He was tanned walnut brown, long and lean, his sinewy arms and legs always encased in a white Bonds singlet and olive-green shorts, both covered in paint. "If I ever die and leave you destitute, Annie," he'd said one day as we all lay on the grass that tumbled down to the river, "you have my permission to cut off one of my limbs and sell it as a Frank Andrews original."

"Just one, Frank?" Annie had replied.

Frank laughed and pulled the Greek fisherman's cap Annie said was welded to his head over his eyes.

He was beautiful, Frank Andrews, and I think I was probably a little bit in love with him from the moment he opened the door and offered an unsure twelve-year-old the worst lamingtons she had ever tasted in her short life.

We had sat at the table that first afternoon—Frank, Annabelle, and I—eating them, while Annabelle's eyes rolled with every bite and his crinkled at the corners with mischief.

"What? You don't like them, Belle? What do you think, Tallulah de Lovely?"

"I think they're very tasty, Mr. Andrews," I'd said, as Annabelle snorted sarcastically.

Then Frank smiled his wonderful smile at me. "When you're ready," he said, "you can call me Frank."

Whenever I came upon him in that house—and that was how it always felt with Frank, that you didn't so much see him as come upon him unexpectedly—he would always say something that made me feel really good inside; he would call me Tallulah de Lightful or Tallulah de Lovely, and Annabelle would say, "More like Tallulah de Mented," and the three of us would laugh like hyenas.

I suppose I didn't meet Annie that visit, because I should imagine everyone would recall their first brush with Annie Andrews.

Annie, with her burnt-copper hair tangled in bobby pins and scarves. With her scarab beetle brooches and bracelets snaking up her arms. You could, as Annabelle always said, hear Annie long before her actual entrance—and it was always an entrance with Annie, even if she was just returning from the bathroom.

The only quiet thing about Annie was her voice, low and raspy; sometimes to hear it you had to lean right in to her, right in to her Annie-ness.

"Men love it, Lulu," she told me once at the River House, and I had no reason to doubt it. Even if Annie hadn't been with Frank; even if she hadn't married into Australian art royalty, their 1964 wedding making the cover of the *Women's Weekly* under the banner "The Perfect Picture"; even if she hadn't re-created that cover in one of her own paintings, replacing Frank's head with a peacock's and her own with a fishhook, Annie would have found a way to get noticed.

They certainly noticed her in Juniper Bay, where Annie had told the local paper, *The Bayside Bugle*, shortly after they arrived, the family had moved to find some peace and quiet.

"Frank and I need to paint," she'd said. "You can't imagine the incessant demands on our time in the city, the ridiculous things we're asked to join and do.

"We're artists, not public servants, and not everyone seems to be able to grasp that."

I'd read Annie's short interview as eagerly as anyone else in the Bay, including the various members of the art-appreciation societies and galleries who quietly crossed the Andrews off their potential patron lists.

~

"So you went to the Andrews' house?" my father, Harry, had said that night at dinner—a typical feast served up by my mother, Rose: roast lamb, herbed potatoes, butternut pumpkin mash, sweet potato gratin, mint peas, honeyed carrots, bread rolls, butter, and gravy, followed by rhubarb crumble with double cream. ("Honestly, Lulu, it's a wonder you're not gargantormous," Annabelle used to say, "it really is.") I nodded as I swallowed a mouthful of peas.

"And . . ."

"And what?" I said, rolling my eyes in a repeat of Annabelle's performance earlier that afternoon.

"And did they roll you in honey and make you bay at the moon? Did they whisk you away to an opium den? Did they"—Harry gasped—"*pierce your ears?*"

I was the only girl at Saint Rita's whose ears remained bare—Rose would not let me pierce them. "Very funny, Harry," Rose said, coming in with more potatoes, but behind Harry's teasing lay the sort of gossip that had ignited around Juniper Bay ever since the Andrews had turned up like exotic cats on the prowl. It was the most exciting thing that had happened there since a suitcase full of American dollars had washed up on Wattle Beach in the fifties—"Mob money," everyone had said, thrilled at the very sound of the words.

The Andrews were usually described as "Australia's premier artistic family," their branches sprinkled with painters, sculptors, architects, playwrights, and poets. They were famous and infamous at once; people who had never stood before a painting in their entire lives still knew who Annabelle's family was.

Frank's father, "Craggy Jack" Andrews, was one of the world's most respected landscape artists, granted the honor of an Australia Post stamp bearing his image. Annie had famously said to a reporter on his death: "Well, at least we can all still lick the back of his head."

Frank's mother, Christa, still alive, still hurling paint at enormous canvases from rickety ladders in her whitewashed studio, was famous in her own right for her work, and for taking back Craggy Jack time and time again, shamefaced and pinpricked at her door, after one of his frequent disappearances.

Fergus, Frank's older brother, was a documentary filmmaker, a man who traveled the world tracking down rare and endangered species, lost tribes, and—Annie said—loose women.

There was, it seemed, no great affection between Annie and her brother-in-law; Annabelle told me once there had been a flurry of letters between lawyers, and very nearly a court case, when Annie had said to a reporter of Frank's famous brother, "Oh yes, Fergus is marvelous, the way he ventures to those remote, undiscovered places, and impregnates all the women." Frank had made Annie apologize, and it had all blown over, but the following Christmas, according to Annabelle, Fergus sent everyone glass beads from Ghana—except Annie.

Annabelle could imitate Fergus perfectly. I can still see her, squatting in her backyard, staring into a nonexistent camera, saying: "And so to the Wahi-Wahi people—as the sands shift in their drought-ravaged region, where to, for them?" while I howled with laughter on the grass.

There was an entirely different tempo at the Andrews house. Instead of running screaming from one of my twin brothers' endless pranks—fake spiders in our shoes, itching powder in our sleeping bags—Annabelle and I would sit barefoot in the lounge room listening to Frank's record collection: "Now what you can hear in this bit, girls, is Coltrane's three-on-one-chord approach—can you hear that? There!" he'd say, shaking his head back and forth.

Annie would come in with her glass of wine and begin to dance; if Annabelle was in a good mood, she'd join her, and I would sit on the rug drinking them all in, Frank, Annie, and Annabelle, and wonder how I got there.

My own family, by comparison, seemed impossibly dull, something I hadn't really noticed before Annabelle entered the picture. Even Simone and Stella, who I'd known since kindergarten, seemed to fade into the background when she was around; next to her vividness, my oldest friends seemed like sepia cutouts of themselves.

Until the arrival of the Andrews family, my own world had been enough, but in theirs I had glimpsed something completely irresistible—the promise of more. Harry and Rose sensed it too, and after my first visit to Annabelle's house, Rose insisted my new friend come to mine, a prospect I fretted about all week.

But I needn't have worried. Annabelle loved my house from the moment she set foot in it. She loved my parents, and Rose's cooking. She even loved Mattie and Sam, my six-year-old brothers, twin catapults of mischief.

"I want to go to your house, Tallulah, come on, let's go see Harry and Rose," she'd say.

"No, we went there yesterday, and anyway, why can't we go to yours?"

"Because, Tallulah, as you well know, we may not actually be able to find mine."

I never did understand why Annabelle was so keen to come to my house; it seemed so tediocre.

But years later, when I thought of my childhood home, I

would ache for it. I would close my eyes and go back to the street with its hot footpaths and its sprinklers pirouetting on front lawns. I could smell the freshly mown grass and hear my little brothers' voices, yelling for Annabelle and me to come and play with them.

"Hey, Lulu; hey, Annasmell, want to kick the ball around?" I hated them calling Annabelle "Annasmell," but she would just laugh and yell back: "No, thanks, we don't play with mini-minors."

After school, we would walk all along Plantation Street, past the Deans' and the Hunters' and the Delaneys', until we would come to my house—a home that, to my eternal shame, had a huge sign out the front that read: DE LONGLAND PLUMBERS—PLUMBING THE DEPTHS OF EXCELLENCE.

The first time Annabelle saw that sign, I thought she would have a conniptionary.

"Oh my God!" she shrieked. "'Plumbing the depths of excellence,' you have got to be joking, plumbing the depths of . . . oh my God, I'm going to wet my pants."

Finally noticing that I was not laughing quite so hard, she stopped clutching at her stomach, sat down, and said, "Actually, it's really very good."

I sat down beside her in the gutter, and she put her arm around me.

"Tallulah," she said, "I'm not laughing at you. I think that if I needed, you know, some plumbing done, I would want someone who, who, you know, could plumb my excellent depths."

We both burst out laughing, and my shame faded to two bright dots on my cheeks.

Then we went inside, where Rose was waiting for us with afternoon tea, singing to herself and smiling, so everything was all right.

Our house might have looked like every other one on Plantation Street—apart from the fact that ours had boasted a huge sign advertising Harry's plumbing business—but things behind the front fence were a little more complicated.

Rose suffered from anxiety and depression, the anxiety coming in panic attacks that left her backed into a corner with startled eyes, the black dog of depression growling in her ear, leaving her weeping at the kitchen table, her floured hands moving restlessly through her hair, and Harry hovering helplessly nearby.

"Come on, Rosey," he'd say, "buck up—Lulu will make you a nice cup of tea, won't you, love?"

Sometimes it would work, she would look up and wipe her cheeks and say, "I don't know how you put up with me, Harry," but other times she would just sit there, lost, until my father, with his red plumber's hands, would go to her, saying: "I know, love, I know," kissing her hair and trying to find her in his great big arms.

"It's not her fault, Lulu," Harry would say to me, while I stood eight years old and bewildered outside her bedroom door. "She'll come out when she's ready. Let's have a game of Monopoly, hey, just the two of us."

Rose's childhood family, Harry told me, had been broken.

Not strong and steady like ours, he said, but a home full of leaking pipes and creaking floorboards, cold draughts and doors hanging off hinges that no one cared about enough to mend.

A mess, Harry said, just a mess, and when a thirteen-year-old Rose ran away from it, no one came looking for her.

"Just as well," Harry said.

I hated hearing about the house Rose came from, hated the people in it who had not bothered to look for her, hated that something they'd done to her somehow did something to us.

Rose was ultimately placed into a foster home where two middle-aged sisters stood on either side of her at their great wood-burning stove and taught her the secrets of measuring, of timing, of adding just enough butter. They took her hands in their own to stir with a wooden spoon, to ladle, to whisk, to dollop, to ice.

They saved her, she said.

At night the three of them would stand at a long oak table in the living room, spread with paper patterns for Rose to cut out, pins to attach to fabrics, ribbons and buttons to take from jars and sew. They gave her restless hands something to do, and it was there in that house that Rose first began naming her favorite dresses.

"Shirley," she'd said, picking up a polka-dot halter-neck to wear to her first dance; "Maria," she'd announced, taking out the sensible black tunic she wore to work on Saturday mornings in the haberdashery department of David Jones; "Myrtle," she groaned at the pleated white shift the sisters insisted she wear to her weekly tennis lessons.

When I was little, I would steal into her room and peek in the box at the bottom of her wardrobe, where she kept three of her most beloved dresses. Pressed between sheets of white tissue paper lay Audrey and Constance, after the two sisters who had first put a pair of scissors in her hands, and Grace, who she was wearing the first time she met Harry.

I loved Grace—she was buttercup yellow, with a Peter Pan collar and a row of pearl buttons down the front to the waist, which fell into a pin-pleated skirt. Grace had two deep pockets and in one of them, still, a rose-pink handkerchief, with the letter R in the corner, embroidered by one of the sisters. I would take the hanky out and put it to my nose, before folding it carefully and putting it back in the pocket.

It smelled like my mother, when she was happy.

The year I met Annabelle, Rose's wardrobe rustled with Phoebe, Greta, Betty, Alexis, Madeleine, Lauren, and Kitty, perched on their padded hangers like a line of gorgeous chorus girls.

She would wear variations of these dresses for years, changing their styles to suit the decades, but not their names, each becoming as familiar to me as sisters. Only Grace and Audrey and Constance remained untouched and irreplaceable, folded between the layers of tissue paper for little hands to caress and wander over.

I could read Rose's mood by the dress she was wearing: Phoebe and the rest of the girls for good days, a succession of shapeless shifts for the bad. I called the shapeless shifts Doris—I don't remember when I christened them that, I just know that sometimes, when Rose had been sitting at that kitchen table for far too long, it gave me some kind of comfort to say to myself, rocking back and forth on my bed: "It's okay, she's just having a Doris day."

One night, after Annabelle had been at Saint Rita's for a whole term, she asked me to sleep over at the River House, and when I got there I saw that Frank had laid out two sleeping bags on the back lawn, a gas lantern beside them.

"It will be magical, girls, you wait," he'd said, striding back and forth from the house to bring us pillows and books and packets of chips.

We had grumbled, I remember, moaning about mosquitoes and sticks in our bums, but Frank was right.

We lay under a tablecloth of stars thrown across the sky, and later, when the moon rose above us, and the opossums began to scurry along the fence line, we whispered our secrets to each other.

"Dad drinks," Annabelle said, her head on my shoulder.

"I know, I've seen him."

"No, Tallulah, you've seen him drink a glass of wine; sometimes he drinks a lot more than that."

"I didn't know that."

"No. I hate it, so does Mum."

"What does he do?" I whispered, scared of the answer.

"He sings."

"That's not so bad."

"Yes it is, he sings and dances and shouts his stupid poems and grabs at things in the house and goes on and on about them: 'Look at this statue, Belle; look at this flower. . . .'"

"Oh."

"He's embarrassing, Tallulah, he's so . . . much."

"What does your mum do?

"She says, 'You're a fool, Frank,' and goes to bed."

"What do you do?"

"I just wait until he falls over, and then I go to bed as well."

Annabelle wriggled her body beside me, her words coming out in little puffs of frost from her mouth.

"Tallulah," Annabelle said, "why do you call your parents Harry and Rose? I mean, I call mine Frank and Annie because they're—well, they're not your usual sort of parents, are they? But it seems kind of weird that you do."

I turned my body toward her, so we lay facing each other, our heads close, and explained that I didn't have the usual sort of parents either.

I told her about Rose's depression, and about how she had never really been—apart from the baking, that is—a "mother" type of mother, especially after the twins came, when she had stopped being any sort of mother at all for a long time.

I told how I had looked after the twins myself—how Harry and I had—and how it was around that time that I started calling her Rose, and how my father became Harry by default.

Then I took a deep breath and told her about my mother's wardrobe.

"Rose names her dresses."

"What?"

"She names them, all of them."

I told her about all the girls—Phoebe and Kitty and Greta—and about how Rose gave them each personalities, stories about where they had come from and what they had seen.

I told her and waited, eyes closed, for her judgment.

"Wow," she breathed, "that's really astoundible."

Our breath danced in the night air.

"So," she said, snuggling into me, "who do you like the best?"

Saint Rita's had a courtyard right in the middle of it, and in the middle of that stood a huge macadamia tree with fading colored benches at angles beneath it for rumpled tunics to sit on.

"Meet you at the tree," girls would say to each other, and if anything was going to happen at Saint Rita's, it was going to happen under those branches.

I was sitting on one of the benches waiting for Annabelle between classes one day when two pairs of stocking-clad legs stood in front of me.

Stacey Ryan and Jacki Goldsmith.

The Piranha Sisters.

"Hi, Lulu," Stacey said.

"Hi, Lulu," Jacki echoed.

I looked at their feet.

"So," said Stacey, "I was wondering if you could help me with a little problem I've got.

"The thing is," she said, "I'm going to this party on the weekend, and I was thinking of wearing Lucy, but then I thought maybe Amanda would be better, you know, because she's so much fun, but Jacki thinks maybe I should wear Ashley because she gets so jealous if I leave her behind . . ."

It took me a minute to digest what they saying, a minute to

understand that she was making fun of my mother, and another minute to wonder who had told her.

Stacey was still talking, saying. "What do you think, Tallulah, who should I choose?"

I stared at her, knowing that by the end of the lunch hour, the whole school would know about my family, know all about my mad mother and her chorus line of dresses and her weepy, floury hands.

"Stacey," I said, "my mum, she's really great most of the time but—"

A blur of chocolate pleats and olive-brown arms pinned Stacey against the tree. Annabelle Andrews, green eyes flashing.

"Actually, Stacey," she said, "Tallulah's mother's got a name for you too."

"Really?" Stacey challenged.

"Yeah," said Annabelle, "it's Stupid Fucking Bitch."

Stacey struggled beneath Annabelle's grasp while beside me Jacki just shifted her feet, opening and closing her mouth like a demented salmon.

"And if you ever," Annabelle hissed in Stacey's ear, "say anything to anyone about this, I will shove your arse clean through your ears, do you understand?"

Stacey nodded, bit her lip.

"Right," said Annabelle, letting her go. "Glad that's sorted."

Then she took my hand and led me away.

~

"'Shove your arse clean through your ears'?" I said. "'*Shove your arse clean through your ears*'? Bloody hell, Annabelle, what are you? One of the Kray brothers?"

We were at my house later that day, replaying what had happened: I was doing my Jacki demented-fish imitation, and Annabelle was rolling on my bed laughing.

It had taken us about two minutes of detective work to suspect that Mattie and Sam had told Jacki's little brother, Marcus, about Rose, and then it had taken ten cents each to get them to admit it.

Later that night, I thought about Annabelle, appearing like an avenging angel in a pleated tunic and how I had never, not even for one second, thought it could have been her who had spilled my family's particular brand of beans.

"Swear," she had said that night under the stars.

"I swear I will never tell about Frank," I said. "Your turn."

"I swear I will never tell about Rose," she echoed. "Now choose."

Annabelle said we had to each pick one star out of the sky and make our vow upon it.

"Right," she said, pointing at the sky, "see that little one right there, there near the Big Dipper, that sort of fuzzy-looking one? That's mine."

I pointed to another.

"Mine," I said.

"Okay," said Annabelle, "now hold my hands."

We had knelt toward each other on the damp grass that night, locked eyes, and promised we would never betray each other.

I had felt her hands digging into mine, closed my eyes, and meant it.

I never really considered that one day it would all change, that it was in fact changing right beneath our feet as we walked back and forth to each other's houses.

Little ripples were forming below the concrete that would eventually split and divide us like the tectonic plates they taught us about in Geography. I had no idea about those cracking, shifting plates beneath us; I didn't even feel them moving.

chapter two

"Housekeeping."

So this was it, then.

I could not spend the rest of my life lying on the tiled floor of the Hotel du Laurent's bathroom, I could not put the DO NOT DISTURB sign on the door and live out the remainder of my years there, becoming one of those urban legends people talk about at dinner parties—"the Woman in Room Fourteen."

I would have to get up, get dressed, and get used to the new me, the one who apparently thought it was acceptable to wake up with someone else's groom after their wedding night.

Oh God.

"Just a minute," I called out, grabbing at a dressing gown on a hook, knotting it at my waist, and making my way out of the bathroom and across the debris of the room.

I opened the door to the smiling face of a woman in her sixties who reminded me of Rose, soft and plump and carrying a pile of fresh white towels in her outstretched hands.

"Housekeeping," she said again. "Is now a good time or would you like me to come back later?"

I looked at the shipwrecked room around me—*What must these people think of us?* I thought. "Would you mind giving me a bit longer?" I asked her, my voice like smashed glass.

"I can come back in an hour or so," she said, still smiling, before adding, "You all right, dear? You look like you've seen a ghost."

"I'm fine, thanks," I answered, and wondered how she knew, wondered how long I had lain on that floor, half awake and half dreaming, visited by the ghosts of a decade's childhoods past.

I shut the door behind her and began to automatically gather up my belongings, picking up shoes, folding clothes, and finding some small comfort in the routine of it.

As long as I kept methodically putting things away, I could pretend that this was just another morning after the night before, but of course it wasn't.

The room was an unholy mess, clothes strewn from one end to another, the exquisite dress my mother had made me to wear to the wedding a discarded heap on the floor.

I could hardly bear to look at it. Rose had, I knew, taken so much care with it, and now it lay rumpled, a small tear, I noticed, on its hem.

Any comfort I felt vanished.

I had taken something beautiful and tarnished it.

I had ruined it.

I had ruined everything.

I understood that from the moment I had woken up with Joshua Keaton beside me.

I picked up Rose's dress and buried my face deep within its silky folds, feeling its coolness against my hot cheeks.

Rose.

What would my mother think of me?

What would my father think of me?

What would Frank and Annie think of me?

And Annabelle?

What would she think of me?

I began to pack frantically, tossing clothes into my suitcase, suddenly desperate to get out of the room, where no amount of tidying up and cleaning could erase what I thought of me.

What had Annabelle said, about leaving your mark in life?

As I sat down on the bed the past rushed back to reclaim me once more, and to remind me of all that I had left behind.

~

For Annabelle's thirteenth birthday, Fergus sent her a Swiss Army knife, and the most impressive thing about it was that it really was from Switzerland, while all the boys we knew only owned ones that came from Snow's corner store, three streets away.

"Wow," I said, sitting on her bed and looking at its red, shiny sides and smooth, white cross. "What can you do with it?"

She flicked open one of its attachments. "This one," she said, "is for filing your nails." She flicked open another. "This one's for when you go camping and forget to take your can opener, and this one"—she flicked up a long, sharp blade—"is for cutting you from ear to ear if you ever go to the movies with Simone and Stella without me again. Joking." She smiled at my stricken face.

Even now, all these years later, I'm not so sure she was.

What she did use that blade for was to carve an intertwined AA and *TDL* on the underside of our kitchen table, gouging our initials deep into the wood while I listened out for Rose, so she could quickly put the penknife in her lap and say, "Great scones, Mrs. de Longland."

It was, she said, whittling away at the pine, verilitaly important to leave your mark in life, but I could have told her, even then, that she didn't need an engraving to do that.

~

In the summer that we both turned fourteen, Frank gave us a gift.

"Frank's building us a tree house," I told Rose one afternoon after school. "He says that now that we are turning into young ladies"—I giggled—"we need a place of sanctuary."

Rose sat down and pushed a plate of Iced VoVos toward me.

I'd always loved those biscuits, with their sickly sweet strawberry and vanilla icing, and Rose would occasionally buy me a packet, in our house store-bought biscuits a rare treat among her home-baked goodies.

She was wearing Greta, a striped pink-and-white seersucker smock dress, and looking not unlike an Iced VoVo herself.

I giggled again.

Rose smiled at me: "What are you laughing at?"

"You," I smiled. "You look a bit like one of those biscuits, Rose."

Rose looked at the plate.

"And you"—she smiled—"look like a Tim Tam."

We both glanced down at the dark chocolate layers of my Saint Rita's School for Young Lesbians uniform and laughed.

"What's this I hear about Frank Andrews building you girls a tree house?" Harry said, home from work and looking for something to eat.

"Harry—tools," Rose said automatically, gesturing outside and shaking her head as he picked up his toolbox from the floor. "I don't know how many times I have asked your father not to bring his tools into the house," Rose said. "*Harry*, boots!"

Harry stood in the doorway, looking down at his feet.

"Sorry, love," he said, walking back outside again.

Rose and I smiled at each other across the table.

"So," Harry said, returning barefoot and pulling up a chair, "what about this tree house?"

"Frank's going to build us one," I replied. "He says that now that we are growing up, Annabelle and I need a place we can escape to—Frank says everyone needs a place they can escape to."

"You're telling me." Harry smiled. "When do I move in?"

"Sorry, Harry," I said, "it's just for me and Annabelle, it's going to be amazible."

"Is that right?" Harry said. "I might have to take a look at it myself, see if Frank needs any help with the plumbing—surely this extravaganza is going to have hot and cold running water for you girls, isn't it?" he teased.

"It's going to have everything," I said. "Annie's calling it Frank's Folly."

"Well, she'd know all about that," Rose said, biting into a biscuit.

Sometimes Greta could be a real bitch.

But it wasn't just Rose's skin Annie Andrews got under; it seemed the whole of Juniper Bay was unsettled by her—and they didn't even know the whole story, as I came to.

Long before Frank, Annie Andrews had been Anne Grunker, a name, she told me, she so hated that, from the moment she was first forced to write it with her pudgy five-year-old fingers, she had become determined to shed it.

At school she had insisted that her increasingly bewildered mother, Ruth, label all her schoolbooks ANNE G., and at seventeen she had met a beautiful but stupid Italian boy called Roman Barantis, a name Annie found so entrancing, she married it.

And when she walked out on her first marriage a full six weeks later, Anne Barantis left with nothing but the newspaper off the front step, and her husband's name.

Both would prove helpful in Annie's new world.

In the paper she would find an advert for artists' models wanted at the Cove studios, and years later Mick Porter, who would become world famous for his *Cove Nudes* series, would recall the moment when six-foot Annie Barantis walked in, dropped her green velvet cloak, and perched her dimpled bottom on the stool.

He had, he later recalled, turned to his students and announced: "Ladies and gentlemen, Eve has entered the garden."

Annie's new name made her daring. Annie Barantis said things and did things that Anne Grunker would never have contemplated, including attending a barbecue at Mick Porter's one October afternoon, where she met a well-oiled Frank Andrews.

The *Weekly* would trill in the story that accompanied the wedding cover: "It was a meeting of the minds and the hearts, as Annie and Frank bonded over Mick Porter's famous king-prawn shish kebabs and Carole King's infectious hits from *Tapestry*."

Annie, however, had her own version: "We got completely pissed, shagged each other senseless on Mick's couch, and moved in together the next day."

And for a long time, the union of Frank and Annie Andrews was a successful one

Frank, always slightly troubled in some way, like a ripple on a perfectly still lake, became, everyone said, steadier, and when Annabelle was born two years after the wedding he was, as he'd say himself, "skyrocket happy."

"I picked you up, and you were like a little pink crumpled starfish," he liked to tell Annabelle over and over again. "I told you, 'It's all right, little one, I am yours.'"

And he was, which was just as well, because, despite wearing the stamp of her mother's name, Annabelle was never really Annie's.

"I don't think I was cut out to be a mother," Annie said once during a radio interview we had all listened to in the River House's cavernous lounge room. "I never really wanted to be one, not like some women, you know, breasts leaking at the very sight of a baby. But for me, the really surprising part is how fond I've grown of her over the years. I don't know if you'd call it motherly love, but it's fierce enough, I think, to be."

On hearing this, Annabelle had walked out of the room and slammed the door. Annie had stood up, sighed, and called after her: "I said fierce, Belle, fierce."

⁓

"American Oregon," Frank announced, "Californian softwood—nothing fancy, nothing posh, just good to work with, flexible, gives you what it has to."

He ran his hands along the wood as Annabelle and I exchanged glances, then smiles.

"But the beauty of this particular timber is that it's also really hardy, able to withstand all sorts of weather, all sorts of conditions, all sorts of assaults on it—even from two teenage girls." He grinned.

We were sitting on a benchtop in Frank's shed, swinging our legs and watching him through the tiny particles of dust that hovered in the air.

"So"—Frank clapped his hands together, making the dust dance—"it is with this wood that I intend to build your tree house, girls, and not just any old tree house either. Now, allow me to show you where it shall stand," he said, opening the door with a flourish.

Leading us out into the backyard, whistling and holding up branches to duck under as he went, Frank stopped at a mango tree at the broken fence line, pregnant with fruit.

"You've got to be kidding, Dad," Annabelle said. "What about the opossums? What about the bats?"

The three of us stood beside the tree, Annabelle and I looking uncertainly up into its shadowy green and black branches.

"Don't worry about that, Annabelle." Frank grinned. "What about the *mangoes*?"

In Frank's hands the tree house grew into a strange, wild nest, springing, it seemed, from the branches themselves, spreading across the breadth of the tree and reaching upward to where the sun peeked through the crescent moon and star shapes he had cut out of its walls.

It was, of course, a work of art—a Frank Andrews original, off-limits to everyone but Annabelle and me.

"We'll need a table."

"Mmm-mmm, and two chairs."

"And some shelves, for our things."

"And some candles."

"Rose won't let me have candles."

"What are you, Tallulah, six years old?"

"I'm just saying, Rose won't like me having candles up here."

"Will she know?"

"No."

"Well then—candles, and definitely food."

"Okay—chocolate, obviously, and some chips."

"Mmm, and lollies— some mint leaves, milk bottles . . ."

"What about rats?"

Annabelle looked at me. "Well, I won't be eating them, Tallulah, but if you really want some . . ."

Our laughter hooted down through the branches.

It was, just as Frank had said, a sanctuary, the perfect place for Annabelle and me to escape to after school, slip away past the knots of boys from Saint Joseph's who had started calling out our names when we walked past, the tectonic plates beginning to shift beneath our feet as our training bras itched beneath our tunics.

We were, as Sister Scholastica beamed at us in Social Instruction, "blossoming into womanhood, flowering," she said, "into perfect, young blooms," while rows of girls sat with shaking shoulders desperately trying not to laugh, especially when she warned us of the dangers of "pollination."

"There will be bees," she warned, while Annabelle moaned beside me in quiet hysteria, "and they will try to take your nectar."

"Oh dear God in heaven," Simone muttered from the row behind us.

Sister Scholastica's "There will be bees" speech was destined to go down in Saint Rita's history, year after year of giggling schoolgirls able to recite it long after its creator had gone to meet hers.

But whenever I looked at our class photo from that year, I could see that Sister Scholastica's horticultural homilies, however disturbing, were right—row upon row of girls with untouched faces, bright eyes, lovely smiles, like a garden.

Like Annabelle.

She was in the back row, her height dictating this position in each year's Saint Rita's snapshot, standing, as always, a little bit apart from everyone else, as if she had wandered accidentally into the frame. Her hands were resting loosely on her hips, her shoulders tilted back, her head tilted forward, her green cat eyes staring directly into the lens. Her lips were plum red and unsmiling, but turned up slightly at the corners, and I wondered if she had been making an effort, thinking of Annie's words when we'd left that morning: "Try to smile in this year's photo, darling, I would like one photo of you at school that doesn't look like you're an inmate on death row."

Her hat was tipped back on her head, her uniform slightly rumpled, and her tie hung loosely around her neck, transgressions she would be in trouble for later.

She had Frank's olive skin and Annie's wild curls, not red, like her mother's, but dark brown, and whenever I looked at her in that photo, I thought of Sister Scholastica's "perfect young blooms" and wondered how I ever thought I stood a chance.

Simone and Stella were there too—Simone, with the long dark braids she would cut off the moment she finished school, staring straight at the camera with a penetrating look television viewers would come to know years later, and Stella, plump and lovely, also staring at the camera, but with an eager smile and a PREFECT badge pinned to her chest.

I was, as always, front and center, holding up a chalkboard with our class name and year written on it, looking, as always, slightly embarrassed to be doing it. I was there because I was tiny, the shortest girl in the class, relegated to this position because I was also the neatest.

No rumpled uniform for me, no messy hair or loosened tie, Rose had primped me and starched me to within an inch of my life: two long, perfect golden braids with chocolate-brown ribbons framed my face, my smile was wide and toothy, a smattering of freckles bridged my nose, and my eyes stared straight into the lens, as chocolate brown as my uniform.

Years later, in grade twelve, Joshua Keaton would demand to see my grade-eight school pictures, study this photo, and declare I look like a Crunchie bar.

"Makes me want to eat you all up" he would say, and I would take those chocolate ribbons out of my hair, and let him.

There was a soft knock at the door just as I finished packing.

I opened it to the smiling woman with the cleaning trolley who asked, "Did you have a good time, love?" I had absolutely no idea how to answer that question.

Instead, I smiled back and asked her if she would like the magazines I'd brought with me.

Shutting the door behind me, I scurried to the lift, head down, praying that no one from the wedding would see me, almost breaking into a sprint past the dining room where a celebratory after-wedding breakfast had been planned.

There was no one there of course, there was nothing to celebrate and nobody would have been able to stomach anything, much less eggs.

The lift door opened and my hands shook as I pressed the

button for the car park. I closed my eyes until the lift door opened again, then I half walked, half jogged to the car, my suitcase bumping behind me. By the time I got in I was crying hot, plump tears and wondering where I should go.

Not home, not yet.

I thought of Simone and Stella—the only two people I knew who had not been at the wedding and who might understand what I had done.

Somehow, I had managed to stay friends with them all through high school and long afterward, when Simone had changed her last name to Severet and become the poster girl for lesbians, and Stella had changed her name by marriage to McNamara and become the poster girl for Catholics.

We had remained close despite my defection to Annabelle, whom neither of them had been particularly fond of, and understandably so. Annabelle didn't like me to stray too far from her side—if I went anywhere with Simone and Stella, she would sulk for days; if I wanted to go home alone, spend time with my family without her, she would turn up on our doorstep half an hour later anyway; if I went shopping without her, she would hate what I bought and demand I return it so she could help me choose something else.

On my sixteenth birthday, which Rose had insisted I celebrate with Annabelle, Stella, and Simone, the four of us sat in my bedroom, where Annabelle demanded I unwrap my present before anyone else's. It was a photo in a wooden frame of the two of us, arms linked, looking up at the camera with huge grins on our faces, and engraved on frame were three words: *Best Friends Forternity.*

"Forternity," Annabelle told Simone and Stella sweetly, "is Tallulah's and my word we made up together. It's a cross between *forever* and *eternity*, and it's actually stronger than both of them.

So," she added brightly, "what did you two get her—some lipstick, I suppose?"

Sometimes the intensity of her friendship felt suffocating, like I couldn't really breathe properly when she was around.

But even Annabelle's sometimes overwhelming attentions did not prepare me for the onslaught that was Joshua Keaton.

chapter three

The bell above the door to Snow's corner store tinkled as I led Mattie and Sam inside and let them loose to ricochet like pinballs through the store.

"Behave," I said, "or I won't buy you a treat."

They raced over to the cabinet so they could spend an inordinate amount of time discussing the various merits of the raspberry versus lime Popsicle, and were opening and closing its glass cover so all the cold air could escape when I felt a shimmer of heat beside me.

Sky-blue T-shirt; long, lean body tapering down to navy shorts; brown arms leaning on the glass.

He smiled, pushing a mess of dark curls from his forehead, flicking his eyes over the three of us before his gaze came to rest on mine.

"So," he said, "see anything you like?"

The question filled the air between us and hovered there until Mattie announced informatively, "She's not allowed to have any ice cream, she's on a diet."

Sam nodded. "A massive one," he added helpfully.

The boy in the sky-blue T-shirt laughed and said, "Really? She looks just about perfect to me."

And that was it, Joshua Keaton and I had met, and the heat between us just about melted every ice cream in the cabinet. "I'm

Josh," he said, his eyes, dark and flecked, still locked on mine. "What's your name?"

"Tallulah . . . Lulu."

"Well, Tallulah-Lulu"—he smiled—"I'll see you around."

Then he left, Snow's bell signaling his departure.

"Ha-ha, you said your name was Tallulah-Lulu." Mattie grinned.

"Shut up, Mattie," I said, leading them both to the counter.

"Lulu's got a boyfriend, Lulu's got a boyfriend," Sam chanted, dancing around me, and right at that moment, Josh walked back in.

"Are they right?" He grinned. "Have you got a boyfriend?"

"No," I said.

"Do you want one?"

Later on, after Josh talked his way into walking us home, wheeling his bike beside us, and further talked his way inside our house, where he charmed Rose by inhaling a plate of her macaroons and impressed Harry by knowing what a snake pipe was, he asked me again.

"So, Tallulah-Lulu," he drawled, a tiny dimple dancing on his right cheek, "do you want a boyfriend? Because I could be interested in applying."

I giggled—at the inanity of his line, at him, at us, at me, standing in the kitchen of my house with the most beautiful boy I had ever seen.

"I'm serious," he said.

Then he put one finger on my lips, leaned in, and kissed me.

Mattie and Sam were playing *Star Wars* outside on the lawn, Harry and Rose were somewhere upstairs, and I was leaning back against the table, eyes closed while Josh's fingers trailed down my neck, brushed against my shoulders, touched my face.

His hand cupped my cheek as he pulled me toward him, his kiss growing deeper, and I don't know how long it went, that first kiss, but I do know that his hands and mouth and tongue made every inch of my pure, untouched, Catholic girl's skin want to be pollinated right there and then on Rose's laminated benchtop.

Later that day, when all the mothers were out on their lawns calling their children inside, their singsong chorus of "Cait-lin," "Aman-da," "Chris-topher" signaling the end of play, he stood on my front step and said, "Well, did I get the job?"

I nodded my head.

"Excellent," he said, turning to walk down the path and pick up his bike from its resting place behind Harry's plumbing sign.

"So I'll see you tomorrow," he yelled, and disappeared down the street.

I watched him go and could not believe my luck.

Lying awake that night I thought about how strange it was that the evening before I had gone to bed a girl who had never had a boyfriend, or even been kissed. Now I apparently had a boyfriend, I was a girl who had been kissed, and I knew, despite my complete lack of previous experience, properly.

I smiled in the darkness, thinking of my family at dinner that night.

Harry teasing, "Tallulah Keaton, nice ring to it, love."

Rose worrying: "Don't be silly, Harry, they've only just met."

And the boys rhythmically chanting, "Lulu and Josh, sitting in a tree, K–I–S–S–I–N–G!" and pounding their fists on the kitchen table until Rose told them she'd tie them to that tree if they didn't desist.

Annabelle had rung earlier, but I'd asked Rose to tell her I was already in bed, not wanting to share Josh with her just yet. I could not, I knew, keep Josh a secret from Annabelle forever; it was in every way impossible.

I closed my eyes, wrapped my arms around my waist, and

thought that if I really did have a boyfriend, if *Joshua Keaton*—I hugged his name to me—was my boyfriend, then I would just have to find a way to fill in all the spaces between him and Annabelle, to be enough for both of them.

~

"No way!" Annabelle shrieked, walking to school the next day. "So you're standing in Snow's and this guy just wanders in and asks you to be his girlfriend? You cannot be serious, Tallulah! What's his name?"

I hesitated before I answered her, wanting to keep everything about him to myself for just a moment longer.

"Joshua Keaton," I said, and waited.

I could not bear it if she made fun of it in some way, turned the letters of his name around or gave him a nickname that would make me wince every time I heard it.

I could not bear it if she spoiled him for me.

"Joshua Keaton," she announced, "sounds completely intrigivating—now tell me every single detail of what happened, I want to know all about him."

Relieved she had not mocked, I told her all I had learned about Joshua Keaton, which was not very much, snatches of information sandwiched in between Mattie's and Sam's romping, Rose's baked-goods offerings, Harry's car talk—"What do you think of the new Holden, Josh?"—and kissing.

I knew that he was seventeen, that he lived two suburbs away with his mother, Pearl—no mention of a father—and that he had gone to Ralston Road High School, but had left the year before to do a mechanic's apprenticeship.

I knew he loved surfing, had a part-time job at DNA Motors, which he liked, working for a man called Mel, whom he did not.

That was about the sum total of what I knew about Joshua Keaton when I was walking to school with Annabelle that morning.

But later, as the days turned into weeks, and weeks turned into six months after the day we met, and he used a penknife and a blue pen to tattoo my initials on his wrist to mark the occasion—Harry calling him a "silly bugger" when he saw it—I could have told her so much more.

I could have told her he was five foot eleven and three-quarter inches tall, that the missing quarter inch drove him to distraction, that he had a shock of white hair beneath all those curls, but you had to lift his hair at the nape of his neck to find it; I could have told her he couldn't whistle.

I could have told her he loved the Saint Kilda Football Club, Saint Bernard dogs, Vietnamese egg noodles with anything, being kissed on his back, the break at Duranbah, and Deborah Harry—"The second sexiest woman on earth, Tallulah-Lulu."

I could have told her his father had left to join the merchant navy three weeks after Josh was born, and that the first time he got drunk he'd tried to call him on the HMAS *Melbourne*, shouting down the phone at the operator that it was a matter of national security he be put through to Davie Keaton, and that when she hung up on him, he had sat on a swing in Ralston Park and wept.

I could have told her that when he told me that story and cried, it looked like he was raining inside.

I could have told her he had double-jointed thumbs, that when he was thirteen he had written a letter to the motor racing champion Peter Brock asking to be his codriver, and that he had slept with the signed photo that arrived in answer under his pillow for weeks.

I could have told her that he tasted like almonds and smelled like lemons and that the softest place on his skin was everywhere.

I didn't tell her those things, but in the end, it didn't matter—she found it all out herself.

I arranged for them to meet for the first time at Wattle Beach, away from Harry's and Rose's or Frank's and Annie's curious eyes. It was hot, one of those days when the road shimmers at your feet and your shoulders are pink even before the sun hits them.

I was nervous, uneasiness pecking at my skin, and Annabelle took my arm and said, "For God's sake, Lulu, will you relax? I'm not going to eat him."

We were walking down the green-tinged concrete steps to the beach when I felt her shift beside me, her fingers pressing down slightly on my wrist.

"Is that him?"

Josh, running through the last of the curling waves, long limbs negotiating a path past little kids on surf mats and mothers with babies on their hips, board tucked under his arm, drops of water catching in his curls, then smiling beside us, as he dropped his board.

"Hey, Tallulah-Lulu," he said, ducking his head to brush his saltwater lips on mine. "How's my girl?"

He shook his whole body, large wet droplets diving off his skin, and lifted his chin toward Annabelle.

"Hey," he said.

That was it, and there was nothing in that moment, in that first meeting—in all the times I replayed it later, when it mattered—that shouted a warning to me, nothing that said he is kissing you and drinking her in, nothing that whispered in my ear to be careful.

It was just the three of us, laughing and talking and finding room for one another on our towels under a perfect sun.

That summer, when I was sixteen, Josh claimed my family as his own, helping the boys build their infamous exploding volcano in the backyard—rocks, mud, sand, sticks, a hose, and a whole lot of trouble—holding the ladder steady for Harry as he cleaned the gutters in the roof; sitting, elbows down, at Rose's kitchen table, chin poised on his clasped hands underneath, huge smile dimpling at his cheeks, waiting to be fed.

Rose had said we could see each other only one night a week during school term, and on weekends after I had done my studying.

She told Josh it was important that I do well, that I didn't need any distractions—Josh, of course, being the distraction. He had smiled and nodded and continued to turn up at our house most nights just before dinnertime anyway.

Rose would hear the bike creaking up the grass and the gate click, and would roll her eyes at me and sigh, but both Josh and I knew there was no way in the world she would turn away a hungry boy from her table.

"Does your mother know you're here?" she would ask, and Josh would nod because it was easier to do that than to explain that Pearl Keaton would barely have looked up from her ciggies and her crosswords for long enough to notice he was gone.

Pearl lived in a veil of smoke, sitting on her couch, her crossword puzzles spread out on the table with its ringed coffee cup stains and a bottle-green glass ashtray brimming with butts in front of her.

"Hello, darl," she'd say when Josh led me by the hand past her up to his room. "You two behave yourselves up there!"

I would feel Josh wince beside me, wince at his mother's crassness, her carelessness, the knot of her dressing gown loose, her feet encased in giant puppy-dog slippers.

"Why didn't get you dressed, Mum?" Josh would ask. "You knew Tallulah was coming."

"Well, excuse me, Peter Prissy," she'd say. "You don't mind, do you, love?" and I'd shake my head, embarrassed for all of us.

Pearl worked as a cashier at the TAB, had one friend called

Caroline she went to the local football club with every Friday night, worked split shifts to put a roof over her son's head, and told him that when his father, Davie Keaton, had gone to sea, it was no great loss.

Maybe it wasn't, but when I saw the way Josh was with my parents, the way he sat at our table and drank in Harry's words, I wondered.

I didn't like going to Pearl Keaton's, didn't like the lies I had to tell Harry and Rose to get there.

I hated the shut-in rooms and the stained linoleum, the inevitable tussle on Josh's bed once we climbed the stairs to his room while he grappled with my clothes and I grappled with my Catholic sensibilities.

It seems faintly ridiculous now, but it was 1982, I was a sixteen-year-old Catholic schoolgirl, and every time Josh touched me, somewhere in the back of my mind was Eve giving Adam that damn apple and cursing humankind for all eternity.

I was scared of sinning, worried Josh would no longer be interested in me if I let him go "all the way," afraid I would fall pregnant and have to move away like Lisa Fitzgerald, banished to a grandmother in outback Longreach, her baby stowed away in the car like a fugitive.

"You don't," mothers up and down every street in our neighborhood told their daughters, "want to end up like Lisa Fitzgerald," as if the direst thing in the world had happened to her, that she had caught leprosy or had been sold into white slavery.

I thought about Lisa, a vague imprint of a tall girl with glasses and a hooting laugh, and wondered how she did "end up." I wondered if she knew she was the poster girl for celibacy at Saint Rita's and that I thought of her every time Josh reached for me.

I would be wrapped around him, our limbs as close as crossed fingers, torn between wanting him and the knowledge that good girls didn't do this kind of thing and bad girls got sent to Longreach.

~

"Oh for God's sake," Annabelle said to me one morning, "all this puffing and panting is nauseating, why don't you just have sex with him and be done with it?"

"I just don't want to yet."

"Why? It's really no big deal."

"Annabelle, I really wish you'd stop going on about this—why is so important to you anyway?" I asked. "You haven't even had sex yet."

"Oh, yes, I have, and let me tell you, it's really nothing to write homosapien about."

"You've had sex?"

"Yes."

"Who with?"

"Mark Morris."

"You've had sex with Mark Morris?"

"Yep, in his car."

"You had sex with Mark Morris in his car?" I didn't even know she knew Mark Morris, the vice captain of the Saint Joseph's rugby team, save for occasionally saying, "Get stuffed, Mark" when he called out something stupid when we walked past.

"Look, Tallulah," she said, "as much as I'd like to stand around while you repeat everything I say, I've actually got some homework to do."

We kept walking down the street together, but now Annabelle was doing this weird, exaggerated sashay, sort of swishing her hips and swinging her schoolbag in front of me, like a pendulum.

I kept my head down and stared at the footpath, confusion prickling at my body and, for some reason I could not understand, tears gathering deep in my lids, hot and salty and childish.

Annabelle could swing her bag all she liked and pretend that this was just another conversation on our way home, but she knew and I knew that it wasn't.

We kept walking in silence until she stopped, put her bag down, and said, "Why are you carrying on about this?"

"I'm not carrying on, I haven't said a thing."

"Presactly, Tallulah. Look, I don't have to tell you every little thing that happens in my life, do I? I'm sure you don't tell me *every* detail of what goes on between you and Josh."

I kept my head down, afraid to look at her, this new Annabelle who had not only had sex but had also started to keep secrets from me.

We came to the corner where we usually had our "Your house or mine?" conversation and I headed straight for home without her, and straight to my room.

"Lulu," Rose called out, "aren't you coming downstairs? There's fruit and cookies on the table," but I buried my head in my pillow and knew I couldn't eat a thing.

That night, Josh took me to the movies in a borrowed car.

Coming home, we pulled over on the street next to mine and he started kissing me, tugging at my jeans and pulling my belt loose.

"Don't, Josh," I said.

"Why not, Tallulah-Lulu?" he mumbled, face in my hair.

"I'm just not ready."

"Jesus, Lulu." He let out a long sigh. "What's wrong this time?"

"Nothing's wrong, Josh, I just don't want to."

Drumming the steering wheel with his fingers, Josh said, "Well, when are you going to want to?"

"I don't know," I answered. "Stop asking me all the time."

He ran his hands through his hair. "There's lots of girls I could ask, you know."

"Fine," I snapped, opening the door. "Ask one of them, then."

"Maybe I will," he said, as I slammed the door behind me, and Josh drove off, and I stood there wondering if that was the end of us, if we would finish as quickly as we had started.

But Josh came over the next morning with a bunch of carnations he'd bought at the service station on the way and said he was sorry.

"I know I shouldn't pressure you," he said, scratching the back of his ear. "Do you want to, like, get married or something? Would that help?"

I laughed and took him in my arms, and told him that wouldn't be necessary.

⁓

To get to Craybourne Island you drove across a dubious bridge in Wattle Beach that seemed to sag every time a car rumbled over it, and where during the day kids jumped like starfish from its railings, shouting to the sky as they leaped.

I had been to Craybourne many times, day trips with Harry and Rose, and later sandwiched between Mattie and Sam, the boot loaded with picnic baskets umbrellas and collapsible chairs.

I'd been there on school excursions year after year to study Craybourne's famous soldier crabs; I'd been with Stella and Simone on a camping trip when we were twelve; I'd been with Annabelle, who pronounced it Cray-boring; but now, driving across the bridge with Josh, I felt like I had never seen it before in my entire life.

The bridge rumbled beneath the car as it always had, the boats bobbed for apples in the harbor, but nothing seemed familiar at all, sitting in Josh's new car with my hands in my lap, rubbing my thumbs together.

He swung into the car park of the Half-Moon Motel, its neon sign flashing a sliver of a crescent every few seconds.

Josh turned off the engine, leaned over.

"How's that for romance, Lulu?" he said. "I've brought you the moon."

"It's very nice, Josh," I answered, trying to find something to say. "Very lunar."

It was my seventeenth birthday and I had spent it lying to Harry and Rose, telling them I was staying at Annabelle's for the night. "Annie's making me a cake," I'd said, half hoping, I think, to be caught out by the improbability of my words.

Josh kissed me, his mouth deep on my neck, his hands underneath my shirt, then, his voice saying, "Let's go inside."

I followed him with my head down, scared stiff that someone I knew—or worse, someone my mother knew—would see me there, loitering with Josh Keaton at the reception desk of the Half-Moon Motel.

"With intent," Annabelle said the next day when I told her not quite everything.

"What?"

"You were loitering with intent."

We giggled together on her bed, and I asked, "With intent to what?"

"With intent, young lady," she said sternly, "to get pollinated."

Then we collapsed in laughter.

But that night wasn't really what Annabelle and I had reduced it to while giggling on her bed.

Not at all.

"Come here," he'd said.

The half-moon outside blinked on and off, so every few seconds I could see his brown arms reaching out for me, his hands clasping the back of my neck, pulling me toward him.

Tracing the outline of my lips with his finger, he took my hand in his and slid it lazily down my body, hooking his fingers onto my skirt.

"Wait," he said, smiling and swinging his legs off the bed.

From his sports bag he took out a candle, his cassette recorder, and a tape.

He set the candle out on the cupboard beside the bed and lit it, its tiny flame finding beauty in the shadows, and clicked the tape into the recorder.

"I made this for you," he smiled.

I closed my eyes as he came back to the bed, feeling his breath on my body, and his hands running over my skin, the two of us laughing at the goose bumps they produced.

"You're beautiful, Tallulah-Lulu," he said.

"So are you," I replied.

And as the sea and his sixteen-track mixtape played the soundtrack of us, so we were.

chapter four

Stella, Simone, and I had been meeting up at Gottardo's Café for years—I loved it because the coffee was excellent, Simone loved it because the owner played Dean Martin songs incessantly, and Stella loved it because she loved anywhere she could get away from her children and breathe for a second.

After I left the hotel I had phoned and asked them to meet me there—it was the only place I could think of to go to, with the only two people I could think of to go to.

It was about a ninety-minute trip from Juniper Bay to the city, plenty of time to think about what I had done, for the shame to gather deep in my bones and rattle all the way.

Plenty of time to think about how stupid I had been to think I could go back and walk away unscathed.

The past was another country and only exceptionally foolish people visited it.

I swung the car into Gottardo's car park.

There was always going to be damage done, but I could not believe I had been the one to do it. I was the one who had put that damn tape back in the recorder and pressed replay.

"Stupid, stupid girl," I told myself in the rearview mirror. "They don't even have cassettes anymore."

Stella and Simone were already there when I arrived and sat

down, Stella's three-year-old son, Riley, curled up in a ball under the table.

"I'm sorry, Lulu," Stella said, "he really wanted to come." Riley began to lick my shin under the table. "He thinks he's a cat," Stella continued. "It's driving me crazy. He won't answer to anything else but Mr. Socks, and I have to give him his milk in a little bowl—"

"For fuck's sake, Stella," Simone interrupted, "don't encourage him, remember when Grace thought she was a horse and you ended up enrolling her in pony club."

"I did not enroll her, Simone," said Stella. "I just took her there and let her have a bit of a run around the paddock. . . ."

"Can you hear yourself, Stella?" said Simone, stirring her coffee. "Can you actually hear how ridiculous that sounds? Now enough kinder talk, I want to hear all about the wedding—spill, Lulu."

I looked at her and thought that, even in her wildest dreams, Simone would have no idea what I was about to say.

"I've done something terrible," I said quietly.

Simone looked at me. "What do you . . . ? Lulu, what's wrong?"

The shame scorched at my skin, sending my hands to my face, fingers pressing deep into my eyes, as the tears came again, spilling through them.

"What is it, Lulu?" Stella said, standing up and coming around the table to stand next to me.

She put one hand on the side of my face. "There," she said, patting my hair and using the voice that must have soothed her five children through all their assorted childhood anxieties. "Everything's all right, Lulu, whatever it is, everything is going to be all right."

I sank into her, burying my face in her dress and hoping that, somehow, some of Stella Maria Patricia Mary McNamara's goodness would seep into me.

"Lulu," said Simone sharply, "what on earth have you done?"

"I slept with Josh Keaton on his wedding night," I whispered into Stella's stomach.

"What?" said Simone.

"I slept with Joshua Keaton on his and Annabelle's wedding night" I whispered again.

"Lulu," coaxed Stella gently, "we can't help you if we can't hear you."

"Tallulah," Simone snapped, "we can't hear a bloody word you're saying."

"*ALL RIGHT*," I shouted at her from across the table. "I HAD SEX WITH JOSHUA KEATON ON HIS WEDDING NIGHT."

Stella's hand flew to her mouth, and Simone, who I am fairly sure was smiling, said calmly, "Oh, Lulu, Annabelle is going to scratch your eyes out."

"Meow," said Riley from underneath the table.

~

When I got home later that night, the phone was ringing, but I ignored it in favor of lying on the couch with a pillow over my head.

I heard the answering machine click on, then my father's voice.

"Hello, this is a message for Lulu de Longland," he announced, making me smile in spite of myself. No matter how many times I told him he could just speak normally to me if the machine answered, he always spoke formally to it first, like he was addressing the United Nations.

"Lulu, it's your father. How was the reception? I'm sorry I couldn't stay, but I'm sure you all had a good time." I winced, thinking, *Well, two of us did.* . . . Then he added, "Look I'm sorry to bother you, love, but your mum's gone a bit downhill. When

I got home from the wedding she was wearing Doris—anyway I've made an appointment with the doctor, but if you've got any time to come see us in the next week or so, love, that'd be great. Thanks, love, this is the end of the message for Lulu de Longland from Harry de Longland—her father."

"Oh, Harry," I said into the pillow.

I stood up, wiped my eyes with the back of my hand, pulled my hair off my face, the way Rose liked it, and was just running upstairs to change when the phone rang again.

"Lulu," a voice I knew well said, stopping me on the fifth stair. "Sorry I didn't call earlier, but we've had all sorts of delays over here—as per usual—but anyway, things are back on track and I'll try you again a bit later. Hope you're well—how was the wedding? Looking forward to hearing all about it. All right, well, take care and I'll try again later."

Ben Moreton.

My boyfriend.

"I'm sorry, Lulu," he had said two weeks earlier, "but it's still beyond me why you would even want to go to the wedding."

I'd watched the familiar lines of his shoulders and neck hunched over as he packed his suitcase on the table by the window, carefully color-coding his shirts and ties as he went.

"Ben," I said, "we've been through this. Annabelle and Josh are my oldest friends, and I know you don't understand—"

He spun around, words tumbling out of his mouth. "You're right," he said, "I don't—I don't understand why you would choose to go to that wedding when you could come to Hong Kong with me. Why, Lulu? Why? So you can be humiliated by that woman all over again, so that Josh can stand there with that stupid smirk on his face and tell you how lovely you look? So that Annabelle can talk to you in that ridiculous language and the two of you can pretend you're still twelve years old and that nothing bad ever fucking happened? Is that it?"

I'd stood, stunned and silent, as he rammed a final pair of navy socks into his luggage.

"Is that it, Lulu?" he had continued, zipping up his case. "Because if it is, I am glad I'm going to Hong Kong, because I am getting really, really tired of dealing with it."

Then he'd walked out of the bedroom and slammed the door.

I heard him go down the stairs and out the front door onto the street below to be snapped up, I presumed, by some other woman out there who wouldn't be able to believe her luck that here in this city there was a perfectly normal, nice man, who usually never raised his voice, or swore, or walked out of an argument, and who separated her whites from her coloreds when he did her washing.

A smart woman.

"Sorry," I had said out loud to the room, which was strangely silent and still in the aftermath of Ben's anger. "I'm so sorry."

But not sorry—or smart—enough to go with him.

Now there he was on the answering machine, trying to make up for the fight, for our awkward good-bye at the airport, making a supreme effort by even asking about the wedding, while I—well, what had I done since he left?

Unwelcome, the memory of the wedding night flashed across my mind.

I saw Josh through the keyhole of my hotel-room door, swaying in the hallway, smiling when I opened it, leaning in to me, half saying, half singing the words from one of the songs from a sixteen-track mixtape he'd once made.

"No, no, no," I said out loud to myself, banishing the picture by shaking my head and resolutely beginning to pack for Harry and Rose's.

But Josh kept singing and took a step toward me.

"NO," I said, shaking my head and hurling a pair of shoes onto the bed.

Usually I just took an overnight bag, but this time I reached for my suitcase—I thought I might be staying awhile.

The phone rang once more and I was running to get it, certain it was Harry asking me if I was coming, wanting to reassure him that, of course, I'd be there, when a different voice cracked through the answering machine.

"Tallulah," Annabelle Andrews said, "I was just wondering if you could have waited until the confetti had actually hit the ground before having sex with my husband."

I stood stock-still on the spot, irrationally certain she could detect any movement through the airwaves.

"I know you're there, Tallulah," she said calmly. "Pick up the phone, immediately."

I snapped the suitcase shut and fled.

The ninety-minute trip from the inner-city apartment I shared with Ben back to Juniper Bay felt like forever, and I kept looking in the rearview mirror to see if anyone was following me, but the only thing that chased me all the way home was my own guilt.

Turning onto Plantation Street, I don't think I had ever felt so relieved to be home, where I could walk through the gate, past the sign—freshly painted every few years—up the stairs and know exactly what to expect. Even if Rose was in the other place she inhabited, with its half-shadow rooms none of us could enter, there would still be fresh flowers in the hall, the kettle would feel warm, and Harry's unlaced work boots would be by the back door. It was as familiar as the pink chenille bedspread on my childhood bed and the sticks that had been placed under it, put there by Mattie's and Sam's hands, no matter how old they grew. Even though they were both away in Canberra on a one-term exchange for the physiotherapy degrees they were studying for, I had still automatically reached under the bedspread the first night I got home, checking to see if my now strapping twenty-two-year-old brothers had left me a present.

I had been home for about a week, looking after Rose and hiding behind the house's familiar walls, when Harry approached me in the garden.

"What's going on, love?" he asked, leaning on a rake.

"What do you mean, Harry?"

"Well, love," he said, "I've just seen Annabelle's mum on the telly."

"On the telly?" I echoed stupidly.

Harry took a long look at the rake.

"Yes, love—talking about how you ruined Annabelle's wedding. It's going to be on that Maxine Mathers show tonight."

Harry was looking at me, one hand moving up and down at the back of his neck, his signature move for worry.

God.

He didn't need this—first Rose and now this, his daughter, caught like a deer in headlights on national television.

There was not much I could do about that—it was done, and clearly I was done for, but I could, at least, still help him with Rose.

"It will be all right, Harry." I smiled at him. "You know Annie, she's always being melodramatic about things—I better go in to Rose."

It wasn't much, but it was all I had, and I left him in the garden with his anxious question mark of a face.

Rose was sitting at the kitchen table, crumpled.

"Hey, Rose," I said, sitting beside her and putting my hand on Doris's sleeve, "the jonquils are out, do you want to come and have a look?"

She stared ahead, her hands folded neatly in her lap. I reached over and put her head on my shoulder, patting her hair. We sat for a while in the quiet, which was broken only by one jagged little sigh from Rose.

I reached into my bag of tricks to find the one that might help her, words and pictures learned as a little girl sitting by my mute mother's side.

"How about I sing, Rose, would you like me to sing to you?"

A slight shift, Rose's shoulders next to mine.

I began to quietly sing an old tune, "Dream a Little Dream of Me."

It calmed both of us; it was always easy to forget the outside world when it was just Rose and me, dreaming in her kitchen.

Later, when I had managed to get Rose to sit outside with Harry in the garden seat, its red hibiscuses faded, its fringes long gone, nicked by an assortment of birds over the years, I sat on my bed and watched, half horrified and half mesmerized, while Annie's heavily kohled eyes blinked from the television.

A video montage of Andrews family moments played, while the voice-over intoned:

> *They are one of Australia's oldest and best-known dynasties, respected internationally across every field of the arts.*
>
> *But the passions that drive the uniquely talented Andrews clan also divide them, and tonight, exclusively on Channel Nine, wife of Frank Andrews and Archibald Prize winner Annie Andrews speaks for the first time about the scandals that have dogged Australia's first family of the arts.*

The montage played out, replaced by a single black-and-white photo of Annabelle and me that filled the screen.

The phone next to my bed rang. It was Simone.

"I'm not sure what exactly Stevie Nicks is going to say" — Simone was not particularly fond of Annie — "but I hope you're going to get a chance to tell your side of the story."

I had no intention of doing so, but if I did, I knew where I'd start: that first summer when we were all together, Annabelle, Josh, and me, sharing the heat of the sun.

———

It was the summer before senior year, and Annabelle and I were lying on our towels beside the Craybourne Island pier in Wattle Beach on a lazy Sunday afternoon, a line literally drawn around us in the sand.

"See that," Annabelle snarled at any tousle-haired surfer who would, lured by her mermaid curls, recklessly amble over to us, only to retreat moments later, cheeks stinging harder than the salt on their skin, "that line means do not cross, do not disturb, and do not talk to us — I drew it because I know how hard it is for you surfer boys to understand English."

"Annabelle," I said, outraged and thrilled at the same time by her rudeness, "you shouldn't speak to them like that."

"Oh, they love it." She shrugged.

The only male allowed to cross the line was, of course, Josh, who was now standing in front of us, his tall, dark body casting a shadow over ours, putting his board down and shaking ice-cold drops of water onto our skin.

"Can I come in, girls?" He grinned, not waiting for an answer but instead dropping to his knees and lying his whole cool body on the entire length of mine, and cocking his head to my ear.

Annabelle, perhaps sensing I would put up a bigger fight for him than I had for Stella and Simone, had never attempted to exclude Josh. She just shuffled across from her seat next to mine and let him in. The three of us had grown increasingly closer that summer — picnics and songs and getting drunk in the park on sickly sweet cider, telling jokes and shouting at the sun — until all our lines blurred, and it was hard to tell where we each finished or began.

We were, of course, too close.

Rose could see it, her brow furrowing as the three of us trooped upstairs to my room; Annie could see it: "Annabelle, why don't you go and find your own boyfriend to eat us out of house and home?"; even the Piranha Sisters could see it.

"Excuse me, Sister" — Stacey had shot her hand up in French class one day, staring directly at Annabelle and me — "but some of us were wondering what a ménage à trois is?"

The rows of chocolate-clad girls tittered as Sister Eltrees, the youngest and most easily unsettled nun at Saint Rita's stopped, *Encore Tricolore* in hand, mid-flutter.

"Oh, I'm not sure, dear, some sort of cake I think."

Which really was funny, I suppose, seeing as Josh eventually managed to get that cake, and eat it, too.

The only person who didn't see it was me, or if I did, I rolled over in the sand and dove in, headfirst.

Besides, there were too many moments that belonged exclusively to Josh and me — laughs and sighs and promises that were just ours — for me to worry about all the others in between.

That was the summer they put an outdoor roller-skating rink next to the Wattle Beach caravan park, and all the parents would gather there in the early evening to watch their children wobble around.

Later, when the stars came out, the DJ would say: "All right, young lovers, don't be shy — choose your partner for the couples' session," and Josh and I would skate out together.

I loved Josh's arm around my back, the two of us swaying back and forth until he would skate around to the front of me and push me into the barrier.

Pressing hard against me he would whisper, "I love you, Tallulah-Lulu," and even the stars would sigh.

Now he was lying along the full length of my body, blocking out the sun.

"Hey, baby," he murmured, "you smell like coconut, makes me want to eat you all up."

Little bumps rose on my skin as I shivered in the sun.

"Oh, get a dune," moaned Annabelle.

He rolled off me and squeezed between us. Annabelle and I both turned toward him, and Annabelle announced: "Annie's entering the Archibald."

"The what?" Josh murmured, his mouth on my neck.

"The Archibald," Annabelle said, "although I wouldn't expect a philistine like you to know what it is."

"A what?"

"A philistine—it means a person who does not appreciate art, someone who is hostile to artistic achievement—an uncultured, uneducated, peasant sort of person, really." She smiled.

"Geez, Annabelle," said Josh, "bit harsh."

"But true, Joshie," she teased, "sadly, all too true."

Flipping over to lie on her back, she continued, "Now, while I tell Tallulah all about it, why don't you run off into the ocean and go pee in your wet suit with all your surfie friends?"

Josh sprang to his feet and swept Annabelle up in a fireman's carry. "I think you're the one who needs to cool off, Annabelle!" He laughed.

Annabelle squirmed out of his hold, shrieked, and ran, tearing down the sand on her long, brown legs with Josh bearing down behind her, their lean bodies casting shadows like stick insects on the sand.

Like twins.

I sat up, shaded my eyes from the sun, and watched them disappear farther and farther away onto the shadowy shore, watched them tumble and wrestle in the sand before Annabelle wriggled out from under him, ran straight to the water, and dove in, a perfect arc of olive skin and flash of white bikini.

Josh charged in after her, and together they went under, while I sat on my towel waiting for them to surface, and it felt like forever.

That night, Josh and I lay under a jacaranda tree by the river, our faces close and whispering.

"Josh," I said.

"Yes, Tallulah-Lulu?"

"Do you want me to get a white bikini?"

～

The next day, on the way home from school, Annabelle walked ahead of me, trailing a stick along the fences.

"We're not going to mine," she said, "so don't even suggest it."

"Well, I don't want to go to mine either."

"Doris?" Annabelle asked me.

I nodded.

"Annie?" I asked her.

She nodded back.

"She's being particularly dramatic at the moment." She sighed.

"Come on," I said, grabbing one end of the stick, "it's so hot, let's go to the river."

Annabelle and I had found a corner of the river we had claimed as our own; it was to the right of the canoe club, a pale gray jetty that jutted out into the water.

Sharp shells clung to its underbelly, and hundreds of tiny, silvery fish darted beneath its uneven boards, swarming together in one direction, then precision-turning into another.

We could strip down to our underwear and lie in the shallows underneath the boards, winks of sunlight shining through, while tiny waves—wavelets Annabelle called them—flirted with our toes.

"You look like a mermaid," I told Annabelle that afternoon, as we lay in the shallows and her hair fanned our around her face.

"So do you." She smiled at me, and added, "I wish we bloody were."

"Me too," I answered. "Then we could just swim away."

"Where nobody could find us," she agreed, adding, "Frank and Annie are really fighting over this Archibald thing."

"Why?"

Annabelle sighed, ducking her head under the water, and reemerged seconds later, smoothing her dark hair off her face. "Because Frank doesn't want her to enter it."

"Why?"

"He says that she's not doing it for the right reasons. He reckons she's just in it for the publicity and the money."

"How much money is it?"

"About twenty grand, I think."

"That's pretty good."

"I know, and Annie says, you know, that God knows we need it, with Frank not doing much art himself lately"—Frank's work was always like Frank himself, haphazard and sporadic—"and who does he think pays for me to go to Saint Rita's, and does he have any idea how hard it is to keep his name out there. . . ."

Annabelle was gone, lost in Annie world with her jangling bangles and her jangling voice.

I wiped some water from my hair, the droplets running down my back.

"But I still don't really get what he's so upset about. The Archibald is pretty prestigious, isn't it, it's not like she's entering a coloring-in competition, or anything . . ."

Annabelle laughed. "I think it would be better if she did."

"Why?" I asked, "I still don't get it."

"Because it's got all these rules and conditions attached to it if you want to enter, and one of them is you have to know the person you're painting, and that they should be well-known in their field, like in politics or the arts or some other verily impressive job."

She sank back down in the water, head tilted back, elbows propping her up.

"And the problem is . . ." I said slowly.

"The problem is that you'd think if Annie was going to choose someone to paint a portrait of, someone she knows well and is a distinguished person in his or her field, she might have, you know, chosen Dad."

"She didn't?" I said stupidly.

"No," said Annabelle, "she chose Fergus."

This did surprise me; I didn't think Annie really liked Fergus all that much. Whenever his name was mentioned, she'd say something under her breath, and Annabelle said she was still cranky about not getting any glass beads.

But Frank adored him.

There were photos on the wall of the River House of him as a kid, following Fergus around, carrying his cameras, copying the way he dressed, rubbing his chin with his hands and curling his hair behind his ears just so, until Frank grew old enough to fit into his own skin.

Fergus sent Annabelle postcards from places we would race to look up in the atlas; he sent her feathers and headdresses and envelopes filled with strange scents from a life far removed from Juniper Bay.

One night, we had been watching one of Fergus Andrews's documentaries at Annabelle's house, when Annie came into the room.

"What are you watching, girls?" she'd said.

"Uncle Fergus's newest documentary, he sent it to me," Annabelle replied.

"What's it called?"

"Um, *Alisterus Scapularis, King of the Parrots*."

"*King of the Wankers*, more like."

"Annie," said Frank, walking in, "what a thing to say."

"Oh for Christ's sake, Frank, Fergus's documentaries get more pretentious with every award he gets, you know that as well as I do."

"What I know," said Frank, "is that Fergus is very talented and hardworking and he doesn't deserve your derision."

Annie turned to look at him with her gypsy eyes.

"You're right, Frank," she said, "he doesn't. I'll save that for his little brother."

Annabelle and I had exchanged looks, and gone back to the *King of the Wankers*.

The truth was I didn't much like Fergus either.

The first time I met him was when he had come to stay a few nights at the River House. He had talked about himself all through dinner, bringing out photos and souvenirs for everyone to sigh over, and never, I noticed, my eyes flicking between the two men, asking his little brother what he had been doing.

At about nine o'clock he had stood up, stretched, said, "Sorry, guys, I guess I'm still on Swazi time," which even though I was only fourteen years old and hadn't learned the word yet, I still knew was a tosser of a thing to say.

He'd walked up the stairs to the guest bedroom, stopping under a huge canvas Frank had recently finished, a lawless clash of colors and collage that would one day fetch a ridiculous sum of money at Sotheby's and said, "It's very busy, isn't it?"

Back then, Annie resented Fergus's success, the way he seemed to be overtaking Frank, who, she said, was more talented than "the whole, damn lot of them."

Frank's work was exquisite, paintings and drawings and etchings of such detail, such beauty, that people found it difficult to believe they came from a man's hands. But Frank was erratic, his timing was always off, his studio scattered with unfinished commissions, earning him the nickname "Half-baked Frank" in less kind artistic circles.

Frank was so interested in the minor details of life—"Tallulah, Annabelle, quickly come in here and look at this marvelous spider's web!"—that it probably never occurred to him to look at the big picture, and when he did it was all too often to find he had painted himself right out of it.

This time, however, it was Annie who was painting him out, leaving for the Solomon Islands about a month later, where Fergus was filming his latest documentary. Her departure was signature Annie: erratic and hurried.

"Keep an eye on Annabelle, Tallulah," she said to me the day before she left as she packed up the huge, flat wooden box that held her paints and rolled up her brushes. "And Frank—actually, keep both eyes on Frank."

"How long will you be gone for, Annie?" I asked.

She shut the lid and looked up at me.

"Obviously you're not an artist, Lulu," she said, "or you would know there is no answer to that question." She smiled, chucking my cheek with her glittering hands. "I will be gone for as long as it takes me to get it right, okay, my little worrier?"

"Actually, I was wondering who's going to take care of Annabelle," I snapped back at her, surprising myself with how upset I was she was going, and not quite understanding why.

"She is perfectly capable, Tallulah," Annie answered, "of taking care of herself."

It rained the morning Annie left for the Solomons, a cracking storm taking photos in the sky, leaving a snapshot of her departure, Frank barefoot and hovering beside the taxi with a huge black umbrella.

With Annie gone, a blanket of calm settled over the River House, like rain damping the dust down after a long, hot spell.

Frank roused himself out of bed each morning to take care of his daughter, who needed to be, he said, "loved, fed, clothed, and shod in that order," as he shuffled about the house ironing her uniforms and making macaroni and cheese.

Annabelle stayed over at our house most weekends for the rest of that summer and into autumn, she and Josh jostling for position at our table, and Rose, especially if she was wearing Greta, muttered things about Annie under her breath.

The rhythm of our days shifted and settled into the new pattern, until Annie's absence drifted into two months, then, a phone call from Fergus later, what seemed like forever.

It was after dinner on a Saturday night—I know because Harry and Rose were watching repeats of *Parkingson*—when Annabelle showed up, knocking on our front door, then joining us wordlessly on the couch.

One good thing about Rose's illness was that it made her highly tolerant of anyone else's strange behavior, accepting what other people might have questioned. So instead of asking Annabelle what she was doing there, she just moved over and made a space for her on the couch.

When *Parky* finished we went upstairs to my room.

"Annie's not coming back," she told me. "Fergus rang Dad and said that he and Mum"—she spat the word out—"have fallen in love, and that they need to stay there together in the Solomons to 'work things out.'" She hooked two fingers on each hand in quotation marks to show exactly what she thought of that particular phrase.

"Oh God, Annabelle," I said, "that's awful." I went to put my arms around her.

"Don't," she said, flicking them away. "I don't care, Tallulah, I really don't. If Mum wants to behave like a perfect slut with Mr. Fucking Khaki, then fine. Frank and I are better off without her anyway."

Frank—my heart lurched. "How is he?"

"Who cares, Tallulah?" she said, looking completely exhausted.

Then she slept on my floor for thirteen hours.

chapter five

"But you did abandon your daughter, Annabelle, when she was in her senior year at high school, didn't you?" Maxine Mathers was asking Annie, somehow managing to look both damning and sympathetic at the same time.

I had just gotten off the phone with Simone and was sitting on my bed, biting my nails and hypnotized by the train wreck that was Annie's interview, watching her eyes widen as she abruptly leaned forward, startling Maxine Mathers into the folds of her chair.

"I find it very interesting," Annie said slowly, "that you would use the term *abandoned*."

"Why's that, Annie?" Maxine asked, her hand tucked underneath her chin, her features rearranged to appear faintly amused.

"Because, Maxine, I did not abandon my daughter, as you so dramatically put it. I left for a few months to the Solomon Islands to paint a picture, which is what I do, and very well. Annabelle was with her father, and I hope that period taught her that she could stand on her own two feet, and that women do not stop being who they are once they become mothers."

"But you ran off with her father's brother," Maxine pressed, as I bit down to the quick of my nail.

Annie sighed. "I did not run off with him, I fucked him," she said, and, as the switchboard at Channel Nine presumably exploded, she added, "which is another thing I do very well."

Maxine Mathers, looking like an extremely well-groomed stunned mullet, turned to the camera, her face in search of a suitable expression.

"After the break," she said, "Annie speaks exclusively to *Today, Tonight, and Tomorrow* about her complex relationship with her daughter, Annabelle, and the heartbreaking betrayal of Annabelle's childhood friend."

I got up from the bed and switched off the television. I already knew how this part of the story ended.

Going to sleep that night, I thought about Annie's words, which gave the impression that she thought she'd done her daughter a favor when she left all those years ago.

It was true that for a time the wheels of the River House kept turning, and Annabelle had never said she felt abandoned—in fact, most of the time she acted as if Annie's absence was a blessing: "No more bloody patchouli candles stinking up the house."

But I was never convinced by her nonchalance toward Annie's absence; it seemed to me like an act she was putting on, although I wasn't entirely sure for whose benefit. Sometimes her own, sometimes mine, but mostly, I thought, for Frank, who was slowly coming undone.

He seemed increasingly incapable of finishing anything: he would leave washing half-hung on the line, dinners half-cooked, and never had the name "Half-baked Frank" suited him more.

A melancholy had settled around him, a quiet sadness that traveled with him as he roamed the River House looking for a place that still felt like home.

"Frank's gone," Annabelle said about a week later, on our way home from school.

"What do you mean he's gone?" I asked. "Gone where?"

"Wouldn't have a clue," she said. "Don't know, don't care."

"Well, you must have some idea where he's gone. Has he gone to get Annie?"

"What? No, don't be stupid, Tallulah. As if Frank could work out how to get to the Solomon Islands; the man can't even work out the bus route."

"Well, how long has he been gone?"

"Two days."

"Two days?" I shrieked. "Have you reported it to the police?"

"'Have you reported it to the police'?" she mimicked. "Stop being so melodramotional, Tallulah."

"Annabelle," I said, "I am not being melodramotional. If Frank really is gone, you should have told me, or Harry and Rose . . . Annabelle, I just don't . . . are you sure he's gone?"

"What do you mean am I sure he's gone? He's gone, Tallulah, as in he's not here anymore, he's not at the house, I came home from school on Wednesday and I called him and I called him and I went to every room and he's gone, all right, as in no longer around, disapanished. . . ."

"Well, we have to do something," I said. "First of all, you have to come home with me until Frank turns up—and he will turn up; second of all, we have to tell Harry and Rose; and third of all, we have to get in contact with your mother and tell her to haul her fat, sorry arse back here."

Annabelle giggled.

"What is so funny?" I demanded. "This is not a funny situation, Annabelle, this is not a joke—"

"You said *arse*." Annabelle smiled. "You never say words like that."

"Actually, I said, *fat, sorry arse*," I corrected her.

Rose made up a bed in the spare room for Annabelle, bustling and fussing around in Phoebe, fluffing the pillows and opening windows to "let some air in."

"Thanks, Mrs. de Longland," Annabelle said.

"Pleasure, treasure. Now, come on, you girls, help me with these sheets," Rose said, billowing white cotton into the air.

Later that night, when the boys had gone to bed, Harry and Rose asked Annabelle and me to sit with them in the lounge room.

"Not the kitchen," I noted to Annabelle. "Must be serious."

Rose came in carrying a tea tray and wearing Alexis.

"Verily serious," whispered Annabelle.

Rose put down the tray, said kindly, "Annabelle, do you have any idea at all where your father has gone?"

Annabelle shook her head.

"Well, I know you don't want us to call the police, but Harry and I both think that if your dad doesn't turn up by tomorrow, or if we haven't heard from him, we really should."

Annabelle looked out the window.

"If he's hurt, or in some sort of trouble," Rose continued gently, "it would be wrong of us not to. You can see that, can't you, love?"

Annabelle nodded, an almost imperceptible shrug of her head.

"All right," Rose said, "that's settled then—now, the other thing we need to talk about is your mother."

Annabelle shifted in her seat.

"She should know what's happened, Annabelle, and I would like your permission to call her," Rose said firmly.

Surprising me, Annabelle nodded again.

"All right," she said. "Can I go to bed now?"

All that night, I shifted in my bed, caught between awake and dreaming.

Words and pictures looped in the darkness: Frank laughing with Annie on the grass; Frank hunched over a picture, paint-brush behind his ear; Annabelle saying, "Dad drinks"; Annie saying, "Keep both eyes on Frank"; and then my own face, my own voice—"Frank says now that we are fourteen and young ladies, we need a place of sanctuary."

I sat up and as a growing wind slapped at my window, I had an idea of where Frank Andrews might be.

Outside, the dark was giving way to light, and I got out of bed and tiptoed down the hallway to my parents' room.

"Rose," I whispered, kneeling by her side of the bed. "Rose," I tried again.

Rose rolled over.

"Lulu? What is it, love, are you all right, is Annabelle all right?" She went to turn her bedside light on, but I put my hand over hers.

"Sshh, Rose," I said. "I think I know where Frank is."

Wordlessly she slipped out from under the covers and followed me out into the hallway. "What's going on, Lulu?" she said, glancing at the clock. "It's half past five."

"I think I know where Frank is," I repeated.

"You know where he is? Is he all right? I think we should wake your father."

"No," I said, still whispering, "Frank wouldn't want that— he'd hate that, and he wouldn't want Annabelle either."

Rose looked at me. "What do you want to do, Lulu?"

"I want us to go to him, on my bike."

I'd thought it through: Rose couldn't, or wouldn't, drive, and riding would be faster than walking.

"Now?"

"Yes, before everyone wakes up."

Rose nodded.

"Go and get changed," she said, "I'll meet you out front."

I went back to my room to pull on a T-shirt and some shorts. At moments like these, I was glad that Rose was my mother. She hadn't asked where we were going or, like most mothers would have, made a fuss. We had been through so many of her own moments of madness, she wasn't about to question mine.

I slipped my shoes on, feeling surer now that Rose was coming with me. If anyone could help Frank it was my mother. When I wheeled my push-bike around to the front of the house, she was waiting for me under the sign, in Phoebe.

She hitched the hem up and perched sidesaddle on my bike, the daisy clips dancing on its spokes. "I haven't done this since your dad used to pick me up from work." She laughed. "Forgotten how much fun it is."

I smiled, climbing on and concentrating on keeping us balanced, arms on either side of her, breathing her in, just like Harry must have done all those years ago.

"Hold on, Rose! Corner!" I yelled, as we lurched to one side, threatening to tip over, shrieking and giggling and half hoping we would.

"That was close." Rose laughed. "I thought we were goners!"

I laughed out loud at Rose suddenly acting like the child she should have had the chance to be.

Nearing Annabelle's house, I slowed down and wobbled the bike to a stop outside the gates guarded by the twin gargoyles, baring their grinning teeth and fat little tummies at us.

"Good morning, Lulu, Annabelle," Rose said, nodding at them.

"Very funny, Rose," I said, leaning the bike against the fence. "Come on."

Making our way past the house and the shed, as the earth sloped toward the river, Rose took my arm, slowing me down. "Are you sure this is where he is, love?"

"Pretty sure," I said, my foot on the first rung of the steps that

Frank had somehow managed to curl around the tree without using a single nail—"You don't want to pierce a tree," he'd explained to us. "Breaks its spirit."

"I'll go up and see."

The wind whipped at my legs as I began to climb to the place where Frank had built our nest, shadowy in the branches that held it in their gnarled claws.

Reaching the last rung, I hoisted myself through the hole in the floor, pulling myself up by the dangling rope to the veranda, and peered through a window.

"Frank," I whispered, "Frank, it's me, Tallulah, are you there?"

No answer. Only the rushing breath of the growing wind and the screech of a flying fox startling me and rousing the shape on the floor.

"Annie?" Frank said. "Is that you, Annie girl?"

When I think of that night, I think of the wind that tore at it, and of the strange journey that was Frank's descent from the tree house.

At first he was hesitant to leave, his eyes flicking from Rose to me, then back to Rose, where they widened for an instant.

"Ah," he'd said, then, "a fellow traveler." And let himself be led.

Rose sent me home to tell Annabelle he had been found, and after that, Frank's mother, Christa, took him in, the apple from his father's tree.

Frank was cleaned up and sobered up, Christa telling an interviewer years later, when Frank's *In My Mother's House* came out, that when he first arrived she had pointed him to his room and handed him a paintbrush.

"It's how the Andrews men heal," she said.

How the Andrews women heal she did not say, but the day Frank left for his mother's, Annie rang to say she was coming home to claim her daughter.

~~~

"How's your dad?" I'd asked a few weeks after Annie's return.

Annabelle shrugged. "All right."

We were sitting at Snow's, waiting for Josh to show up.

"Is he doing any work?"

"Don't know."

"Yes, you do, Annabelle, he writes to you all the time."

"Well, he writes to you too, Tallulah, so you already know the answer to that question."

"Are you going to go and see him soon? Maybe I could come with you. We could go during the holidays?"

"No."

"Annabelle, why don't you go see him?"

"I don't want to," she said. "Stop going on about it."

"I'm not," I said. "I just think it would be good for him if we went to see him."

"Well, I don't want to see him," Annabelle said, holding up her hand. "End of conversation, Tallulah."

I sighed and looked out the window for Josh, Frank's latest letter burning in my pocket.

Dear Tallulah de Lightful,

Well, things at Christa's are going as well as can be expected.

She watches over me like a hawk and swoops in if she sees me falter, a mother's prerogative, even if I am fifty-seven years old.

I am painting again, a new series, which I think you might like, and Annabelle also. I think it's quite enchanting, if you'll forgive some immodesty.

How is Annabelle?

I do not wish to burden you with all our family's ills, and I do not intend for you to become our go-between, but as she does not answer my letters could you tell Annabelle this for me?

Could you tell her that I think of her every day and the last thing I do when I close my eyes at its end is to kiss her good night?

Tell her I have not touched a drop.

Did you know that the name Tallulah has its origins with the Native American Indians, the Choctaw people of the Mississippi region?

It means "leaping waters," and having seen you in the swimming pool, I do not doubt it.

Good-bye, my friend,
Whatever happens, don't stop leaping.

Frank X

chapter six

"Just hear me out, Lulu," Simone was saying. "That's all I'm asking you to do."

We were sitting in the Royal Albert's beer garden in Juniper Bay, sunlight spilling through its lattice onto tables with beer coasters shoved unceremoniously beneath their legs.

I loved the Royal Albert; it had been my local go-to my whole life. It was a redbrick, beer-soaked relic where the bartenders called everyone "sweetheart" and placed frosty glasses on long, wet mats that ran the entire length of the bar, long after all the other hotels in the area had nailed their furniture down and painted their walls cappuccino.

I had sat perched in its "Ladies' Lounge" with Rose, and later with Sam and Mattie too, drinking something red and frothy through a waxy straw, while Harry bought chips for everyone and drank beer until Rose said, "That's enough now, Harry."

I had danced with Annabelle in its now long gone Cabaret Room, screaming the words to songs we loved into each other's faces, hers smudged and beautiful under the red and blue lights.

Josh and I had kissed underneath its dark green awnings, hot nights drowning in sweat and love and too much underage vodka.

And now I was back, sitting opposite Simone, executive producer and presenter of *Our Time, Our Stories*, and one of the most successful young lesbians ever to graduate from Saint Rita's.

Our Time, Our Stories was no *Today, Tonight, and Tomorrow*—no startled, shady businessmen opening their front doors to a flash of lights and a determined brunette asking: "Would you like to tell the people whose lives you've ruined where the money's gone, Mr. Stevens?"

It was instead a gentler journey, narrated by Simone herself, her melodious voice inviting viewers each week to "come with me, Simone Severet, as we celebrate our time, our stories."

And now here she was, trying to convince me to appear on it.

"The thing is, Lulu," Simone was saying, "normally we wouldn't touch 'Woman Shags Ex-boyfriend on His Wedding Night' with a ten-foot barge pole. Sorry," she added, seeing my face, "but we wouldn't. In this case, however, I think, I really think, we've got a valid story to tell, and I want to tell your side of it."

I sipped my wine and thought: *Come with me, Simone Severet, while I talk you into doing something you don't want to do.*

"This is not just a story about love, or betrayal," she said, "this is a story about dynasties, about what happens when classes collide."

My eyebrows shot up involuntarily.

"I mean, look at the family portrait—there's dear old Frank, an institution in this country, an absolute bloody institution, sloshing around with his red wine and all that marvelous hair. And there's Annie, swirling about in those awful kaftans, and then there's Fergus, trying to get into the pants of anything that accidentally wanders into his camera range." Simone drained her glass. "And then, of course, we have the lovely"—she raised an eyebrow—"Annabelle."

Stella had a theory that Simone and Annabelle could never really get on because they were too much alike. "They're pretty much exactly the same person," she told me one day, "the same animal, so they feel threatened in each other's presence."

"Is that right, David Attenborough?" I had smiled.

"Yep," Stella answered. "Think about it, Lulu, they're both really good at everything, and really, really bossy."

Simone intruded on my thoughts, leaning toward me and smelling, as she always did, of vanilla, musk, and other women. "Lulu, are you listening to me? Now, what I think is the really fascinating part of this whole thing is not the family itself—Australia's chockablock with artistic families trying to outpaint each other to death. No, what I am interested in is what happens when two kids from the suburbs—you and Josh obviously—find yourselves tangled up with them, two beautiful twin Icaruses flying too close to the sun."

"Oh God, Simone," I said, "I think I liked 'Woman Shags Ex-boyfriend on Wedding Night' better."

"Fine," she snapped, dropping both the coaxing tone and all pretense, "we'll go with that, then."

We sat back and smiled at each other.

"Seriously, Lulu," Simone said, "this is not a story that's going to go away anytime soon. Believe me, I know—it's got the big five written all over it."

"The big five?"

Simone unfurled one finger at a time, like she was firing off a round of bullets at the table. "Fame. Money. Love. Sex. Betrayal. The only way this story could get any bigger would be if Annabelle had actually murdered one of you that night."

"Well, I'm sorry to disappoint you—" I began, cutting myself off as I looked up to see a young guy swaying in front of our table. He was wearing a T-shirt that said *Bernie's Bucks Night* and had the face of another bloke, presumably Bernie, grinning across it.

"You're that chick, aren't you?" he said. "The one who got off with her friend's husband?" He turned to call out to his mates at the bar, "Hey, it's that chick, you know, the slutty one from the telly."

"Oh God," I said into my wineglass while Simone put a cool hand on his arm.

"What's your name, mate?" she asked, using her television voice, all dulcet tones and velvet.

"Dougie," he answered.

"Well, Dougie, I think you might be getting my friend a little bit confused with me—you might know my show, *Our Time, Our Stories.*"

Dougie's eyes clouded, trying to place her.

"Anyway, I don't mean to be rude, but my friend and I are in the middle of a really important discussion, so what I'd like to do is buy you and your mates a round, and I'm also going to write down the number of our network sportsperson so he can arrange some tickets for you all, how does that sound?"

"Excellent," said Dougie, tipping his head and sending a dribble of beer down his shirt. "Ex-cel-lent."

"Right," said Simone, scribbling on a piece of paper and putting it in his top pocket. "Now, go and tell the bartender the next round's on me."

Simone and I sat and watched his retreating back, both knowing that any chance she may or may not have had of convincing me to do this thing went with him.

Still, she was nothing if not persistent.

"Lulu," she began again, but I held up my hand.

"It's over, Simone." I sighed. "End of discussion."

I drove home and thought about all the things Simone had said to try to convince me—and how disappointed Dougie was going to be the next morning when he woke up, dry-eyed and throbbing-templed, to find Simone's note in his pocket. He would take it out and read through sandpaper-scratched eyes: "Dear Dougie, piss off. Maxine Mathers."

Simone and I had made our peace, and for the moment, she had withdrawn her fire. Stella, however, was another matter. I hadn't heard from her since I had confessed my crime to her and Simone at Gottardo's.

She'd left that day, quickly scooping up a still-meowing Riley from under the table, and I knew just by watching her panicked exit that she would pray for me the moment she got home.

Stella McNamara née Kelly: possibly the only student at Saint Rita's who had seriously considered joining their order until she'd locked eyes with William "Billy" McNamara at the Franciscan Brothers' end-of-year dance.

Any thoughts she may have indulged of lifelong chastity went right out the window to the tune of Madonna's "Like a Virgin" as Stella had her very own immaculate perception.

"I'm going to marry him," she'd whispered to Simone and me—Annabelle had refused point-blank to attend ("Why should I stand around waiting to be groped by some pimply juven-vile delinquent?")—as we waited outside for Mr. Kelly to pick us up. "I'm going to marry Billy McNamara."

Simone snorted. I whispered, "How do you know?" and Stella said dreamily, "You just do."

Apparently she did just know, because on her eighteenth birthday Stella Kelly and Billy McNamara stood together in the Saint Rita's chapel, promised to love each other in sickness and in health, through thick and thin, and, as it turned out, Billy's mercifully brief career as a stand-up comic.

Dragging me and Simone along for support, Stella would valiantly sit at the front table at the Royal Albert every Thursday night, laughing slightly hysterically as she drove her fingernails into her own legs underneath the table, while Billy died a thousand deaths onstage, tapping the microphone and saying again and again, "Is this on?"

Stella and Billy had survived not only that but two miscar-
riages and five heaven-sent children, and never once did they
waver, never once did they look out of the corner of their eyes at
what else was on the table and think *maybe*.

So that day at the coffee shop I understood when Stella's hand
flew to her mouth and she said, "But Lulu, it was their *wedding*
night."

The last time I had seen her so shocked was five years earlier
when Simone told her she was gay and had dragged me along for
immoral support.

We had discussed how to tell Stella beforehand, talking
through different ways we could bring it into the conversation,
and ultimately deciding to break it to her gently and with respect
for her beliefs.

Which was why I could not believe it that day when the three
of sat down at a wine bar and ordered our drinks, and Simone had
turned to Stella and said: "Knock, knock?"

"Who's there?" chirped Stella.

"A lesbian, now who wants cake?"

Stella had downed her just-arrived wine in one gulp, giggled
uncertainly, and burst into tears. Stella always burst into tears
whenever she felt unsure of herself. Annabelle had called her
Old Faithful. It was a little cruel, but I preferred it to Annabelle's
other nickname for Stella—Virginia Intactica.

I had known Simone was gay since her eighteenth birthday
party, held in the somewhat ambitiously named Swan Lake Room
on the top floor of the Royal Albert. I have a photo of her cutting
the cake with her parents, Bob and Viv, on either side, three sets
of hands clasping the knife, Bob's buttons straining at his suit, Viv
resplendent in lavender feathers.

I had stayed until the end, the band winding down for the
night, halfheartedly playing "I Just Called to Say I Love You," the
last few couples still sort of standing.

Simone and I were outside on the veranda, draining our drinks.

"Did you have a good time?" I asked her.

"Yeah—you?"

"Yeah, you should be in there dancing," I said. "It's the last song."

"No one to dance with," she said.

"You could dance with anyone, Simone," I answered, "there are boys in there who would cut off their right arm to dance with you."

"Don't want to," she said, and I asked the question that had been hovering on my lips all through high school, where Saint Rita's girls paired off with Saint Joseph's boys or, if they took the road less traveled, tumbled with the boys from Ralston Road High. Kisses were stolen and hearts were broken—Stella's and Billy's eyes met under a canopy of fake stars, Josh Keaton arrived on a push-bike, Lisa Fitzgerald went to Longreach, and through it all, Simone, so beautiful with her pixie face and cheekbones you could ski down, had remained removed, not interested, it seemed, in anyone.

"Simone," I said, "have you ever liked anybody?"

"You mean like-like?" she asked.

"Yeah."

"Yeah."

"Who?"

"Penny Watkins."

"Oh," I said.

"Oh," she echoed, and there was a little pause while the air settled between us, and we both looked inside to see Penny, arms looped around her boyfriend Scott's neck, both swaying drunkenly to the music, her head on his chest, and her skirt caught up at the back in her knickers.

Simone and I laughed.

"Well, she's not very stylish," I observed, and Simone smiled at me.

"So," she said, "now you know my secret, I'm a big fat old *lesbian*."

"You're not fat, Simone," I said, and that was it, really.

Simone was gay, I wasn't, and it remained not so much a secret between us but something we both understood she was not yet ready to share. I never said anything to Annabelle, although I'm sure she probably knew and yawned it away, or Josh, who I thought would probably make some schoolboyish jokes about it, and both Simone and I agreed to wait a few years before we told Stella.

Now Stella was avoiding me, not answering her phone, or making Billy answer it — Billy, who said uncertainly, "I'm very sorry, Lulu, but for some reason Stella doesn't want to talk to you. Is everything all right with you girls?" Billy McNamara, the only person in Australia who apparently had not seen the now infamous episode of *Today, Tonight, and Tomorrow*.

"Everything's fine, Billy," I said. "Just ask Stella to call me when she's ready."

A few days later, she rang.

"I'm sorry, Lulu," said Stella stiffly. "I'm very sorry I haven't returned your calls."

"That's okay," I said. "How have you been?"

"Good, really good."

"And now tell me how you've really been, Stella," I said, falling into an old rhythm.

"Oh, Lulu, it's been awful. Patrick and Thomas were sent home from school with stomach flu; Grace has started that whole horse thing again — Sister Margaret wants us to send her to a counselor — and I've got to make Claire a costume for her ballet concert by Friday, which of course I haven't done."

"I'll make it," I said automatically. "What is it this year? Bee, dog, frolicking wood nymph?"

Stella burst into tears.

"See, Lulu," she said, "this is why I am a bad person. . . . I spend all this time judging you and not returning your calls, and you just carry on as if nothing at all's happened."

"It's fine, Stella—" I said, but she interrupted me.

"No, Lulu, it isn't fine. I'm a dreadful prude; I know I am, I can't help it. I think it's because my parents were so religious, you know— PATRICK, GET YOUR HANDS OFF YOUR BROTHER'S NECK! I mean they were always sending me off to Bible camp and going on at me about mortal sin and how you had to sleep with your hands outside your duvet."

I was smiling now, smiling at Stella, who had apparently spent much of her youth lying rigid in her bed, feverishly praying that her own hands wouldn't wander.

"It's okay," I said. "It really is okay."

I sat down on the stool beside the telephone table.

"I'm just glad you're still talking to me."

"Of course I am."

"So, did you pray for me?" I teased, already knowing the answer.

"Yes."

"Which saint?"

"Jude."

"Which one's that?"

"Lost causes."

"Right."

"Lulu?"

"Yes?"

"I think you should go to confession."

"I don't think so, Stella."

⌒

"Bless me, Father, for I have sinned," I said quietly in the dark. "It has been—" How long had it been since I had done this?

Sat opposite a stranger and whispered my secrets to him? Not
since I was a child, trying to catch a glimpse of the priest's bowed
head, even though I knew it was Father Duffy trying to pretend
he didn't know me.

Now, all those years later, the priest opposite me shifted in his
seat, probably used to people blowing in off the street outside his
church on a whim and a prayer, desperate for redemption.

But I hadn't chosen this church randomly: I knew Saint Se-
bastian's well, and was familiar with how it could wrap its cool
sandstone arms around a little girl feverishly lighting candles
for her vanishing mother. Sometimes, when Rose had too many
Doris days in a row, I would walk the seven blocks from my house
to this church and its quiet embrace.

Kneeling in its wooden pews, I'd close my eyes and pray:
"Dear God, please make Rose better. Dear God, please make
Rose better. Dear God, please make Rose better." I would say
the words over and over, rocking back and forth on my knees and
hoping that, if I said them often enough, someone would have to
hear them.

"God," I'd put in as an addendum, "I know you're probably
really busy, so if there's anyone else there—one of the saints who
hasn't got as much to do as you—I don't mind if they help either."
An eight-year-old girl bargaining with her idea of heaven.

Now I was back and not really sure why; maybe just because
Stella had wanted it.

And possibly because nothing else, not the tears that fell until
I thought there could not possibly be any left to cry, or the letters
of apology I wrote and discarded, or the marks I left on my skin by
digging my nails into it, had made me feel one iota better.

I had done something I had no idea I was capable of, and the
guilt of it gnawed at me night and day, and I didn't think I would
ever, ever get over the shame of it.

It was ironic, I thought, that it had been years since I had stepped inside a church, years spent shedding much of the guilt it clothed its daughters in, and now it was guilt, and great big dollops of it, that had driven me right back inside again.

The priest made a quiet noise in his throat.

Right.

Better get on with it.

"It has been quite a few years since my last confession," I said, remembering every word of the ritual. "These are my sins."

The cool air hung between us. Outside someone was moving around in the church, probably a volunteer doing the flowers.

I closed my eyes, rubbed them.

"Yes," the priest said, and I had no idea how to get the next part out.

"I recently had, well, what occurred was I, had fornication"—*was that even a word?*—"that is to say, I spent some time with a married man, Father," I said.

He nodded again.

"On his wedding night."

Even in the shadowy cubicle, I could see his eyebrows shoot up.

"I'm terribly upset about it, Father," I said, the words rushing out, the cool air suddenly feeling uncomfortably hot.

Gently, he said, "And why did you do that, my daughter?"

"I don't know," I answered him, bringing my hands to my face. "I don't know why."

But, of course, I did.

chapter seven

In the last few weeks of school, Annabelle had grown a different skin, shedding who she used to be when I wasn't looking. A new, brittle layer masked any softness she'd ever shown. I saw less and less of her as the year wound down; we didn't always walk home together, and when we did she would walk slightly ahead of me, and I could never quite catch up.

She didn't want to talk about Frank, still licking his wounds under his mother's roof, and she certainly didn't want to discuss Annie, ensconced again at the River House, her affair with Fergus, for the time being at least, over.

Annabelle had asked me to be there for Annie's homecoming, probably the last conversation we'd had that had scratched the surface, the two of us waiting on the front steps for the taxi to arrive.

"Are you all right?" I'd asked.

"Yeah," she said, "just a bit nervous."

"Are you glad she's coming home?"

"I don't know, sort of, I guess, in between being really pissed off with her."

We laughed, sipped our Cokes.

"Do you want to go inside and wait?"

"No, I want to see her get out of the car."

"Why?"

"I want to see her face, Tallulah."

"Okay," I'd said uncertainly. But the instant Annie got out of the cab, and Annabelle drew back beside me, I knew that whatever expression the prodigal mother wore to greet her daughter was apparently the wrong one.

Annie arrived as she'd left, in a hurry, slamming the cab's door and striding up the path carrying her paints and bags filled with sarongs, shell necklaces, and two grass skirts, one for Annabelle and one for me.

She had quickened her steps to get to her daughter, fallen into her.

"You look beautiful, darling," she said. "I missed you every day," and I looked at Annie's face and knew that it was true.

Not that it helped any.

We had gone inside and Annie had unpacked her treasures, telling us stories about where she had been, but not who she had been with, and then giving us the grass skirts.

"Thanks, Annie," I said, studying the row of perfect white cowrie shells sewn into the skirt's waistband. "Let's go and try them on, Annabelle."

Annabelle glared at me, and I realized I had made a mistake. "No, thanks, Tallulah," she said, tossing her skirt on the floor.

"Oh, come on, Annabelle," Annie said, "try it on. What else are you going to do with it?"

Annabelle stood up, looked into her mother's face. "I thought I'd burn it," she said coolly. "I wouldn't want to catch anything off it."

Annie had put her head in her hands. "So this is how it's going to be?" she said.

"You started it," said Annabelle, and walked out.

After that, the two of them cohabited under the one roof, Annabelle affording her mother only the merest hint of herself, silently complying with domestic instructions and answering when she had to.

Annie tried.

I saw it the few times I visited, but the absence of Frank throbbed through the house as Annie tried to repair the damage under its roof.

"How long," she asked one day, appearing at Annabelle's bedroom door while we were studying, "is this marathon sulk going to go on for, Annabelle? Because I have better things to do than spend my life dealing with an obdurate teenager."

"Then don't," Annabelle answered, flipping over on her bed to her stomach. "Do what you like, you always have."

"Do something with her, Lulu," Annie said, "before I go back to the bloody Solomons."

But there was nothing I could do; Annabelle was slipping through my fingers too.

I missed her.

But in between studying for my exams, helping Rose look after Mattie and Sam, and being consumed by Josh Keaton and his determination to get under every inch of my skin, much of the drama being played out at the River House coursed by me, and I didn't miss her enough.

~

We were going to travel.

We were going to Indonesia first, so Josh could surf Uluwatu, then Japan so I could see the cherry blossoms, then Europe, where we were both going to see everything.

While I studied for my exams, Josh studied Lonely Planet guides, working out our route, when was the best time to go where, what we would need to take with us, what jobs we could do to pay our way.

"I'm going to learn how to say *I love you* in seventeen languages," he told me, "and then I'm going to show you."

Josh had it all worked out. All I had to do was tell Rose and

Harry. Because while Pearl Keaton would one day look through her haze of smoke, realize her son was gone, and keep doggedly puffing away without a moment's pause, my parents were another matter.

Harry was growing wary of Josh, worrying that we were too serious, too young, never mind that when he was nineteen, he had fallen head over heels for a girl in a buttercup-yellow dress that swished when she walked.

And Rose . . . well, I hated to think of Rose without me. She had been good for so long—Doris had not put in an appearance for months—but Rose was, I knew, unpredictable. She needed me beside her as she moved around the house making her cakes and casseroles, knitting her jumpers for Harry and the boys, in case she dropped a stitch.

So I put off telling them, and Josh grew more and more impatient.

The last week of school came, and I still hadn't told them.

"Have you said anything to your parents yet?" Josh had asked me by the river.

"No, but I will, Josh, I told you, after exams."

"I told my mum this morning."

"What did she say?"

"She said it was fine, that she'd always wanted to travel herself, you know, how she never got the chance, the usual guilt trip."

"Oh," I said, "well, at least you've told her."

"What do you reckon your folks will say?"

"I think they'll say we need to slow down; I think they'll say I should go to college first before traveling; I think they'll say that I need something to fall back on." I snuggled in a little closer and looked up at his face. "And I'll say I've already got something to fall back on."

"Lulu?"

"Mmm." My mouth on his earlobe.

"We really need to do this thing."

"I know."

"You need to tell them we're going. And I need to start booking tickets."

"I told you, Josh, I will, after exams."

"Promise?"

"Promise."

"Lulu?"

"Yes, Josh?" I smiled.

He sat up.

"I've got to get the hell out of Juniper Bay," he said.

On the last day of school, Annabelle didn't show up, so when we all threw our school hats in the air, hers was missing, and in all the photos taken that day—me and Stella and Simone grinning from ear to ear, poking our tongues out, squashing our faces together, Simone making stupid rabbit ears behind Stella's head in every single one—there was nothing of her.

There was not one image from that day to record that Annabelle Andrews ever sashayed through Saint Rita's stained-glass doors and left her reflection there wherever I looked.

But I needed to share the final school day with her somehow, so when the last bell rang, I tore myself away from all the other girls going crazy on the oval, Stacey Ryan taking off her shirt to do cartwheels in her bra, and ran all the way to the River House.

"Annabelle," I yelled, letting myself in through its never-locked door and running up the stairs. "Annabelle, I can't believe you didn't come today, where were you? Where *are* you? Annabelle, ANNABELLE!"

My uniform was covered in felt-tipped scrawls from over-excited schoolgirls who'd drawn flowers and love-hearts beside their names. My hat was pulled low over my ears, completely destroyed by Bata Scout–clad feet stomping all over it, and in my bag, bumping all the way against my legs as I ran, was the book I had planned to give Annabelle.

It was a journal of every single word we had made up together, and its meaning—starting with *Absolutely: absolutely/completely—To agree wholeheartedly with*, and ending with *Zigot: zealot/bigot—Person with very extreme views they insist on shouting at people.*

"She's not here," Annie said, materializing at the bottom of the stairs. "I thought she'd be with you, Lulu, celebrating the last day of Saint Rita's serfdom."

"No," I said uncertainly, not wanting to get Annabelle into trouble, "we didn't go home together—do you mind if I wait here for a few minutes, Annie?"

She shook her head and floated away.

I waited on the stairs, perspiration trickling down the back of my neck, between my legs, and biting into the back of my knees, making me thankful for the cool silence of the house. It was so quiet there these days: no dinner parties with guests who filled the house with smoke and laughter; no glasses tinkling or music playing.

I thought about Frank, sitting on that step, about how much I missed him and how much Annabelle pretended not to, remembering what she had said at the beach the previous weekend, when the two of us were under the shower.

Josh was running up from the water, holding his board under his arm, his board shorts low and long on his hips, and Annabelle and I were arguing—again—about Frank.

Annabelle switched off her shower and shook her body from head to toe, covering me in salty droplets. "Will you let it rest, Tallulah?" she said. "Honestly, you're like a dog with a bone over this thing."

"I'll let it rest when you tell me what exactly Frank did to deserve the silent treatment and when you tell me what your problem is."

"My problem," she said slowly, watching Josh run toward us, "is that I have a father who was too stupid to see what was going on right in front of his own eyes, and with his own brother." She reached down and picked up her towel, eyes still on Josh. "And if people are too stupid, or don't care enough, to see what's going on right in front of them, Tallulah, then they get what they deserve."

Before the thought was even completely finished, it seemed like my legs stood up all by themselves from the River House's stairs, to run down them, out the front door and past Annie's "See you, Tallulah."

I ran down the side of the house, past Frank's workshop, the tree house, the tiny moon-shaped beach, along the scrappy paths with the branches that snatched at my skin all the way to the canoe club with its graying jetty sighing with the lovers who lay beneath it.

As I ran, images clicked through my head, like I was looking through a viewfinder: Josh tucking a curl back behind Annabelle's ear; looking down at Snow's to see their feet swinging together under the table; the two red dots on Annabelle's cheeks when I'd walked into Frank's shed last Saturday morning and Josh was there, with no shirt on—"It's so hot," he'd said. "It's so hot"; Josh's urgent "I've got to get the hell out of Juniper Bay."

I ran until I saw them, and the last image clicked into place, the two of them, naked, silvery fish beneath the dock.

Josh sat up with his hand on his mouth, and said "Lulu." Annabelle brought her knees to her chest, as my own buckled beneath me and I fought to stand.

I said their names, my arms outstretched—for what?

For what? I always asked myself later, long after I had turned on my heel and ran as fast as I could all the way back the way I had come, stumbling and tripping on my own feet, not bothering to push branches away as they scratched at my face so that by the time I ran to my own front gate and past the DE LONGLAND PLUMB-ERS—PLUMBING THE DEPTHS OF EXCELLENCE sign and straight into Rose's bewildered, outstretched arms, my chest was heaving with shuddering sobs and I was bleeding outside and in.

Annabelle and Josh would spend the next few years doing all the things Josh and I were meant to do: Josh helping Annabelle put on her backpack, laughing as she fell with the weight of it. They would travel and take pictures with the camera Fergus had given them as a going-away present; they would drink too much red wine in crooked little bars in Spain; they would squint their eyes against the whitewashed walls that hold up the Greek islands; they would land like lemmings in Earls Court in London, and I would stay at home, on the streets I grew up on.

I would stay at home with Harry and Rose, look out my window, and wonder which one of them I ached for more.

part two

chapter eight

"I don't want you working here anymore, Lulu."

I looked up from my desk to see Harry standing beside it in his navy boiler suit, rubbing the back of his neck as if he were trying to erase it.

"I don't want you in the office anymore," he repeated, still rubbing, and I knew from the way he said it he'd been practicing the words.

"Well, that makes a lot of sense, Harry," I smiled. "Your books are finally up-to-date, the billing system's sorted, all the apprenticeships are done. Sheesh, what more do you want from me?"

"Not from you, *for* you, love."

"What?"

"It's not what I want from you, it's what I want for you."

"Very deep, Harry, you really are plumbing the depths today."

My eyes flicked back to my computer screen as Harry shut the office door, his work boots leaving tiny mounds of black dirt on the carpet—Rose would have a fit, I thought automatically.

Harry rolled a chair from across the room and sat down beside me.

"It's time for you to start living, Lulu."

"What?"

"You're twenty-two now, and you've been moping around this

office and at home since you were eighteen, ever since Annabelle and Josh left."

I put my hand up to stop him.

"No, love, I know we're not allowed to mention their names, but it's bloody ridiculous. What's happened has happened, and they're long gone. You can't keep flogging a dead horse, especially after it's bolted." Harry took the hanky out of his pocket and handed it to me, just in case. "You've been wonderful, Lulu, with the business expanding the way it has, but it's not right, love, it's wrong of me to keep you here running the show."

"I've liked it."

"No, you haven't, Lulu, you've borne it out, that's all."

I stared at the computer screen.

Of course I had borne it out.

My ambition had not been to say: "Good morning, de Longland Plumbers, how can I help you?" or driving my car to work sites where men in hard hats wolf-whistled long and low, and only stopped when someone told them I was the boss's daughter. I had never sat on my bed and dreamed of doing spreadsheets until my eyes burned behind their lids.

This was not the life I had been hurtling toward through the school gates on that last day, my hat caught on the sky's breath, every nerve singing with what was to be.

I had never imagined I would stay so still.

But if my life did not remotely resemble the one I had planned, it was at least, a life. I had found comfort in its inertia, in the familiar rhythms of the office, where I arrived at half past seven and flicked the kettle on a minute after that, and at home, where even Rose's moods, mercurial as they were, had their own pattern. Her depression waxed and waned, leaving our house in shadow or light, but always there; Rose, our very own paper moon.

We lived around it, Harry reading his paper quietly in the garden, the boys thundering down the stairs to be picked up for swim squad, flicking their towels at me on the way. Sixteen years old now, they ate like bears and looked like giants and came to me when Rose crumbled.

The thought of leaving them, or any of it, filled me with panic.

"Harry, I don't want to do anything else."

"Yes, you do, and you know you do. Your mother and I want you to try something else, Lulu. Go to college, like you were meant to; go traveling; do anything, love, but do something—and do it somewhere else."

There it was.

"You're firing me *and* kicking me out?"

"That's about the size of it." He grinned and took the hanky back to blow on it loudly.

~

Rose came down to my car in Betty—blue-and-white seersucker bumps, big pockets—and thrust a basket filled with cakes and buns and biscuits covered in checked tea towels into my hands.

"Rose," I said, "it's an hour-and-a-half drive, there's enough food here for a week."

"I know, but you can give some to Simone when you see her—I saw her on television the other night and she's as skinny as a stick! Now, you'd better go if you want to miss the traffic."

I put the basket in the passenger seat, smiled at Rose, who smiled back, our eyes holding.

"Off you go," she said, crossing her arms.

I kissed her, got in, and pulled out of the driveway, stopping briefly at the end of the street to take a look at her in the rearview mirror, waving until the very last moment when I turned the corner and headed for the city in a car that smelled like a cinnamon bun.

Simone was already ensconced in city life, clawing her way up the television ladder and hanging on with grim determination as those above her fell, and sharing a flat with a girl called Beth who wore kimonos and smoked a lot.

"You can stay with us for a few weeks until you find your feet," Simone had said on the phone, "or until Beth dies of emphysema—then you can have her room."

I moved in temporarily with the two of them, unpacking Rose's offerings before an incredulous Beth, who said: "Are those *baked goods*? I didn't know anyone did *baked goods* anymore," then proceeded to work her way through Rose's basket, in between puffs.

After Harry had told me it was time to end one sort of life and begin another, I'd gone home to appeal to Rose—but she'd simply echoed everything he'd said. So had Mattie and Sam, who'd professed that they too wanted me gone so they would no longer have to share a room.

A few days later I'd told Stella, who'd said, "It's time," and burst into tears, and Simone, who'd sighed over the phone, then said: "Just get here, Lulu, stop fucking around."

Having not much of a life had its advantages—there wasn't much of it to pack up: just my clothes, my résumé, and the "city survival kit" the boys who worked for Harry presented me with on my last day.

Pete, Micko, Chook, Simon, Lizard, and Alexi had stood in a half circle around me and shifted their feet while I opened it. A torch, a penknife, an oxygen mask, a street directory, and, finally, a pair of faux-fur-trimmed handcuffs and a box of "maximum pleasure" ribbed condoms.

"You never know your luck in the big city, Lulu!" Micko had shouted while they all fell about laughing, and our first-year apprentice, Lizard—so called because he was always flat out like one—grew pink at his ears.

They toasted me with warm chardonnay out of plastic cups and surprised me with a ludicrously large card that said, *You'll be*

missed, on which Chook had crossed out the *m* and replaced it
with a *p.*

We were all half-drunk when we left the office, Micko ruf-
fling my hair with his red hands and saying, "You're a good girl,
Lulu, you'll be all right."

Two weeks later, I was curled up on a mattress in Simone's spare
room, praying that I would be.

Something had happened that day by the jetty all those years
ago, something had burrowed its way beneath my skin through
the damp earth and stayed there. It stamped me with a sourness
I could almost taste. It made me feel both invisible and obvious,
the sort of person it would take people a long time to notice, and
then, when they did, wonder why they had bothered.

When men looked at me with interested eyes, it made me
flinch. Not that it happened often—none of the single blokes,
names emblazoned on pockets, who worked for Harry over the years
ever asked me out, maybe because I was the boss's daughter, maybe
because there was not one thing about me that invited them to.

When snippets of stories about Josh and Annabelle filtered
back to our hometown, Mrs. Delaney calling from behind her
fence: "Well, your two old chums are certainly making a name
for themselves, photojournalists, aren't they, dear?" it made me
want to slap her stupid, doughy face.

Once, an accidental sighting of them in a magazine in the
news agency made me sway where I stood as I held their faces in
my hands, awash with bitterness.

But mostly, whatever had gotten ahold of me that day by the
river made me sad. Not Rose-sad, not lost-in-another-place hope-
lessness, but face-pressed-to-the-window sad, watching from behind the glass.

I had left home without much of a fight, not having much

fight left in me. But somewhere along the drive to the city, I felt a shift, as if my body was uncoiling a little from its confines. It might have been that I was only twenty-two and youth has its own way of shouting in your ear and making you sing, but driving to Simone's that day I began to let go.

Stella was right. Harry and Rose were right. It was time. All I had to do was let the air in.

That night I closed my eyes and went to sleep in Simone's flat, and felt Rose's hand on my cheek.

The next morning I was in the kitchen looking through the classifieds when Beth came in, adjusting the sash on her kimono as she sat down beside me.

"Watcha doing?"

"Looking for a job."

"What sort of job?"

"I don't know, really. Something that's not working for my father's plumbing company."

"Right, so obviously you're very picky—what are you good at?"

"I don't know," I said, and realized it was true.

"Are you a leso?" she asked, reaching for her pack of cigarettes and fishing one out.

"I'm sorry?"

"Are you," she whispered dramatically, "a friend of Dorothy's?"

"I don't think so," I said uncertainly. "Is she a mate of Simone's?"

Beth threw her head back and laughed so hard she immediately began choking on her cigarette, screwing up her little face and clawing at her throat until I passed her some water.

She gulped it down, wiped her eyes, and blinked at me.

"You know what?" she said, "I've a feeling you're not in Kansas, anymore, Toto."

Later, when Simone and Beth had left for work—Simone to a production meeting and Beth to the dental surgery where she worked, I presumed, as the anesthetist by breathing on people—I took the number out of my handbag.

Are you a secret worrier? the woman's voice on the radio had asked, about halfway between my house and Simone's. *Is the only person holding you back you? Do you want to reclaim the power that you know is in you?*

"Yes," I had whispered in the car. "I do."

Then call the Epstein Institute, a respected name in personal growth since 1982, and join our Worrier Women Workshop—we'll teach you how to roar.

I felt a bit ridiculous dialing the number, but something had made me pull over in the car and write it down, and after being so quiet for so long, I was pretty sure I was ready to roar, or at least howl a little.

"Hello, the Epstein Institute," a woman's voice—not the one from the radio, I noticed—said. "How can I help you?"

"Hi," I said. "I'm interested in one of your workshops, the one for women who worry too much."

"I, I'm sorry, which one?"

"The, um, Worrier Women Workshop," I replied. "You know, ah, for women who want to roar."

There was a long pause, then a snort of laughter.

"It's Warrior Women, love, *Warrior* Women."

"Oh," I said, "'Warrior Women.' Of course, well, I'm sorry to trouble you, but no, I don't think I'm one of those."

I hung up, not with a roar but with a whimper.

Simone laughed even harder than the woman on the phone

when I told her and Beth what I had done over two and a half
bottles of red wine and takeaway curry that night.

"I'm glad you didn't sign up, Lulu," Simone said. "You probably would have had to go on some ghastly weekend away where
they make you kill a pig and smear its blood on each other's boobs
or something. . . . Actually, maybe I should go!"

"Well, I think," Beth said, swaying in her kimono and talking
through the cigarette dangling between her lips, "that it was very
brave of you to call, Lulu, and you know what else I think?"

"No."

"I think you *are* a warrior woman, setting off for a new life
with your basket of baked goods. . . ."

"More like Red Riding Hood," Simone said, yawning. "I'm
off to bed."

A little later, as I passed by her room a little unsteady on my
feet, I said in a half whisper, "Simone, are you awake?"

"Yes," she answered.

"I wanted to say thank you."

"For what?"

"For letting me stay."

"No problem."

"Simone?"

"Mmm?"

"I love you," I told her.

"I love you too, Lulu."

"But not in that way."

"In what way?"

"I'm not a friend of Dorothy's," I whispered. "I'm very sorry,
Simone."

"Good night, Tallulah," she said, and I felt her smile in the
darkness.

The next morning Simone had gone out for a run—I had no idea how—and Beth was sitting slumped in the chair at the corner of the kitchen, reaching into her pockets for cigarettes, putting one to her mouth, taking it out again, and saying, "No, even I can't do it this morning."

"Would you like a cup of tea?"

"Love one—that was a pretty good night, wasn't it?"

"Yeah, it was."

"I still can't believe," she said, a laugh forming in her throat and slowly working its way up to a hack, "I still can't believe you said 'the one for women who worry too much.'" Her little body seized up as a cough rattled at her throat.

"Here," I said, handing her a glass of water to put out the fire.

When she finished coughing she said, "So, what exactly do you worry so much about, Lulu? For example, what's the one thing that is worrying you the most right now?"

I looked at her, so tiny, curled up in the wooden chair, her feet barely reaching the floor, and thought about all the things that were on my mind that morning—that I wouldn't find a job, or a place to live, that I would have to go scurrying back to Harry and Rose, that everyone would say knowingly, "I see the de Longland girl's home again," that I would always, despite the long drive between me and my hometown and the air rushing through the window, continue to feel the way I had felt for the last four years for the rest of my life.

Then I looked at Beth and thought of the thing that was really, really bothering me.

"I am really worried," I said, pointing at the packet of cigarettes on the table, "that those things are going to kill you."

~

I spent that day looking for a job in the paper, and by the end of it had three appointments, all at temp agencies, all for places who wanted someone to come in, answer the phone, type a few letters, file a few orders, arrive on time, leave on time, and not nick anybody's lunch out of the fridge.

Perfect.

I wonder what would have happened if I'd got a job like that.

Instead, Simone insisted I go and see her friend Loreli Marks, of the Marks and Abbott recruitment agency.

"They do mostly media work," Simone said, "in television or radio or advertising or marketing firms, and then they have a creative arm where they work with galleries and theaters and agencies. It's still office work, but at least the offices have a bit of life about them—you might meet someone famous."

"I already know someone famous—you!"

"Not yet, Lulu"—she smiled—"but I will be."

~

"Your reference is terrific," Loreli beamed at me, her bright red lipstick like two glossy ribbons stretched across her face, "even if it is from your father."

"I haven't really worked for anyone else, I'm sorry."

"Don't be," she said crisply. "Your typing is excellent, your shorthand's very good, your bookkeeping skills are completely up-to-date, and your presentation is terrific. I wish I had a hundred of you, Tallulah," she said, "but I don't, so the question is where to send you where it will do you and me the most good—and I think I'm going to give you to Duncan."

"Give me to Duncan?"

"Not in the biblical sense, dear, don't look so alarmed. No, I thought I might set up a meeting between you and Duncan McAllister's people—you've heard of Duncan McAllister, no doubt."

"Yes," I said, "he's the fellow on the radio, the one with the magic tonsils."

"Platinum."

"Oh, yes, platinum. So what sort of help does he need?"

Loreli smiled at me. "Where do we begin, dear?"

~

"Duncan's a great bloke," one of the men in the restaurant told me.

"He's very energetic, very on the ball, it's a lot of fun working at 3KPG with him, never a dull moment."

"Oh, absolutely," said the other one, who was called PJ or JP, something with initials anyway, and who clicked his fingers at the waitress.

I hated people who did that.

"So where is he?" I asked.

"Duncan?"

"Yes, I just think that if he is looking for a PA, wouldn't he need to interview the candidates himself?"

"Lulu," PJ said, "it's midday. Duncan does the morning show, which means he's been up since about three a.m., and right now he'll be home in bed, having a well-deserved rest. But I'm very much Duncan's right-hand man, and he trusts me with these sorts of decisions."

In the six years I worked for the man with the platinum tonsils, first as his PA and then as his producer, I never saw JP, or PJ, or whatever his name was, again.

chapter nine

Duncan McAllister.

King of the airwaves, darling of the talkback set, smoker, red-wine drinker, and serial ex-husband with three former wives—Kiki, Kerry-Anne-with-an-E, Karen, and another one, Kimmy, on the way—his only criteria for marital bliss apparently being that the bride's name begin with K.

Besotted father to Duncan Junior (Kiki), Rhees (Kerry-Anne), twins Jasmine and Jarrod (Karen), and owner of Barney, an enormous dog of uncertain origins and highly questionable dietary habits.

An original.

An old fraud.

A mess.

~

"You cannot be serious, Lulu," Simone had said when I told her who my new boss would be." Duncan McAllister, what the hell is Loreli thinking?"

"Do you know him?" I asked.

"Everybody knows him, Lulu," she said. "He'll eat you alive, Little Red Riding Hood."

"Why?" I asked. "Why is everybody so afraid of this person?"

"Because, Lulu," Simone answered, "he is the most powerful

person in the media, therefore he is one of the most powerful people in the country, therefore he is a first-class wanker."

"I heard he once set fire to a waiter's hair because he thought he was ignoring him," Beth said, coming in from the bathroom.

"I'm sure it was an accident," I said, already displaying a portentous level of loyalty to my unseen employer.

"It was pubic hair, Lulu," Simone said.

"Oh."

"Anyway, if you survive, you'll have to have him over for dinner. It would do my career no harm at all if Platinum Tonsils became a personal friend of mine."

"You said he was a wanker."

Simone smiled at me. "It's the media, Lulu," she said. "We're all wankers."

On my first day at 3KPG, I pulled my car into the visitors' car park, the security guard not appearing to understand when I explained I was a new permanent employee—personal assistant to Duncan McAllister, actually.

"They all are, love," he said, slapping a purple VISITOR sticker on my windshield.

I walked up the half-lit hill to the studios, hushed and still in the early hours of the morning, wandered around its labyrinthine halls by myself, and eventually found Duncan's office—hard to miss with the glittering microphone painted on its door.

"Right," I said to myself, borrowing one of Mattie and Sam's childhood expressions, usually used when they were poised on the edge of some sort of danger: "Let's *do* this thing."

I took a couple of deep breaths and knocked on the door, which was swung open moments later by a man with a red face, a red-wine stain on his upper lip, and a red shirt patterned with giant hibiscuses, with all of its buttons undone.

"Please tell me you are here to deliver my very late morning coffee, because if you are not, you can fuck right off," he said, hibiscuses swaying.

Duncan McAllister, I presumed.

Determined to remain professional, I held out my hand and smiled. "I'm Tallulah de Longland," I said. "Your new personal assistant."

"Really?" he said, ignoring my outstretched hand. "How very exciting for you. Now, Tabitha—"

"Tallulah."

"Tallulah—my apologies to both you and Miss Bankhead. Now, do you think you could possibly make me a coffee or would you prefer to fuck off?"

He swayed a little more on his feet, and behind him, the beginnings of a little fire sparked in the ashtray on his desk.

"I beg your pardon?"

"Oh, wonderful, they've sent me a deaf person—*Mungo!*" he suddenly roared. "Get me a fucking coffee and get rid of this person from the sheltered workshop."

Then a wolf attacked me.

It came from somewhere behind Duncan, a great lolloping beast bearing down on me like a shaggy freight train, barreling into my knees and wedging its head firmly between them.

Then it backed out from between my legs and, with a surprisingly fluid and graceful leap, pinned me against the corridor wall, one great paw on either side of my chest.

"Oh dear God," I said as its breath assailed me from all angles, "what on earth have you been eating?"

The beast nuzzled me, its wet nose poking at my neck, its tongue dripping drool, and its owner clearly not in a hurry to call it off.

"Could you tell it to get down, please?" I squeaked to Duncan, now sitting back at his desk, making a great show of going through some papers and ignoring the fire now raging in the ash-tray beside him.

"Pardon?"

"Could you call it off?"

"*It* has a name—Barney," he replied. "He is a dog, and for some strange reason he seems to like you, Talisa."

"Tallulah," I said again, this time through gritted teeth.

Duncan whistled and Barney released his paws as my knees buckled beneath me.

"Now that you've finished playing with my dog," Duncan said, continuing to shuffle papers from one side of the desk to another, "do you think you could possibly personally assist me by making me a fucking coffee, or should I send out for one?"

"You should send out for one."

"Pardon?"

"You should send out for one, Mr. McAllister," I said, picking up my handbag off the floor where the wolf-dog had knocked it out of my shaking hands and heading for the door.

I could not, I realized, work for this person.

Not because of his rudeness—although no one had ever spoken to me as he had—or his swearing—I had heard it all before and then some on building sites—or even his questionable taste in shirts.

It was because I was a plumber's daughter.

Specifically, I was Harry de Longland's daughter, a man who plumbed the depths of excellence day in, day out, with one of Rose's handkerchiefs crisply folded in his pocket. Harry, who spent his life up to his elbows in other people's U-bends and got into his work truck every morning with a smile and a wave; Harry, whose office was always tidy, and whose apprentices were taught to be courteous and interested in what little old ladies living in apartment buildings with blocked drains had to say.

I looked at the squalor of Duncan's office, with its overflowing ashtrays and growths on top of scattered coffee cups, the bulging in-trays and papers on the floor, and I could see he didn't give a damn about any of it.

I looked at Duncan and thought of my father, sitting at home late at night, using a pencil to fill out the rosters so he could carefully erase any trace of mistakes, standing on a ladder on his bandy legs repainting the sign that stood outside our house every year or two, and I knew I was in the wrong place.

"I'm sorry, Mr. McAllister," I said, "but this isn't going to work out. I'll go straight to the agency and explain. I'm sure they'll send you someone, um, better." I started to walk out the door.

"You're leaving? Even for me that was quick," he mused, looking pleased with himself. "Could even be a personal best."

The smugness of his tone made me childishly determined to have the last word. After all, I would never be seeing him again.

"I shouldn't think that's something to be particularly proud of, Mr. McAllister," I told him coolly, and turned on my heel.

~

"Geez, that was quick," the man at the sentry gate said, echoing Duncan's words. "I think you might have set a new record."

"Mmm," I replied, handing in my VISITOR card and leaving the studios of 3KPG far, far behind me.

Pity.

I quite liked the dog.

~

Later that night I was sitting on the floor with a glass of wine, resting my head against the sofa and describing my encounter with Duncan to Simone and Beth when our doorbell rang.

Simone went out through the kitchen, then came in again with Duncan behind her, his hair brushed, his shirt ironed, his white shoes tasseled.

"Good evening." He nodded to Beth and me, then addressed me directly. "Tallulah," he said, articulating every syllable of my name, "I have come to apologize to you for my oafish behavior this morning."

"Oh, right," I said, getting to my feet, my thoughts scrambled. "Come and sit down, Mr. McAllister."

"Duncan."

"Duncan—would you like a drink?" I said, stupidly pointing to the bottle in my hand as an illustration.

"No, thank you, Tallulah," he said. "Stomach feels like it's been licked out by a rabid Afghan dog, so no, I'll just grovel awhile, if I may."

"You may," said Simone, clearly delighted.

"In private, perhaps?" Duncan said.

We sat in Simone's kitchen, Duncan eating some of Rose's muffins I had heated up for him in the oven.

"Mmnff," Duncan said through a mouthful, "these are very, very good."

"My mother's," I said. "There're about two hundred more in the freezer if you'd like to take some home with you, some jam-drop biscuits too, if you like those."

"Jam drops?" said Duncan. "I didn't even know people knew what they were anymore."

"My mother does," I said, and told him about Rose's baking.

I told him about Harry too, because he asked what my father did and if I had any siblings and about the town I'd grown up in until I looked at the clock and realized that at least one of the reasons he was called Platinum Tonsils was because he was very good at asking questions with them.

Duncan glanced at the clock too, nudging eleven, and straightened on his stool.

"Now, Tallulah," he said, dabbing at sultana scone crumbs with a napkin. "I want to apologize sincerely for this morning; it was very rude behavior, even by my standards."

I nodded, wondering if I should tell him he had one crumb still hovering on his nostril.

"The thing is, Barney likes you, and he's rarely wrong about people, although he liked my second wife, Kerry-Anne-with-an-E, too . . . God, she was a pain in the arse about that, always going on about it whenever some poor bloody hotel clerk had to write down our names: 'It's Kerry-Anne—Kerry with a Y, Anne with an E,'" he mimicked, then mused, "Mean of me, really, to spell it out that day in the divorce court . . ."

"Duncan."

"Oh, yes, getting off track, the thing is, Barney likes you. . . ."

"So you are here because your dog likes me?"

"Yes, exactly." He beamed, then caught my expression. "Well, not entirely. The thing is, Tallulah, well, the thing is, I'm a bit of a dickhead, really, and a lot of that is unquestionably me, but some of it is because I'm surrounded by other dickheads—you see?"

I nodded again, not quite knowing what else to do.

"I've been in the media for a long time, and it's been marvelous, but it does tend to turn us all into little monsters, and then I meet you and I think you might be just the person to help me be less of a monster, you see?"

"I don't know if that's in the job description." I smiled.

He smiled back, a little world opening between us.

"All right," I said, finding myself agreeing to work with this strange person. "But we have to clean up your office."

"Done!" He beamed. "We'll start fresh on Monday, bright and early, the curse of morning radio, I'll pick you up just after five—I live quite near here, you know."

He stood up, grabbed his sports coat and another scone, and beamed some more.

"We're going to have the most wonderful time, Tamara."

———

We settled into a friendship, Duncan and I: one that began that first morning he picked me up, his green station wagon rumbling up my driveway with Barney sprawled along the length of the backseat, happily dribbling on the car mats.

Duncan kept his word, and after he came off air, we cleaned the office, people stopping to gape at Duncan McAllister on his knees with a dustpan and brush and waltzing around the 3KPG hallways with the feather duster between his legs.

It was, I suppose, an unlikely friendship, but it suited us, and the only way I can think to describe it was that I taught him not to be too much and he taught me not to be too little—"Go on, Tallulah, do it, what's the worst thing that can happen?"

He was, I learned, a good man, and if his demons sometimes rose and turned him into a bad one, shouting and railing his way out of restaurants, smashing glasses and spluttering, "Do you know who I think I am?" nobody felt worse than the protagonist, shuffling into the studio the next day saying, "Don't look at me, Lulu, I'm wearing the cloak of shame."

It helped, of course, that we didn't find each other remotely desirable, Duncan once explaining he could never be attracted to someone with freckles: "They're like little red crabs marching across people's faces, aren't they, Lulu—oh, shit, sorry."

But with our own sexual dynamic sorted out, it still bothered him that I wasn't actually having any, and I would regularly catch him eavesdropping on my calls, hoping there was a man at the other end of the line.

After I had worked for him for about six months, he wandered into my office and said, "Tallulah, I have something to say."

"You've always got something to say, Duncan, that's why you're a talkback host."

"Very funny, Lulu, now listen, you're a good-looking girl, you really are. You remind me a bit of my second wife, Kerry-Anne, before she went off."

"Duncan!"

"Sorry, sorry—before she grew old gracefully. The thing is, you're a good sort, and I just can't understand why there's no bloke in your life, and I think it's about time you had some fun, got back on the horse."

"What horse, Duncan?" I asked, to annoy him.

"You know what I'm talking about, Lulu—Simone tells me you haven't had a canter in years."

Simone and Duncan occasionally attended the same wine-soaked industry dinners, and I hated the thought of the two of them talking about me.

"What? Oh, Duncan, that's disgusting, I can't believe Simone would tell you that," I said, even though I could.

"Calm down, Lulu, I'm only trying to help. And I think you might be blocked."

"Blocked?"

"Yeah, I think it's been so long since you've done the deed, you're terrified you've forgotten how to do it."

"You're insane," I said.

Duncan looked at me seriously.

"Would you like me to have a go?"

"What?"

"Would you like me to take a crack at it, get things moving again?"

"Oh God, Duncan," I said, "that's disgusting, that's the most disgusting thing I've ever heard."

"Only trying to help, Lulu," he said, shuffling back into his studio, and I couldn't be angry with him because I knew in his deeply misguided, completely unacceptable, totally repellent way, he was.

Duncan was right though. I hadn't saddled up in years.

Hadn't wanted to.

Wasn't ready to.

Too busy to.

Still aching somewhere.

I certainly kept busy though. I was up early and at the studio, home in the afternoons to potter around the flat, or to meet Simone for coffee. Stella and Billy had moved not too far away and I'd visit them too, playing with their kids in the backyard, rubbing Stella's tired feet and staying for macaroni and cheese. I swam one night a week at the local pool, went to yoga on Saturday mornings and to the markets with Beth on Sundays, until she announced she was moving back to the small town she had fled from.

"It's my dad," she told Simone and me. "His heart." Packing up her kimonos and Benson and Hedges, she explained, "I'm the only daughter, comes with the territory, brothers won't do a thing—don't want to face it, you know men."

"Not really," said Simone and I simultaneously, but for different reasons.

We waved her off. "See ya, Simone. See ya, Warrior Woman," she yelled later through the car window, and she was gone, in a little white puff of smoke.

The day Beth went back to the small-town streets she grew up on, she left behind much more than the lingering pall of smoke that seemed to hover for years afterward in Simone's apartment, or the half-empty packets of cigarettes we kept finding in potted plants or behind saucepans, soft-pack mementos of a girl who thought she could give up her vice by hiding it from herself—she left a question mark in the air.

Maybe it was the ripple of change her departure caused, the

slight shift in my small world, but whatever it was, almost from the moment her little car disapanished at the top of the hill, I began to feel restless.

It had been over a year since I'd arrived in the city, and while I had found what lots of people would call a pretty good job, and a place to live with Simone, I hadn't really met anyone new, apart from Duncan, since I'd arrived.

I'd let the air in, but not much else.

chapter ten

"What's the problem, Lulu?" Duncan said about a week later, "got TNT?"

"No, Duncan." I sighed. "I do not have premenstrual tension, which is, as you well know, PMT, not TNT. I just feel really, you know, really . . ."

"Boring?" he said.

"No," I said, "bored."

"Right," he said, "let's go, then."

"Where?" I said.

"Everywhere," he said, and meant it.

One of the perks of having platinum tonsils was that everyone wanted them at their party, but Duncan rarely obliged, preferring to stay at home with whichever wife he was cohabiting with at the time.

Weekends were spent with all of his children from his various marriages at Lingalonga, his beach house on Willow Island, about two and a half hours away from the city.

Sometimes their mothers came, sometimes they didn't, and sometimes I went along too, piled into Duncan's station wagon with Duncan Junior, Rhees, Jasmine, Jarrod, and Barney, his great big bullethead panting out the window.

I liked these weekends away with the various branches of my

employer's family tree, its own complications making my family seem almost normal, Rose's quirks not withstanding.

Willow Island itself was beautiful, and I felt myself exhale the moment my bare feet touched its sands, the shock of the waves hitting my skin, shaking off the city.

Mostly, I liked being with Duncan away from the microphone. On Willow, he was a toned-down version of himself, less amplified, the relief of not having thousands of people hanging on his every utterance making him quieter, making him listen.

We had some of our best conversations walking along the island's beaches, free-ranging, uncensored, never having to worry about when the commercial break was.

~

"Is Dad going to marry you?" Jarrod asked the first time I went away with them, little Jasmine's hand sitting softly in my lap.

"Don't be stupid, Jarrod," Rhees said, "as if he'd marry Tallulah—her name doesn't start with K."

"Ha-ha," said Duncan, "very funny."

"Daddy," said Jasmine, "Barney's eating the picnic rug."

Duncan loved weekends at Lingalonga, a name that both amused and appalled him but which he was stuck with because that was the name the old couple he had bought it from years beforehand had given it and, as Duncan said, "You don't muck around with history, Lulu."

Willow Island was reached by a car ferry, its captain Walter Prentice and his men in boiler suits shouting out unintelligible words to guide drivers up its ramp, their hair permanently stiff from working in the salty breeze, rolled cigarettes between their lips, which curled in smiles whenever they saw Duncan.

"G'day, mate," they'd say as we all piled out of the car. "Coming back to the real world, are ya?"

Duncan would smile, shaking hands all around and instantly

turning into the old man of the sea: "Winds up," "Sou'easter, is it?" or "Have the mackerel been running? I'm thinking of taking young Rhees here out for a go."

"They've got it made, those blokes," he told me, "working outside, fresh air, no worries, no ratings, no mad bloody ex-wives, no phone stalkers."

"No box at the cricket, no personal line to the prime minister's office, no adoring fans begging you to tickle them with your famous platinum tonsils—you'd last about a week, Duncan," I teased him. "Tops."

Then we'd all climb the barge's rickety old steel steps to the café perched like an eagle's nest at the top, settle into a booth, order Cokes and hot chocolates and something for Barney under the table, and Duncan would look out the salt-smeared window and say, "Well, here we go, kids, off to paradise."

"You always say that, Dad," Jasmine said one crossing when the wind was so strong, it felt like it was blowing the barge across the water.

"Because it's true, Jazzy," he said.

But after I told Duncan I was bored, he gave up Lingalonga for the next two weeks, sending his wives in his place and squiring me for a solid fortnight to parties, balls, charity auctions, gallery openings, and concerts, until we both collapsed in the studio, exhausted.

"Tallulah," he said one morning when he picked me up, having only dropped me off in a taxi a couple of hours earlier, "I can't do this much longer."

"But you said I had to get out there and meet new people; you said I was old before my time; you said, if I remember correctly, I had to scratch the itch before I forgot where it was."

"I know," he said, miserably, "but it's killing me."

The truth was, it was killing me too, I was just enjoying watching Duncan squirm every time we went out and he was set upon at the door: "Duncan McAllister, you old dog, where have you been!"; "Don't tell me you're still alive, McAllister, which wife are we up to now?"; "Oooh, Mr. McAllister, you're even more handsome in the flesh than you are on the radio!"—encounters he seemed to relish and be repulsed by at the same time. I was watching him one night, standing by a wall at a cocktail party at a gallery he had insisted we go to—"Lots of arty types there, Lulu, you might meet someone *vigorous*"—when a man came and stood beside me.

"Hello," he said to me, leaning his back against the wall, "do you mind if I share your wall? Nowhere to sit, of course, never is at these things."

"No, I don't mind," I said, looking at him—blue eyes; short, wavy blond hair; open-necked checked shirt; navy pants, and wondered if you could call him vigorous.

"I'm Ben Moreton," he said, holding out his hand.

"Lulu de Longland," I said, taking it.

"Great name."

"Thank you."

"So, what brings you here?" he asked.

Not vigorous, I decided. "I came with my boss, actually," I said. "I'm not sure why."

Ben Moreton smiled.

"I came by with a mate," he said. "I'm not sure why either."

Not vigorous, but nice.

We both stared out at the party, watching as a shout of laughter and a ripple of shoulders erupted from the group where King Platinum Tonsils was holding court.

Ben said, "That's the radio bloke, isn't it, Duncan McAllister? I really can't stand him, can you? He's so, I don't know, predictable."

"Actually, he's my boss." I smiled.

"Oh God, I'm sorry," said Ben. "I really don't know why I was going on about him like that, I mean I don't even know the man, I expect he gets that a lot."

"It's okay," I said. "Duncan's that sort of person—people either love him or hate him."

"What about you?"

"I love him," I said, watching Duncan blowing smoke rings across the room and poking his fingers through them.

"Then I take back every single thing I said about him, Lulu de Longland."

Not vigorous, but very, very nice.

Later, as Duncan, Ben, and I walked to the car—Ben's mate was long gone, but Ben had stayed on, offering to drive us home—there was a flurry at the door of the gallery as Annie Andrews walked in just as we were walking out.

"Platinum Dick!" she cried—Annie, hair graying, kohl a little thicker, perfume a little more cloying, but still unmistakably Annie.

I had not seen her since I had run from her house that final day of senior year, except once, on television, accepting the 1985 Archibald Prize for her "raw, intimate, and engaging portrait of Fergus Andrews, documentary maker and brother-in-law to the artist."

Now, there she was, right in front of me, her eyes widening as she realized who I was.

"Tallulah!" she said, "you've no idea how much we've all missed you."

Annie, drunk, grabbing at me with her jeweled hands.

I couldn't see anything except those hands scrabbling at me to take me back to where I did not want to go, her purple mouth saying, "This is amazing, this is amazing, Annabelle will be so pleased I saw you," until Ben somehow stood between us and shut the door, dragging Duncan and me with him.

"Time to go, I think," he announced.

"Our hero," Duncan simpered, then collapsed in Ben's arms.

"Right," he said, "let's get old Platinum Dick home."

I giggled.

"Then maybe you could tell me who that woman was, or maybe not, or when you're ready."

Very, very, very nice.

~

Ben worked in his family's shoe company, Moreton's Shoes—"Keeping Australia on Its Feet Since 1967"—mostly in the import department, which meant he traveled to Asia frequently and that by the time we moved in together exactly twelve months later, I had amassed a ridiculously large shoe collection.

"Lucky you've got such tiny feet, Lulu," he would say, kissing my toes. "So many great styles fit you." I loved Ben kissing my toes, but I didn't love him saying, "So many great styles fit you," just like I didn't love him telling people that between his family keeping Australia on its feet and mine plumbing the depths of excellence, we had the nation's best interests covered, or the way he rang me at work when the show was on to ask things like, "Are we still set for Tony and Kate's on Saturday night?"

"Uh-huh," I'd say, keeping an eye on the flashing phone lines, "six thirty."

"Great," he'd say. "Great, do we have to bring anything? I could do that rocket-and-feta salad if you like."

"That sounds good," I'd say. "I really have to go now."

"Okay, Lulu, sorry to interrupt, see you at home later."

"'*Rocket-and-feta salad*'?" Duncan's voice boomed through my cans. "How very Martha Stewart of him."

"Shut up, Duncan," I said, "and stop listening in on my calls."

"They're my calls, actually, Lulu," he said. "Remember

Mornings with McAllister, the name of the show? You're actually meant to be answering the phone for *moi*!"

"Fine," I said, and put Peter the mad postman from Hobart through to punish him.

⁓

Ben was twenty-nine to my twenty-three when we met, but he still had the baby-faced cheeks of his youth, making him look like a schoolboy in his suit, and he was an excellent shoe salesman; women, in particular, were unable to resist buying once he had their heels in his hands.

His father, Jeremy, looked just like him, except for some graying at his temples. He was a quiet, solid man who worked hard, played tennis two nights a week, and wrote thoughtful letters to the papers about import tax.

I liked Jeremy Moreton very much; I liked Ben's mother, Fiona, too, a pale, blond woman with an excellent shoe collection who always had a whiskey and soda at five o'clock.

Ben had three older sisters—Maria, Gwen, and Lois—who adored him and had always been vaguely suspicious of his girlfriends, the three of them hovering around me at family functions and asking questions like, "What do you think we should get Ben for his birthday this year, Lulu?" to see if I knew the answer.

But I liked them, especially Maria, who was an animal lover and, despite her family pedigree, absolutely refused to wear leather. The Moreton girls seemed to like me too, accepting my presence by their brother's side pretty much seamlessly.

Seamless.

That was the thing about Ben and me: after the night we met, and he called the next day to see how Duncan was and to ask me out for lunch, our lives blended neatly one into the other with no messy edges.

We went out to dinner together, he started swimming with me one night a week, he sent me funny postcards when he went on buying trips, and when he asked me to move in with him I did, my furniture fitting neatly into all the empty spaces in his apartment.

I left for work while he was still sleeping, would get home a few hours before he did, so I would have some time to myself before we had dinner together. Then I would go to bed early, Ben padding around the apartment carefully in order not to wake me.

In between, our lovemaking was easy, unhurried. Not what you'd call vigorous, but nice.

Sometimes, however, when Ben had tucked me in and kissed my forehead with a "Sweet dreams, Lulu," I would close my eyes, and another man would whisper, "Hello, Tallulah-Lulu," and I would know every inch of his skin.

chapter eleven

It could get quite exhausting catering to the two main men in my life: working for Duncan was like being the mother of an overgrown adolescent, and while Ben was, in comparison, much more mature, both were capable of sulking like teenagers if they felt the other was getting more attention.

So when Ben's work took him to Asia every few weeks, I spent the time half missing him and half not, and half feeling guilty about it and half not.

I had more time to spend with Simone and Stella, or on long phone calls with Harry and Rose, Harry surreptitiously updating me on Rose's health.

"Good," he'd say quietly into the phone, "getting out in the garden a bit more, went over to the Delaneys for their daughter's birthday, all the girls have had an airing . . ."

Harry's reports, like Morse code from home, were reassuring, but I still needed to visit Rose every few weeks to see for myself.

Mattie and Sam were growing up and out of the house, about to turn eighteen and in their final year of high school, their limbs like giant branches jutting out from their joints.

"Hey, Hallabalulu," they'd say, running down the stairs, "see you at dinner," slamming the screen door with their sports bags over their shoulders, on their way to soccer or rowing or football, where people would say, "There're the de Longland twins —

they're very good," and my heart would sing like a mother's to hear it.

If Rose's illness had touched them, it did not show, just as Harry and I had hoped. We had worked together, shielding them when they were small from the worst of Rose's sadness, Harry and I holding twin umbrellas over their heads.

On Doris days we had sent them to friends' houses, on Scouts' weekends away, or I would take them upstairs to their bedroom to distract them with the latest installment of Zac McCain and his very large brain.

They had loved those books, about a boy whose enormous brain contained all sorts of things—hidden doors into other worlds; secret passwords; recipes for disgusting dinners like blowfly pie and lemmingtons; lists of girls in school to be, in capital letters, AVOIDED AT ALL COSTS. There were codes to each portal of Zac McCain's very big brain, which Mattie and Sam solved with ease, hooting with laughter at my attempts to do the same.

"Lulu, it's easy," Sam would say, jumping up and down like a pogo stick on the bed. "You just take the third number and add it to the number of the last letter, then multiply it by the first number of Zac's name."

"What?" I'd say, squinting at the numbers. "You two are making this up."

"We're not," they'd chorus, their fingers digging into my ribs, their scratched and Band-Aided legs wrapped around mine on the bed, "it's you."

"Probably because you're a girl," Mattie would add, "and you haven't got a very big brain like Zac McCain."

I would snuggle down between them, wondering how Harry was doing downstairs in the kitchen, and wish that I did have Zac McCain's very large brain, because maybe then I could figure out how to help my mother.

Still, as big as they were now, and as strong as Rose appeared to be getting, I was drawn back to all of them every few weeks, just to make sure.

"Can I have next Monday off, Duncan?" I asked him one morning on the way to work after Ben had left for a two-week buying trip to Thailand. "I've set up all the interviews, you've got four pre-records done, and the 'What's Your Car Worth?' guy is coming in as well, so you don't really need me, and Suzanne said she'd do the call lines."

"Not Suzanne," he said petulantly. "She's a lesbian, and you know all lesbians hate me."

"All lesbians do not hate you, Duncan," I said, "and may I remind you yet again that refusing to sleep with you does not make a woman a lesbian, all right? Suzanne is not a lesbian and even if she was, it would not affect her ability to answer the phones. So can I have Monday off or not?"

"Only if I can come with you."

"What?"

"I want to come home with you, Lulu," he said. "I want to see little Sleepy Hollow, I want to sit at the counter and order a malted milk at White's . . ."

"Snow's."

"Snow White's . . . whatever. I want to swing on the porch, stand at the gates of your high school; I want to see where you have come from, Tallulah." He peered at me intently. "I need a day off myself, and I really, really want to get away from Kimmy."

"What happened, Duncan?"

"Slight indiscretion at the Radio Awards on Thursday night."

I sighed and thought, not for the first time, that when Duncan McAllister finally shuffled off this mortal coil, the words *Could Not Help Himself* should be carved into his tombstone.

"All right," I said, "you can come, but only if you stay where I can see you."

"You've become very possessive of me, Tallulah," he said, pulling into the station. "Not sure if that's healthy in a young woman."

⁓

Driving home to Juniper a few days later with Duncan, Jarrod, Jasmine, and Barney in Duncan's sauna-on-wheels, I looked in the little mirror at the two kids sprawled out on the giant dog behind me.

"Sound asleep," I said to Duncan.

"Angels," he replied. "Let's hope Barney doesn't eat them." He shifted in his seat. "Thanks for letting us come, Lulu, I know it's probably not the weekend you were thinking of with all of us here, but Karen's off on one of her bloody Men Are from Mars and All They Think of Are Their Penises weekends, and Kimmy's talking about the *L* word."

"Don't tell me you've turned her into a lesbian, too."

"Not lesbian," he breathed. "Lawyer."

I shook my head, watched the heat rise off the road, and flicked a fly out the window.

We drove on in silence, the car radio off because Duncan hated listening to anyone other than himself on air. "No point," he'd say. "Only makes me gloat unbecomingly."

Instead, we were tuning in to the dulcet sounds of Barney's snores and the occasional random word from Jasmine's lips.

The heat hung in the car, reducing our conversation to lazy snatches that went nowhere in particular for the rest of the trip.

As we got closer to home, I checked off all the familiar milestones for Jazzy and Jarrod, now awake with their heads hanging out opposite windows.

"That's where I went to primary school," I said. "That's the pool I learned to swim in! And that's my old high school, Saint Rita's."

"That's the oval I shagged the entire football team on," Duncan said under his breath.

I ignored him. "This is my street—and there's my mother!" I said, waving at Rose, who was standing in Kitty on the footpath, smiling.

We pulled over, Duncan bounding out of the car before I'd even unbuckled my seat belt.

"Hello, hello, you must be Rose, who by any other name would surely smell as sweet," he beamed, crushing her in his arms.

Back off, I thought, *back off, Duncan, you're too big, too much for her.*

But Rose was laughing and patting her hair, *purring*, I thought, in Kitty.

She'd been, I realized with a shock, and to use a phrase from the radio industry, *McAllistered*.

"And Harry!" Duncan was booming. "Let me shake the hand of the man who brought excellence back into plumbing. And now may I introduce Jasmine and Jarrod, two of the finest fruits from my loins, and Barney, who I believe may be eating your sprinkler as we speak."

We all turned to look at Barney, and I was about to say something when I realized everyone else was already heading inside, Duncan's suitcases at my feet.

"Hurry up, Lulu," he called from the door, "Rose has made some sort of fruit punch!"

Once Jasmine and Jarrod were upstairs in the spare room, coloring with the felt pens Rose had bought them, stomachs down and ankles up on the beds, Duncan and Harry had been sent outside with cold beers and a cheese platter.

Barney was somewhere under the house gnawing at its foun-

dations. I sat with Rose in the kitchen as she took the lamb out
of the oven.

"Saved you the shank." She smiled. "Don't let the men know."

"Rose," I said, "you've gone to so much trouble."

"I love it," she said simply.

"I know you do," I said, and added, "You look great, Rose."

"I feel it."

"Really?"

"Really." She smiled. "You've got to stop worrying, Lulu. I
really am so much better."

"How long have you been good?"

She smiled, twinkling—I loved it when Rose twinkled—"Now
there's a question. Might be better to ask how long I've been well."

"All right, how long have you been well?"

"Fourteen and a half weeks."

"That's so good, Rose."

"Well," she said, handing me the shank to chew.

~

That night at dinner we sat shoulder to shoulder around the
table while my fingers, as they always did, led themselves to the
AA and *TDL* carved underneath, tracing them from start to finish
and then traveling to the *JK* that Josh had carved next to them one
Christmas, making me wonder all over again about the girl who
had inextricably linked us together forternity.

Pointing out the signposts from my childhood to Jasmine
and Jarrod, I had seen Annabelle everywhere, coming out of the
school gates, caught in the slipstream of schoolgirls, ducking her
head under the showers at the pool, standing on corners with her
hat pulled low. I saw her beside me in the tree house, leaning out
the window and fluttering down notes to Frank below—*PLEASE
SEND LEMONADE ASAP*—and hauling up the provisions in
the basket attached to the rope Frank had made us. I saw her at

my door, taking off her school hat to show me her hair, dyed jet-black; I saw her flailing arms, hitting out at Stacey Ryan: "I will shove your arse clean through your ears."

I smiled, looking out the kitchen window, looking for Annabelle on the street where we grew up, always a step or two ahead of me, her face turning back to me to laugh at something we'd shared.

Josh was there too, looking up as we had driven past Snow's, wheeling his bike up Ladbroke Hill, sweat forming a V on his back, sitting on the wall outside Saint Rita's, waiting for me, legs swinging, Sister Bonaventure shooing him away. I saw him with Sam and Mattie in our backyard, the boys tumbling over him like waves, Josh rolling on the grass in laughter. I saw him at our door: "Hi, Mrs. de Longland. Anything to eat?" I saw his face in the half-light of a streetlamp as he bent down to kiss me, and I heard him whisper, "You're my girl."

They were everywhere I looked but nowhere I could touch them, and only by tracing their initials under my mother's table could I be certain they had ever once sat at it.

I felt Harry's eyes on me, willing me back into the conversation.

"So, Duncan," he said, carving the lamb at the head of the table, "what brings you to our neck of the woods?"

Duncan answered with a long spiel about the joys of small-town living, but I knew there was more to his visit than his professed longing to see Juniper Bay—it was there in the way he kept glancing at me, then lifting up his eyebrows in exaggerated ponder.

Later, when everyone else had gone to bed and we sat sipping red wine on the garden swing, I turned to him.

"So, Duncan," I said, "you want to tell me why you're really here?"

"Annie Andrews."

I sucked in my breath.

I hadn't mentioned Annie to Duncan since that night at the cocktail party where I had met Ben, and she had shocked me with her entrance, then her tears, and Duncan hadn't either, but I assumed that might have been because he had no recollection of it. I still didn't know how they knew each other, although I could probably guess.

"What about Annie Andrews?"

He leaned in toward me. "The reason I am here, Tallulah, is because I am interested to know what happened to you in this little town that made you so boring when I first met you. . . . Honestly, you were like a little Amish person."

"Oh, come on, Duncan, I'm sure you've extracted the whole story out of Simone by now."

"Only bits here and there, Lulu, bits and pieces. Simone only tells me what she wants me to know, infuriating woman—another lesbian, you know, town's bloody full of them in their cowboy shirts—and when I tried to get your friend Stella drunk at your birthday party to loosen her lips she had one glass of wine and burst into tears." He leaned in further. "But I do know that it's something about Annie Andrews and her family"— he narrowed his eyes—"some deep dark secret you've all harbored for years."

"It's not that big, Duncan," I began, but he silenced me, putting his fingers to my lips.

"It's all right, Lulu," he said. "I've figured it all out anyway, figured it out the night we ran into Annie and you went all limp and I had to carry you outside."

"*You* carried *me* outside?"

"Yes, and for the record, I do wish you could control your intake a little more when we're in public—but anyway, I figured it all out and I want you to know that your secret is safe with me."

"What secret, Duncan?"

He stopped mid-swing and peered at me.

"That Annie Andrews . . ." He paused dramatically, Sherlock Holmes in tasseled shoes. ". . . is your mother!"

I stared at him.

"Born out of wedlock and left to a then-childless Harry and Rose as a changeling on their doorstep to grow up, become best friends with Annabelle, Annie's legitimate daughter, only to discover years later that she is, in fact, your half-sister, and leave you wondering evermore who your real father is."

I was completely speechless.

"It's all right, my dear," he said soothingly, "your secret is safe with me, I'm an old bastard myself, you know."

"A silly old bastard."

"I beg your pardon?"

"You, you're a silly old bastard, Duncan McAllister," I said, starting the swing again.

"Not right?"

"Not even close."

"Well, what then?"

"You really want to know?"

"Yes I do."

"Why?"

"Because it matters to me."

"All right," I said, and told him.

"That's it?" he said about half an hour later.

"What do you mean, that's it?"

"That's it? Some pimply-faced adolescent walking around with a permanent erection broke your poor little small-town heart by running off with your best friend, and you didn't get to be king and queen of the prom. That's the terrible past that made you the most boring woman on earth when I first met you? That's the big secret, the love that dare not speak thy name? Jesus, Lulu, who didn't get their heart broken in high school? My first girlfriend gave me the clap and then ran off with her driving instructor."

"What was her name?"

"Who?"

"The girl, the one who ran off with the instructor."

"Chloe," he said.

"Oh," I said.

"With a K."

We both laughed so hard we nearly fell off the swing.

~

"I'm sorry, Lulu," he said later. "I shouldn't have belittled your story, as pathetic as it really is."

"That's all right," I said. "You're right, anyway, I let the whole thing go on for far too long, made it much bigger than it really was."

"No, I'm not right," he said. "Perhaps if I had loved so deeply I would not be on my way to divorce number four."

He patted my arm, moved closer.

"Don't even think about it, Duncan."

"I'm not," he said, "furthest thing from my mind, actually."

Then he put his arm around my shoulder and told me the real reason why he had come.

The man with the platinum tonsils had throat cancer.

With treatment, radiation, chemotherapy, perhaps surgery, they could, he said, buy him some time, but how much was hard to say, and the bloody doctors wouldn't give him a straight answer.

Either way, Duncan said, he would probably lose his voice, which some people, Duncan smiled, would probably think was not such a bad thing.

When I was eight Harry had taken me to a squash court and had accidentally hit me in the chest with the hard black ball, sending me to the floor, the breath knocked out of me.

Duncan's words felt exactly like that, like someone had hit

me with a hard little sphere of rubber, leaving its imprint stinging on my chest, my hands flying to it automatically.

I felt it, the body blow.

From the moment Duncan told me, I began to ache for him, the physicality of it surprising me, all the little pains of a heart breaking.

Driving back to the city on the Monday evening, after a weekend of sightseeing and pretending not to know Duncan's secret, I could hardly bear to look at him, hardly bear to think about his action plan, as he called it.

"Time to tidy up," he had said that night on the swing. "Tie up loose ends, finish unfinished business, fix what's broken." He had looked at me with his watery eyes, not from tears, of course, but from the huge Cuban cigar he'd been smoking. "And that includes you, Lulu."

"I'm not broken," I said. "I told you, I'm all right about all that now."

"No, no you're not," he said, "and that is why, when Annie rang me recently to try to put some sort of meeting together, I said I would."

I put my hands over my eyes.

"I know." He puffed contentedly on his cigar. "If I wasn't dying, you'd kill me."

"I don't want to talk to her, Duncan, I don't want to talk to any of them."

"Ah, but you see you have to, Lulu, to get closure."

"Did you just say *closure*?"

"Yes, I did." He nodded sagely. "Kimmy says you need it."

The mist began to clear. "Kimmy? You've told Kimmy all this?"

"Well, I told her my illegitimate-daughter-left-on-doorstep theory—backed the wrong bloody horse there, didn't I?—but no matter, you have to do this, Lulu. If there's one thing I've learned in the last few weeks, it's that you must have your chance to say good-bye. It's the words we don't say, Lulu, not the ones we do, that linger longest."

But I had said good-bye. To both of them.

~

I had said good-bye to Annabelle in the tree house.

Harry came into my room about a week after I had found Annabelle and Josh by the river and told me they were leaving for Canada at the end of the month, where Fergus had arranged some work experience for them on one of his shoots.

"I'm sorry, love," Harry had said, patting my knee from the end of the bed where he sat rubbing the back of his neck. "I know this has got to hurt a lot—still, might be best that they go, out of sight, out of mind and all that rubbish." He had kissed the top of my head, turned out my light, and shut the door behind him, leaving me panicking in the dark.

I'd felt like I was being erased, that things I said and did no longer mattered, that I could literally disappear into the shadows of my room, spill silently into its corners. It felt like Annabelle had taken over my life, slipped into my shoes when I wasn't looking, and that if I wasn't careful no one would ever know about the other girl who had once worn them.

I did not sleep most of that night, and in the early hours of the morning I got up, took the book from my bedside drawer, put it in my backpack, got dressed, and let myself out of the house.

Then I rode my bike over to the River House and ran across the backyard with my heart thumping in my chest and my neck craned toward Annabelle's window, and climbed up to our nest in the mango tree for the last time.

I took the book I had written for her, the one with all of our sayings and phrases, and put it down in a corner.

Then I pressed my face against one of Frank's windows—

the diamond one—and looked out at the still sleeping River House.

"I was here," I whispered into the early-morning light, feeling everything slip away from me. "Don't ever forget that I was here."

~

I had said good-bye to Josh at the skating rink.

About a week before he and Annabelle were leaving, he had rung and asked me to meet him there, so we could talk, he said, in private.

"Without Annabelle," I said, "without your girlfriend?"

"Don't," he said. "Don't, Tallulah." And I didn't, I just met him at the rink, where he stood waiting at the entrance, green-checked shirt I'd bought him for his last birthday, jeans, sneakers, hair curling around his collar.

I bit my lip, played at it, drawing blood, tasting it in my mouth.

"Lulu, I'm glad you came."

I nodded, stupid.

"Do you want to skate?"

The moon hung over us, watching as I sat on the steps, bag by my side, struck dumb, immovable in its light.

"Do you want me to put your skates on?"

He unzipped my bag, took out my skates, bent his head, and held my foot in his hands.

"I'm so sorry, Lulu," he whispered.

He slid my shoes off, put my skates on, tying and checking the laces, and I could hardly bear his touch, his hands on my feet, holding them firmly, turning my ankles and threading each lace so carefully with those hands I knew so well, the swollen knuckle, the bitten fingernails, the touch of them on Annabelle's skin, reaching for her face as I turned mine away.

"Look at me, Lulu," he'd said. "Please look at me."

But I could stare only at my white skates, my head to the ground.

Josh lifted my chin and stood up.

He led me to the rink and put his arm around my shoulders.

We began to skate swaying, as we always did, against each other, and when my tears came, he pulled me to him, took my face in his hands and said, again, "I'm sorry, Lulu," and I knew that he was leaving.

He had not come here to tell me it had all been a mistake, an anomaly, that it was me he wanted, not Annabelle, that he was not going away and had never really intended to.

I looked at him and realized he was already gone.

"It's complicated," he was saying. "It just kind of happened; I know it's really bad for you. . . ."

I closed my eyes, thought it was true that you could actually feel your heart breaking.

"But I love you, Tallulah-Lulu," he said. "I always will."

He leaned in toward me.

"You're my girl," he whispered.

That is what Josh Keaton said to me as the moon rose and his tears fell with mine on the night we said good-bye.

chapter twelve

Duncan swung the car into my driveway.

"I had a really great time this weekend," he said. "Thank you."

We hadn't spoken about his cancer after that night on the swing, a night that ended up with the two of us underneath a blanket Rose has brought down for us, Duncan further outlining his action plan, which mostly involved keeping his news from as many people as possible.

"Join us, Rose," he'd said.

"No," she'd answered, "I think I'll just turn in."

"God," Duncan sighed, snuggling in beside me, "it's just like being on Walton's Mountain."

We hadn't spoken about it on the way home either; Jarrod and Jasmine were in the car and small ears did not need to hear such big stories.

Instead, we'd listened to the tapes he flicked in and out of his cassette recorder.

"Hello, I'm Johnny Cash," Duncan had said again and again, rewinding the tape back to the beginning of the phrase, smiling to himself each time he said it.

On any other day I might have stopped him, snatched the cassette from its box, but on this day I let it go, not knowing how many other ones he had left to annoy the hell out of me.

"I'm glad you came," I told him as he walked me to the door. "Though I think my mother has a little crush on you."

"Well, she's a woman, isn't she?" he replied, and I knew then how we were to play it, like nothing had been said at all.

"See you at work," he said, turning back to the car.

And for the next few weeks everything did go back to normal, at least on the surface, or normal if it was on cocaine. Duncan's illness didn't slow him down at all; instead, it seemed to me he was living his whole life on fast-forward, and with the volume turned up. If he was going, he was going kicking and screaming, caressing and cajoling his listeners from behind the microphone, and getting the best ratings of his career.

In the first warm days of the summer of 1990, no one could touch Duncan McAllister, who was at least four points ahead of his nearest rivals, and no one but me knew it was dying that had made him fearless.

He told the prime minister on air to "grow some, sir"; he started a petition to deport the entire South African cricket team on account of their "appalling accents"; and, in what he said was the proudest moment of his entire life, he was named *Who* magazine's Sexiest Man of the Year. He was dressed on the cover as a boxer—hooded gown, red gloves, swinging on the ropes as a platinum microphone dangled from the ceiling, *The Champ* emblazoned on his satin boxers.

"God, I am sexy, aren't I," he said every time he looked at it. "How you manage to work in such close proximity to me and not just *erupt*, I'll never know, Lulu—you must have loins of titanium."

But as weeks turned into months, his voice started to lose its rich honeyed timbre, growing hoarser, his breath more labored, his skin sometimes turning, I thought, an alarming gray beneath his stubble.

He asked for, and received, a three-day working week, belligerently telling management he wanted more time to go fishing, and they, desperate to keep him, had agreed. They also agreed I could reduce my days at the station—Duncan needed me, he told them, "to bait his hooks," when in reality I sat outside the oncologist Dr. Patrick Stephenson's door while Duncan underwent radiation therapy.

Surgery had been ruled out—Duncan didn't like the odds—so instead we took a ridiculously complicated route, and a different one every time, to Dr. Stephenson's office. We always went when the receptionist was on lunch, or on an errand, or wherever it was she went when she was pretending she didn't know Duncan McAllister was her boss's patient.

She must have known, of course—lots of people must have, especially as time went on and Duncan's voice grew hoarser—but somehow we managed to escape detection for quite a while before the whispers grew into shouts.

After the radiation treatment, Duncan's throat swelled and scratched, his energy levels plummeted, and we needed every one of the four days between his shifts to get him ready for the next round.

But somehow he managed to pull it all together for the three hours that made up his show, and only if you listened carefully did you hear the cracks in his voice.

He wasn't well enough to attend my twenty-fifth birthday dinner, instead thoughtfully sending a male stripper dressed as a courier to the quiet restaurant where Ben, Simone, and Stella had taken me.

"Special delivery for Tallulah de Longland from Duncan McAllister," the stripper called, bursting through the restaurant's front doors and startling the waitstaff.

"Over here!" Simone yelled, pointing to me, while Stella blushed and Ben held my hand under the table.

"Don't worry," he whispered, then added, "How bad can it be?" just as my personal delivery boy stood in front of me, whipped off his shirt, pointed to his chest, and said, "Sign here please." Then he pressed play on his CD player and began dancing to "It's Raining Men," glancing at Ben through the entire performance while Ben and Simone screamed with laughter and Stella stared, fixated, at his chest.

At the studio the next day Duncan walked in, grinning.

"How was your birthday?" he smiled. "Did you like your special package?"

"Oh, you mean the gay male stripper you sent me?" I asked. "He was great; I think he and Ben will be very happy together."

"What? That's not what I ordered—oh, never mind, we have far more important things to discuss. Such as this," he said, flourishing a white envelope in his hand. "Do you know what this is?" he asked, holding it so close to my face I could have opened it with my teeth.

"A birthday card?" I asked.

He shook his head.

"A summons?"

"Very amusing, Lulu, no, this, my darling heart, is your ticket to Closureville."

"Closureville?"

"Yes, you've never been there before, that's why you may not have heard of it, but it's by way of Time to Move On and Stop Being Such a Drama Queen Street."

He opened the envelope, put the white card from inside its folds on my desk, walked to the door of my office, and added: "Might see you there if you can man up for it."

He shut the door, and I looked down at the thick white card on my desk.

Enchanted, it said, *an exhibition by Frank Andrews*. And

there, filling the edges of the card, were two gray-penciled little girls, heads close together, features blurred, expressions unseen but with their arms around each other, forternity.

~

I had no intention of going, not unless Duncan came up with some story about how it was his dying wish that I should do so—and I wouldn't have put it past him—but in the end it was Harry who changed my mind.

He and Frank had become friends after Frank had moved back to the River House from Christa's.

Annie had moved out—the fault lines between them caused by her affair with Fergus too deep to mend—and Annabelle was long gone, leaving Frank moving among his wife's and daughter's shadows in the house's cluttered rooms.

How silent that house must have seemed as he walked its floors, and how loud his steps must have sounded without the jingling of Annie's bangles or the giggles from Annabelle's bedroom, falling like quavers down the staircase.

He listened to the radio out in the studio, where he drank instant coffee made with hot water straight from the tap and painted for hours, only venturing out for supplies, and it was on one such trip he'd met Harry.

They'd run into each other in a hardware store soon after I'd left for the city; Harry had been there to pick up some storm-water pipes and Frank some methylated spirits—"Don't worry, mate, it's not for me," he'd said to Harry at the counter—and the two men had laughed their way into a friendship.

After their chance meeting, Harry and Frank had begun meeting up once a week in the Uxbridge Arms—Harry for a beer, Frank for the one glass of red wine he now allowed himself a week—and found they fitted each other "like a pair of old overcoats," Harry said.

After they'd been meeting for a few weeks, he'd rung to tell me and ask if I minded.

"We don't talk about you and Josh and Annabelle, Lulu," he'd said. "That's all past now, but I wanted to check with you if you had any worries with it."

"No, Harry," I'd said, and I meant it.

Harry had spent so much time plumbing the depths of excellence and looking after all of us, he'd never been the sort of man to go for a knock-off drink with the other tradies after work.

So I was pleased he and Frank had found each other among the hand drills and glue guns, although sometimes I wondered what the barmaids at the Uxbridge Arms made of them—Harry in his overalls and work boots, Frank in his paint-splattered singlet and fisherman's cap.

I'd asked Harry once what they talked about, and he'd said sometimes they didn't say much at all, just sat there, "letting the day settle." Other times, he said, they spoke about Frank's painting. Once, Frank had told him, "I can't get the black right." Harry had said, "What do you mean you can't get the black right? Black's black, isn't it?" And Frank had answered, "No, mate, there's all kinds of blackness." And Harry, thinking of Rose, had understood.

Harry had rung a few days after Duncan had showed me the "Enchanted" invitation, and asked if I would go with him.

He wanted to go, he said, to be there for Frank, and because it was at Bloom, the local gallery, it meant he wouldn't have to leave Rose too long by herself. Even though Rose had been doing well, we never really knew when her depression would make its appearance from behind a door somewhere, announcing its arrival in a shapeless beige dress and marathon bouts of baking. It would just begin, and sometime later it would end, and in between Harry hovered.

This time, although Rose was in the middle of a long stretch of good days, she wasn't well enough to walk into a room full of people; instead, she said, she would send along a tea cake.

"Don't make me walk in carrying a cake tin by myself, Lulu," Harry pleaded with me.

"I don't know, Harry—who's going?"

"Everyone," he'd answered, "the whole kit and caboodle."

"I don't know," I repeated. "I'm just not ready, I don't think."

"We never are, love," he'd replied, "but it's probably time."

The day Harry invited me, I went home, and I told Ben about the exhibition over dinner.

"How do you feel about that, Lulu?" he asked.

He knew about Josh and Annabelle—when we first started seeing each other, we'd swapped edited versions of our previous relationships, Ben's largely consisting of girls his sisters had maneuvered in front of him.

"No one really serious," he'd told me, "before you."

I had told him that since Josh and Annabelle, I'd had a few casual relationships also, which was, of course, not strictly true, but how do you tell someone you've been frozen in time since high school? Even to me it sounded ridiculous.

I poured us each a glass of wine. "I feel fine about it, actually," I told him. "A bit nervous, sort of like going to a school reunion, I guess."

Ben smiled at me. "You'll be fine," he said, "and I'll be there, and your dad, and Rose's tea cake."

I smiled back. "Which is the only reason you're going," I teased.

"No, it isn't," he said, surprising me by coming around to my side of the table and kissing my neck. "I have to protect my woman."

That night when Ben went for his run, I stood in front of our full-length mirror practicing being normal.

No, not normal, nonchalant.

"Oh, hi, Annabelle; hi, Josh."

No.

"Hi, Josh; hi, Annabelle."

"Hey there, you two!"

Hey there, you two?

What the hell was wrong with me?

"Annabelle, Josh, how lovely to see you."

Better.

"It's been so long, hasn't it? I keep up with your travels—Ben and I subscribe to *Gourmet Traveller*, actually."

Ben and I subscribe to Gourmet Traveller?

Clearly, I needed professional help.

~

Duncan was sitting at his desk in the studio, a pile of newspapers fanned out in front of him.

"I'm going," I told him, not needing to explain where. "Harry's going as well, and he needs me to go with him. And Ben's coming too."

Duncan looked up over his reading glasses and smiled. "And I'll be there as well, so you'll have a whole battalion of blokes there to protect you from the evil ones, a veritable army. Perhaps we should wear great knobs of garlic around our necks. . . ."

"Don't, Duncan," I said, "I'm actually a bit nervous."

He nodded, waiting.

"The thing is, I don't know what I'm going to say when I see them. . . . I have nothing to say. They've spent the last seven years traveling the length and breadth of the planet, winning bloody awards and seeing the world, and I've been stuck here."

"With me."

"Oh, Duncan, I'm sorry, I didn't mean it like that."

"I know you didn't, Tallulah, but the truth is you have rather been stuck with me of late, and Barney, and all my children and my ex-wives. Then, of course, there's your father, your mother, your friends, and Ben, all of whom, my dear, would be utterly lost without you."

"Duncan . . ."

"Don't stop me, I'm on a roll. Also, I am, in case you have forgotten, dying, and you can't interrupt the terminally ill." He smiled his watery smile at me. "Now, as I was saying, you've been stuck here quietly going about your business, which is, of course, to keep us all sane and out of prison, fussing over me, dislodging God knows what from Barney's throat, babysitting Stella's children, staying at Simone's when one of her leso girlfriends dumps her, sorting out your father's business, ironing your mother's mad bloody dresses, attempting to make Ben more vigorous. . . ."

I smiled back at him.

"So who cares? Who cares where Annabelle and Josh have been, climbing the Andes or sailing the Amalfi Coast on some bloody boat. Anyone can get on a boat, Lulu, you just buy a ticket. There're thousands of us out there flailing about in the ocean, but there's not that many of you. You're the one standing on the shore and shining the light, guiding us all in safely." He picked up a newspaper and pretended to read it. "So fuck 'em," he said.

chapter thirteen

"Enchanted" had sent a frisson through art circles: the return of Frank Andrews with a major exhibition after an almost seven-year hiatus had the critics and collectors welcoming him back into the fold with open arms and, it was rumored, deep pockets.

Within days of the white envelopes arriving in various mailboxes across the city, people were saying that "Enchanted"—thirty-six paintings and line drawings—was Frank's best work to date.

They were also asking whether Annie would have the hide to turn up.

Fergus had discarded her long ago, Frank had not taken her back, and Christa, it was said, remained furious with her for driving a wedge between her sons.

Still, I thought Annie would show up, because I was fairly sure the years wouldn't have changed one of the things I had admired about her.

"I don't give a stuff what people think about me, Tallulah," I heard her voice echoing from a long-ago afternoon at the River House, "and neither should you. No one who ever truly matters does."

Frank had chosen to show "Enchanted" not at one of the major city galleries, like Rafferty's or Slater's, but in our hometown, at his friend Laura Metcalfe's art space, Bloom.

People moaned and grumbled—it was too far, what was Frank thinking, making them trek from the city on a Saturday? But they would all go, I knew, because it wasn't just Frank's pictures they wanted to look at.

They were going to see the other show as well, the one starring Christa, Frank, Fergus, Annie, Josh, and Annabelle—"I could sell extra tickets just for them," Laura Metcalfe had said to me a few days before the exhibition.

With Duncan resting at Lingalonga, I'd headed home the week before the opening to check on Rose, and had run into Laura outside Bloom.

I'd known Laura since I was a little girl—Harry had done all the plumbing at the gallery, and Sam and Mattie had gone to school with her son, Brett.

"Tallulah"—she smiled—"how are you, my love?"

"Good, thanks, Laura," I answered. "How are things with you?"

"Mad," she said, and told me how her phone hadn't stopped ringing since the invitations had gone out. "It's crazy," she said, "usually I have to beg the local rag to run up to one of my openings, but everyone's coming, all the papers, some TV stations, and they're all asking the same questions: Is Christa going to be there? Is Annie invited? Is Fergus? They're all hoping for a fight, of course." She laughed. "You know—Fergus and Frank rolling around the footpath, Christa and Annie at each other's throats, stabbing each other with their hatpins . . ." Then she told me how grateful she was to Frank for giving her the exhibition, instead of Slater's or Rafferty's, adding they were mightily pissed off he hadn't gone to them. "But that's Frank for you, always there for an old friend," she said, walking into Bloom. "Of course, I've got no bloody idea where I'm going to put everybody."

There's a photo of Ben and me from that night, taken for some newspaper's social pages—Rose cut out the clipping and kept it in one of her albums.

Ben is wearing a white shirt and olive tie, black trousers, his hair cropped close to his head in a number two buzz cut he'd just had, saying it was easier for traveling. It made him look much tougher than he really was, and with his arm wrapped around my waist, he looked faintly menacing, when all he was really doing, I see now, was trying to hold on.

I'm standing beside him wearing a dark blue satin wrap dress Rose had made for me, a silk flower of some sort in my hair, and a fake smile stretched wide across my pink cheeks. I have smoky eyeliner on, and red lips, and my hair is down, out of its usual ponytail and falling in big, loose curls around my face and past my shoulders. I look nothing like the sort of girl you would leave standing by the river.

"You look amazing," Ben had said that night at Harry and Rose's, where we were staying.

"Thanks, I don't know why I'm doing this."

"I don't know why either." He smiled. "But if we are doing it, let's just get it over and done with."

We walked to the car, and when we got in he reached across the seat for my hand.

"You can do this, Lulu," he said. "You can do this with your eyes shut."

We were meeting Harry there; he worked on Saturdays and wasn't sure what time he'd finish.

After driving past the gallery and seeing the crowd already gathered on the footpath, smoking and gossiping, we'd parked a couple of blocks away, the walk giving me time to breathe a little in my satin dress.

By the time we arrived, there was a queue, which Laura was sensibly keeping well oiled, sending out waiters with champagne and beer while she ran around inside, rearranging paintings she had rearranged from their previous rearrangements.

On the edge of the footpath, a fidgety knot of media waited, and from where Ben and I were standing we could see who was arriving, illuminated by silver flashes of lightning from the photographers' bulbs.

Fergus Andrews was first, blithely strolling up the street with his own camera around his neck, looking, I thought, exactly as I remembered him—"Where to, for the Wahi-Wahi?"—but as he got closer, I saw how life had marked him.

He was still wearing the same clothes, khaki pants and shirt, with lots of complicated pockets with zippers and netting—"Wanker still thinks he's in the Kalahari," I heard one of the snappers say—but deep lines were carved into his skin, mottled by the sun.

He had lost none of his swagger though, and as the photographers swung their glass eyes upon him, he raised his own camera and began snapping them snapping him all the way to the top of the stairs.

I took a step back to let him pass just as a taxi rolled up and Duncan rolled out. "Good evening, wonderful night for Frank Andrews, isn't it? Or are you here for me? No? What a pity. So, who's here so far? Christa? No? What about Annie? Has she arrived? I wonder if she'll turn up with a great big scarlet A attached to her frock, don't you?" Then, spying Laura at the door, he strode toward her, saying, "Lana, what a pleasure it is to see you, my dear!"

A few minutes later, in a show of solidarity for Frank, I supposed, Christa and Annie arrived together, arms improbably linked.

They looked, I thought, standing in the queue, like two jewels, Christa wrapped up in an emerald kimono, her shock of white hair pulled tightly off her face in a bun, and Annie beside her wearing layer upon layer. "It's my Sara Lee signature look," she used to laugh, and tonight she was wearing a confusion of tights and tunics, skirts, scarves, and a wide-belted coat, like a pirate, all in varying shades of purple.

Both women smiled at the cameras but then hurried inside, Christa murmuring, "It's Frank's night!" to a question from a journalist. Annie demurely followed her, saying nothing at all, for once playing the dutiful, albeit ex, daughter-in-law, but in reality desperate (I would find out later) for a drink.

Then Frank arrived with Harry behind him, clutching Rose's tea cake in a metal cake tin with a kitten on it.

"Frank, Frank, over here, Frank!"

"Look up here, Frank, just to your left!"

"Frank, Gary Clarke, *Insight*, how are you feeling about tonight?"

"Christa and Annie arrived together, can we take it family relations are thawing?"

"Frank—Pete Taylor, the *Bulletin*, is it correct half of the works inside have already been sold to the Flintoff collection?"

"Frank, can you just look over here? Sorry, mate, would you mind getting out of the way?"

"No worries." Harry stepped back, looking embarrassed to be there, hating being accidentally caught up in Frank's limelight.

Frank put up his hand, silencing the mob.

"Thanks very much for coming along tonight. It is, as you say, a big night for me, and it's a night I'm very glad to be sharing with all my family. So thank you all once again." He nodded his head, signaling to Harry to follow him up the stairs.

"Who's that codger?" Gary Clarke, *Insight*, said as he walked past me.

"Dunno," Pete Taylor, the *Bulletin*, answered. "Someone said he's a plumber."

"Come on," Ben said, "let's go inside and find your dad."

I nodded and followed him through the door, feeling, I realized with a shock, not so much relieved but slightly shortchanged that Josh and Annabelle did not seem to be coming after all.

God, I thought, looking down at Rose's beautiful frock and patting the flower behind my ear, *all this for nothing*.

Then I looked across the room and saw Harry standing in the middle of it, stiff as a board and clutching a cake tin.

Not quite for nothing. I smiled to myself as Ben and I made our way over to him, a slow, complicated journey through arms and elbows and shoulders and a woman who laughed like a hyena.

"Harry," I said, "saw you with the reporters outside, suppose you think you're big-time now."

"Hi, Harry," said Ben. "Want a beer?"

"Oh yeah, mate," Harry said, reaching for his wallet.

"They'll be complimentary, Harry," I told him. "It's the only way they can get people to come to these things."

Ben left to get the drinks, and Harry and I smiled at each other.

"Complimentary, probably should have known that," he said, then looked down at the cake tin. "Probably shouldn't have brought this either."

"I'll take it," I told him, "don't worry about it."

Harry smiled at me again.

"Well, love, you did it."

"I did."

"I'm glad you came, Lulu."

"And I'm glad you're here."

"I stick out like balls on a bull, though, don't I?"

"You're fine," I said.

"So are you," he answered.

When Ben came back with the drinks, I took the tin off Harry and went to the bathroom, checked no one was looking and dumped the cake into the bin, crossing myself for the sin I was committing against both my mother and her favorite recipe.

Then I went into a stall, closed the door, and sat down to breathe.

"Lulu," came a hoarse whisper from outside the door, a pair of white-tasseled shoes underneath it.

"Duncan," I hissed, "what are you doing in here?"

"Let me in," he said, then, affecting a girlish giggle. "I'm busting."

"Duncan, get out before someone catches you."

"Open the door," he said again.

"No."

"If I'm in there with you, there's less chance of someone see-ing me out here, now isn't there?"

I opened the door. "What do you want?" I whispered as he barged his way into the cubicle. "What *are* you doing? Duncan, I am not doing cocaine in here with you if that's what you're after."

"Don't be stupid, Lulu, it's about six hundred dollars an ounce at the moment, not that I can't afford it, I just refuse to pay such ridiculous prices so that some pimp in Colombia can get a diamond in his tooth. . . ."

"Duncan," I clenched my teeth.

"What? Oh yes, I came in here to talk to you privately, now get up on the seat."

"What?"

"Get up on the seat—didn't you ever smoke in the toilets at school? Of course you didn't, Miss Goody Two-shoes—you get up on the seat so there's only one pair of feet under here and it won't look suspicious."

"Oh no, as if we don't already look suspicious."

"Ssshh," he said, putting his fingers to my lips. "Someone's coming." We stood stock-still, facing each other and holding each other's shoulders in the small cubicle, while I held my breath and Duncan pulled a series of what he thought were amusing faces at me.

When the woman left he said, "Right, up on the seat."

"I am not getting up on the seat, Duncan."

"Fine," he said, "but don't blame me if Sister Scholastica catches us."

"Duncan, enough . . . What do you want?"

"Well, I just wanted to tell you that I have just seen Annabelle and Josh arriving, so you don't get a shock when you go outside—forewarned is forearmed and all that."

A little knot began curling its way around my stomach.

"Now, Lulu," Duncan was saying, "I know this is not an easy night for you, and I am very proud of you for coming."

"Thank you," I whispered, resigned to my fate of listening to "Monologue in a Toilet" by Duncan McAllister.

"I also wanted to tell you that you look absolutely breathtaking and I have checked out Annabelle, who I have never seen in the flesh before in my entire life, but who I can tell you is far too skinny and has aged badly, and also Josh, who I can tell you has definitely had his teeth whitened, and not very well."

The bathroom door opened once more, and we both stood still and waited for whoever it was to leave.

"The coast is clear, my dear," Duncan said a few minutes later. "Now, we may make our escape—you go first, I'll follow in a few minutes."

I made it as far as the door when he whispered again.

"Lulu?"

"Yes," I said, "what now?"

"I just wanted to let you know I also brought Barney. He's on a lead out the back and I have told him, should this toothy Josh person give you any trouble, he has my permission to eat him."

I walked out of the bathroom with the now empty cake tin in my hands and gave it to a passing waiter.

"Could you please put this in the kitchen?" I asked him. "I'll collect it later." Then I walked over to where Ben was standing in the crush.

"What were you and Duncan doing in the toilets?" he asked, more curious than concerned—he had known my employer long enough now not to be bothered about any departures from normal behavior.

"Did you see him follow me in?"

"Lulu, everyone saw him follow you in. He did everything but drop to the floor and roll in behind you."

Wonderful.

"Lulu," Harry's voice beside me said, "here's someone who wants to say g'day to you."

I turned and looked straight into Frank Andrews's familiar face, older, a bit more weather-beaten, whiskery, graying at the temples, and that lovely mouth breaking into one of its wide-split smiles.

"Lulu," he said, "I've missed you."

He held out his arms, and I went to him.

Deep breath.

Coffee, cigarettes, turpentine, red wine, paint.

I breathed him in and nothing had changed; I flew through the green door, back to that house with its flickering river, back to the Andrews' yard swinging on a rope as Frank held on to my legs saying, "It's all right, Lulu, I've got you."

Safe.

I closed my eyes and breathed him in, my friend Frank.

We stood close.

"So, Lulu, your dad's been filling me in on what you've been up to all these years. You've done really well," Frank said.

"Thanks, Frank, but what about you? These paintings are beautiful, and there're so many people here to help you celebrate—you even got Harry into an art gallery, and that's not easy."

"I'm sorry Rose couldn't come," Frank said.

"Yeah," I said, "me too. She just wasn't up to it."

"I know. Harry keeps me in the loop."

I nodded, watching impatient arms begin to pull at him.

"I shouldn't monopolize you, Frank, there're lots of people

who want to congratulate you—but I'd love to come to the Uxbridge Arms with you and Harry sometime."

He nodded and held his arms out once more, brushing his
mouth to my ear.

"Before you go, see Laura Metcalfe, the gallery owner. She
has something for you, Tallulah de Lovely."

When Frank walked away I was left by myself for a few minutes. Harry was advising the art critic from the *Bulletin* about in-
stalling a gray-water system, and Ben, I could see from the corner
of my eye, was at Laura's makeshift bar.

I decided to get another champagne, scanning the crowd for
Josh or Annabelle, so I could hide if I spotted them, and headed
for a table sprinkled with amber flutes.

"So, I see you're finally old enough to drink legally."

Josh.

Standing just behind me, his voice in my ear.

I turned around to face him. Josh who, unlike Fergus, did not
seem marked by life at all. He looked, I thought, exactly the same,
except his hair was longer and he'd filled out more, a man version
of the boy I had known.

All the times I'd rehearsed this, what I'd say, how I would
behave (I'd thought the right move might be to act like I had just
run across a long-gone and distant friend: "Josh?" I'd say, a slight
question mark in my voice, "I thought it was you, gosh, I'm not
even sure how long it's been, how *are* you?" putting the inflec-
tion on the "are" just the way I'd heard Simone do it) proved
fruitless as I stood there struck mute by the shocking familiarity
of him.

I am not sure what I expected, but I did not expect this, for
him to look and sound so much the same that I almost tucked my
head under his arm, almost took a step toward him.

Instead, I saw him move toward me, saw the way his eyes
opened slightly, his mouth forming a half laugh, his hand leaving

the pocket of his corduroy jacket to reach out to my cheek and stroke it, like it still belonged there.

And I stood there, letting him, somehow stuck beneath that stroking hand until my father released me.

"Well, here's a turn-up for the books."

"Harry!" said Josh. "How are you?"

"Good, thanks, Josh. . . . Well, this is something to tell Rose later, all of us here together after all these years."

"Yeah, yeah it is." Josh smiled. "It's really great to see you, Harry."

I stood between the two men whom I had spent years watching through besotted eyes, standing at the bottom of the ladder as they cleaned the gutters of our house, stamping about the roof in their big work boots, calling out for someone to put the kettle on. I had seen them stand together at the smoking incinerator, rubbing their chins, drifts of their conversation floating up on curls of smoke to the veranda, and I had watched Harry let him go after the night I came home from the river.

"What's happened, love?" he'd said when I came through the door. "What's wrong? You look terrible; I'll get your mother."

They had put me in my pajamas, and into bed with a cup of tea, while Rose soothed and patted and Harry turned his back on Joshua Keaton.

Josh had gone to see him once, Rose had told me, just before he and Annabelle left. Josh had gone to Harry's office and waited until Harry came out. Harry had said a few words to him, then refused to shake his hand.

Rose was upset and told Harry that no matter what had gone on between his daughter and Josh, we were young and who knew at that age what they really wanted? People, she told Harry, fell in love with people they weren't meant to all the time. She said that Josh was immature, with no father to guide him, but Harry was having none of it. "I trusted him to take care of our daughter," he said, "and he didn't."

And now they were standing together, the years and Josh's obvious delight at seeing him mellowing Harry as Josh spoke eagerly to him, his hand all the while resting on the small of my back.

"How's Rose?" Josh was saying, "I was hoping she might be here tonight. . . ."

I excused myself and weaved my way back through the crowd and out onto the street, needing to get away from the gallery and Josh's hand on me.

It had left me confused, unsure of what was more shocking, the fact that he would, after all these years, after everything, touch me so casually, or the fact that I had enjoyed it way more in the Deep South, as Simone would say, than I had a right to.

I sat down on a step outside a closed café, pressing the backs of my hands into my eyes.

"Tallulah."

So this was how it was going to happen.

I looked up and saw her face, Annabelle, pale under the café light, long and angular and thin beneath a strapless black dress, a silver choker around her neck, some sort of talisman hanging off it.

Annabelle, like Josh, the same face, but older, surer.

Her green eyes danced.

"I've just met your mate Duncan"—she smiled— "in a whirl of polyester." She gave an awkward laugh. "He warned me off you actually, said I wasn't to hurt a hair on your head—must be nice to have a friend like that."

"It is." I found my voice and thought, *Do you not remember, Annabelle? Do you not remember? "I will shove your arse clean through your ears."*

Annabelle grinned down at me.

"Move over," she said as the years fell away and Sister Scholastica bustled between us. "I'll just sit here."

We sat shoulder to shoulder on the steps, and it felt like that first day of school when we circled each other at lunchtime, offering up bits of our lives to each other for approval—Annabelle saying, "*Dolly* magazine's 'Poet's Corner' makes me want to varf."

"Varf?"

"Yes, Tallulah, varf, it's a cross between *vomit* and *barf*."

"Oh, well, then it makes me want to varf too."

It felt like we hadn't moved since that first day in Sister Scholastica's class. While I had been struck dumb upon seeing Josh at the gallery, with Annabelle I couldn't stop talking.

There was so much to tell her, so much to fit in, and it wasn't until I began speaking that I realized how much of a void she had left in my life, and how eager I was to fill it.

I could talk to Duncan and Simone and Stella about anything, but there was something in Annabelle's green gaze, something that gathered at the corners of her eyes and in the way she threw her head back laughing, saying, "Stop, stop, I can't stand it, wait, yes I can, go on!" that had always made me brighter, funnier, more vivid than when I was with anybody else.

I talked and talked. I told her about how I'd met Duncan, how Harry and Rose were—"Rose," Annabelle said, "how I have missed Rose." I told her about my job at the radio station and living with Simone and Beth, and meeting Ben, and it seemed like there weren't enough words to tell her all I needed to say, except of course the one thing I couldn't bring myself to speak about.

When I finally stopped talking—nerves, I see now, nerves and that same old feeling of wanting to be enough for her—and the silence played out between us, she said quietly, "Tallulah."

She turned to face me, her eyes on mine.

"I know what Josh and I did was wrong, inexcusable actually, and I wish we had told you earlier that we were falling for each other, but it was just so hard, you know, because we so didn't want to hurt you."

What I should have done at that moment was told her.

Told her how I had never been quite the same since the day by the river, how I'd spent years after it suspended in time, how angry I had been, and how it sometimes simmered still just beneath the surface.

I should have told her that seeing them together made me want to varf.

I should have told her that they broke my heart.

I wish I had.

I wish I had, but instead I faltered, caught up again in the excitement that was Annabelle Andrews sitting next to me.

I smiled at her.

"Honestly, it's fine; it was so long ago now, Annabelle. We were teenagers—everything seems so dramatic, doesn't it, when you're a teenager? I'm happy," I told her, "we don't have to go back there."

"Are you sure?" she said, "because I could try and explain what happened."

I did not want her to explain what happened, I did not want to hear how she and Josh didn't mean to fall in love, how they tried not to see each other, how they kept apart until they could not stand it for one more minute.

How I got in the way.

"I'm sure," I told her. "Absolutely," the lie falling like a lifetime of incorrect names from Duncan McAllister's lips.

~

When Ben found us a couple of hours later we were passing a joint between us "like drunken teenagers," as he said on the way home, Josh, Annabelle, and Duncan all asleep in the backseat,

Barney spread out over the top of them like an enormous throw rug.

Ben wasn't happy when he found us. He'd spent most of the evening at the bar with increasingly inebriated men who kept looking at the soles of their shoes to see if his company had made them, and cheering each time the Moreton's logo was discovered on a pair.

He'd also been keeping an eye on Duncan, getting louder in the center of the room and rapidly moving out of his "Hail, fellow, well met" phase to dip his toes into more belligerent shoes. Usually when this happened it was my job to distract him, and Ben had been about to try to find me when Josh joined him at the bar and introduced himself.

"If you're looking for Tallulah and Annabelle," he told Ben drunkenly, "they're outside." Josh had raised his glass. "To old times, good times."

Ben had hated him on sight. "For you maybe," he had muttered in response.

When he found us sitting on the café steps, I half stood and introduced him to Annabelle. "Ben, I was just coming inside—this is Annabelle Andrews."

"Hello, Annabelle."

"Hello, Ben."

The silence gathered under the awning above us.

"Well, that went well, didn't it?" Annabelle said brightly, and the two of us—Annabelle and I—dissolved into giggles.

With that, Ben walked off toward the gallery and said, "I'm leaving in five minutes, Lulu." Somewhere through my marijuana haze I understood it would be a good idea to go with him.

"Jesus, Lulu," he said in the car. "I feel like a bloody chauffeur service."

"Ben, nobody could get a taxi, you offered to take people."

"No, Lulu, *you* offered for me to take people."

We drove on in the sort of brittle silence only late nights that have gone on too long can bring.

"I don't know why you're so angry, it's not far, and they're all staying at the same hotel," I said.

"That's not what I'm angry about, Lulu, and you know it."

"What then?"

"You want me to spell it out to you?"

"Yes, Ben," I answered wearily, "I do."

"Fine," he said. "I'm angry that you left me at a party for more than two hours while you went outside with the one person you have told me has really let you down, and when I finally find you, you're smoking marijuana with her like some loser drug addict, and the two of you sit there and laugh at me—"

"We weren't laughing at you, Ben."

"Well, that's how it looked to me."

We drove on in more silence until I thought about Ben calling me a drug addict after seeing me have one joint in the two years I had known him.

I started to giggle.

"What are you laughing at?"

"You," I told him.

"Me?"

"Yeah, you."

"Why?"

"You called me a drug addict."

Ben smiled. "I know, you'll be dealing crack cocaine next."

I reached over, put my hand on his knee. "I'm sorry, Ben, I shouldn't have left you there."

"It's just not like you, Lulu."

"I know," I said, looking down at my hands.

He was right, it wasn't like me, but then again, I hadn't been the girl he knew from the moment I'd felt Joshua Keaton's hand on my back.

Frank Andrews's exhibition at Bloom would, over the years, achieve a sort of mythical status, with every single painting and sketch sporting a discreet little red sticker by the end of the night, most of them fetching record prices.

Anecdotes about the evening would be told at dinner parties for months afterward, people would brag about being there, and someone would steal the green cherub knocker off Bloom's front door.

"There was far too much drink," Laura Metcalfe would sum up a decade later on the *Sunday Arts* program. "My fault, I over-catered, and everyone was overexcited anyway . . . it was just one of those nights, I guess."

Two women would physically fight over Frank's *Twelve Apostles* painting, Annie Andrews would leave very publicly with Fergus, Maxine Mathers would turn up at Duncan's hotel room and demand to be McAllistered, and Harry and I would lie to Rose and tell her everyone had enjoyed the tea cake.

I would wake up the next day with Frank's gift to me beside the bed, a small frame holding the merest hint of two little girls behind its glass.

Ben had already gone for his run, and for once I was thankful.

Usually his insistence on running every morning, even on Sundays, annoyed me and made me resentful as he slid out of our bed, creeping around the room getting dressed even on those mornings when I reached for him.

But on that particular morning I was glad to be alone, feeling strange and unsettled, closing my eyes to the frame beside me and remembering Josh's hand on my skin.

chapter fourteen

The week after the exhibition, on the way to work—after bragging about Maxine Mathers's late-night visit to his hotel room: "Now, there is a woman whose reputation exceeded her . . ."—Duncan announced he would not be renewing his contract when it came up in a month's time.

"Can't do it anymore, Lulu," he said. "Got to get ready for my final turn on the floor. I wanted to wait until you'd had your little high school reunion to tell you, but the tumor's hanging on tighter than Kimmy to the prenup, and there's a few more of the buggers now, apparently."

We pulled into the station and made our way inside, Barney snaking in and out of our legs as we went. It was cold. Duncan was rubbing his hands together and blowing on them, pacing back and forth in our little room beside the studio, and all I could think was how I should get him a scarf. I should get him a scarf so his neck wouldn't get cold, surely that couldn't be good for him.

"I'm getting you a scarf," I said.

"What?"

"I'm getting you a scarf, it's too cold in here for you."

"Lot colder where I'm going, Lulu."

"Duncan, don't say that."

"It's true, Lulu," he said, flicking the shutters of our office closed. "There," he said, "now when everyone arrives they'll all

think we're in here shagging ourselves senseless, could do wonders for your reputation."

"Or yours." I smiled.

"Mine doesn't need any help, Lulu—now where was I? Oh,
yes, it's time for my action plan to kick in." He began to outline
it, telling me how he had been meeting with his lawyer for weeks,
working on a plan to distribute his not inconsiderable fortune eq-
uitably between his ex-wives and children. "The will's sewn up
tighter than a gnat's arse over a rain barrel," he concluded cheer-
fully. "I don't want any fighting after I'm gone. They've all been
more than adequately compensated for the ignominy of being married to me—particularly Karen. God, I was a bastard to her. . . ."

"I don't think you were that bad," I said.

"I called her Katie at our wedding ceremony, Lulu, and don't
start being nice to me now just because I'm dying," he said. "It's
very patronizing." He took a sip of his coffee, holding it in both
hands. "Now we need to talk about what we're going to tell everyone—so far, only you, the specialists, and I know that I'm to shuffle off this mortal coil sooner rather than later, and that's exactly
how I mean to keep it. No one must know, Lulu—not Kiki, not
Kerry-Anne, not Katie—"

"Karen," I said automatically.

"What? Right, not Karen, not Kimmy, not the children, and
certainly not the Mephisthophelean bastards I work for."

I sat on his desk swinging my legs, wondering how he thought
we were going to pull this off.

"Here's what we're going to do," he said, pacing the room and
rubbing his hands.

Gloves, I thought. *Gloves.*

"In a couple of weeks' time, we'll make an announcement
that I'm retiring, that after forty years I'm giving the tonsils a rest
and looking forward to spending more time with my family—they
all say that, whether they're retiring or have been given the flick.

We do no interviews, no specials, do not, for Christ's sake, let them do one of those *This Is Your Life* TV specials—I'll do my last shift, then we leave. Got it?"

I nodded.

"Then, I retire quietly to Willow Island to while away the hours. I've sorted it all out with Dr. Stephenson. I'll visit the specialists when I have to, and he'll provide me with whatever painkillers I may need.

"You take some leave without pay from the station, but stay on the same wage, on my own payroll as my personal assistant—by the way, I'm going to need you to get me some pot."

"Get you some pot?"

"Yes," he said impatiently. "Pot, Lulu, you know, weed, grass, dope, herb, skunk—apparently it's marvelous for pain management—oh, stop looking at me like I've asked you to smuggle cocaine in your undies! Really, Lulu, it's not that hard, you just wander around the corridor for a bit and ask if anyone's got some, this *is* a radio station, you know. But I don't want any rubbish—no leaf, just some nice, sticky heads, got that?"

"Yes," I said, "go outside in the hallway at my place of work and ask people who pass by if they have any skunk for me."

"Good girl." He beamed. "Now about the children. They are not to visit when things start to get ugly. I do not want those children to see me unless I'm up and about, with a fishing rod in my hand, do you understand?"

I understood.

Duncan McAllister had relied on me to handle just about every aspect of his life for the last few years—now he wanted me to do the same for his death.

~

"Is Duncan holding out for more money, Lulu, is that what this is all really about? Well, tell him we'll give it to him."

"Tallulah, I don't think you or Duncan realize how vital it is for us to retain his services. . . . We've just repainted his name in the car park, for Christ's sake."

"Fuck him, Lulu, all right, fuck him, if he wants to play this game, then fine, tell him we've got a line of people champing at the bit to take over."

On and on the questions went, asked by those farther and farther up the ladder until I was summoned by the man who sat on the very top rung, every now and again poking out a polished shoe to knock someone clawing their way up off it.

"Is there nothing you can do?" Jack Abraham, owner of Oz-Radio, was asking me, having flown from London, it was rumored, specifically to change Duncan's mind—which he hadn't, because Duncan was hiding from him on Willow, saying, "You deal with it, Lulu."

I shook my head.

"I'm sorry, Mr. Abraham."

"Call me Jack."

"I'm sorry, Jack, but no, I don't think I can do anything at all."

"Is there nothing anyone can do, Lulu?" His canny eyes met mine.

"No, I don't believe so."

"Well," he said, getting up, "better let the man go then."

On Duncan's last morning, the media camped outside the security gates waiting for his car to creep through the predawn fog, and although the papers and airwaves had been full of his departure for days, we were both still surprised to see so many of them there, like guests we never expected to turn up at a party.

"Eat them, Barney," Duncan said, before pulling up beside the pack, rolling down his window, his arm resting on the door, squinting at the lights.

"Slow news day, is it?" he said, "Or has someone died? Bernie Hanson, you old fraud, I thought your dick was the only thing that got up this early in the morning. . . ."

He pulled them all out, all the old tricks, the insults, the one-liners, and as the security gate lifted like a game-show hostess's arm, the pack stepped back to let Duncan McAllister through for the last time. Then they put down their cameras and recorders, and clapped.

"Geez," said Duncan, taking in their standing ovation, "if I didn't hate half the bastards I'd be quite moved by that."

Duncan's last shift broke all the ratings records, but even when it was over, it wasn't over.

While he quietly moved to Willow Island, I had to stay behind at the station to "tidy things up," answer the listeners' letters that still arrived weekly, long after he and Barney had left the building, which had been a strange procession of man, dog, and well-wishers who opened their doors to shake hands and paws along the way.

I'd also stayed to take the phone calls, the lies falling from my lips like casually dropped stitches: "No, Duncan's fine, he's just ready to take a well-deserved break after forty years in the business." "No, I'm sorry, he's not doing any interviews at all at the moment, too busy fishing." "Thank you so much for making Mr. McAllister that beautiful commemorative quilt; he thanks the ladies of the McLean Valley with all his heart."

Duncan would call every day or two from the island to bark instructions at me, ordering books and newspapers, any special food he wanted brought over, names of people he wanted called, and outlining elaborate plans to keep the truth hidden for as long as possible.

This involved furtive trips to and from the ferry, into town and the hospital, where he had somehow contrived a separate entry from the general public for us. We would drive into the basement car park and catch a service elevator to a third-floor storage room, which we would stroll out of—Duncan motioning "One, two, three, go!" at me with his hands—and down to a passenger lift to take us up to Dr. Stephenson's office.

I don't know how many people we fooled, or for how long. We certainly did not fool Kimmy.

She and Duncan were no longer together, a quiet divorce and an even quieter settlement having ended their union legally, but they kept in touch and she had turned up at Willow Island one day, roaring up the driveway in the red BMW the divorce had bought her.

Duncan told me afterward how he'd opened the door and she'd said, "What's all this bullshit about you retiring here, Duncan?" And he, unable to deflect her steady gaze, had answered with the truth.

"Hard luck, Mac," she'd said.

He also told me he'd apologized to her for "stuffing things up" between them, and she'd said it was all right, that they'd had some fun together, and asked if he was still up for some more.

"I told her I wasn't dead yet." He beamed, completely delighted with himself.

chapter fifteen

It wasn't just Kimmy who had seen through Duncan's elaborate—
and increasingly exhausting—ruses. Other people were beginning
to suspect he was not well too.

The papers started hinting at his demise, people asked me
outright what was wrong with him, and a few months after Frank's
exhibition, a letter fell through the slot in our doorway, landing
so softly on the carpet I did not hear it drop, or the footsteps that
had brought it.

> *Dear Tallulah*, bright green ink looped large across the page.
> It went on:
>> *I'm very sorry about your friend Duncan's illness. I
>> liked him very much when I met him at Bloom—I think.
>> Anyway, he told me something that night I would like to
>> talk to you about. This is where we are, come anytime.
>> We're here for a couple more months.*
>
>> Love,
>> *Annasmell Andrews*

She had underlined *anytime*, and I longed—instantly—to go
to her, laughing at the childhood nickname she had signed off
with in her emerald-green pen.

Its color, and her mention of his name, also reminded me I had not yet got Duncan his pot—but at least now I knew where I would get it from, and it gave me an excuse to go to them.

I looked at Annabelle's letter again, the address in town where they were staying, and tried not to think about the plurality of her words—*you know where we are, we are here for a couple of months*—Annabelle and the boy she stole from me by the river as green as the ink in her pen.

A few days later I was walking up a street lined with laurel trees to the town house Annabelle and Josh "maintained" in the city while they traveled. I had read that once in a magazine feature on them—*The stylish couple maintain an inner-city sanctuary that is home to the two nomads* (which Duncan later crossed out and changed to *gonads*) *when they return to Australia.*

And now I was right outside that inner-city abode, as agitated and nervous as if I were on a first date with both of them.

Annabelle opened the door before I rang the bell. "I've been waiting," she said, "all morning actually; Josh went out, said he couldn't stand watching me pace."

"Oh," I managed, following her up the stairs leading to the lounge room. With huge black-and-white photos on every wall, it was like being surrounded by a giant checkerboard. I put my bag down and sat on a couch, my hands in my lap.

"You look like you're waiting outside Sister Scholastica's office." Annabelle smiled at me, and I relaxed a little and managed to reply: "Not likely, considering I'm here to score drugs. For Duncan," I added, "not me."

Annabelle nodded, never easily thrown, and asked if I'd like a coffee or tea.

"Tea, please," I said, "white and one."

"Still the same, then," she said, and a small part of me, for some reason, bristled.

"Not quite," I answered, determined not to be thrown by her either.

When she came back with the tea, she sat opposite me on a huge, deep couch, her legs tucked under her, thin and angular, and almost, I thought, to coin an old phrase, disapanishing within its folds.

She was beautiful, no matter what Duncan said. The hollows of her cheeks had filled out, and she'd cut her hair so a blunt fringe now fell across her forehead.

It suited her, dammit. Everything, I thought, looking around the town house, suited her.

The checkerboard walls were filled with shots of Josh and Annabelle on their travels and images of wild-eyed men and women, though none as startling as a picture of Annie, naked and panting on the floor.

"When she had me," Annabelle said. "I don't think you've ever seen that one, have you?"

"No, it's very, well, it's sort of confronting, isn't it?"

"Confronting? No, I don't think so; I think it's very comforting."

"Well, she doesn't look very comfortable to me."

Annabelle laughed and said, "God I've missed you, Tallulah."

I wasn't ready for it. I wasn't ready for her, and so I said nothing, just sipped my tea.

"Your friend Duncan, he said you missed me."

"What?"

"Duncan, that night at Bloom, he said that he was your dearest friend in the world, a position he understood I had left vacant, and thanked me for." She was holding my eyes steady with hers, but her words—Duncan's words actually—were coming out in a rush. "He said that although he had done his best, you, for reasons he wasn't entirely sure of, still missed me, and then he said that due to unforeseen circumstances he would soon be leaving the position vacant once more and he was offering it back to me—provided I met certain requirements."

I sat there, hearing Duncan's voice, the words sounding so utterly like him.

"What were they?" I asked, trying to keep my voice as steady as her gaze.

But she had dropped her eyes. "He said I could have your friendship back provided I didn't go off and shag your current boyfriend underneath some rickety pier."

The silence filled every space between us.

"And then he said"—Annabelle lifted her head and cocked it—"'Not that I personally have anything against water sports, my dear.'"

I couldn't help it, I laughed, at Duncan, at Annabelle's near-perfect imitation of him, and at me, sitting in Annabelle and Josh's "inner-city sanctuary"—which Duncan had, also, rather predictably I told him, crossed out and changed to *wanctuary*—like I was the sort of girl who knew the sort of people who maintained them.

Annabelle laughed with me, then abruptly took the cup from my hands and disappeared into the kitchen, coming back with a refill and saying, "So, tell me about Rose, Tallulah, how is she? Every time I saw a kimono in Japan, I thought of her. I bought her one, actually, I've kept it for a couple of years; it's in a box upstairs. I thought she might like to call it Cherry, after the blossoms, of course. I'll show it to you if you like," she said, almost running up the stairs, and I realized two things.

First of all, Annabelle Andrews had missed me, and my family, just as much as I had missed her. And two, she was nervous.

When we'd last met, it was me who couldn't stop talking; this time it was Annabelle tripping over her own tongue in her hurry to get the words out.

She kept asking questions: How was Harry? Was he still plumbing the depths of excellence? What about the twins? How old were they now? "I bet they're handsome," she said, "I'd love to see them." She even asked about Simone and Stella, and when I was leaving, as she was handing me the kimono for Rose, she said, "We should catch up again; I'd like to meet Ben properly. Maybe the four of us could all go out to dinner."

I felt a tiny, delicious—and childish—sense of power, that for once it was her doing the asking, and me doing the deciding.

"Maybe. I'll check with Ben. He's away a lot on business trips—overseas," I added unnecessarily, looking, I imagined, like a woman who was not easily thrown.

~

A fortnight after I visited Annabelle, Ben went away on a buying trip to Malaysia, but not before the four of us—Josh, Annabelle, Ben, and I—endured dinner together at a Nepalese restaurant.

Ben hadn't wanted to go, but I had pushed, wanting, I suppose, to show them that I had a life of my own, with a man who went on buying trips to Asia and knew what wine to bring.

I'd told Ben it would be fun, that Josh and Annabelle knew the owners. "Of course they do," he'd said under his breath, just loud enough for me to hear.

But we had gone, and sat at a booth festooned with prayer flags, Annabelle and I on one side, Josh opposite us, arms spread out across the back of the seat, lazily interrogating Ben in a chair at the end of the table.

"You're in shoes, aren't you, Ben?" Josh drawled, taking a swig of his Corona.

Ben nodded. "It's a family business, Moreton's Shoes—"

"Keeping Australia on its feet since 1967." Josh smiled, then added, "You must be exhausted, mate."

Annabelle and I laughed, but Ben didn't, grimly plowing through a plate of momos. "Actually, Lulu and I like to tell people that in between my family keeping Australia on its feet and hers plumbing the depths of excellence, we've got the nation's best interests covered."

I was embarrassed, for him, for me, and sent a prayer up to the flags that I could just disappear from this booth where Josh was saying, "Well, that's very patriotic of you, mate."

Sitting with Josh and Annabelle made me realize how suburban Ben and I had become, how pale in comparison.

Everything about Ben seemed wrong that night: his hair; his checked shirt; his blue jeans, too low on his hips; his voice, too high; his shoes, too polished. He looked, I thought, too try-hard, and I was too stupid back then to realize that was exactly what he was doing, and to love him for it.

On the way home I said to him in the car, grouchily, bitchily, "You know, Ben, it's not me who likes to say that about our families having the nation's best interests covered, it's you."

Ben kept his eyes on the road. "Sorry, Lulu," he said, not flinching. "I thought it was us." When he left early the next morning, he did not wake me, and I did not mind.

With Ben away, Duncan at Lingalonga with his first wife, Kiki, and their son, Duncan Junior, Mattie and Sam studying for university exams, and Rose, according to Harry, the best she had been in months, I found myself with days to fill.

So I filled them with Josh and Annabelle.

Annabelle rang and suggested that the three of us do lunch, then a dinner, then a walk in the mountains, and in between there was a blur of bars and basement art galleries—places in my city I did not know existed and would not be able to find again in the daytime.

We roamed the streets with arms linked, through back alleys that rose and fell like breaths, and tumbled through doorways into bars with no names and people determinedly wearing black behind them.

I felt heady between them—Josh's laugh against my ear, Annabelle standing beside me in nightclub bathrooms, our eyes meeting in the mirror. "You look splendifigous." She smiled at me.

We shared breakfasts in sunny cafés, Annabelle quiet behind her sunglasses, Josh pretending he knew how to do the cryptic crossword while I sat eating cinnamon toast, feeling like I belonged to both of them.

On about our seventh night out, we were at one of their friends' places, with people strewn like scatter cushions around it, when Annabelle said she was not feeling well and wanted to go home.

I remember half getting up, saying, "I'll come with you," but she shook her head.

"No need," she said. "You stay and have fun. I'll see you at home later, Josh."

She slipped through the door, and Josh and I sat on a couch with a woman who kept insisting she had met him before, and I knew long before she did that she was irritating him.

"Come on, Lulu," he said, standing up, "let's go."

We couldn't get a taxi, so we started walking our way out of the city, through the backstreets, past low-slung telephone wires with quivering opossums running along them.

It was the first time we had been alone since the night we'd said good-bye, the same white moon, it seemed, watching us.

I could hear our breathing, our boots on the road, and if nothing else but to break the silence, I said, "This feels strange, doesn't it, Josh? Sort of strange and familiar at the same time."

He smiled. "Strangely familiar, you might say."

A garbage truck roared around the corner, its orange lights making me jump back to the footpath, Josh close beside me. The truck's huge arm reached out to pick up a bin, a huge claw plucking chocolates out of an arcade machine, then it rumbled off into the early morning, its steel belly swaying like a pregnant woman's.

We walked a few more steps, then Josh stopped underneath a street lamp and tilted my chin up to its light.

"So I can see you," he said, and leaned over and kissed me.

Somewhere not too far away I could still hear the truck's rumble, but I was caught in a memory where nothing had changed, my head filling with sadness and elation and the same, delicious rush of him.

Driving my car onto the barge to Willow Island the next day, I sat in it long after I felt the boat pull away from the dock, closing my eyes in the sun that warmed its way through the windows.

I reclined my seat and felt the steady rhythm of the boat's engines somewhere beneath me, dozing until Walter Prentice's tanned-leather face appearing at the window woke me.

"You all right, Lulu?" he said. "Going across to see Duncan?"

"Yeah, just visiting for a few days," I said.

"Better get a coffee into you before we get there," he said, "we're only about fifteen minutes away."

"Thanks," I said, opening the door and heading up the narrow steel steps to the café, the steel rail gritty beneath my hand.

I was glad to be visiting Duncan and leaving behind the imprint of Josh's kiss. I could still feel it, the hardness of it on my lips, his hands trailing from my face to my neck, marking my skin with his, as surely, I thought, as a bruise.

"Did you want a coffee? I'm about to shut down the machine."

I was, I realized, standing at the counter with my own fingers on my mouth.

"I'm sorry, miles away, yes, I'd love one, if there's time," I answered the man standing behind the counter.

He smiled.

"Always time for a coffee—Tallulah, isn't it?"

"Yes," I answered him, realizing I had never seen him on the barge before and wondering how he knew my name.

"Will Barton," he said, putting out his hand for me to shake, "I'm a mate of Duncan's actually. I've been doing a bit of work for him over on Willow. He said you'd be on the barge and asked me to look out for you—I've just started a bit of deckhand work for Walter too."

"Right." I smiled, not knowing what else to say, then added completely unnecessarily, "I'm a mate of Duncan's too."

"Well, mate of Duncan's, let me make you a very fine coffee and help that hangover of yours."

"Is it that obvious?" I smiled back.

"Yeah," he grinned, "you've got that whole sweaty thing that women get the next day going on."

Charming, I thought, surreptitiously taking a serviette to dab at the sides of my nose.

"So, are you from the island?" I asked as he frothed my milk, in an attempt at polite conversation.

"Yes and no," he answered. "It's a bit of a long story. I'll tell it to you sometime"—he raised his eyebrows—"maybe when you're in a better state—not so sweaty."

He smiled, and despite his obvious obsession with perspiration, I smiled back.

Even through my bloodshot eyes I could see Will, friend of Duncan's, was a very attractive man—tall; salt-and-pepper hair; crinkly, dark eyes; dimple in his chin—the sort of man a girl *could* get herself in a sweat over, should she be so inclined.

I wasn't—life was complex enough—so I thanked him for the coffee and sat at a booth looking out at the sea, watching as Willow came into view, glad there was now an ocean between Josh's lips and mine.

Somewhere between the start of that kiss and the end, a taxi had turned onto the street and I was suddenly desperate to get in it.

I uncurled myself from Josh's arms and began flailing my own about, like a woman caught in a rip, trying to attract a lifesaver's attention instead of just hailing a cab.

Not waving, but drowning.

The taxi slowed to a stop, and I fled.

~

When I got to Lingalonga, I unpacked my bag in the guest room, taking in the familiar fishing photos on the walls, the faces of sun-glazed children smiling at the camera through hot-pink zinc-smeared noses, and the women holding them tight against the sea.

I had relaxed the moment I walked through the door, giving myself over to the timelessness of the place, the mobiles dangling in the doorway, knotted with sticks and twigs and shells and feathers made by little hands, still grainy with sand.

I took the bag of pot out of my bag and went to the kitchen, where Duncan was making tea.

"Here you are, you old hippie," I said, tossing the pot on the table.

"Well done, Lulu." Duncan smiled. "Where did you get it?"

"Annabelle."

Duncan raised his eyebrows.

"I've been spending a bit of time with her, actually," I said. "Her and Josh."

Duncan's eyebrows lifted a fraction higher.

"Does Ben know?"

"Know what? That you've turned me into a drug dealer?"

"No—don't be arch, Lulu, it doesn't suit you. Does Ben know that the band's back together again?"

"Not really, but he's away a lot at the moment."

"How very convenient."

"Shut up, Duncan, you're the one who wanted me to get closure."

"I did, but now I look at you and I'm not entirely sure that's what you're getting. . . ." He put the tea down in front of me and let the sentence dangle in midair.

Later, he was lying on the couch, his hand buried deep in Barney's fur beside him. I was sitting opposite him, reading aloud from one of his favorite books, *The Swimmer*, something I would do more and more of as he rested his voice and his bones. Neddy Merrill was about to take the plunge into one of the many suburban pools he would attempt to swim his way home in when Duncan's voice interrupted me.

"I think you'd better stay here until Ben gets back," he said, "where Barney and I can keep an eye on you."

I kept reading, half annoyed at his proprietary tone, and half relieved to hear it.

~

I stayed on at Willow with Duncan for about a week, but there wasn't much for me to do.

Later there would be brow-wiping and hand-holding; later still there would be pain I couldn't relieve no matter how many morphine patches I slapped on him; later there would be long nights of trying to calm his dreams, but for now Duncan was still upright.

The pain had not felled him, it had only slowed him down, lending everything we did together—walking, throwing a stick to Barney, cooking mussels from the trawler in the big, silver saucepan—an unhurried feel. But whatever we did, we could only do it for about an hour at a time, before Duncan would make his way back to the sofa and I'd arrange the commemorative quilt from the ladies of the McLean Valley around him.

I left when his second wife, Kerry-Anne, arrived—he had, by now, told all the Ks, if not the children. She was on her own, without Rhees, and called from the door: "Where are you, you old bastard?"

"Still got a thing for me." Duncan smiled from his chair.

chapter sixteen

W hen I finally returned from Willow Island, I cleaned the flat
for Ben's homecoming, put fresh sheets on the bed, dusted, vacu-
umed, and opened the windows "to let the air in," as Rose would
say, although I knew inside that what I was really doing was trying to
get the odor of my own transgressions out.

I stocked up on Ben's favorite foods, put a six-pack of beer in
the fridge to chill, threw some blue irises in a vase because someone had once told me they were "manly" flowers, and then, in
another frenzy of delayed guilt, I picked up the phone and called
Simone and Stella.

I'd neglected them, I knew, had pushed them aside once more
for Annabelle and Josh, but when Stella picked up the phone she
just said, "Lulu, how lovely to hear from you—I was only just
saying to William the other day"—Stella had started calling Billy
"William" just after his short-lived stand-up comic career, in an
attempt to give him back some of his dignity—"that we haven't
seen you in a while; the kids have missed you."

Simone, however, was more direct.

"Oh," she said when she heard my voice, "back from the Ber-
muda Love Triangle, are we?"

We met the following day at Gottardo's, ordered toasted sand-
wiches and fat chips with our coffees, and settled into an initially
easy conversation about Simone's new producer, who she hated,

Riley's new teacher, who Stella loved, and Thomas's tap recital, which I had missed.

Thomas was Stella's first boy, my godson, and I had been—unless I was sick or looking after Rose—to every concert he'd been in, and either Rose or I usually made his costumes as well.

"I'm sorry, Stella," I said, "when was it?"

"Last Friday," she answered. "I did leave you some messages, but don't worry about it—Simone came instead."

Simone went?

I looked at her, smiling at me across the table. "Auntie Simone," she corrected Stella, "the one who doesn't drop her friends like a schoolbag the moment Josh and Annabelle blow back into town."

"I didn't drop you, Simone," I protested. "I just wanted to spend some time with them, I haven't seen them for years. . . ."

"No, not since Annabelle 'stole your life'—I think that was what you used to wail at me."

"Don't fight." Stella put one hand on each of our shoulders. "I hate it when you two fight."

"Stella," Simone said, "you've been as pissed off as I am at Lulu, and don't pretend you haven't. You should tell her how upset Thomas was that she didn't show up, instead of pretending you didn't mind." Simone looked directly at me. "It was really shitty of you, Lulu, and you know something? I really thought you'd got past all that, but you're behaving like we're back in high school."

"Well, so are you," I shot back at her, unsettled and angry at the sudden lurch in our conversation. "You've always been jealous of Annabelle."

"That's not what this is about and you know it," Simone said. "This is about you putting yourself at their disposal—you're making a fool of yourself, Lulu, only this time it's much worse because we're not in high school any longer, and none of us bounces back like we used to."

Stella burst into tears.

"Like my breasts," she wailed to no one in particular.

⌒

When Ben came home, he looked around the flat, took a beer out of the fridge, and said: "So you missed me?"

"I did," I answered. "I'm sorry about that night with Josh and Annabelle. I was rude to you, I think."

Ben nodded. "Don't worry about it, Lulu."

We watched the football game together, Ben's arm around my shoulders, his feet up on the coffee table, a beer in his hand.

"This is nice," he said.

"What?"

"This," he answered. "You and me."

Later, when we went to bed, I tried to apologize for my behavior again, but he said, "It's okay, Lulu. Look, I'm completely exhausted, and it's been a really good night, so let's just not go there, all right?"

I nodded my head against his chest, not telling him I had already been.

⌒

On a roll of atonement, I left Ben at home to rest from his trip for a few days and went to visit Harry and Rose.

I hadn't been home for a month, and although Harry had told me how well my mother was doing, I wanted to see for myself.

I parked the car outside the house, walked past Harry's sign, and headed up the path to the front door.

"Rose?" I called out, "Rose?"

"Lulu," Rose said, rustling across the lino in Madeleine's red and green checks and putting both hands out to me. "It's so lovely to see you. Your father has just gone down to the office for a bit, and then he'll pick up some dinner on the way home."

"Pick up some dinner?"

"Yes."

"From a takeaway?"

"Yes, people do it, you know, Lulu."

That was true, lots of people did it—I did it a couple of nights a week—but Rose, endless purveyor of the cooked meal? "What are we having?"

"Thai, I love it."

"You love Thai?"

"Yes, Lulu, I love Thai, why do you keep repeating everything I say?"

Because my mother was wearing Madeleine, because my mother was ordering Thai food, and there was no flour on her hands. Because my mother looked happy.

The twins were away at a uni soccer camp and the house was quiet without them, smaller somehow without their long, rangy bodies filling every corner of it, sprawled out on couches or swinging their legs at the breakfast bar.

Sometimes, when Rose was depressed, the house needed their noisiness to fill it, the way couples who are no longer talking use their children to color in the lines between them.

But this time it was Rose's voice that carried down the hall-way and into the garden where she watered the strawberry plants, humming to herself and reminding me of a story Harry had once told me about when they were courting.

They had gone swimming at an out-of-the-way swimming hole, and Harry, shy about Rose seeing him in his swimmers, had been astounded when she had slid out of her dress in one easy movement, laughing up at him: "Come on, Harry, get your gear off, or are you afraid the eels will get your gilhoo-lies?"

Now, hearing her singing in the garden, I could easily imag-ine that Rose, the one who just dived right in.

Later that night, Harry and I sat swinging in the dark.

"She's doing so well, Lulu," he said. "Best she's been in a long time."

"That's great, Harry."

"It is. Dr. Reynolds, that's the new bloke we're seeing, she likes him, seems to trust him; she hated Dr. Shaw, she called him Dr. Not-So-Shaw."

"I know," I said, laughing.

"Anyway, we've been to the pictures a couple of times, and yesterday she nipped down to the news agency."

"On her own? Did she take the car?" I asked, thinking of Rose's station wagon, sitting on its haunches in the garage for what felt like forever.

"No, she walked down—one step at a time, Lulu."

"I know, I'm just glad she's getting out." I put my head on his bony shoulder. "I'm sorry I haven't been down much, Harry. I've just been so busy at the station sorting out all of Duncan's stuff."

"He's on his way out, isn't he, Lulu?"

"Yeah, he is. Cancer, throat cancer—it's terminal."

"Better for you to be there with him then, love. We're all right, Rose and me. I think she's really coming along well, she's been giving me a hard time about all sorts of jobs around the house, and that's always a good sign."

"I'm so pleased, Harry."

"Me too, love—do you want to turn in?"

"I do, I'm pretty tired."

"Want me to carry you?"

I smiled, remembering long-ago nights of flannel-pajama-clad arms wrapped around his neck, fingers clasped at the back, legs hooked to his waist, and Rose saying, "For goodness' sake, Harry, bring her inside, she'll get a chill."

"I'm twenty-five now, Harry, not twelve," I reminded him.

"I'd still give it a go."

"I know you would, you lunatic; come on, let's go in."

We walked through the garden to the back door, and I looked up to see Rose watching over us from her bedroom window, hands deep in Madeleine's pockets.

chapter seventeen

Leaving my parents—Rose in Betty, Harry in his boiler suit, both of them waving me off from the driveway—I headed back to the city, letting myself into the flat and throwing my keys on the hallway table.

A white envelope sat in our mail basket, with embossed and scalloped edges, two wedding bands in the corner, and my name in a silver pen across it.

I picked it up, running my fingers along the scalloping, as Ben entered the room.

"Hi." He smiled. "So who's the lucky couple this time?"

"Not sure," I said, although I had known straight away, recognizing the familiar, broad loops, "but I think it might be Josh and Annabelle."

I opened it, and one tiny, perfect, blush-pink rosebud fell out.

Annabelle and Josh, the card said, were getting married on August 27 at 5:00 p.m. at Saint Alban's Church in Juniper Bay, and afterward, guests were invited to join them for a party at the Hotel du Laurent.

They had booked the entire hotel out for the night, so everyone was also invited to stay for a celebratory breakfast the next morning.

There was a note as well, which I didn't read then, not in front of Ben, but saved for later, when he had finally left the apartment to meet some friends from work for a drink and had stopped looking at me from every angle, checking if I was all right but never asking.

When I was sure he was gone, listening for the click of the downstairs door, I went to our room, lay on the bed, and took it out.

Tallulah, Annabelle had written, *I hope you will come, we would really love you to be there, but if you can't for any reason, I want you to know we completely comprestand. Love always*, A.

I put the note down on the bedside table, rolling the tiny rosebud between my thumb and my finger.

Stupid really, to feel like this, as though someone had, as Rose would say, "knocked the wind out of my sails."

But I did feel like that, I felt stupid, and foolish.

I turned my face, buried it deep into the pillow, and let go of the stupid, bloody rosebud.

What had I been thinking? That Josh would leave Annabelle for me? That Annabelle would leave Josh for me? That they would take me with them wherever they traveled to next? That they would realize that out of all of us, I was the one worth hanging on to?

No, but they would love me to come, and if I didn't, they would completely comprestand.

Well, how very genanimous of them.

I turned off the light and closed my eyes, hearing Ben come in a couple of hours later to lie beside me and say with his beery breath that he understood why I was "a bit upset."

"We don't have to go, Lulu," he said. "I'm in Hong Kong that week, anyway, you could come, bit of retail therapy."

But I had already made my decision.

~

"You can't go, Lulu," Stella said, "it will only upset you."

"Jesus, Lulu, why don't you just wear a sign that says KICK ME, and save yourself all the trouble?" said Simone, somewhat less diplomatically.

"Just come with me," Ben tried again.

"You have to go, Lulu," Rose said firmly. "It's the right thing to do."

"I think you should do want you want, love," Harry said.

"You could always poison her at her bachelorette," Duncan said.

In the weeks leading up to the wedding, I didn't really have time to think about it; I was too busy trying to calm down Duncan—who, unsurprisingly, was not going gently into that good night.

He had begun to rail against his treatments, refusing to have any more chemo on the grounds that he was not going to lose one more single strand of hair—"A man's hair is his strength, Lulu, look what happened to Samson"—demanding I come to the island, announcing that no, he was better off alone, then summoning me once again, meeting with Andrew Lyons, his longtime lawyer, to sort out the minutiae of his life to such an excruciating degree that the usually indefatigable Andrew had taken some stress leave.

Duncan would be serene one minute, agitated the next, panicking wildly over the smallest things: "Lulu, I can't find Barney's striped rubber ball; we've got to find that ball for him," he urged one day, and sent me down to the beach to search for hours. When I finally returned, sunburned and empty-handed, he had looked at me and said dismissively, "What are you so upset about, Lulu? It's only a ball."

He was losing weight and had taken to tying a bit of rope around his falling-down tracksuit pants to hold them up; his skin was sallow and his step unsure; sometimes when he opened the door to me I would wonder who this old man was.

But other times, if one of his former wives or colleagues—

especially if it was a former colleague—visited, the slackness of his jaw would tighten, the roped tracksuit pants would be replaced by a pair of perfectly ironed jeans, his back would straighten, his hair would be concealed by a white cricketing hat, his smile would be welcoming, and he would become the suntanned retiree, hale and hearty and stronger than any of the winds that whipped at Linga-longa.

He would walk on steady legs beside his guests on the sand, arms out wide, face turned toward the sun, an old conjurer pulling out one last hoax from his bag of tricks.

When the children came—and they came most weekends—he would rest in his bed right up until the minute he heard the car in the driveway and then be at the door to greet them as they tumbled out of their mothers' cars: Duncan Junior, Rhees, Jasmine and Jarrod, racing to get into the house first and the room with the bunk beds in it.

"Bags it," Jarrod would shout from the top bunk.

"You did not, I got here first."

"That's not fair, you always get it."

"Da-aaad!"

On hearing the familiar wail, Duncan would dive in, Barney right behind him, and enter the fray.

When they left, leaving their trail of sand and sticks and half-eaten lollies wrapped in waxy paper stuck under pillows, Duncan would wave them off, turn and go inside, close the door behind him, and sleep for hours.

I spent most of the next month on the island. Ben was away, and Rose, Harry reassured me again and again, was doing well, so I crisscrossed back and forth on the ferry, sipping lukewarm coffee out of polystyrene cups, surrounded by bags of fruit I knew Duncan would refuse to eat and knowing that, no matter how much I wanted to, I could never bring this particular ship home to shore.

Duncan, I discovered, had made a new life on Willow, one that had nothing to do with who he was on the mainland. People always seemed to be popping in and out: Will, the deckhand I'd met on the barge, often sat with Duncan poring over blueprints for goodness knew what—a boat probably—the people from the post office hand-delivered his mail, and a salty collection of fishermen could usually be found there at sunset, waiting at the back gate for a beer and a chinwag with the man with now not-so-platinum tonsils.

I hung around for as long as I could, just drinking Duncan in.

Rose made me a dress for Annabelle's wedding.

She was not up to coming herself, but had made me a pale pink, knee-length lace shift with three-quarter sleeves and a mandarin collar. It had a matching cream bolero and a pink lace flower I could pin on it, or in my hair—"Whichever you like, darling," she said—and I knew my mother could not have taken more care with it than if it had been my wedding gown.

Harry and I had mostly listened to the radio on the way to the church, and when we pulled up outside he had given my hand a squeeze and said, "Your turn next, Lulu."

My father, the man with no idea.

The church was beautiful. Someone—Frank, I thought—had tied bunches of tiny pink rosebuds to every pew and set out sandalwood candles with rings of ivy at their base.

I stood at the door, Harry's hand on my arm, and took it all in.

"It will be all right, you know, Lulu," he said as we walked in, and just as we did Josh had turned his head and smiled at me.

I smiled back, and somewhere inside the look that passed between us, I left the church to go to a corner store where my brothers were curled like question marks around my legs, and a boy in a sky-blue T-shirt was pushing the hair from his eyes. Then

Harry pulled at my arm, and we sat down between two groups of people I didn't know. A woman with a red face and a puffy skirt asked me if I was a friend of the bride or the groom, and I told her truthfully that I didn't know.

A harp began to play on the balcony above us, and Christa walked in, wearing another kimono and a complicated hat, followed by Fergus in a white linen shirt and khaki trousers, Annie in her layers, swaying slightly as she made her way to the front, too much jewelry, too much makeup—too much scotch, everyone would say later.

Josh's mother, Pearl, walked in quickly and scurried to her seat at the front, not looking at anyone. As she passed I got a strong, sharp whiff of the cigarette she had just put out, her lipstick smudged from its tip.

Then Annabelle, on Frank's arm, Frank in a suit and his fisherman's cap.

Beautiful, tall Annabelle in a full-length, aquamarine vintage gown and lilac coat, shimmering in its folds and holding a bouquet of tuberose and ivy. Someone—not her, Annabelle could never be bothered with makeup—had painted her eyes and given her lashes; her curls were dark and loose about her face, and she was as beautiful to me as she was the day she first sat down beside me, one of Sister Scholastica's finest flowers.

I didn't really listen to the ceremony; I just sat in the pew with my arm against Harry's shoulder and passed tissues from my handbag to the woman with the red face who cried noisily throughout.

Then we went to the reception at the hotel, where I smiled and laughed and clinked my glass at the speeches and danced with everybody and spent time with the older relatives and spoke about the flowers, and said, "Yes, they were lovely, weren't they?" and "No, you wouldn't think of frangipanis as your first choice."

I ate the food and the cake and had my photo taken again

and again, and my champagne refilled again and again, and not once did I speak to Annabelle or Josh, because I was far, far too busy smiling.

Harry left early; he and Frank were not staying at the hotel, Harry because he needed to get home to Rose, and Frank because he said he needed to not be near the open bar.

So I made my way to my room alone, falling backward on the bed when I got inside and sleeping in my clothes and shoes until a knock at the door woke me.

I got up and looked through the keyhole.

I opened the door.

"Josh," I said, "what is it? Is everything okay?"

He swayed a little, and smiled a lopsided smile at me, and closed the door behind him.

Then his hands were in my hair and on my face, and I was holding his tie tight in my fist and not letting go when we sank to the floor. And I didn't care that it was Josh, who shouldn't have been there, or that Annabelle was somewhere upstairs.

I didn't care because I felt his skin slip into mine, I felt the bite of his teeth and the breath from his mouth as he said, "Tallulah-Lulu," his hands retracing the path they had traveled so many times before, and somewhere in the aching I led him all the way home to me.

chapter eighteen

"I'm really sorry, Ben."

"I know you are, Lulu, but it doesn't change what happened."

"I know."

"It's so, I don't know, tawdry, or something."

Ben and I were standing in our soon-to-be empty apartment, about a fortnight after the wedding, when he came home from Hong Kong.

After my lunch with Simone and Stella, I'd hidden out at Harry and Rose's, making a few trips back to my city apartment to collect the belongings I knew could no longer stay there once Ben returned from his buying trip.

I'd wanted to stay in my old room at Harry and Rose's forever, but I knew I owed Ben more than that.

Much more than that; at the very least an apology to his face, which I could hardly bear to picture.

I'd been waiting for him most of the morning, pacing the rooms of our apartment and letting my eyes fall on the life we had shared, coming undone at the "World's Best Girlfriend" mug still sitting in the drying rack.

When I heard the cab pull up, I watched him through the window and knew I was not the only one undone. Everything about him seemed different: the way he walked, the way he picked up his suitcase, the way he didn't look up at the window, like he had always done, to see if I was there.

Now we were sitting on the end of the bed that was no longer ours and I was watching him let me go.

"I know, it *is* tawdry, and so stupid, and I'm sorry, Ben, I don't really know how to say how sorry I am."

We sat still for a while, then he got up and started unpacking.

"Where's all your stuff?" he said, opening the closet, seeing the empty spaces.

"At Rose and Harry's, I thought you'd probably want me . . . not here," I said, waving my hand around our bedroom. "So I've sort of half moved there for a while."

He nodded and sat down again on the bed, put his head in his hands.

I moved nearer to him and put my hand on his back, felt him inch away.

"Don't, Lulu," he said, then, "Have you got somewhere to go tonight?"

I nodded, thinking of Simone.

"Good," he said, "because you're right, I don't want you here."

He stood up and went into the bathroom, and the steam from the shower curled under the door while I sat on the bed and waited.

I could still hear the hiss of the water hitting the tiles when I left.

Later, we would sort out who owned what and who owed what, all the little unpickings of a relationship, and much later we would wish each other well, but for now I left him to it, standing under the shower, washing us away.

I didn't see him again for months, until everything had changed and the guilt I felt over losing him would be diminished by another loss, one that cut right through to the bone.

"Dear God, Lulu," Duncan rasped, opening the door a crack, "come in, come in, are there hordes of press behind you trying to get a shot of the Juniper Bay Wedding Shagger?"

"Shut up, Duncan," I said, "and let me in."

He did, and I noticed a spring in his step that I had not seen the last time I was there—nothing like a scandal to get Duncan going again.

"You look well, Duncan," I said. "I should sleep with the bridegroom more often."

Duncan sat down and peered at me.

"You know, Lulu, when I said you needed closure, I had no idea you'd take it so literally."

"No, neither did I."

We sat down on the couch, Barney under our feet, as Duncan threw his arm around me.

"What happened?" he asked eventually.

"I drank too much."

"Always a good defense, not honorable, of course, but more than adequate for many occasions."

"And I wanted to."

"Aha."

"Aha?"

"Yes, Lulu, aha, as in, now we get to the seed beneath the husk—go on," he said, "I'll hold your hand if it helps along the way."

So I told him.

I told him what I had not been able to tell the priest when he had said, "And why did you do that, my daughter?" and why I kept silent and began to pray instead, asking whoever was listening to forgive me for, apart from the obvious transgression, the sin of omission.

Because I had omitted to tell the priest with the soft voice and the warm hand over mine that the real reason I had fallen to the floor with Josh Keaton was not because I loved him. It was not because, as Rose had offered, I had been "carried away" by the emotions of the day, and not because, as a mad-eyed Annie had said on television, I had "always been pathologically jealous" of her family. None of those things were Duncan's seed beneath the husk.

I did it because I was tired of being the girl who brought the ships home to shore. I was tired of standing over the stove in my school uniform cooking the family dinner and babysitting Mattie and Sam every time Rose had one of her Doris days, tired of keeping Harry's books and ironing Rose's dresses and trying not to mind as days then weeks then years went by before Josh or Annabelle came home, and pretending I didn't mind when they did.

I was tired of looking after Duncan and making him meals he wouldn't eat and telling him it didn't matter when Barney molted all over clothes I had just washed, tired of traveling back and forth on the barge with half my clothes on land, the other at sea.

I was tired of pretending to be interested in Ben's work and acting as if I cared whether wedge heels would be in this summer.

I was tired of being the girl by the river, at the skating rink, standing beneath a perfect moon as silent as the stars that hung beside it.

I didn't want to be that girl anymore.

So there it was.

"Are you shocked?" I asked Duncan.

"No," he said idly, "not at all, not by that."

"What, then?"

"Well, I was just wondering," he said, "what took you so long." Then he gathered me a little closer to him and rasped, "And now, my dear, we await the fallout."

It didn't take long.

While I had switched off the television before I could catch Annie's ravaged face answering Maxine Mathers's caramel-clipped questions about the wedding, and while my name had not been broadcast, it didn't matter.

There had been a photo of me in my blue satin dress at the exhibition at Bloom, standing just behind Josh and Annabelle and beaming at the lens. They are looking straight into it, and I, although I had no recollection of it being taken, am considering them, my head cocked to one side—"Like the specter at the feast," Simone had offered.

The interview had concluded with a still from Frank's "Enchanted" series, two little girls with their arms about each other, one of them destined to become the Juniper Bay Wedding Shagger.

Annie's appearance on *Today, Tonight, and Tomorrow* would become a part of Australian television folklore, replayed again and again on "Top Ten moments" and anniversary specials, mostly because of Annie's infamous "I fucked him" comment, always bleeped out, and Maxine's stunned expression following it.

It would, for a little while, not just be my undoing, but Annie's also. There had clearly been something not right with her the night of the interview, drunk, or on something, or both, staring at the camera, tugging at her ear, staring into space, smiling her cat's smile at the camera, as if she knew something that nobody else did, or ever would.

Poor Annie, that interview left more than one reputation in tatters.

Mine didn't matter so much, and while for months afterward people would hear my name and I would watch while they tried to recall how they knew it, my infamy was soon eclipsed by the Moonlighting Minister, a conservative politician caught soliciting at a well-known gay beat. I can still see his wife by his side in pearls and Laura Ashley at the press conference, her mouth a grim little line of public service.

But for a while I knew what it felt like to be the person strang-

ers talked about on trains, and, in the eyes of people who did love
me, to fall from grace.

~

"Hello, I'd like to speak to Tallulah de Longland, please," the
girl's voice said on the phone.

"This is Tallulah," I said.

"I have Dr. Patrick Stephenson on the line for you."

"Thank you."

"Hello, Lulu."

"Hello, Dr. Stephenson."

"Lulu, I've just left Duncan and he's in a bad way. He won't
go to the hospital, as you know, and frankly even if he did go I
don't know what good it would do."

"I see," I said, even though I didn't.

"He's on his way out, Lulu," Dr. Stephenson said, "and he has
made it known to me that at the time I feel it is appropriate, I am
to ask you to let certain people know—he says you have a list."

"I do," I said, thinking of the big brown envelope with DUN-
CAN'S DEATH LIST written on it in my employer's scratchy hand,
with a skull and crossbones drawn underneath it, the skull with a
knowing, leery grin on its bony face.

"I do," I repeated, "I do have a list, Doctor."

"Well, it's time to use it," he said crisply.

When he hung up, I stared stupidly at the phone for a long
time, then ran up the stairs to my room and began throwing
clothes in a bag, pulling out shirts from drawers and grabbing at
hangers, and it was only when I sat on the floor with everything
spilling out of the bag and tried to do up the damn zip that I realized my hands were shaking.

Rose came into the room, walking across the floor to kneel
beside me, taking everything out of the bag and folding it, going

to my closet and taking out dresses and shoes, and calling out to Harry for a glass of whiskey and milk.

"For you," she said, "not me," then, "You know you haven't packed any underwear," and then I was laughing and crying at the same time while she wordlessly took the whiskey from Harry at the door and closed it behind him.

"Now," she smiled, handing the drink to me, "we'll do this together."

I left the next day, holding a basket of warm sultana scones for Duncan from Rose and with a slightly aching head from Harry's two glasses of whiskey with a shot of milk.

"He won't eat them, you know," I told her.

"I know." She smiled at me. "But he'll smell them."

I sat on the barge and thought about Duncan, and how tears were made of salt, like the sea.

Then I drove up the road to his house and let myself in, finding him asleep on his bed, hands curled like a child's under his chin, and tasted the sea on my lips.

Then I tucked the blanket in around him and told him what Rose had told me.

"Now," I said to him, "we'll do this together."

~

We used a roster system, spacing visitors out, blocking in the ex-wives and children's times when we thought he would be at his best, and leaving every afternoon free for a nap, which seemed to me, I thought, tiptoeing into his room late one day, to be getting longer.

Barney was lying, as always, at the end of the bed, ready to spring up at a moment's notice if he smelled something vaguely edible, and Duncan was having a good rest, not like some days, when he grimaced and cried in his sleep, yelling out random words and sometimes grabbing at his own throat.

When he was like that I would try to comfort him, stroking his forehead and whispering, "It's all right, Duncan, everything's all right, sleep now," until one time when he suddenly woke up, batted my hand away and said, "Jesus, Lulu, you scared the shit out of me, I thought you were Grammy McAllister coming to get me." After that I left him to fight his demons alone.

I was just tiptoeing out of the room again late one Sunday afternoon when I heard his raspy call.

"Lulu."

"I'm here."

"I know; I can hear you creeping around the room like a bloody ghost."

"I'm sorry."

"Don't be—have the hordes finally left?"

"Yes."

"It's just you and me," he whispered.

"Yes."

The sun wrapped its last rays around the room.

"Take me outside."

"You sure?"

He nodded.

He stood up, shuffled into his slippers, and I grabbed his dressing gown.

"Not that," he said, "not old man's clothes."

"Well, you need something," I said, and took a jacket out of the wardrobe for him.

We walked slowly into the backyard and through the white wooden gate onto the dunes, sea grasses clinging to their curves.

We stood there together for a little while, and I was just about to say that we needed to get back inside, out of the cold, when he touched my arm. "Look," he said, his fingers tightening on my skin, "the pipis are blooming."

Duncan had told me about this, had told me again and again

with the light dancing in his eyes about how not once but twice he had witnessed this performance: the first time as a boy, and the second time a few years back with his old fishing mate Hugh Brearly when they were enjoying a few sundowners at Nelson Bay.

He had told me how people had laughed at him, said he and Hugh had been at the rum, not believing in this strange, silent dance that began when, at the command of some unseen hand, all of the pipis that lay buried and dormant beneath the sand suddenly popped up at the same time.

They huddled in small groups along the shoreline, salty clumps of eugaries knotted tightly together like men gossiping on the corner, and then rolled together back into the sea, in perfect, tumbling unison, somehow knowing which wave would be the one to take them exactly where they needed to go.

Duncan called it a bloom, or in his more romantic moments "the Dance of the Eugaries," and we stood there watching their strange water ballet until they were all gone, leaving little pockets in the sand to show where they had been.

"Bravo," Duncan whispered, turning on his heel.

We walked back through the house, and I settled him in his bed, watching as he dozed, wondering where the morphine was taking him and knowing that there were some places I could not go.

"Lulu." His voice surprised me. "Lulu?"

I leaned forward as he patted his bed and whispered, "Barney." Hearing his name, the great dog jumped from his place at the foot of the bed and stood beside Duncan's hand, trailing over the mattress. "Up," he said, "up, boy."

In one movement, before I had time to say, "I don't know if that's a very good idea, Duncan," Barney was up and in, placing his head on the pillow beside Duncan like a very hairy, very ugly old woman.

I started to laugh at the two of them, lying there together, when Duncan patted the other side of the bed, and I realized he wanted me in there too.

"All right," I said, "move over—but if this ends up in the papers—"Duncan McAllister Found Dead in Bed with Mad Wedding Shagger and Dog"—I will never, ever forgive you."

Duncan laughed a long, low, rolling chuckle, and Barney and I both curled our bodies closer to him.

"Lulu," he whispered.

"Yes."

"Your breath is atrocious."

"Shut up, Duncan, you know it's Barney's."

"And your legs are shockingly hairy," he said, each word an effort. Underneath the sheets, his hand found mine and curled around it.

"Well," he said, turning to look at me with eyes that still twinkled even as the fire in them was damping down, "I would have liked to lingalonga. . . ."

Duncan never regained consciousness, and after five long days' journeys into night, and people coming and going and pressing their lips against Duncan's forehead, the eugaries danced on the shore and rolled back to the sea, pulsing and quivering inside, safe within their perfect, imperfect shells.

chapter nineteen

"Hello, Tallulah."

"Nice to see you again, Andrew."

"Please sit down. Do you want anything, tea, coffee, a glass of water?"

"No, thank you, I just had a coffee at the café downstairs."

"Right, well, let's get straight to it," Andrew Lyons said, tapping a pencil against his palm.

"I could have phoned you with all this, Tallulah, but knowing you as I have over the years, when you and I have both been a party to some of Duncan's little imbroglios, I thought I should talk to you in person."

I nodded, knowing what was coming; had known it ever since Duncan had fallen ill and begun dropping hints about my own future, intimating that I "wasn't to worry," that I would be "taken care of," words that unsettled me every time he had spoken them.

I didn't want to be taken care of, I didn't want a single thing from Duncan McAllister, didn't want to be sitting here in the offices of Ferris and Lyons, perched on the edge of a familiar sofa, with Andrew buzzing around me like an attentive beige fly.

All I wanted—stupidly, impossibly, childishly—was Duncan back.

I wanted Andrew to say, "This might come as a shock to you, Lulu, but Duncan is not, in fact, dead, but is now, as we speak, relaxing on a little-known island in Melanesia, having cleverly staged his own death in a bid to avoid paying tax."

Since Duncan had died, my feet had remained firmly on the first rung of Elisabeth Kübler-Ross's famous five stages of grieving: denial, my mind running through a series of impossible scenarios about where he really might be, each more fantastical than the last, and all of them, I supposed, designed to keep me from the aching truth—that my friend was gone.

But it was becoming increasingly difficult to keep up the charade in Andrew's office, the backs of my legs sticking to the leather sofa, perspiration plodding down the back of my neck, and Andrew about to tell me what Duncan had bequeathed me.

I had no idea what it would be—the man was capable of anything—and although it had been generally presumed before Duncan's death that he was a wealthy man, no one had any idea just how wealthy, and even Kimmy had reportedly gasped after being told of the extent of her more-than-generous slice of the McAllister pie.

Andrew excused himself and walked through the heavy, paneled door to the room Duncan had always called "the inner sanctum of the inner sanctum," so I sat, looking at the degrees on his walls, wishing I had asked for a glass of water.

There was a photo of Duncan on the wall, sitting on the same sofa I now occupied, with Andrew's children, a blurry gaggle of limbs and missing-tooth smiles, wrapped around him.

A memory of one of the last conversations I had with Duncan flitted by.

"Lulu," he had said one morning when I was making up the guest room at Lingalonga, "do you think you'll have children?"

"I don't know," I replied. "I'd like to—but in case you haven't noticed, there's a distinct lack of a potential father at the moment."

"I don't think you'll need to worry about that, my dear," he had said, adopting one of his maddeningly enigmatic "I know something you don't know" countenances. "No." He'd chuckled. "I don't think you'll have a problem with that at all."

Oh God, I panicked, as a thought struck me, making me sit bolt upright on the sofa so suddenly the leather ripped at my sweaty skin.

Had Duncan left me some of his own sperm? I wouldn't put it past him; in fact, the more I thought about it, the more likely it seemed, so that by the time Andrew reentered the room, I had convinced myself he would be carrying some sort of gold-plated petri dish.

"Sorry about that, Lulu," he said. "I just had to check on something—well, I won't keep you in suspense any longer."

Putting his fingers to his lips, he whistled, a sharp, shrill sound that jerked though the air.

Through the inner sanctum of the inner sanctum, a familiar shaggy figure banged the door open with his mighty head and came barreling toward us.

Barney.

Duncan had left me Barney.

Andrew passed me a letter while Barney gamboled around our feet and pressed his great head between our legs, before settling himself between us as I opened it.

Dear Lulu,

By the time you read this I WILL BE DEAD—I've always wanted to write that, so dramatic, isn't it? Like an Agatha Christie novel on a wild and stormy night, everyone gathered at the mansion to hear the old boy's will. Anyway, by the time you read this I really will be dead, and you will be in possession of one of my most treasured possessions, Barney.

I know how hard it is to find a place to live these days with an animal, particularly one who may or may not be a wolf, so I have also made arrangements, through Andrew, to house him in the sort of premises to which he is accustomed.

To that end, I have bought Barney a home of his own on Willow Island, not too far from the one where I no longer lingalonga, which, as you probably know, I have left to the children.

You may not have noticed it, as it is nothing fancy, just a nice little shack by the sea with plenty of room for Barney to run around in, and lots of trees for him to claim as his own.

Unfortunately, because the archaic laws of our country are yet to recognize what we both know, which is that Barney is, of course, human, I was forced to purchase his new home in your name, as its caretaker.

Now, don't get all huffy about this, Tallulah, it is yours in name and legality only; in reality it belongs to Barney to happily eat his way through for the remainder of his years. In the meantime, you are most certainly welcome to visit, or indeed, as I suspect will be the case, live there for as long as you wish or as long as it takes for you to become happy.

I know you're not happy, Tallulah, and it is my greatest wish that by caretaking Barney's home you may find on Willow some shelter from the storm you have found yourself in.

Don't be mad at me—I can't bear it when you're mad

at me. Also I cannot answer back, so it would be more than
a little unsporting of you.

Your friend,
Duncan

PS I wonder where I am, don't you? Personally, I'm hoping
for Hawaii.

"So," Andrew said, "what do you think?"

I looked up, and the sight of Barney, his leash dragging on the ground with no familiar hand tugging at the other end of it, finally undid me.

Duncan was not swinging in a hammock strung up between coconut trees, not being spirited away in the dead of night by a speedboat driven by a woman in a white bikini with a fishing knife between her teeth.

Duncan was dead, and I knew it in the moment I saw his lost, riderless horse.

"I don't know," I said. "I don't know what to think. I didn't want anything from him."

"He knew that, Lulu," Andrew replied. "That's why he gave it to you."

~

"Well, what sort of a house is it?" Simone asked, excited, impatient, revved up on the three coffees she had managed to inhale in the half hour she, Stella, and I had been sitting in the café across the road from her work.

"I don't know, I haven't seen it yet."

"God, I wish someone would give me a house," she said.

"Well, I wish he hadn't."

"Don't be ridiculous, Lulu. Besides, you already told me, he gave it to Barney, not you."

We both looked down at Barney, rhythmically licking Stella's shoes with his great, lapping tongue.

"What are you going to do?" Stella asked, nudging Barney off her right foot with her left. "Are you going to move there?"

"I don't know, I thought I'd see it first, maybe spend some time there. I don't really have anywhere else to stay at the moment anyway. . . ."

"You know you can always stay with me, Lulu. But you should go over—check the place out, decide what you want to do with it. Want us to come with?" Simone asked—lately she had grown so busy, she had decided to do away with what she called "superfluous" words.

"No, I think Barney and I should do this on our own, but thank you."

"Suit."

"Stop it, Simone, it's suit yourself, suit *yourself.*"

"You knew what I meant, didn't you?"

"I didn't," said Stella. "Anyway, let's get back to this house business. When are you going to go?"

"This weekend."

"At least let us run you to the ferry," Simone offered.

"No, thanks," I said. "I've done it a million times, I'll be fine."

"When can we come and see it?" she pushed.

"I don't know," I said. "I'll call you once I've settled in."

"Here," Stella said, taking a small gold medal from the enormous green carry-all she was always toting, "take this with you."

I looked at the bright circle in my palm and found Saint Christopher, patron saint of travelers.

"Bloody hell, Stella," Simone said. "Who carries religious medals around in their handbag? Who else have you got in there?"

"Um, let me see," Stella said, fishing around in the green abyss. "Therese, I think, and Jude and Florien."

"Florien?" Simone snorted. "Who's he? The patron saint of hairdressers?"

"It's chimney sweeps, actually," said Stella primly.

"Oh, well, he'll be getting a lot of work around these parts, then."

"Stop it, Simone," I said. "Thank you for the medal, Stella, I'll put it in my backpack."

"Oh, Lord save," said Simone.

"It's Lord save us, Simone, Lord save *us*." Stella sighed.

~

Everyone, it seemed, was determined to make the first trip to Barney's new home with me, including Rose, who I visited a few days before I left.

"I'm coming with you, Lulu," Rose said firmly.

"Rose, it's not necessary, really, I'll be fine."

"I know it's not necessary, Lulu," she said, "but I'm still coming."

"But I don't need you to."

"Well, I need me to."

Harry was looking on, enjoying every minute, I knew, of this battle of wills between his wife and daughter, watching Rose fight her own corner.

"Rose," I said, "you can come later. It's a bit of a hike; it's not like we can just jump in the car and we're there."

But if we were to just jump in, I knew it would be, for the first time in a long time, Rose behind the wheel. Harry had told me that a few weeks earlier, at Rose's request, he had taken her station wagon out of the garage, cleaned it, checked it from top to bottom, turned it over, and taken it for a run around the block a few times, before Rose slid behind the wheel, turned the ignition, and took off, wearing Phoebe and a new hat.

Since then, she had driven a little farther each day, until they discovered her license had expired and she'd had to retake the test for a new one. Now it was in her wallet, where she had shown it to me, saying, "Can you believe it, Lulu? I don't look too bad for an old girl, do I?"

"You look great," I'd said, and we'd both sat staring at a miniature Rose smiling out at us from behind the plastic.

I was thrilled for her—and for Harry, his Rose reemerging as the laughing girl who slipped out of her dress and jumped into waterholes, who now took off in the car wearing a hat and came back brandishing takeaway dinners: "Just like that," Harry had said.

But I'd also learned not to trust this Rose, the one in full bloom. I'd seen her like this before, watched how easily her shoulders could drop, like petals to the floor. When she was like this, she was always in a hurry to throw herself back into the family, impatient to mend the frays at its edges. Now she wanted to come with me to Willow, but I wasn't ready for that, for her, yet.

"Rose," I said, "I promise you can come next time; just let me go over by myself first."

"Fine," said Rose, "but I'm baking you some biscuits."

chapter twenty

I didn't take the barge over to Willow.

Instead I went on the new "Day Tripper" service, run by Will, the deckhand I'd met in Walter Prentice's café, the one, I remembered, who'd said I had a sweaty face.

"It was Duncan's idea, actually," he'd told me when I'd rung the number to book. "He said Willow needed a service for people who didn't want all the palaver of packing up a car, or were only going to stay a day or two."

Or, I thought inwardly, for people who are carrying so much baggage all by themselves, they really don't need to take any more.

"Anyway," Will was saying, "I'll be happy to take you and Barney across whenever you like," adding, "Duncan said I was to take good care of you both."

"Did he?" I said, feeling, as I always did, both annoyed and comforted by Duncan's proprietary tone, now apparently still booming at me from beyond the grave.

"Yup," he answered. "I've got a boat-building and handyman service on Willow as well, so Duncan said to keep a bit of an eye on you."

I bristled a little, and when I hung up, said into the air, "Duncan, I am not a five-year-old girl on a kindy excursion, you know!" and began stuffing clothes into a backpack to take over to Willow.

How many other people had Duncan asked to "keep an eye on me" over there, I wondered, but when I told Simone and Stella about it later, Simone had leaned back and said, "Well, Duncan probably had a point, Lulu, I mean look what happens when you're left to your own devices."

Stella had insisted on driving me down to the point where Walter's barge and now Will's much smaller boat picked up the passengers for Willow. Walter had raised his hand from the deck when he saw me, and I waved back, wishing for a moment I had taken my car, if only to see his leathery face at the window saying, "All right, Lulu, bit of a nor'easter coming, but we'll be sweet."

"Man looks like a half-eaten pecan pie," Duncan always said once Walter had walked away.

Duncan.

I had not, right up until the moment I saw Walter Prentice, realized how difficult this trip to Willow was going to be. Some-how, in the midst of everyone's voices asking me about the house, it had escaped me that this would be my first trip to Willow with-out him beside me or waiting for me at the gate of Lingalonga. It felt wrong, as if I had no business being there.

I had no business anywhere, for that matter. No job, no one counting on me to turn up at a certain time, and no real idea of just what I planned to do once I opened the mammoth gift Dun-can had given me.

No, given Barney, I reminded myself firmly, *it's Barney's house, not yours, remember.*

I smiled at the absurdity of it, and at what I was doing, or not doing.

I hadn't really worked in months. I had no partner, no profes-sion, and no, as Simone would say, clue.

What had Duncan said I was to be in his final letter?

A caretaker.

I looked out at the water.

Perhaps, for the time being, that would have to be enough.

I would become the caretaker of my own life, until I figured out what I was really meant to be doing with it.

Besides, it was not as if there was anyone around to take care of me.

I put my backpack down and knelt beside Barney, letting his chocolate eyes steady me until he ran barking toward Will Barton, who was bringing his boat into the bay.

"Hey, Barney boy," he shouted, "good to see you, mate." He guided the boat in and shut down the motor, dragging the dinghy onto the wet sand.

"Hey, Tallulah," he said. "Nice to see you, want me to take the backpack for you?"

"No, thank you, I'm used to it," I said, wishing I had taken Simone's advice to sew a few badges on it—"So it looks like you've been somewhere, Tallulah."

Barney had already leaped into the boat and settled himself across its width, and I followed him, but in a decidedly more ungainly fashion, the backpack threatening to take me with it when I swung it off my shoulder.

I don't know why I'd bought a brand-new backpack for Willow; it just seemed more appropriate than a suitcase—"More 'islandy,'" Stella had offered, while Simone had looked at it and said, "How very Lonely Planet of you."

Now, I wished I had taken one of them with me, as Will started the motor and we cut across the water in a steady slap of small waves hitting the bow.

I felt strangely nervous, the intimacy of the small space we were in not helping, making me feel like I should make conversation, then finding I had none.

Will Barton filled the space between us, telling me about the house Duncan had bought me.

The owner before Duncan, Will said, had been a bloke called

Terry Danvers, a big-talking, smallish man who had tried to turn it into a recreational club, the Willow Island Aqua Sports Association.

"That's a bit of a mouthful," I offered.

"Yeah," grinned Will, "he tried to shorten it to WIASA, but it never really took off."

Terry had spent a couple of months fixing it up, Will said, then done a runner, taking off in one of his own canoes, never to be seen on the island again.

He'd bobbed up on the mainland a couple of years later, leaving a mountain of debt his mother eventually took care of and an abandoned clubhouse in which the island kids lit bonfires and shared their first kisses.

Since then, it had stood empty, a shell of a house with the horsetail casuarinas creeping closer, and sand billowing into its corners, and people thought Duncan was mad to buy it.

Will smiled. "He didn't listen to any of them; he said it had excellent bones."

Duncan had asked Will to be in charge of the renovation, to supervise the contractors and tradies, and after it had been repainted, rewired, had the plumbing "sorted" and the giant yawning holes in its walls replaced by windows, Will had realized Duncan had been right, it did have good bones.

Speaking of bones, Will went on, his last job for Duncan had been to load the new deep freezer with a supply of them for Barney. "You've got enough in there to last you for years," Will said. "I'm coming over to you if there's a nuclear war, by the way." It was then that I threw up over the side of the boat and into the bay's pristine waters.

"I'm sorry," I said when I'd finished, red-faced. "I'm normally okay on this ride, but I'm just a bit nervous, I think."

Unnerved and undone by Duncan's gift, at how hard he had worked to make it work for Barney and me, at how much I wished he was sitting beside me, fingers deep in Barney's coat.

"I miss Duncan," I found myself telling Will Barton, who was handing me a bottle of chilled water he'd grabbed from a nearby shelf, "stupid old bastard."

"You'll be all right," he said.

I took a quick sip and looked down at Barney—who was staring reproachfully at me from beneath the seat. "Oh, stop it," I said to him. "As if you haven't done worse," and Will Barton let out a snort of laughter.

"Duncan told me you were funny," he said.

Oh God, I thought, what else had he told him?

Then the familiar lines of Willow Island came into view— at first a smattering of casuarinas, then, through their fringes, a small, rocky bay and then the long wooden dock visitors hauled their luggage along.

"It's beautiful, isn't it?" Will said. "I never get tired of this place."

"Mmm-mmm," I said through the water bottle, still raised to my lips. I felt I had already committed enough indiscretions on this trip, and I saw no need to add vomit breath to them.

Will idled the boat, cut the engine, and threw a rope around the cleat. Then he hoisted my backpack on one shoulder and stepped onto the dock.

Barney had already jumped ship and was running up and down the shoreline before disappearing entirely up a sandy path.

"Barney!" I called after him. "Come, come back!"

"He'll be all right," Will said, and I wondered for a moment if that was his answer to everything.

He put my bag on the old-fashioned wooden luggage trolley and walked beside it until we reached the end of the dock.

"I'll walk you up to the house, if you like," Will said. "It's not very far."

"No, thank you, I'll be fine from here, I've got a map," I said, taking out the piece of paper Andrew Lyons had given me, and, seeing Barney come bounding back into view, adding, "and I'm pretty sure he knows the way."

"Okay," said Will, "but I might check in on you a bit later, see how you're settling in."

"Great, thanks," I said, my voice high and suddenly not my own. "I'll see you later, Will." I began to walk up the path, feeling the eyes of the island on me, some of them, I imagined, peeking through twitching, netted curtains.

Duncan, Will had told me, had remained uncharacteristically tight-lipped to the rest of the Willowers about what he was doing with the former WIASA headquarters, and who was going to live in it.

As a result, who I was had become part of an island guessing game—some Willowers said it was one of Duncan's former wives, others said a mistress. One of the wilder theories was that it was his little-known, horribly disfigured brother sent to live on the island away from cruel stares and prying eyes.

"You didn't believe any of it, did you?" I'd asked Will.

"No," he answered. "I believed what Duncan told me."

"Which was?"

"He said he bought it for you because you were his friend," Will replied, "and Barney's godmother."

Now Barney and I had come to the visitor's board, as marked on my map.

Willow Island, the sign said, was officially known as Casuarina Island, after the she-oak, or horsetail casuarina trees that studded its dunes, but locals had adopted the name Willow in the early 1950s for the way the trees bent over, a lifetime of winds forcing them to bow to the inevitable. However, the notice jauntily reminded visitors, Willow Island was not a place to weep but rather to celebrate the strengths of the casuarinas, still standing strong against the winds that buffeted them.

Bloody hell, Duncan, I thought, *how many messages can one man send from the grave?*

The island, the sign noted, was sixty-three kilometers long and fifty-seven kilometers wide, and currently home to roughly 376 permanent residents—the number written in chalk for easy alteration—although its ranks swelled on weekends and holidays.

I reached for the stub of white chalk to change the number to 377—378, I thought, if I included Barney—but then I put it back in its place again.

Don't get ahead of yourself, Tallulah, I thought, taking Barney's lead.

I followed him as he loped down the path, more subdued now, no more scrabbling through the bushes or darting ahead of me. I walked behind him, ducking my head under branches, hearing the whipbirds from somewhere within them and taking in the sharp, wet air, and the long drag line of a snake's belly on the sandy path in front of me.

Putting my hand up to hold my hat down against the wind, I tramped after Barney, then stopped to put my backpack down outside the high, curved rock wall he had led me to.

Avalon Road—home to the former WIASA, and now to Barney and me.

Barney pushed open the wooden gate with his bullethead, then began to run up the path toward a white house, which was perched like a drunken ship pitching a little to the left. I began to run too, backpack bobbing against my shoulders, toward the house with three roof lines like sails against the sea.

Barney had pushed open the unlocked front door and was sitting on the gray slate tiles in the hallway waiting for me when I arrived panting behind him. I took my shoes off so I could feel their coolness on my skin, and then began to wander through the house, and the whitewashed rooms that filled it.

They were generous, airy spaces, with timbered windows and rough, concrete floors, a kitchen with a pitched roof and a long table, big enough for a dozen people to eat at—"If we knew a dozen people here, Barney," I said—its cupboards, I saw, already stocked with essentials.

I made a cup of tea, my hands groping about the unfamiliar drawers and cupboards for mugs and sugar, and feeling ridiculously triumphant when I found them.

I felt better with the tea in my hand and padded down the three stone steps into the lounge room, where two fat, overstuffed sofas sat beside a bookshelf that ran along an entire wall, crammed with books.

I ran my finger along their spines, smiling as I realized they had belonged to Duncan, who had loved books and wanted everybody else to as well.

My eyes took in his favorites, and I saw him pressing his nose deep into their folds, looking up at me and saying, "Sometimes, Lulu, I just can't get close enough."

Barney was nudging me, also impatient to get on, to lead me up the stairs to the bedrooms—six of them, I counted. I'd never fill them, surely.

Then we climbed some steeper, smaller steps to another bedroom, a storage space that had been converted into a loft, which Barney claimed for both of us by performing his customary three complete circles before collapsing on the rug he had decided was his bed.

"I don't know, Barney," I said. "Those stairs could be a problem for you, mate."

He looked at me with watery eyes, snorted something disgusting out of his mouth, and immediately fell asleep.

Well, I thought, so much for the ludicrously expensive Snoozy Paws custom-made dog bed I'd brought him for his new home.

I lay down on the bed that felt like the house beneath it—big, white, billowing—and listened to the sounds of my new home, Barney's snores, the she-oaks creaking against the window, the rumble of the ocean, and then, making me sit up in bed, a knock at the door.

Barney stirred, shot skitter-pawed down the stairs, and sniffed at the gap underneath the door.

"Who is it?" I called.

"Julia Bendon, your neighbor."

I opened the door to a plump, creamy woman carrying a warm dish covered by a tea towel.

"Hello," she said, holding it out. "I've brought you this dinner to welcome you to the island, and also because I wanted to come and have a good look at you."

I laughed, taking the dish from her, absurdly happy to meet someone who lived nearby.

"Well," I said, "at least you're honest."

"Not always," said Julia Bendon.

Later, when our friendship was as robust as the dinner she had brought over that first night, Julia would tell me how she had indeed watched me through her window that afternoon.

"I'm not usually a curtain twitcher," she would say, "but Duncan had made you so damned mysterious I couldn't help myself!"

She would also confess she had been a little disappointed at what she saw.

"Because I didn't have a hunchback, you mean?" I asked.

"Or at least a small limp," she replied. "Boris"—Julia's husband—"kept trying to get me away from the window. 'Leave the poor girl alone,' he said. 'Give her a chance to settle in.'"

"What did you say?" I asked her.

"I said I was giving you an hour, then I was taking you up some dinner."

We would both laugh, remembering, but that first afternoon was far more awkward, loaded with polite questions that fell from my lips as if I were conducting a job interview, "And what is your husband's name, Julia?"

"Boris."

Boris? "And do the two of you work on the island?"

"Not anymore, both retired, we were in retail over on the mainland."

Julia, showing admirable restraint, hadn't asked me too much about myself, but later she would also tell me how she had collared Will on the beach that afternoon to pump him for information.

Will, she reported, had said I seemed "nice," which was, Julia sighed, just what a man would say. "So unobservant," she'd sniffed.

But Will Barton was not as unseeing as Julia thought.

He did, I was to discover, know everything about me, including the fact that, for a girl who'd arrived on the island with only a backpack, I was carrying a lot of baggage.

Oh well, at least I'd thrown up some of it on the way over.

~

My first few weeks on Willow were lazy ones, spent exploring the island with Barney, reading Duncan's books, and getting to know some of the people who lived there.

I had saved up quite a bit of money and had no real need to start looking for work yet, and although I knew, somewhere between walks through the rock pools at Lonergan's Bay and throwing a stick again and again to Barney on Spanish Beach, that this indolence could not last forever, but in the meantime I was enjoying the sensation of treading water.

Julia was becoming a friend, and a guide to the island, and most days, when the sting of the sun had waned, she and I would walk the steep path to Racey O'Leary's seat, Julia sometimes taking a cloth to polish its olive-tinged copper plaque.

In 1902, it said, Douglas O'Leary had run all the way up here

to light a fire to guide any survivors of the famous *Brereton Ven-
turer* shipwreck to Willow's shore, and by the time he got back
down again "Douglas" had been dropped for "Racey," and an island legend had been born.

Racey O'Leary had been only ten years old at the time, and
Julia liked to sit on his seat and imagine him all those years ago
racing through the scrub, the pepper trees scratching at his face,
dragging the branches through the spindly grass, making his big
fire and not stopping until he had it raging, then collapsing beside
it, his face blackened and his tiny rib cage heaving from exertion.

"How are you, Racey?" she'd say. "It's Julia, just stopping by
on my way to the lookout to pay my respects."

I never added anything to these pleasantries, but instead listened to Julia, who said it was important to let people know they
were still thought of after they went, wherever it was they had
gone. Racey eventually raced off at the age of eighty-five, when
he was still, as the plaque proudly noted, making his way up this
very track almost every day.

No, Julia had said, just because people no longer walked the
paths, it didn't mean you couldn't feel their footprints beneath you.

Like Duncan's.

I thought of him constantly—and of Josh and Annabelle, the
two of them somewhere overseas, trying to get their marriage on
track after its false start.

That's what Harry had called it, as if the three of us were
swimmers lined up on the blocks, and one of us had accidentally
tumbled into the water, or, as Simone had put it, "into Joshua
Keaton's trousers."

My cheeks still burned every time I thought of them, and a
hard little ball of anxiety would gather in my throat, but Duncan
had known what he was doing when he'd sent me to Willow,
neatly whisking them mostly out of sight and out of mind, "Like
people in Tasmania," I could hear him boom.

When I could bear to think of them, it was mostly to wish them well and hope that whatever damage I had done was not permanent. Now that Josh's breath wasn't on my skin, or his voice against my ear, without the *distraction* of him, I could think about Josh with a clearer head and realize he belonged to Annabelle; the two of them, I had come to see, were far better suited than Josh and I ever had been.

I would never have been enough for him — even Annabelle in all her brightness struggled to keep him in her light.

"He's a crack slipper," Duncan had told me one day at Linga-longa, just after he'd imparted the rather startling information that Josh had once visited him there.

"What? Josh came here? Why did Josh come here?" I'd asked, my voice rising.

"Because I invited him," he'd answered maddeningly.

Duncan was still quite well then, padding about the kitchen, making tea, getting out biscuits, and saying, "I could see the way the ship was sailing, and I wanted to have a little talk with him, man-to-man."

Josh's visit, which neither of them had mentioned to me at the time, came not long after the Bloom exhibition, and Duncan had taken it upon himself to "have a chat" with the bloke he said he knew was trouble the moment he spotted him.

"Not the teeth thing again," I'd begged.

Duncan had ignored me, then continued, explaining he'd asked Josh over to Willow "for a bit of fishing."

"Reeled him right in." He'd smirked.

They had shared a beer on Josh's arrival and then headed down to the beach to cast their lines.

"If you want a man to talk," Duncan said, "you shut up, so I did."

Josh, he said, had been edgy, finally filling the silence by asking Duncan what he was really there for, and Duncan had answered, "Well, it's certainly not for your fishing prowess, mate." Then, Duncan recounted, he had warned Josh off. "I told him I knew all about him—old man shooting through, mother chain-smoking her way through his childhood, barely noticing if he was coming or going. . . ."

I winced. I had not told Duncan any of this for him to recite later in "Duncan McAllister—Monologue on a Windy Beach."

"The thing is, Lulu, growing up like that, you can't help but become a crack slipper, someone who just slips through the cracks of other people's lives, you know, riding your push-bike around the neighborhood, always looking for somewhere to park the bloody thing, someone to let you in.

"Someone like you, Tallulah, with your ready-made family sitting around the table eating one of Rose's roasts, Harry cracking a beer and pouring the gravy, Mattie and Sam kicking each other's shins under the table." Duncan sighed. "If Josh had been smart, he'd have stayed there forever, and he might have been happy, but he didn't—and do you want to know why?"

"Why?" I asked automatically, rolling my eyes.

"Because, Lulu, I'll tell you what I told Josh—men like us: we can't leave it alone, because deep down we can't believe that girls like you would want someone like us. We know we're not good enough, never have been good enough. My old man shot through too, remember?

"He left when I was twelve, just walked out the front door with a bag in his hands, and when I said, 'Don't go, Dad,' he said, 'Nothing here to stay for.'"

Duncan shrugged his shoulders.

"And the only time men like us do feel good enough, Lulu, is when we're finally in bed with a woman we never in a million years thought we could have. We're skirt chasers, Lulu, not a very honorable profession, and not a very smart one either.

"I told Josh: 'I've got four marriages behind me, four good

women let down because I couldn't keep it in my pants. I've got kids running from one end of the beach to the other, and some days I can't remember which mother they belong to. . . .'" Duncan sighed again. "I told him it was a bad show, I told him to give it up, to give you up, or Annabelle, or both of you, before he did something just to see if he could."

"Bloody hell, Duncan," I said, "you said all that?"

"I did." He smiled. "More tea, vicar?"

Now Duncan was gone, having once again been proven right.

Josh and I had never discussed his trip to Willow; somehow I had managed to put it from my mind after Duncan told me about it, and Josh . . . well, who knew what Josh had thought of it.

It certainly hadn't stopped him.

Thinking about Josh and Annabelle and Duncan constantly sometimes made me feel like I was sharing the former WIASA headquarters with three ghosts—perhaps not, I realized after a few weeks, the healthiest of living arrangements.

So I picked up the phone to ask Harry and Rose over, and invite a little bit of my present into my past.

"Your mum will be thrilled, Lulu," Harry said. "She's been champing at the bit to get there, you know, and Sam and Mattie would love to come too. They were just saying the other day they haven't seen you since they got back from Canberra."

I'd hung up the phone and glanced at the enormous kitchen table, happy that at least some of the places at it would be filled. Then I began to get the house ready, plumping pillows and opening windows, setting up the spare bedrooms and stocking the shelves in readiness for my brothers' gargantuan appetites.

They came on a Sunday morning and stayed for three weeks that melded effortlessly into one another, days into nights and back again. I had not spent so much time with my brothers since they were small boys; now they were young men. Mattie and Sam hadn't chosen to continue the family tradition of plumbing the depths of excellence, but if Harry was disappointed not to add "and Sons" to the de Longland company name, he never let it show. He loved having two boys at university, both of them studying physiotherapy, both of them, he'd brag to anyone who'd listen, capable of fixing his back, crooked from years of bending over pipes.

Will seemed to be around much more during my family's stay too, taking my brothers out to collect the crab pots, or showing Harry all the work that had been done to WIASA, Harry happy as always for a bit of tradie talk.

"I hope my father's not stalking you," I said to Will one morning in the kitchen after Harry had been chatting to him about fixing up the boat shed.

"Nah." Will laughed. "I like having him around, he's a good bloke."

Then he reached out for my cheek.

"And it gives me an excuse to hang around you a bit more."

My stomach did a little flip as our eyes locked together for an instant, but I stepped back out of his reach.

The truth was, from the moment I first saw him, it registered that Will Barton was a very attractive man, in the same way that you register that the sun comes up every morning, but I was in no shape to contemplate any sort of dalliance.

I didn't deserve it, so I stepped out of the way, brushing Will, and what he'd said, aside.

His eyes dropped from mine, and I saw a slight flush rise to his cheeks as he awkwardly turned away from me, murmuring something about tide times.

He was still murmuring when he walked out the door.

Over the next few days, it was easy to forget his words, lost in the cacophony Mattie and Sam created. I loved having my brothers around, so grown-up now, so loud, so *busy*. Sometimes, as much as I loved Willow, there were days that hung empty in the afternoon and nights where the casuarinas nudged at my window, and I would lie and listen and wrap my fingers deep in Barney's coat.

Now my brothers' long bodies and strangely deep voices seemed to fill every room, where they ate and strummed at guitars and still played tricks on their big sister—for example, I discovered the day after they'd gone, putting rotting crab shells in her laundry basket.

On the morning they left—Harry warning me not to get too fat on all the food Rose had packed into the deep freezer, Rose pretending to be offended—I watched Will take them all the way across the bay, then turned to walk home, Barney close beside me, the weight of his body against my legs. He leaned into me along the path, his head knocking against my knees, up to the front door and onto the couch, where he lay panting beside me.

I lay back and took in the silence: no Harry banging away at the gurgling pipes of the WIASA, no Mattie and Sam playing soccer in the front yard with Boris and Will, and no Rose.

No Rose singing in the kitchen in Lauren as she rolled and sliced and cut and mixed and told me, for the first time, about us.

Harry and the boys had gone out with Will in the boat and we'd had the whole afternoon to ourselves. Rose, making two lasagnas—one for us, one for Julia and Boris—had put it out to cool and said, "Let's go for a walk, Lulu, it's too nice a day to be stuck inside."

I had thought so too, but a childhood spent watching her in the kitchen and not daring to ask if she would like to come anywhere at all still lingered. So I had not suggested a walk myself, despite the fact that every day of my family's visit, most of her dresses had an airing—and I knew, without having to peek in her suitcase, that there would be no Doris days on this holiday.

"Let's go," I smiled, whistling for Barney.

We walked, my mother and I, along the edge of the water all the way to Pipers Point and back again.

Then Rose looked out at the water, slipped her arm around me, and began to speak.

"When I was about sixteen, Lulu, I started to panic," she said, keeping her eyes fixed on the ocean. "I don't know why. It felt like all these little knocks just behind my heart, hammering away inside me.

"I managed to hide it for a long time, but it wouldn't go away, and the knocks got louder and louder, and when I was nineteen I was sent to the hospital for treatment, and then I was in and out, and in and out of there for months, and one time when I was out I met your father."

We began to walk again, her arm still around my shoulders, her eyes still on the bobbing sea.

"I told him how I was, Lulu, I told him I was too much to take on, but he said, 'I'll take you on, Rose,' and he did.

"The next few years were up and down, but Harry and I were in it together, so I was lucky, and then I fell pregnant with you."

She turned to face me and took both my hands in hers.

"I'm sorry, Lulu," she said, "but I was no good at it, no good at *you* from the moment you were born.

"All the other mothers were holding on to their babies like their life depended on it, but on the day I took you home I was holding you and I needed to get something from my bag, and a nurse was passing by, and I held you out to her and I said, 'Here, can you hold that for a minute?'

"I hated myself for calling you 'that,' even though the nurse laughed and said, 'Don't worry, Mrs. de Longland, it's just sleep deprivation.' But I knew it wasn't.

"We took you home and Harry carried you inside, and I went into the kitchen to make a cup of tea."

Rose shook her head. "I spent years in that damned kitchen," she said. "I'd look out the window and see you and your father playing in the backyard; I'd watch the way he'd throw you into the air and I wanted to run outside and push him out of the way so I could be the one to catch you, but I couldn't do it. All I could do was stay in that kitchen and try to bake my way to goodness."

I smiled at her, remembering the packets of Taylor's self-raising flour sitting on our kitchen bench, the company's high-topped slogan known by generations of Australian women: "Bake Your Way to Goodness."

"Oh, Rose," I said, both of us now smiling at the absurdity of trying so damned hard to follow a slogan—its writer could never have known how literally at least one woman took it.

"Then," Rose continued, "then the twins came."

I remembered that too, my two squawking, squealing brothers who, it seemed to me, took what little my mother had left to give, then sent her scurrying back into the kitchen, where she stayed and stayed and stayed, until Harry and I knew it was up to us to help them grow up.

"You were marvelous with them, Lulu, you did everything I should have done. Everyone kept saying what a wonderful little mother you were—do you remember that?"

I nodded. "I hated being called that."

"I hated it too," Rose said, "because you were not a little mother, Lulu, you were my daughter, and I failed you."

"No, you didn't," I began, but she shook her head.

"I did, I didn't mean to for a second, but I did."

We had begun walking again, this time in silence, picking our way across the smooth, gray rocks strewn between a small arc of coastline.

We walked toward the end of the headland, and she linked her arm with mine.

"What I wanted to tell you, Tallulah, what I probably should have told you years ago was that all that time, when it was Harry you'd run to when you'd hurt yourself, all those times when it was his arms that caught you, not mine, I loved you.

"It might have been from afar, Tallulah," she continued, taking my face once more in her hands, "but I loved you with every single breath I had in me."

There was a loud knock, bringing me abruptly back from the beach with my mother to the screen door where Julia stood, asking me over for dinner.

"Thought you might be a bit lonely with your family gone," she said.

No, I told her, I was all right, and there was no need for her to cook, Rose had left both of us a lasagna, enough for several dinners, to keep us warm.

Besides, for the next few weeks I had very little chance to feel lonely, much less alone. Duncan had always told me you never knew how many friends you had until you moved to the beach. "No man is an island, Lulu," he'd say, "especially when he lives on one."

chapter twenty-one

It was about a week after my family left, a week spent finding my brothers' belongings scattered throughout the house like pieces of flotsam and jetsam—a sock here, a CD there, some boxer shorts under the bed—when Barney's staccato visitor's bark rang through the rafters.

I went to my bedroom window to see a figure coming up Avalon Road, knowing instantly from each loping step who was paying me a visit.

Ben.

Barney tore out the front door, careering toward him like a hairy bowling ball heading for the pins, knocking him to his knees on impact. Ben laughed and threw his arms around Barney's neck, the breeze carrying his voice up to me.

"Barney boy," he said, "oh, mate, is it good to see you."

It felt strange to see him, both familiar and unfamiliar at once, and I was torn between running down the stairs myself to bowl him over, and shrinking back behind the curtains and pretending I wasn't home.

The last time I had seen him was at Duncan's funeral, a strange, brief moment where we had hugged awkwardly and he had left straight after the service. Before that, we'd met a few times to divvy up the domestic spoils of our previous life together—"Do you want the IKEA wine rack?"—and for me to return my keys to our old apartment.

"I'm so sorry," I'd said—again—as I handed them over.

"I know," he'd answered, taking them.

Since then, I'd heard bits and pieces about him from Simone and Stella, who imparted the rather startling information that she sometimes saw him at church. Since he'd never gone when we were together, I could only think he now went to fall on his knees and thank God I wasn't in his life anymore.

"How did he look?" I'd asked Stella one day when she reported a sighting.

"Pious," Simone answered for her.

Ben was, I thought, well shot of me, but it didn't stop my missing him, or our old life together. Sometimes I'd think about our flat, the twenty-seven steps up to its front door, Ben's bike in the hallway, the newspaper spread out on the kitchen table in the morning, and I would find myself aching for the normality of it. Even though I knew deep down that he was probably not the right man for me, he was a good man, and there were times I had wondered if that could have been enough.

Now he was here, and I could not stand hiding behind the curtains forever, so I ran down the stairs and flung open the door.

"Ben," I said, "what a nice surprise!"

He smiled, tucking his hair—it had grown, I noticed, and suited him—behind his ears, like he always did when he was nervous, then thrust a package into my hands.

"Here," he said, "this is for you."

Then he told me he was getting married.

Monica Golliana wore a size six shoe, had dark brown curly hair that she mostly wore pulled off her face, was a devout Catholic (ah, that explained the church business), and was originally from Napoli but had left when she was a child, her parents starting their own small shoe-importing business in Australia and building it up into "quite the going concern."

All of this Ben told me after he had blurted out his news at the front door, and we had sat down in the lounge room together, having a glass of wine with Barney happily ensconced between us.

I was glad to hear it—all of it—because once he'd stopped apologizing for the abrupt way he'd delivered his news, he could not stop talking about her, Monica Golliana, whom he had met six months after we broke up, and who did not mind him saying things like "quite the going concern," whereas I always had.

"Have you got a photo?" I asked, and he took one from his wallet—Monica Golliana, with the curly hair she mostly wore pulled off her face blowing in the wind as she stood looking out from what was once my balcony.

"She's lovely, Ben," I said, and she was, dammit.

"Thanks," he said, adding, "You should open your present." Then, once again suffering from premature explanation, he said, "It's those shoes you liked from our autumn collection a couple of years ago, remember the ones with the bows you said were like the ones on a chocolate box?"

I did remember, and was inordinately touched that he had too—Ben who was not right for me, just as I was not right for him; Ben who was not at all vigorous, but very, very nice.

"So," he said after I had tried them on, "who's that joker who brought me over here?"

"You mean Will?" I asked.

"Yeah, big boofy bloke, knows a lot about ropes."

"He's got the boat service between the mainland and Willow, and he does a few odd jobs around the place," I answered.

"Bit macho, isn't he?" Ben asked.

"I hadn't really noticed," I replied. "He's a nice guy actually, Ben."

"Mmm," Ben said. "I could tell he was dying to ask me how I knew you—I wouldn't tell him though, he annoyed me with all that rope tying."

"Ben, he was on a *boat*," I said.

"I know," he said, "but you know how that sort of bloke intimidates me, with all that 'Oh, I'm Will, and I fix engines and take fishing charters out to sea.' 'Oh, hi, I'm Ben and I'm a shoe salesman.'"

We laughed together, and then he asked, "So are you seeing him, this manly Will person?"

"No," I replied, "I am not seeing 'this manly Will person,' but he's been a good friend to me here on the island, and he was a good friend of Duncan's."

Barney's ears pricked up, as they always did, at Duncan's name.

"What about Josh?" Ben asked quietly. "Do you hear from him, or them?"

"No."

He nodded.

"I've let it go, you know, Lulu, what happened."

"That's good," I said, my throat tightening.

"Have you?" he asked.

"No," I answered.

"I'd still like to smash his face in though."

"Really?"

"Yeah, the way he just came in and ruined everything, and then left you to clean up the mess afterward."

"I let him in, Ben," I said.

Ben nodded again, then got to his feet.

"I should go, Lulu," he said.

I walked him to the door, then all the way to the jetty where I could see Will's boat slowly making its way toward us to pick Ben up.

"You shouldn't be too hard on yourself, Lulu," Ben said, kissing my cheek, "and that manly Will person seems like a pretty nice guy, actually."

I cried just a little watching him go — Ben Moreton, still keeping Australia on its feet, walking all the way out of my life.

chapter twenty-two

Kimmy McAllister, née Varagos, was my favorite of Duncan's ex-wives.

The newest and the youngest, most people believed she had married him for his money, calling Duncan an old fool and worse. But while Duncan's wealth was undoubtedly part of the attraction—when a reporter had facetiously asked her what she liked to read, she'd answered, "The *BRW* Rich List"—Kimmy was far smarter than people assumed, and there had been a crackling spark between her and Duncan from the moment they met.

Kimmy had been working for a cosmetics brand in a department store, spraying passers-by with perfume and saying: "Have you tried our new fragrance, Detour? You never know where it may lead you."

Duncan, as he later recounted at their wedding reception, had been one of those passers-by, when he stopped to watch her spritz shopper after shopper before walking over and saying, "Detour? How ridiculous, come on, we're taking one."

Then they had gone back to his flat, to resurface two days later, engaged.

"We just thought what the hell," Kimmy told me one day at the studio. "And my mother said he'd make an excellent starter husband for me."

But behind Kimmy's flippancy lay a deep fondness for Duncan, who, she told me, was a kind, funny, and generous husband, who had been unfaithful to her since the day they met.

"Who cares?" She'd shrugged. "I'm hardly Mother Teresa myself. But I love him." She added, "I bet they'd all be surprised to know that."

Duncan's death had left her, at twenty-five years old, a very wealthy woman who, like all of Duncan's ex-wives, remained loyal to the man who'd picked her up in the perfume department, refusing all interviews or the offer to pen a tell-all of their life together.

"I just told them I couldn't write," she laughed.

Kimmy was good to Duncan's kids as well, with Kiki, Kerry-Anne, and Karen all trusting them to her care from time to time, which was why she called me one afternoon on Willow, just as I was heading out the door for a walk with Barney.

"Hello?"

"Hi, Lulu, it's Kimmy."

"Kimmy! Nice to hear your voice, how are you?"

"Good, really good—fabulously wealthy, actually."

"I heard."

"How's Barney boy? Still eating for Australia?"

"He's good—you know, Kimmy, if you ever wanted to visit him, you'd be more than welcome."

"No, thanks, Lulu, can't think of anything worse than being stuck on some crappy island—no offense. How's the house?"

"It's lovely, Kimmy, it's really wonderful—I hope you don't mind me having it . . ." I began to say, still feeling unsettled by the size of the gift Duncan had given me, but Kimmy interrupted.

"Couldn't care less . . . Listen, are there any gorgeous men over there?"

"No."

"Definitely not coming over then—but can I send Duncan Junior?"

"Duncan Junior?"

"Yes, he ran away from Kiki's and has been living at my place for the last two weeks."

"Why?"

"Dunno, probably fancies me, but the point is, Lulu, he's here, he's dropped out of school, and he doesn't do anything but mope around the house and look at my boobs."

Duncan Junior was the oldest of the McAllister children and as Kimmy talked, I saw his pinched face at his father's funeral, his arms stretched all the way around Rhees's, Jasmine's, and Jarrod's smaller shoulders.

He would be sixteen now, I realized, Rhees about fourteen, the twins eight, I thought, maybe even nine, and all of them, according to Kimmy, dealing with the death of their father in different ways, Duncan Junior not very well.

"He says he's an emo now," she was saying.

"A what?"

"An emo, Lulu, you probably don't have them there on Chestnut Island."

"Willow."

"Whatever—anyway an emo is like a kid who wears a lot of black and won't go out in the sun and is always fucking miserable and plays the worst fricking music I've ever heard in my life. He's driving me crazy; I really think he needs to get some fresh air and maybe see Barney. So, what about it, Lulu? Can he come and look at your boobs instead of mine for a little while?"

"They'll be a little bit of a letdown after yours."

"I know," Kimmy agreed. "Most people's are."

~

"Up, Barney boy," I said a fortnight after Kimmy's call. "We've got a visitor coming."

I walked down Avalon Road, past Julia's house and down the

sandy track toward Luggage Point, Barney sticking his nose down in the sand the moment I opened the gate, trembling with excitement as he picked up a scent and took off after it, hind legs frantically trying to catch up with the rest of him.

So Duncan Junior was coming—very reluctantly, Kimmy had told me—to Willow.

"He doesn't want to go," she said, "Says there's no point, he hates the sun and won't go swimming."

"Great," I said. "So why's he coming?"

"He says he wouldn't mind seeing you."

"Right," I said, and wondered why.

We were not, I thought, particularly close, but I had always been fond of Duncan's eldest son—and felt more than a little sorry for him for having to bear his father's name.

I'd once asked Duncan about it. "Not my idea," he'd huffed in reply. "It was Kiki's. The woman had just gone through thirty-six hours of the most unmitigated gut-wrenching pain it has ever been my displeasure to witness, and quite frankly if she had wanted to name him Vlad the Impaler, I wouldn't have denied her."

I reached the pier that stretched out from Luggage Point to the ocean, sat down, dangled my legs over the edge of it, and waited, trying to reconcile this new version of Duncan Junior, the one who hated the sun and wouldn't go swimming, with the boy I knew.

I could see him at Lingalonga, a tall, skinny kid with the angular body of a surfer, wearing the same pair of board shorts, it seemed, all summer long, running in and out of the house, slamming the screen door behind him, making his way each time to the sea.

From the mainland, a gray speck of a boat came into view, but the wind and spray crossed its lines and blurred my vision until it came closer and I could see the shape of Will at the back, and at the front, hunched over, something flapping at its face in the wind, a jagged, little black crow.

Will raised his hand when he saw me. The black figure at the front did nothing, remaining at its perch until the boat came all the way in and Will threw me the rope.

"Duncan," I called out to the strange, black creature, "I'm so glad you're here."

The face looked up at me with no smile of recognition, and for a moment I was unsure what to say to this new version of the boy I had once known.

"He can't hear you," Will called. "He's listening to one of those Walkman things. . . ."

"Right," I said as Duncan shuffled off the boat, the frayed hem of his long black coat trailing in the water. "Thanks for picking him up, Will, I'll take it from here."

"You sure?"

"Mmm, Duncan's an old friend of mine, aren't you, mate?"

But he was gone, his hot woolen coat flapping in the wind.

"Better you than me." Will grinned.

~

"So this is your room," I said as Duncan nodded, mute on the bed. "There're fresh towels there, for swimming."

"I won't need them."

His words surprised me, not because it was the first time he had actually spoken since he arrived, but because of the deep baritone that he uttered them in. Even through his ridiculous coat I could see he was thin, too thin, huddled up on the bed and looking, I thought, despite the manly voice, about six years old.

A six-year-old wearing his father's overcoat.

"Duncan," I said, "would you like Barney to sleep in your room tonight?" He nodded wordlessly, but nothing else was forthcoming, so I took that as a sign to retreat.

He didn't eat dinner that evening, said he wasn't hungry, and, the moment he possibly could, escaped up to his room, shutting the door behind him and leaving me standing uncertainly outside it, cursing the father who had begat this particular son.

"What now, Duncan?" I asked the air. "What on earth do you expect me to do now?"

Later that night there was a mad scrabbling down the stairs as Barney rushed for the door, followed by the hunched figure of displaced youth behind him.

"He'll want to be let out," I explained, "to go to the toilet."

Duncan Junior nodded as I opened the door.

"Do you want anything?" I tried. "I'm just about to make some hot chocolate." I wasn't—I didn't even know if I had any hot chocolate, but for some reason with the wind blowing and the sea howling, and the sad, ghost-white boy looking out the window, it seemed like the right beverage for this particular occasion.

He nodded again.

"Right," I said.

I put the saucepan on the stove, watched the milk bubbling to the surface, took it off the boil, and poured it into two mugs, stirring in the chocolate, and carried them to the lounge room, waiting to see if Duncan Junior would follow.

It was a wild night, a night Duncan Senior would have called not for the fainthearted, as the wind whipped through the dunes and the horsetail casuarinas' branches belted against the eaves.

His son came in and sat beside me.

I handed him his mug and heard the vaguely tinny sounds coming from his earpiece. If I was going to talk to this boy tonight, he would not hear me. I sipped my chocolate and decided that this was fine by me. I was not sixteen; I did not know what it was like to have a famous father whose name you carried on your shoulders; I did not know how it felt to lose that father, or to love and hate your mother, and deeply fancy one of your stepmothers.

I did not know how it felt to be warmed by the sun one day and turn your face away from it the next.

I was not a sixteen-year-old boy.

I did not know.

I drank my hot chocolate.

~

A few days later we were both up early, sitting across from each other at the kitchen table, separated by its wide expanse and the tinny sounds still emanating from DJ's ears. (I had taken to calling him DJ; it was less confusing for when I was cursing his father.)

Enough.

I motioned to him to remove the plugs, took a deep breath, and dived in.

"Here's the thing," I said. "I'm glad you're here, I want you to be here, and you can stay as long as you like, but sometimes, you're going to have to speak to me, because right now it feels like there's a ghost living here with me and that's all right some of the time, but not all of the time."

He nodded.

"Also," I said, "I'm going to ask you to help me around here a bit . . . not too much"—I smiled, seeing the grimace—"really just with Barney. It would be great if you could walk him in the mornings."

Another nod.

"Good." I smiled, pointing to the earbuds. "You can put them back in now, if you want to."

I kept in touch with Kiki during Duncan Junior's stay—and with Kimmy, Kerry-Anne, and Karen, who all rang wanting to know how he was.

"He seems okay," I told them, "although to tell the truth I just don't really know what to do with him."

But I knew who might.

"Hello," Will called out, "you in, Lulu?"

"I'm here, Will, out the back."

Will let himself in through the front door and walked through the house, no doubt noticing the many signs of Duncan Junior's presence littered along the way.

"Teen debris." He smiled, joining me at the gate. "So," he said, "how's it going?"

"Fine," I said, "though I spend half my life here hanging around the gate waiting for him to come home, and then when I see him coming I run inside so he won't know I've been doing it."

"Still wearing the cloak of death?"

"Yep."

"Any progress at all?"

"A little. He's started to talk to me a bit more."

"That's a good sign."

"But it's not enough, Will. I'm not equipped to deal with all this stuff. I don't mind him being here—in fact I'm glad he's here—but I don't know how much good it's doing him. I'm not enough for him. I'm not his father—I'm not even a bloke." I looked straight into his eyes. "But you are," I said.

"So, you *have* noticed," he said, one eyebrow arching higher than the other.

It was a both a challenge and an invitation, one that had been coming since our awkward encounter in the kitchen, when I had sidestepped his touch.

I knew exactly what he was asking me, and I knew the answer too.

Of course I'd noticed Will Barton was a bloke, he was far and away the most masculine man I had ever encountered. In fact, I was fairly sure he had some sort of strange, musky scent wild animals could pick up in the woods. But he was also a good man, and a simple one who didn't need the sort of baggage I now permanently traveled with.

So I kept sidestepping.

"Is that a trick question?" I asked flippantly, reducing the conversation to lighthearted banter.

When Will was concentrating on something, I'd noticed, he had a habit of clenching and unclenching his jaw.

He was doing it now, as he considered my response.

"I guess it's tricky for you," he answered heading back toward the house, then softening his words somewhat by promising to take DJ out crabbing the next day.

After he left I stood at the gate and watched the sea.

"Dammit," I said to the sky.

～

The next morning, Will and I were both standing by the crab pots waiting for DJ, when his familiar, dark figure came shuffling toward us.

"Oh God," Will said, "is he wearing mascara?"

"Just wave," I replied, raising my hand and calling out, "Ahoy there, me hearty."

"'*Ahoy there, me hearty*'?" Will echoed. "Are you serious?"

"I told you I needed help," I said, smiling at DJ, who was now hovering uncertainly around the pots.

"Hey, mate," Will said, "ready to do some crabbing?"

DJ nodded, lifting his coat to step into the boat.

Will put up his hand. "I'm sorry, mate, but that coat's not coming."

DJ stared at him.

"Too much weight," Will said. "It will upset the equilibrium of the boat."

I had no idea if Will was telling the truth or not; all I knew was that shedding the coat's heavy weight, DJ looked like he had never felt so relieved in his sixteen years of life.

They were heading down the river in search of sandies, leaving the open sea behind them and rigging up the mackerel frames, looking for the deep drop-off to set the pots, DJ surprising Will, he later told me, with his quick hands and knowledge of what Will called the fine art of crabbing.

"Who taught you, mate?" he'd asked him.

"My dad."

"Well, he knew what he was doing."

"Yeah, some of the time."

"I knew him," Will had offered. "We fixed up the house together."

Another nod.

"Anyway, he was a good bloke."

"Yeah."

Will had passed him a spare T-shirt, saying, "Lulu will kill me if I return you as red as a lobster."

DJ had smiled—"It was like the sun coming out," Will had said—and opined that I wouldn't hurt a fly.

That's what you think, I'd thought instantly.

Will and I were sitting on the side porch after DJ had headed up to his room, and he was recounting the day's events to me, including the moment he'd persuaded DJ to jump into the river's green embrace.

It was stinking hot, and Will had gone in first, curling his legs up under his arms to perform a classic bomb dive, knowing, he said, there was no sixteen-year-old boy on earth who would be able to resist joining in.

"Come on, mate." Will had laughed up at him. "Jump in; just jump in, mate."

DJ had paused for a fraction of a second before standing up

and surprising Will by executing a perfect swallow dive into the water.

He'd stayed down for a long time, long enough for Will to start getting a bit antsy, before he'd shot back up again, breaking the surface.

"Thought you were swimming to China, mate," Will said, but DJ had dived deep down again, listening only to the water.

———

After that, the two of them were pretty much inseparable, DJ heading out the door first thing to join Will on his boat runs, or to help him out in his shed doing, as Ben would say, "manly things" together.

Sometimes I'd join them, the three of us racing one another down Bramble Bay's giant sand dune on bits of cardboard, Barney barking like mad at the bottom, or, on some lazy afternoons when it was too hot to do anything, not doing anything much at all.

DJ stayed for three more weeks, until his mother could bear it no longer and came to collect him.

I had always been fond of Kiki; I liked the way she watched the endless procession of Mrs. McAllisters who came after her with good humor, even acting as witness to Duncan and Kimmy's registry-office wedding, wearing a new pantsuit and a resigned smile.

I liked the way she let her son spend as much time with his father as he liked, and the way she had let that same son come to me.

"I don't mind at all, Lulu," she had said on the phone when we'd talked just prior to DJ's arrival. "Just see if you can get that coat off him long enough for me to at least wash the damn thing."

Now, a month after he had arrived, it hung on a hook behind the laundry door, looking, I thought, even more depressing than it had when it had had an owner to cling to.

I folded it up and put it in a bag for DJ to take home. I walked up the stairs to his room and found him lying on the bed, Barney splayed out on his feet.

"So, your mum will be here tomorrow. You okay about going back?"

"I'd rather stay here."

"Well, you're welcome anytime, sweetheart, you can ask your mum if you can come for the September holidays."

"Cool."

"Cool," I echoed, and sat down on the bed. "Here's your coat."

"I don't want it."

"All right, I'll keep it here for you, for next time."

"Throw it away, Lulu."

"Are you sure?"

"Yeah, I wasn't ever really an emo, I don't reckon."

"No, perhaps not."

"I still like the music though."

"Well, that's something, JD," I replied, trying out his new name, trying to make it sound effortless and everyday on my lips.

It had happened the night before.

We had fallen into a pattern of having dinner together after he had come home from a long day spent with Will. We would eat, take Barney out into the night for a final run, then return home to sprawl out on the couches reading in companionable silence, save for Barney's dreaming snuffles and grunts.

Occasionally I would steal a glance at Duncan's son, noting with pleasure the pallid, hollow cheeks filling out more each day, the limbs bare and brown again, the shoulders relaxed, one hand idly scratching Barney's head, and I would hope that whatever it was that had troubled and brought him here had, at the very least, been softened by his stay.

We had not spoken at all about why he had come, and I had

no intention of introducing the subject, but on that last night, he had brought it up himself.

"Lulu?"

"Mmm-mmm?"

"Thanks for having me."

"My pleasure."

"My dad told me to come."

I sat up, looked at him.

"He told me that if I was having any sort of trouble after he died that I should come to you."

"I see. Well, I'm glad you did."

"He said you were very restful."

"Oh, well, that's—am I?"

"Yeah, you are."

"Good."

"Because you don't keep prodding at me, you know?"

I smiled at him.

"That's because I am not your mother. It's a mother's job to prod."

"My mum never stops."

"Because she loves you."

"I know."

We went back to our books, but after a minute I felt his eyes on me and he spoke again.

"I miss my dad."

"I know."

"I wish it hadn't happened."

"Me too."

Then out it came, in a rush of words mixed with snot and tears and the tale of a girl at school, Marlena, another emo, who had, apparently not seeing the irony, dumped him for being "too depressing."

Blowing his nose continually on his T-shirt while I tried to look like I didn't mind, but later soaked it in laundry detergent for hours, he told me how Duncan had broken the news he was dying by jovially announcing that his son could finally drop the junior part of his name, because the senior part of the equation wasn't going to be around much longer.

Then came the confession of how desperate he was to do just that: change the name he had always hated.

"I've wanted to for ages," he said, "and even though Dad said I could, now that he's gone I think it would be really wrong to do that, you know?"

"I'm sure it would be fine," I told him. "Did you have any idea what name you might like to change it to?"

"I thought Raoul, maybe."

"Raoul?"

"When I was an emo."

"Right," I said, trying not to laugh, and failing.

DJ, I was pleased to see, was laughing too.

"Stupid, really." He grinned.

"Well, what about what I call you—DJ?" I tried. "That sounds pretty cool, and it kind of fits you, don't you think?"

"Nah."

"Why not?"

"Too try-hard, everyone will think that I reckon I'm some sort of deck spinner."

"Right," I said, though I had no idea what a deck spinner was.

"But I don't mind JD."

"JD?"

"Yeah, for Just Duncan."

Just Duncan left with his mother the next day, Kiki explaining that his school had given him compassionate leave and had said he could return to finish the year out if he wanted to.

He was certainly smart enough to catch up, but his mother thought he might want to finish it by correspondence, then start university as planned the following year.

She added: "He said he wants me to call him JD."

"Well, it's better than Raoul," I said, patting her shoulder.

Will came to see me the week after JD left.

"I miss him," he said, "which is not something I would have predicted the day I picked him up in his vampire outfit."

"I miss him too," I replied, "but he'll be back."

"I know," Will said. "I told him he could come and work with me anytime."

"Thanks, Will," I said. "It was really good of you to take him under your wing. I don't actually know what I would have done with him."

"No problem. He was a big help, in the end." He leaned on the door, one arm on its frame, his torso, I noticed, running half the length of it. I had told Kimmy there were no gorgeous men on the island, but I had been lying through my teeth. Will Barton was gorgeous, every salty inch of him, and I wanted, I realized, looking at him leaning in my doorway, his hands on me.

Will caught my gaze and made a half move toward me, before I turned awkwardly out of his way.

I was the last person on earth who deserved a man, let alone a decent one.

"Oh God, Lulu," Will said softly, but I pretended not to hear him.

chapter twenty-three

After JD left, and I had ceremoniously dumped his coat in the outside bin, the house felt quiet and still again, as if all its windows had exhaled.

I did a quick clean-up, threw on some washing, grabbed a book from the shelves, and headed for the back veranda.

"How's the serenity?" I smiled at Barney, who was lying sprawled across the stairs, but even as I said it, the phone was ringing inside.

It was Simone, still apparently using her word shorthand. "Lulu," she said, "How are?" I hadn't seen her or Stella since I'd moved to Willow, but I spoke to both of them at least once a week, and planned to invite them over after I'd caught my breath from the last round of visitors.

"Good," I answered. "How are you?"

"Fine," she said, "but Stella's not."

"Why, what's wrong?" I asked, instantly feeling anxious. Stella was the one person I'd never had to worry about.

"You'll find out when she gets there."

"She's coming here?"

"We both are. Your boyfriend, Will, is bringing us over at five o'clock."

"Today?" I ignored her comments about Will, far more concerned for Stella.

"I just said that, didn't I?"

I bit my tongue. "Okay, I'll get the beds ready."

"Good," she said crisply. "I'm only staying tonight, got to get back for a meeting with the network head of misogyny, but Stella might be longer, she's having a crisis."

"What sort of crisis?" I asked.

"Well, it turns out Saint Billy might need some sort of religious medal of his own to pray to."

"What do you mean?"

"I don't know, Lulu, is there a patron saint for complete bastards?"

"So it's a marriage crisis?" I said, trying to piece it all together.

"Yes, but it's much worse than that."

"In what way?"

"I think she's having a crisis of faith."

Then she hung up, leaving me confused and in a rush to get their rooms ready.

I gave Stella the prettiest one, with the bay window overlooking the southern end of Spanish Beach, and the nicest linen I had, white cotton sheets and a broderie anglaise bedspread.

Then I went into the garden to pick some hibiscuses for her.

They were her favorite flower, and sometimes she'd wear one to school, tucked behind her ear, until one of the nuns made her take it out, saying, "We are not in a Gauguin painting now, Miss Kelly." I put the flowers in a vase next to her bed, then I opened the windows wide and went downstairs again to choose a book for her from the bookshelf.

Stella was usually too tired at the end of the day to read, but she loved books, and Billy often found her asleep in their bed with one still open in her hands.

Stella and Billy.

Billy and Stella.

If what Simone had hinted at over the phone was true, Stella would be devastated.

I grabbed some books and ran back upstairs to put them beside her bed.

I would do anything to make her feel better.

They arrived at sunset, the two of them standing on the doorstep, with Simone looking uncomfortable and Stella looking, I realized, *angry*.

"Well, here we are." Simone gave a tight little smile. "Thelma and Louise."

"If that's meant to be some sort of lesbian joke, Simone," Stella snapped, "I don't find it particularly funny."

Behind her, Simone rolled her eyes as I slipped my arm around Stella's waist and tried to lead her into the kitchen for a cup of tea, or a glass of wine, or, as Simone suggested later, a horse-size shot of Valium.

"We'll have something to drink first," I said, "and then I'll show you around the house."

"Just show me to my room please, Lulu," said Stella flatly.

"Oh," I faltered. "I thought maybe we might have a quick look around and maybe a walk on the beach before dinner."

"No, thanks," Stella answered, "I just want to go to bed."

"But you haven't eaten anything," I protested. "I made your favorite, beef stroganoff with parsley potatoes." I had, begging Will to do a late-afternoon trip to the mainland for supplies.

"No, thanks," Stella said again. "I really just want to go to bed."

"Well, do you want to just have some now? We could forget the walk—"

"Leave it, Lulu." Simone's voice cut in. "She wants to be by herself. I think that's fairly."

"Obvious?" I said, exasperated. "Just say it, Simone."

Stella sighed. "Stop it, both of you, I'm going to bed," and she began walking up the stairs. I followed her and opened the door to her room.

"This is you," I said.

She nodded and closed the door in my face.

~

Downstairs, Simone and I attacked my best bottle of red before dinner and sat out on the back lawn to drink it while she filled me in on the precarious state of the McNamara marriage.

Her name was Nadine, Stella had told Simone on the way over. She was a rental manager at the real-estate agency where Billy worked, and it had meant nothing, he had said, though he had admitted, when she pushed him, that it had meant nothing several times, in between open houses.

And I was right, she was angry, as I'd noticed at the front door, in a simmering rage even Simone had been a little unbalanced by—"Seriously, Lulu, the woman is about to *erupt.*"

Billy had confessed to the affair one morning after church, where all the little McNamaras—scrubbed within an inch of their lives—had sat in the family pew while Billy helped to hand around the collection plate.

"What a hypocrite!" Stella had hissed to Simone when she told her. "What a fucking—yes, Simone, I said fucking—hypocrite, going on and on at me all those years about how we were a team, Team McNamara he called us, and then he goes and plays on someone else's."

Billy had wept, she said, cried and cried and promised her it was over, that Nadine had left the firm of her own volition after Billy had told her it could not go on. He had promised Stella it would never happen again; the whole thing, he said, had made him realize how precious Stella was to him, how much their family meant to him, and how stupid he had been to risk losing it.

He was staying at his mother's with the children, after she, Stella, had personally rung the other Mrs. McNamara to tell her she was sending him over and exactly why.

Simone had gulped at that piece of information. "You told Mary Josephine?" she'd said, remembering, as I did, Billy's formidable and determinedly Catholic mother.

"Yes, I did," Stella had said defiantly. "I hope she *crucifies* him."

"Is she leaving him?" I asked Simone.

"I don't know," she answered, "but I think that's why she's here, to find out."

~

Simone left the next morning, and I found I was living with my second ghost in as many months. Stella glided from room to room, barely making an imprint on the furniture and not eating anything. "I'm sorry, Lulu," she would say, "I'm just not hungry." I would take the plate away and wait for the phone to ring.

Billy rang repeatedly, his calls ranging in tone from affable and anxious to demanding and desperate, but she would not take them, shaking her head at me silently, or gliding out of the room.

"Look, Billy," I would say, "I think she just needs a bit more time. I promise I'll try to get her to ring you the moment I can."

"I need to talk to her, Lulu."

"I know."

"When is she coming home?"

I had no idea.

About a week after Stella's arrival, we had Will over for dinner. I had asked him because I needed a distraction, and there were other reasons I refused to even begin to entertain, starting with the fact that since JD had left, I missed having Will around.

He brought a bottle of wine, and Stella, to my surprise, said yes when he offered her a glass, drinking it quickly and asking for another. It did not, I knew from experience, take much at all to get Stella drunk, and she hadn't really eaten for days, so I should have seen what was coming.

After we'd eaten, and she was onto her fourth glass, she started twisting her hair, moving closer to Will and saying, "No, really, do I look like I have five children? I do, you know—five, can you believe it?"

"No, I can't." Will smiled. "You look terrific, Stella."

"I do, don't I?" Stella agreed, then, lifting her shirt up added, "Look at this stomach."

We looked.

"Very impressive," Will said, gently withdrawing his hand as Stella tried to guide it to her navel. "Well, I think I should probably turn in."

"No, don't go," Stella said, pouring the last of the wine into his glass, giggling as it splashed over the edge. "We've got some more wine, don't we, Lulu? This party's only getting started."

I winced for her, Stella, who had never in her entire life said, "This party's only getting started," who didn't realize that *nobody* said, "This party's only getting started"; Stella, who was clearly floothered, as Duncan would have said—an Irish expression, apparently, meaning completely and utterly stonkered.

She was standing up now, behind Will's chair, whispering something into his ear.

He stood up and put his hands on her shoulders to steady her. "I'd love to go for a walk on the beach," he said, "but I really do need to get going. I've got a really early start in the morning."

Picking up his jacket, he pecked us both on our cheeks.

"Good night, girls. It was lovely to meet you, Stella, and we'll take that walk tomorrow," he said, and ducked through the door, leaving me to my floothered friend, who watched him go and said, "Is he gay, or what?" before sliding to the floor at my feet.

~

The next morning I held Stella's hair back with one hand as she emptied the contents of her stomach underneath a struggling azalea bush—which now had absolutely no chance of survival—and held Barney back with the other.

"Get away, Barney," I said, pushing at his wet nose. "Even for you this is disgusting behavior."

I'd woken up to the low wails of the curlews nestling in the casuarinas outside my window, and the slightly less pleasant wails of Stella doubled over in my garden.

"I tried to seduce that man, didn't I?" she asked me sadly, when there was nothing left in her poor stomach to get rid of. "That Will person?"

"No," I answered, "you just asked him to go for a walk on the beach. It was hardly a full frontal attack; you didn't get the peekaboo nightie out."

"I don't even own a peekaboo nightie," she said, sadder still.

"Nobody does," I told her, putting a wet washcloth to her forehead, "except maybe Kimmy."

As it turned out, getting as drunk as a lord seemed to do Stella the world of good, once she'd stopped being sick. That night she came down from her room, where she had slept all day, ate a huge plate of pasta, and asked if I wanted to go for a walk on the beach.

Whistling for Barney, we went through the back gate and padded barefoot to the water. Barney walked in front of us with the long, stately gait he used when he had no energy left but was still determined not to miss out on anything.

"Don't you get scared here, Lulu?" Stella asked, flexing her toes in the sand. "Living by yourself?"

"No, not when I've got Barney."

"But do you reckon he'd actually attack anyone?"

"Not sure, but then he doesn't really need to, all he has to do is breathe on them."

Our eyes went to him, scrabbling at a dead jellyfish in the sand. Stella leaned down to pick up a spiky green seed and rolled it in her fingers.

"I don't know if I could live here alone. This is the one of the only times since I was married I've slept in a bed by myself," she said, inspecting her find.

"You're kidding."

"No, Billy and I made a pact when we got married that we would never spend a night away from each other, unless we couldn't absolutely help it. Ridiculous, isn't it?"

I considered the idea, and also the fact that she had said her errant husband's name aloud for the first time in days.

"Well, it wouldn't work for me, but you and Billy are different."

"No, we're not, Lulu," she said, and I felt the sadness in every single word.

A wave came in, nibbled at the hem of my skirt.

"Yes, you are, Stella," I said. "I know he's apparently had some kind of slip-up—"

"Oh, is that what you call it? A slip-up?"

I caught the accusation in her voice but did not flinch. There was a certain irony, I could understand, in me of all people trying to navigate my friend through the murky waters of adultery.

"What? No, it was just an expression—look, Stella, I know you are very hurt and confused right now, and not sure whether you can take Billy back."

"Oh, I'm taking him back."

"You are?" I said, surprised. She had not given any hint of this decision as she had glided seemingly aimlessly through my house.

"Of course I am, Lulu. I've got five children who are at Mary Josephine's thinking their mother has gone on a holiday right in the middle of their school term, two sets of grandparents who adore them all and could not bear to see us split up, no job, no skills, no money, nowhere to go, and the entire primary school Christmas Pageant Committee waiting for me to get back and tell them how to make papier-mâché angels."

"You don't want to let those committee gals down." I smiled. "I hear they're pretty ferocious."

"No"—she smiled a little—"you don't." She let out a sigh as long as the night and turned back toward the house.

"So you've decided to forgive Billy?"

"It's not Billy I'm angry at, Lulu, it's God."

"I see," I said, even though I didn't.

"I think I'm past all that Leviticus stuff by now. . . ."

"Leviticus?"

"You never listened in Sister Monica's Bible study, did you?" she sighed. "Nobody did, except me. . . . You know, Leviticus: 'If a man commits adultery with another man's wife, both the adulterer and the adulteress must be put to death.'"

"Sounds a bit harsh. Couldn't you just make her sit through one of Billy's old stand-up routines?"

She laughed, and it made me ridiculously happy to hear it. I had always loved Stella's laugh, like little tinkling musical notes rising through the scale—Simone used to say she'd like to catch one and keep it.

"Listen, Lulu, I can forgive Billy because Billy's a man and their flesh is weak." She shot a warning glance at me. "But God is another matter altogether."

We were at the gate. Barney walked straight in and up to his bed, without a backward glance, while Stella and I sat, then lay down on the grass and looked up to see faint ribbons of lightning darting over the sky.

"I'm angry at God," she began, "because when we were growing up and you and Simone and all the other girls were collecting pop-star cards, I was collecting saints—*saint cards*, Lulu, all right? When you went to the beach on the weekend, I went to church; when everybody went off to the beach for their holidays, I went to Little Mountain Bible Camp, and do you know how we spent our time there?"

"No."

"We made hook rugs, Lulu, for a whole week."

I patted her arm softly to let her know I sympathized but without letting her know I had no idea what a hook rug was.

"When you all had part-time jobs in dress shops or cafés or cinemas on the weekends, I did volunteer work, and after school finished, when everyone else I knew was traveling overseas or studying at university or doing some sort of amazing job, I was getting married at eighteen years old and walking up that aisle as possibly the last virgin ever to graduate with honors from Saint Rita's—and don't think I don't know that Annabelle used to call me Virginia Intactica."

I remembered, trying not to smile at the nickname Annabelle had given Stella, trying not to think about Annabelle.

"So," Stella continued, "I have kept my marriage vows and I have gone forth and multiplied with not one but five children, and I am still doing the flowers for church every Sunday, and I am still getting down on my knees and thanking the Lord for my good fortune every night, and I understand that has been my choice.

"But you would *think*," she said, stabbing at the word in the darkness, "you would think, wouldn't you, that this would earn me some sort of *reward points*, you know, or at the very least some sort of nod from him"—she jerked her head at the sky—"some acknowledgment that I have been his faithful servant for my entire life—but what happens, Lulu, what happens?"

I knew there was no answer required, so I kept still and quiet in the dark.

"People like my husband go out and screw some twenty-two-year-old rental girl, but he will be all right because he will still have five beautiful children who adore him and a stupid wife who will take him back because she loves him. And people like you, Lulu, go out and sleep with your best friend's husband on their wedding night, their *wedding* night, and what happens to you? You're given a bloody beach house."

This time I did flinch.

"So," she said, standing up and brushing the sand from her jeans, "I think I'm done with God now." She walked toward the house, following in Barney's footsteps and not looking back.

I lay on the lawn, feeling its dampness creep through my wind-cheater, my body completely still, flattened by her words pouring over me in a hot rush. All the shame I had felt descended on my chest like a cloud of black insects beating their wings against it. She was right; I didn't deserve this, any of it.

A spray of rain came in from the sea, and I stood up to go inside my house of ill-gotten gain to Stella. As terrible as I felt, she would, I knew, be feeling worse, and the important thing was, I decided, that in the midst of her tirade, she had said she still loved Billy. That was something we could work on together, and what she thought of me—and God—could wait until later.

"Oh, Lulu," she said, bursting into tears the moment I walked into her room, "I don't know what I'm saying, I just hurt so much and everything's gone wrong, and I think I'm just really tired, you know, all those children, and now Billy . . ."

"Shh," I said, climbing in beside her, "it's all right, I'm not upset with you."

"Really?" she asked.

"Really," I said. "I know what I did was wrong, Stella, and I'm trying to work through it myself in the best way I can. But in the meantime, I want to tell you something Duncan told me not long before he died."

She nodded.

"I don't know if it will help you, but it seemed to help him," I said, handing her one of Rose's embroidered hankies.

"Okay."

"He told me that he wasn't sure about exactly who or what he believed in, but that he did believe in something, that he had faith. He said he thought it was what we could still hear through all the shouting."

Stella smiled.

"Then he said he wanted some chicken."

She laughed, her tiny chimes filling the room.

~

"Ex-boyfriends, runaway teenagers, lapsed Catholics—man, Willow Island has certainly livened up since you moved here, Lulu," Will was saying, peeling another prawn and throwing the shell to Barney.

"Don't encourage him, Will," I said. "That's disgusting."

"Not as disgusting as the dead bat he tried to eat yesterday."

"True," I said as we both contemplated Barney, now chewing on the dead crustacean's head.

It was the week after Stella had left, her skin flushing a deep red when Will came to the house to collect her.

"Hey, Stella." He smiled. "Have a good stay?"

"Yes, thank you, William," she'd answered, "very pleasant."

William? Very pleasant?

"I didn't realize we'd moved to Brideshead," I whispered in her ear as I kissed her good-bye.

"Shut up," she whispered back.

"It's 'Shut up, m'lady,'" I replied.

Then she left, Will carrying her bags down Avalon Road, back to Billy, her five children, and the Christmas Pageant Committee, and I could only pray they all knew how lucky they were to have her.

"So, who's next?" Will was saying. "Who's the next visitor?"

"No one for a while, I hope. I'm exhausted."

Will had come over to watch cricket with me, bringing a six-pack and some prawns. I loved sitting there with him, watching the game with Barney at our feet.

"This is perfect," Will announced from the couch. "It's a beautiful day; I've got beer, prawns, the cricket's on, Barney's not eating my shoes, and you."

He smiled a tiny, lopsided smile at me, one that said, "There it is, Lulu, take it," as he moved a little closer.

Warmth filled my body, like I'd just downed a shot of very good whiskey.

This would not do at all.

"Thank you," I told him primly, revisiting Brideshead myself, and shuffled a little farther down the couch.

Will suddenly stood up, startling both me and Barney, who stopped chewing his front paws long enough to register the movement.

"Actually, Lulu," he said, "I've just remembered I promised Deano I'd watch the game with him."

The obvious lie hovered between us.

"Sorry," he said, his jaw clenching and unclenching, "but I've got to go."

"That's fine," I started to say, but he was already out the door, leaving behind the beer and the prawns in his hurry to get away from me.

The screen door slammed shut, and I looked sadly down at Barney.

"And that," I told him, my tears surprising me, "is how to ruin a perfect afternoon."

chapter twenty-four

Julia and I were sitting on Racey O'Leary's seat late one afternoon, trying to spot whether there were any whales moseying by the island, when our talk turned to Duncan's funeral.

"I saw you there. I didn't know it was you, of course, but I noticed you among all those people," Julia said, her eyes trained on the ocean. "It's funny, isn't it? And now we're friends."

"Really?" I said. "Well, I'm sorry I didn't notice you in particular, Julia, but I did notice all the Willowers."

The truth was, they'd been hard to miss, allotted three pews, the Willow Islanders standing out like mollusks stuck to their seats as all the glittery fish in Duncan's life—politicians, film stars, journalists, and glamorous ex-wives—swam by.

It had been a solemn service, and while a spirited eulogy was delivered by Duncan's first radio producer and oldest friend, James Clivedon, the morning was cloaked by an underlying sadness, as worn by the slump of his children's shoulders.

The wake, however, was just as Duncan would have wanted it, a party that took on bacchanalian proportions by the end of the very long night, which saw Kimmy performing a strangely moving rendition of "Islands in the Stream" to an empty bar stool.

"Did you notice Will there?" Julia was asking, still looking out to sea.

"No, I did not notice Will, Julia." I smiled at her, neglecting to add that while that may have been the case then, it was the exact opposite now.

"Well, he was there," she said, adding, "Duncan loved him, you know, used to call him a loin melter."

"A what? Oh God," I groaned as we both started laughing.

"He said Will was exactly the sort of bloke he'd go for if he was gay, someone with a bit of marrow in his bones, not some bloke getting by in life by knowing how to pronounce *focaccia*."

We laughed again, then, as the sun began to dip behind Crook's Rock, headed back down the trail, parting ways at my letter box.

"I better get back to Boris," Julia said, "cook him some dinner—you wouldn't know it now but, boy, was that man a loin melter in his day."

I waved her off, and then checked my letter box before going into the house. I didn't get a lot of mail on Willow, but today there were a couple of catalogs and a letter. I knew the handwriting instantly; it could not have been more familiar to me.

It was from Duncan.

I looked around, peering down Avalon Road, then whipped my head around to the house, half expecting to see him standing in the doorway, saying, "What's the matter, Lulu? You look like you've seen a ghost."

Instead, I held one in my shaking hands.

How had it come to me? It was so like Duncan to do this, I thought, but who had he talked into posting it? Turning the letter around to examine its front, I realized with a small shiver that there was no postage stamp. It had been hand-delivered.

I ran inside the house into the library, where I sat down on the couch, and opened it.

Dear Lulu,

How are you, my dear? I am fine, although a bit cold.

Well, have you settled in? What do you think of Barney's new home? Marvelous, isn't it? So many questions to ask and so irksome not to be able to know the answers—unless of course I'm floating about the corners of the WIASA and lurking behind you like Patrick Swayze at the pottery wheel. You should take up pottery, by the way, it's just the sort of thing a young woman who moves to an island would do, isn't it?

Which brings me to the point of this latest missive— what are you going to do?

I'm sure it's all very pleasant wandering about Willow picking up seashells and the odd shipwrecked sailor—how is Will Barton, by the way?—but you've been there for three months now, and the time is probably coming when you'll need to decide whether to return to the mainland or to stake your claim on Willow and become one of those colorful local identities they'll write about in those marvelous local history books:

Well worth a look is the Willow Island Aqua Sports Association, once home to the infamous Juniper Bay Wedding Shagger, Tallulah de Longland. Tallulah was a much-loved if eccentric Willower, who spent her days making rosella jam wearing nothing but a wedding veil on her head. She lived until the age of eighty-seven, when it is believed her dog, Barney—once owned by the famously virile Duncan McAllister—ate her.

Anyway, my dear, should you choose to stay, I'm sure you'll find something useful to do.

*In the meantime, enjoy Barney's new home — I do hope
it's not too big for the two of you, all those empty bedrooms
and that enormous kitchen table with all those empty
chairs just for you to sit at.*

Oh well, I'm sure you'll think of some way to fill it.

From your old friend to his dearest friend,
Duncan

*PS What did you think of the funeral? Did you think Ver-
di's "Requiem" was a bit much? Kimmy wanted "Let's Get
It On" but Kerry-Anne wouldn't let her.*

At the top of letter was the embossed imprint *From the desk of
Duncan McAllister* — a vanity that had always amused him.

"Love it," he'd say, "makes me sound like a ship's captain. I
wonder if I should get a set done for every room I'm in — "From
the bathroom of Duncan McAllister," "From the garage of Duncan McAllister," "From the unmade bed of Duncan McAllister."

"What about 'From the unhinged mind of Duncan McAllister'?" I had suggested one day, and I smiled, remembering the
arch of his eyebrows.

My eyes fell back on the page, on Duncan's neat, precise
handwriting so incongruent with the man who had guided its
pen with nail-bitten fingers.

A man should have good penmanship, he often said; it meant
you cared enough to take the time to form your letters, to leave
enough space between words so the reader had an easy passage
through them, no matter if the words themselves were harsh —
especially if they were harsh, he had said.

I ran my finger underneath the words, tracing him.

"So, from the desk of Duncan McAllister," I asked the air,
"what's all this about? Who do you want to join me at my table?"

I knew there had to be more—with Duncan there was always more—and the answer came the next day, with another hand-delivered, extra-celestial message from my former employer, this time headed: *From the unhinged mind of Duncan McAllister.*

Dear Lulu,

My apologies for stealing your line, but I was rather taken with it, and besides, we both know I've been stealing other people's lines for years.

The truth is, my mind has never been sharper, and as I lie here and my own days get shorter, I feel a great sense of urgency to share what I have learned these sixty-eight years I have been allowed to freely wander about this earth without some sort of license.

Don't worry, this is not to be one of those awful "I wish I had danced more" missives, the truth is, I wish I had danced less, as do, I'm sure, many other people.

I have made many friends in my life, Lulu, and many enemies as well. I have loved the wrong women and the right ones and somehow I have managed, one way or another, to hurt all of them with only one exception—you.

Yours is the one great love of my life I haven't managed to stuff up—I have not, I hope, ever really let you down, or kept you waiting too long, or told unimaginable lies to you.

We have always been honest with each other, have we not? Well then.

The truth is, bedding Joshua Keaton on his wedding night was not your finest hour.

I know it was partly an act of defiance against your relentless do-goodery, the manifestation of a long-suppressed wish to be a good girl gone bad.

But it was also rather mean-spirited, and not like you at all. You are not a bad girl, Lulu, and never will be.

And so we come, at last, to the real point of this letter.

What I have learned in the years allotted to me is that we can't fight who we are, Lulu. We can't—every time I have tried to, it has ended in tears, furtive taxi rides home, and the occasional night in jail.

I, for example, am a borderline alcoholic with questionable hygiene habits, a know-it-all, a habitual liar, an occasional substance abuser, a secret coveter of other people's lives, a shameless publicity seeker, a wearer of bad clothing, and a serial adulterer, a man who never, ever should have married and yet, ignoring all the signs did it not once but four times, because the other indisputable truth about me is that I can't resist a happy ending.

This is who I am, Lulu, I can't help it any more than you can help being an almost unnaturally decent sort of person, a hand-holder, and a believer in even the worst sort of people.

I know you believe this is a boring sort of person to be, so I hasten to add you are also funny, sharp as a switch knife, and utterly, utterly delightful.

So, having established who you are, the question is, what are we going to do with you, now that I am no longer there for you to fuss over?

Well, I have an idea, a rather good one, I think. Here it is.

Willow Island has many attractions, but nowhere decent to stay so people can enjoy them. Barney's home is big and beautiful and crying out for people to rattle its rafters. Rose's cakes and breads and biscuits lie idle in boxes in her kitchen, and her busy hands need somewhere to put them. Harry deserves a regular holiday. You deserve a life you love.

In short, my idea is to turn the Willow Island Aqua Sports Association into a bed-and-breakfast, a B and B, I believe they're called by people who wear a lot of linen.

You would be the ideal host—brimming with bonhomie, charming, organized, efficient, punctual, not too nosey, not likely to bore your guests with long-winded tales—would that I were alive so that could be my job.

Rose's cakes would be devoured, Harry could fix things around the place to his heart's content, Mattie and Sam could come during the holidays, and all the freeloaders who I am sure will beat a path to your door will find the inn is full.

The point is, Lulu, you've always looked after people, so you may as well get paid for it.

Anyway, that is my idea for you to do with what you will.

In the meantime, my greatest love to Barney, and, of course, to you. I hope my letter has not upset you—I tried to put the proper spacings between the harshest words, and in case these messages from the other side are having an unsettling effect on you, don't worry, this is my final letter.

So, this is it, the famous last words bit.

I wish I could think of something devastatingly clever, but all I can think of is something my mother used to tell me. She was a great gardener, Lulu, and her pockets were always full of crushed petals or leaves or seeds or bits of twigs—you could never put your hand in one of her pockets without finding something in there. She'd say, "I know it's silly, darling, but I like to take a bit of the garden with me wherever I go."

When she died, I went into her backyard and collected all manner of green things and took them to the undertakers with me. Then I slipped her garden into her pocket.

I've never had a green thumb, so I don't have a garden

to take with me, but I do have a hand to hold, and a place to rest my weary head. When I get scared—and I do get scared, Lulu—I think of you, I think of all the wonderful years we had together, and I marvel, I absolutely marvel that I, Duncan Rowan Slattery (don't ask) McAllister, lived long enough and apparently decently enough to be given such a friend.

I don't need a photo of you, or a lock of your hair to take with me—when my time comes, and it is coming, Lulu, I feel it one step behind me at each turn—I plan to close my eyes and concentrate on you.

You're the garden in my pocket.

                                                      Thank you,

                                        Duncan McAllister

chapter twenty-five

"Well, I think it's a marvelous idea, Lulu, I really do."

"I'm not sure, Julia, I've never done anything like it before."

"No reason not to."

"No, I don't suppose so, it just seems pretty overwhelming."

"Well, you've got to do something."

"Do I?"

"Of course," Julia said, kneading the dough on her kitchen bench and then dropping the mixture with a decisive thump. "You can't spend your whole life in a cave, Lulu. Sooner or later you've got to come out and face the wild animals."

A memory stirred; where had I heard that before, the rhythm of it?

"Julia?"

"Mmm?"

"Do you have any idea how Duncan's letters got into my mailbox?"

~

A few days after Duncan's last letter arrived—it was, of course, part of an elaborate plan set up by Duncan before he died, beginning with enlisting Julia to drop off his letters after I had been on

Willow for a suitable amount of time, and ending, I presumed, with a star-crossed wedding between Will and me beneath the casuarinas—I decided to visit Harry and Rose.

I wanted to talk them through Duncan's idea, and catch up with Simone and Stella, probably by now up to her armpits in papier-mâché angels, on my way back to Willow.

Will took me to the mainland, raising his eyebrows when he saw my luggage.

"I didn't know you were moving back to the big smoke."

"Very funny."

"How long are you going for?"

"A few days."

"Where's Barney?"

"He's at Julia's, sulking."

Will nodded. "I'll go visit him while you're away, take him some rotten fish."

He was loading my bags onto the boat and put out his hand to help me. I'd always liked watching Will's long body move around the boat, pumping the fuel line, giving the motor a little choke, quick and graceful, far more balanced on sea than land. Mostly, I liked the way, once we got going, he sat back, and smiled his lazy-man grin at me.

Only this time, he wasn't smiling. Instead he was looking straight out to sea, and I felt the whole ocean between us. We hadn't really spoken since the afternoon he'd left my house so abruptly. We ran into each other once at the post office, where we exchanged some cursory observations about the weather. Now I found myself in the space of Will's silence, filling it once more with inane meteorological references.

"It's cold," I said.

Will nodded. "Really breezy," I added, and he nodded once more.

"Brrrrr," I said, shaking my shoulders at the same time, just in case he needed a visual to illustrate what I was saying.

Will ignored me and I didn't blame him. Who says "Brrrr"? A girl on a boat with a man who was clearly annoyed with her, that's who.

"Will," I ventured.

"Yup," he answered, keeping his eyes on the water.

"Is everything okay?"

"Yup," he said again, and then added, "Why wouldn't it be?"

"No reason," I answered, although if I had been more truthful I would have said, "Because you never say 'yup,' and also because if I really was doing a weather report from this particular vessel, I would have said conditions were glacial."

The rest of the trip passed in silence, and when we got to the mainland Will passed me my bags and nodded once more.

"Have a good time," he said, starting the motor, not waiting for my reply, and not asking, as he always did, when I would like him to take me back to Willow.

"Will," I called out, "I should be about three days—I'll give you a ring and let you know."

He mouthed something at me from across the water, and although I couldn't be sure, it looked a lot like "Whatever."

Back home in Juniper, I put Will's "Whatever"—and whatever it meant—out of my mind while I told Rose about the possible transformation of my island home. She was folding clothes, her quick hands moving through the pile of laundry as she listened, deftly transforming it into orderly lines.

"Well, Lulu," she said, "I think it sounds wonderful, and I'm sure you're just the girl to do it." She smiled. "Let's go and tell your father about it, see what he thinks."

We went out to the garden where Harry was reading, putting the paper down and his arms out when he saw me.

"Lulu, I was just looking at a horse called Island Girl—and here you are," he said, still squinting.

"Put your glasses on, Harry," Rose said.

"Can't find them."

"They're on the table beside you."

He grinned at us. "So they are."

"Your father is getting vainer as the years go by," Rose told me.

"Vainer or vaguer?"

"Vainer, and you know it. Who's going to see you in your glasses apart from me?"

Harry patted the seat.

"Nobody but you, Rosey-girl, but you're the only one who matters."

She sat down beside him. "Lulu's got an idea, Harry. She's thinking about turning the house into a bed-and-breakfast. Well, it was Duncan's idea, but she's thinking about doing it." She was rushing over her words, as if she couldn't get them out fast enough. "Julia would help her run it—you know, with the linen and things—and Will might take guests out on fishing trips, and they could hire some of those old canoes and kayaks in the shed."

"What would you do, Lulu?" Harry asked.

"Well, she'd be Lulu," Rose answered, so sure, as usual, of my capabilities, before rushing on. "You'd have to do all the plumbing and put in the extra bathrooms, and she wants me to supply some cakes and biscuits."

"What do you think of that?" Harry asked Rose, knowing the answer.

"Well, I'd like to help out. Lulu says probably the best way would be for me to cook here during the week and then we could go over on a weekend—not every weekend—and I could leave her with some supplies."

Harry was smiling at her, tripping over her tongue, his Rose, tickled pink.

"Lulu says I have to think of a name for my range, Harry—*my range*."

"Very flash," he said, grinning at me.

"It's just at the talking stage at the moment," I told them. "Nothing's set in stone or anything like that."

"Do you want to do it, love?" Harry asked.

"I'm not sure; I think so, I think I'd like to give it a go."

"That's my girl."

The first night I was back in Juniper, I lay on my bed reading interior-decoration magazines for ideas about B and Bs, which mostly seemed to involve wicker baskets, and listening to the faint sounds of Michael Parkinson's theme song playing on the down-stairs television.

"Can I come in, love?" Harry said, poking his head around my bedroom door, hands in the pockets of his olive dressing gown, feet tucked into his checked slippers.

"Harry," I said, "you've been wearing that same outfit to bed since I was seven."

"I know," he said, sitting on my bed, flexing his feet to inspect the well-worn shoes that encased them.

I smiled at him.

"So," he began, "I thought I might give you an update."

I nodded, looked toward the door.

"Engrossed in *Parky*."

"So . . ."

"So, it's all good, Lulu. I know we all have issues with the medication, your mother the most, but Dr. Reynolds has been slowly taking it down, month by month. He reckons she might be able to come off it completely by the end of the year."

"What do you think?"

"Oh, I think the usual, love, I think I'll just keep an eye on it, you know, see how she's going."

"What does he say about the dress thing?"

"Reckons it's marvelous, says we should all wear clothes that make us happy."

"That sounds good," I said. Dr. Shaw had told us we should throw all the girls out one day when Rose wasn't looking—"The shock of it might jolt her into reality," he'd said, and Harry had gone pale beneath his skin.

"He's got her going to an acupuncturist as well. Don't see the sense of sticking needles into yourself myself, but Rose reckons it makes a difference."

I looked at my father, the lines in his face deepening, the tufts of hair at his temples growing grayer each time I saw him.

"She's really well, and staying well," he was saying. "We haven't had a Doris day in months, and she's getting out more and more."

"So," I said, "on a scale of one to ten?"

"About a three," Harry answered, his eyes locking with mine. "Don't worry, love."

Our eyes met, my words our own code for Rose's state of mental health, one being optimal, ten being the day we never spoke about.

Annabelle had left me at the gate, after walking me home "to keep you company," she had said, then running back to her house for her bagpipe lesson—Annie's idea, short-lived, of course. (Annabelle did about three lessons, then gave her bagpipes to a "poor

Scottish man" down the street who turned out to be about as Scottish as we were, and who sold them to a pawnshop.)

I had collected the letters out of the box and pushed open our never-locked, stained-glass front door.

"Mum, I'm home, Mu-um, Mum, I'm home," I said, singsonging the words, like I always did, but I knew straightaway something was not right, feeling the weight of it caught in the stillness of the house.

The letters dropped from my hands to the floor as I ran to the kitchen door, a towel wedged beneath it. I pushed the door open, and the poisoned air made me feel instantly dizzy as I ran for the stove, pawing at its knobs with hands that no longer seemed to belong to me. Then I raised the sash window with a jerk and went to my mother, who was on the floor. I dragged her from the kitchen into the lounge room, my bony fourteen-year-old arms around her, and ran to the telephone to call an ambulance.

I sat next to her and waited, listening for the sounds of her breath, and it felt like the whole time I was holding my own, not exhaling until the paramedics came through the door. Then I had run the length of the street to where I knew Mattie and Sam would be getting off the bus, waylaying them as they did so to take them to Mrs. Delaney, who was hovering uncertainly in her front yard, wanting to help, dying to know, caught between curiosity and compassion.

"Mum's had a bit of a fall. I have to stay at the house in case the doctor calls, but you two go next door to the Delaneys', there's some cake for you," and they had been far too young, and too hungry, to question the logic of it.

I went back into the house to call Harry and methodically clean up, straighten the chairs I had knocked over, wash the dishes, sweep the flour from the floor, and spray the room with Forest Glen's Mountain Mist, guaranteed, the can said, "to remove even the most stubborn household odors."

Except, of course, for the scent of that day, which lingered on my skin long after it was over.

That was the ten.

～

I stayed in Juniper for a week, talking through ideas for the B and B with Harry and Rose, and vacillating between deciding I would definitely do it and dismissing it altogether in favor of leaving Willow and returning to the life I'd once had.

But before I could make any of those decisions, I knew there was one thing I should do, at least one part of my past I needed to redress on the way to my future.

After saying good-bye to Harry and Rose, I swung my car out of the driveway and down the road to a familiar intersection—left to my house down Laurel Terrace, or right to Annabelle's down Beddington.

Frank still lived at the River House, and I owed him an apology.

I'd decimated his daughter's wedding, been instrumental in sending her away just as she'd come back into the family fold, cost him thousands of dollars for a wedding reception no one wanted to remember and photos of the happy couple no one wanted to see.

I had wanted to say sorry, of course, to Frank, to Annie, to Annabelle, to all of them, but I had balked every time. Easier to retreat behind the she-oaks that guarded my house on an island hardly anyone went to.

I'd done it my whole life, I thought, hidden myself away when the going got too tough. I'd done it when Harry and Rose had let me stay at home all those years ago, and I was doing it again now, on Willow.

Well, if I really was going start my own business there, then perhaps it was time I started minding my own. What had I always told Mattie and Sam, twisting like corkscrews to get out of my way when they were little and I was trying to take a Band-Aid off their grazed knees?

"Hold still," I'd say, "it'll hurt more if I do it slowly. If you let me rip it off, you won't feel it so much, I promise."

I swung the car onto Annabelle's street.

"Rip the Band-Aid off, Lulu," I said to myself.

~

I parked well away from the house, feeling pit-of-the-stomach nervous.

I walked toward the house, waiting for the moment when the white glare of the footpath would give way to shadow as the poinciana tree behind Annabelle's fence reached over to brush the path with its branches. Red flowers tossed casually across its canopy, I took a few calming breaths, then let its cool fingers claim me and lead me inside.

"I live in a jungle," Annabelle whispered as I walked through the gates, the gargoyles grinning at me with their green mossy teeth.

"Evening, Annabelle; evening, Lulu," echoed Rose as I passed beneath them to walk toward the stairs where two little girls sat with their heads together writing words in a book, and closing it wordlessly when they saw me, standing on pale legs to disapanish into the house.

Green tendrils curled around doors, in and out of windows, and traveled all the way across the roof, the wisteria, it seemed, trying to take the house down with it. I stood outside the front door, shut, but needing, I knew, just a slight push to open, and for one of those tendrils to reach down and pull me in.

Putting one hand against it, I called out, "Frank, are you home?"

"In the kitchen, Lulu," he called back, as if it was the most natural thing in the world that I should be here in this house where everything and nothing had changed.

"Tallulah," he said, "how wonderful to see you."

Frank, sitting at his table, covered in papers and pots of paint and bits of ribbon and staples and notepads and coffee cups and a jug filled with water and frangipanis dripping their milk into it. "They say you should burn the stems or something, to stop their leaking," he told me, "but I can't see the point."

"No," I said, thinking that one of the things I had always liked about this man was that he rarely could.

"I'm so glad you've come."

"Really?" I said, "Because I wasn't sure if I should, I actually wouldn't blame you if you weren't overjoyed to see me because" — *rip the damn thing off, Lulu* — "of what I did at the wedding. It was inexcusable, Frank, and I've come to apologize to you."

"No need."

"No need? Frank, I did a terrible thing, and I am so sorry, it was petty and spiteful and wrong" — now the Band-Aid was off, there was no stopping the bloodletting — "and I don't think I can actually stay in this house and look at you, Frank, with your beautiful milky frangipanis in that jug." I burst into tears — big, shuddering sobs that sprang from my eyes and set my nose coursing.

Frank handed me a tissue.

"Blow," he said, guiding my hands up to my nose. "Blow the living daylights out of it, Lulu."

He lit the gas, put the kettle on, put some leaves in the blue enamel pot, and two mugs on the table.

"Sit down and have some tea." He smiled. "There is very little in the world that can't be solved with a cuppa."

I sat, and began apologizing all over again.

"Enough, Tallulah," Frank said. "I am happy to see you. I am happy you are here in this house with me, drinking my tea and destroying my tissues."

"Stop being so nice to me, Frank," I said. "I can't stand it."

He poured out the tea, handed me my cup.

"Lulu," he said, "you don't have to explain your actions to me, just as I don't have to explain my daughter's to you. I told your dad the same thing when he tried to talk to me about it all."

"He did? I didn't know that."

"Well, he did—and I asked him if he could remember what King Edward said, when he abdicated."

"What did Harry say?"

"He said, 'Jeez, Frank, I'm not that old.'"

I laughed and Frank laughed with me.

"Anyway, King Edward said, when nobody could understand why he was throwing it all away, all of it, an empire no less, for a woman who even the kindest person could only say had an interesting face, he said, 'The heart wants what it wants.'

"Anyway," he said, "enough of this. I am glad to see you, Lulu, and in fact, you may have come, as they say, in the nick of time."

"What do you mean?"

"They want to pull our tree house down."

The letter had arrived weeks ago, Frank said, telling me how dismayed he had been when he found it among the clutter on the kitchen table.

It had lain between some pen-and-ink doodles—one rather good one, he thought, of Harry and his truck—and now he had just three weeks or thereabouts to lodge an application for building approval from the local council, an application he could see had bugger-all chance of being successful.

"You read it, Lulu," he said, "see if I'm right."

I scanned the pages, seeing Frank's chances ricochet from bugger-all to not-at-all as I did so. Because of its size and character, the letter said, the tree house was "an extension," which had not been approved by council. Furthermore, when the "extension" had been inspected by Mr. K. Munroe on September 7, it had been found to contravene local building codes 34, 36 A, 36 B, 42, and 78, copies of which were attached.

Not that there would be much point in doing that, when the letter also said that the "tree in which the extension was housed" — *"Tree house,"* I muttered, *"just say tree house"* — had been found to be outside of Frank's land's designated boundaries. Therefore, it was actually on council land; therefore, we were, as Harry would say, completely stuffed.

I had no legal training whatsoever, no concept of council by-laws, and the letter was making my head spin, but nevertheless I immediately launched into some spirited straw-clutching.

"Frank," I said, "did you give your permission for this Munroe man to come onto your property?"

Frank said at first he thought that no, he hadn't — but then a few days ago he'd remembered a bloke a month or so back, asking if he could have a bit of a wander around his garden. Frank had been working on a portrait of Annie in his studio — he didn't usually go in for portraits, he said, but had been working on this one for ages. It was from a Polaroid photo taken years ago, when Polaroids had just come out and everyone stood around at parties waiting for the photos to emerge from the camera's belly. Annie had hated those cameras, Frank said — happily veering completely off course — believing it was unnatural to capture people so instantly. "Annie liked a more languid getting-to-know-you process." He laughed. But he had kept quite a few shots, and he had been working from one of Annie, taken at, of all things, a fondue party, when that bloke had stuck his head in the door and asked him if he could have a look around. Frank had said yes and waved him away — people were always wandering into his home, or turning up in his garden, "down there with the fairies."

"So have you done anything about it?" I asked, trying to lead him back to the real problem sitting atop a mango tree in his backyard.

"No, I just put the letter away until someone came and helped me work out what to do—and here you are, Tallulah," he said as the tendrils came down through the window and yanked me all the way back in.

"I'd like to see it," I said, "the tree house."

"After you, Tallulah de Lovely," Frank said, standing up.

We went down through the garden and stood at the bottom of the tree, climbing the rungs, then pulling ourselves up with the rope to the veranda. Ducking our heads through the doorway with the moon and the stars dancing over it, Frank asked me, "You remember it, Lulu?"

I breathed it all in.

"Yes," I said, thinking that although I might have done it once, I would never let Frank Andrews down again.

"Give me the letter, Frank," I said. "I might know someone who can help."

chapter twenty-six

Before I was due to return to Willow, I had an appointment with Andrew to talk through Duncan's plans for the WIASA.

Andrew, as he did with all of Duncan's schemes, had taken his idea and run with it, producing a spreadsheet of costs and budgets, making detailed lists of each step that should be taken, and enjoying, I realized as I listened to him, every minute of it.

I had been back from Harry and Rose's for a couple of weeks when Andrew called to say he'd drawn up some initial plans for the business and would like to meet with me, Julia, and Will to go over a few points. We'd already had two meetings since I'd been home, and things seemed to be back on an even keel between Will and me, the awkward boat trip—for the moment, at least—forgotten.

I was beginning to think that Andrew rather liked coming to Willow, loosening his tie on the way over on the barge and talking about tide times with Walter Prentice and his boys. There was no doubt about it, there was something about those boiler suits that had every man I knew wanting to hide his clean fingernails in his pockets.

I was at the kitchen table waiting for everyone to arrive when Barney pricked up his ears and shot out the back door, letting me know that one of my guests was on their way down Avalon Road. Will.

Julia would have received an enthusiastic greeting at the

door, Andrew a few halfhearted licks, but for Will, Barney delivered the works. I smiled, thinking of Will on the path, seeing Barney barreling toward him, putting out his hands to try to stop Barney from leaping up at him, and Barney placing his paws on Will's chest to shout hello in Will's ringing ears.

Still, you couldn't blame Barney for wanting to knock the man to the ground.

Sometimes I wanted to myself.

Well, too bad — Will Barton was a good man, a decent man, a damn fine man if you wanted to put a point on it, and he deserved a much better woman than me.

I would not go near Will Barton if he was the last eligible man on Willow — which of course, not counting Paddy Stuart down at the bowls club, he was. (And Paddy, who was in his fifties, lived with his mother and was trying to get into the *Guinness Book of World Records* for catching the world's longest sandworm and so probably didn't count.)

I looked out the window and saw Barney proudly bringing Will to my door, trotting just ahead of him on the path, every now and again swiveling his head around to check that Will was still there, then swiveling it back again, legs prancing just that little bit higher.

"Well, look who the horse dragged in," I said as they came to the kitchen door.

"Lulu," Will said, trying to extricate himself from Barney — who was now looking at me from where his head was wedged triumphantly between Will's legs — "call off the hound!"

"I can't," I said, filling a jug with some water. "I think he's in love with you."

"Well, that makes one of you," Will said, slipping inside the door and deftly shutting it behind him, a whisker of a moment ahead of Barney's bullethead pushing its way determinedly through.

"So," Will said, leaning against the door, hands behind his back, "more meetings."

"Yes," I agreed, choosing to ignore his "that makes one of you" comment. "Andrew's a bit of a stickler for them."

"I've noticed."

"Do you mind?"

"What?"

"Coming here for them."

Will put his head down, said something to the floor.

"Pardon?"

"I said I never mind coming here, not if I get to see you."

"Oh."

"Oh?"

Will tilted his head to rest on the doorframe, crossing his arms.

I had, of course, seen this moment coming, caught it in other moments between us, but I was still unprepared for that "Oh?" and all that it carried with it.

But what to do about it? What to say to him, standing at my door with such a small word looming so large between us?

"Will, I— Look, the others will be here in a minute, so it's probably not a good time, but I don't think that you and I, if that's what you're, if that's where you're heading, well, I just don't think it's a good idea."

"Because you're the Juniper Bay Wedding Shagger?"

I dropped the glass jug, just opened my hands and let it go, falling in slow motion to the floor, and we both stood there and watched it shatter on the flagstones, sending shards of glass splintering across the uneven ridges.

Long after it smashed, we both kept looking at it, while I stood there and thought that if there was ever a moment I would choose to voluntarily disapanish, this was it.

Duncan, bloody, bloody, bloody Duncan.

"He told you?"

"No."

"Yes, he did."

"Well, he did, but only after I told him I knew the whole story anyway."

I went to the cupboard, took the broom in my hands, and began to sweep up the glass, methodically pushing its bristles deep into the floor, until Will was beside me, trying to take the broom from my grasp.

"I think you've got it all now, Lulu."

For some reason I could not let go of the damn broom, so we stood there with it between us, both holding it as if our lives depended on not letting it go.

Will smiled.

"Unhand the broom, Lulu."

"No."

"I said unhand it!"

"No—you."

"No—I said you."

We started to laugh, Will and I, at the stupidity of it, and were still laughing when Julia came through the back sliding door.

"I gave Barney the slip," she announced. "He's most put out." She looked at the two of us, still holding the broom. "Been an accident?" she asked.

"I dropped a jug," I said, and her eyes went to the neat pile of glass on the floor.

"So I see—was it a special one?"

I looked at Will Barton, who I did not deserve.

"Not especially," I said, walking away.

~

After Andrew and Julia had finally left—following a heavy, clumsy sort of meeting with Julia looking at me with a question-mark face and Andrew saying, "I really need everybody here to focus on this, people"—I wandered outside to sit beside Will, watching the trawlers on the prowl out at sea. It was cool and still, no casuarinas whistling, and somehow, just the fact that everyone had gone had lessened the space between us.

"I'm sorry you broke your jug," Will offered.

"It's all right."

"I shouldn't have said that, Lulu, that Juniper Bay thing."

"Why not? It's true enough."

"No."

"Yes it is, Will, you don't know the half of it, you don't know what I did."

"I don't really have to, do I?"

"Of course you do, if you want to . . ." I looked out at the trawlers, at their spiky black outlines. "Well, if you ever wanted to take me on."

"I'll take you on, Lulu," he said, and I thought instantly of Harry and Rose, all those years ago.

That was the night Will told me about how he had come to Willow, how he had grown up there with his parents and sister before they had moved to the mainland so the kids could go to a "proper" school. He had hated every minute of that, insisting on walking barefoot and finding bitumen and broken glass no match for the loose, grainy sands of the islands.

"I was useless, Lulu," he said, "couldn't get my bearings."

His parents had settled in well—they were still "over there," running a small hospitality hire office—and his sister, Judy, had a massage therapy practice on the mainland. She came to Willow now and again to get the kinks out of some of the islanders, backs bent over like the she-oaks that held them there.

Will had studied too, making a "half-arsed attempt at a marine biology degree," and a half-arsed attempt at several relationships along the way. There had been a girl—of course, looking at Will, there was always going to be a girl—but it hadn't worked out. He had taken her to Willow a few times, and although she had tried, he remembered, seeing her staggering across the deck of his boat, smile fixed to her face by the wind, it was, they had both realized, not going anywhere except in different directions.

"What was her name?" I asked.

"Melissa," he said. "She's married to a dentist now—three kids, all with excellent teeth."

He had floated around for a while, working at his mum and dad's office, in a boat design company, and in a pub, which was where he'd met Duncan McAllister.

"I knew who he was, of course," Will said, "pretty hard not to, really, but I also knew him from around Willow. He'd bought the house there a few years back, and I'd see him every now and again on weekends."

Duncan had been drunk, the bad kind of Duncan drunk, obnoxious, sweaty, leering at the female counter staff, spouting Joyce, and mocking the bewildered drinkers around him if they did not sit, mouths agape, mesmerized by his words. I knew that Duncan well, and was not fond of him, the terrible things he'd say, then slink into the studio the next morning saying, "Don't look at me, Lulu, I'm wearing my cloak of shame."

It had been one of those nights that Will had met Duncan, and Will, recognizing a fellow islander who had well and truly lost his sea legs, had called him a cab and taken him outside to wait for it in the fresh air. "I know you." Duncan's eyes had narrowed. "You're from Willow, aren't you? What are you doing in this cesspit of a city? You should wrest yourself from its clutches"—Duncan had steadied himself to look straight into Will's eyes—"and throw yourself back into the ocean, where we both know you belong."

The taxi had arrived, Will had put Duncan in it, and the next day Duncan had rung the pub and asked to speak to last night's bartender.

"Hello," Duncan had breathed into the phone, "are you the fellow who poured me into my cabbage last night?"

"Yes," answered Will, "did you get home all right?"

"Home?" answered Duncan. "Oh, I didn't go home, son, I went— Well that's neither here nor there. I just wanted to thank you for helping me out, buy you a drink— What's your name?"

"Will Barton—and that's all right, Mr. McAllister, you don't have to shout me a drink."

"Duncan."

"Right, well, thanks, Duncan, but you don't need to do this, honestly."

"I insist—what time do you knock off?"

"Six o'clock."

"I'll see you then."

He had turned up right on time, bought Will a beer, sipped lemonade himself throughout their meeting, and apologized profusely for any offense he might have caused the night before.

"It really is all right," Will had told him, surprised that so powerful a man could be so obviously shaken by his own fault lines.

"No, it isn't," Duncan had answered him. "Poor form, really. But enough about me—now tell me why you're here and not messing about on a boat somewhere."

So they had talked—well, Will had talked and Duncan had listened, and by the end of that conversation Will had found himself agreeing that yes, he would be interested in the deckie job going on Walter Prentice's barge, and no, he wasn't too bad with his hands and he could probably help Duncan out with the renovation of the Willow Island Aqua Sports Association, which had, Duncan told him, very good bones.

"So," Will had finished, "here I am—largely because of Duncan McAllister, I suppose."

"And I'm here entirely because of him."

A ripple of a breeze, just the petticoat hem of it, lifted over us. Will shifted beside me.

"Do you reckon we're just like two puppets to him, Lulu? That he's up there somewhere, sitting on a cloud holding one of those wooden cross things, you know, that they jerk the marionettes around with—just sitting up there pulling our strings and laughing his head off?"

I thought of Duncan, his maniacal grin, and nodded.

"It's entirely possible." I smiled.

Will put his arm around my shoulders.

"I think he wanted us to be together, Lulu."

"I think so too," I whispered.

"So," he said, drawing me closer, "what do you think about that?"

I thought it was probably one of Duncan's better ideas. I thought I loved the feel of Will's arms around me, the way I fit perfectly beneath them. I thought I could just stand up, take his hand, and lead him straight back into the house.

Then I thought better of it and wriggled out from under his arm.

"I think just because you want something doesn't make it right," I said, "and believe me, Will, I know."

Will had sighed, then told me what he wanted.

He had found those meetings with Andrew and Julia increasingly uncomfortable, particularly with Andrew referring to him as my "business partner." Duncan's idea of Will taking guests on fishing trips had expanded; he was now, Andrew said, "water sports director," in charge of fishing, kayaking, canoeing, sailing, teaching guests all of these skills as well as maintaining the boat shed and all the craft in it.

But Will did not want to be my water sports director.

Instead, he told me how sometimes as he sat in his boat late at night, casting his line in the deepest part of the bend, he would look through the trees to my house, and it was all he could do not to dive into the water and make his way up the bank through the trees to my door. "That's what I want, Lulu de Longland," he said, his eyes fixed on the trawlers as he stood up to go. "I want to stand dripping water on your front doorstep and demand you let me in."

Opening the back gate to head home, he turned back to me.

"That's not very businesslike, is it?"

I couldn't answer, rendered mute by the image of a shirtless Will Barton on my doorstep as little rivers of water meandered down his chest.

After Will left that night, and I watched his retreating figure all the way down the beach until he disappeared into the black- ness, I went back into my house and pressed my face against my bedroom window.

I wondered if Will could see my house from the his boat, if the reverse was true, but I couldn't see the river for the trees.

Will's words had rattled me, and although I hadn't said any- thing, I thought that if I could not find my own words soon, I would explode, just spontaneously bloody combust in frustration.

Duncan had told me once that was how he'd like to go. "There are people, Lulu," he had said, his bloodshot eyes opening in wonderment, "there are people who actually spontaneously com- bust from the inside. One minute they're there having a beer, and the next"—Duncan had clicked his fingers and made a noise like an explosion—"everyone's at the bar saying, 'Where's Lionel? He was here a minute ago' and there he is, smoldering on the carpet beneath them, like a cigarette someone's ashed!" At which point, Duncan had taken a long drag of his own, and added, "Bloody marvelous."

But I didn't tell Will that was how I felt. I had not come to

Willow to find a love I knew I didn't deserve, and besides, everyone knew it was foolhardy to mix business with pleasure.

I closed my eyes against the windowpane—if Will was going to be Barney's B and B's water sports director, our relationship would be all business, no pleasure.

Dammit to hell and back again.

chapter twenty-seven

"Hello, Lulu."

"Hi, Andrew."

"Well, I've had a look at that letter you gave me about Frank Andrews and the tree house, but it seems pretty watertight to me—I'm sorry, Lulu, but I'm not overly optimistic I can help at all."

"Are you sure? Have you really had a good look through it?"

"Lulu."

"Sorry, Andrew, of course you have, so what can I do now?"

"With your permission, I'm going to pass it on to a colleague of mine—Linda Mayberry, whose firm specializes in these sorts of things. She's very good—not cheap, of course."

"Doesn't matter," I said automatically.

"Really not cheap, Lulu, about two hundred an hour the last time I dealt with her."

"Doesn't matter," I repeated, even though my savings were being depleted at an alarming rate.

"I'll get back to you on that when I hear from her. I'll stress to Linda that obviously we don't have much time, but it should be all right, she's a good egg and I'll tell her to get cracking. Now, how's the B and B going?"

"Good," I said. "Will's finished repainting all the canoes, Julia's sorted out all the linen and towels for the different bedrooms, the plasterers are here fixing that ceiling in the downstairs bath-room, and the first night's booked out already."

"How did that happen, Lulu? It's weeks away, and we haven't even begun to advertise it yet."

"It's all Willowers," I said, "coming for a stickybeak."

"As long as they pay, Lulu," he said. "No local discounts, re-member."

"Yes, Andrew, you've told me, now just back to Frank for a minute, do you think your friend might find some loopholes for us to work with? You must or otherwise you wouldn't bother giv-ing it to her, right?"

"Lulu," said Andrew, "you concentrate on getting Barney's Bed-and-Breakfast up and running, and I'll concentrate on stop-ping them from pulling down Frank's tree house."

"Thanks, Andrew," I said.

"Don't thank me, Lulu, just get on with things at your end."

I put down the phone and was just going to start sorting out the old storeroom when the front doorbell rang.

"Surprise!" Stella said, beaming as I opened the door to find both her and Simone standing behind it.

"Don't freak out," said Simone. "We've come to help, your boyfriend, Will, brought us over."

"He's not my boyfriend," I said automatically.

"Well, you're mad if he isn't," Simone said. "He even got old Saint Stella's motor running on the way over, didn't he, Stell?"

Ignoring her, Stella said, "Anyway, Lulu, we've come to help, we're only here for a couple of days, but your mum told us all the linen and crockery's arrived so we thought we could help make the rooms up for you, fill the cupboards."

"Roll the bandages for our boys on the front line, that sort of thing," added Simone. "Are you going to let us in?"

They wouldn't let me make them a cup of tea, instead getting straight to work—Stella stocking all the cupboards I hadn't got to yet, and Simone helping Will clean up the old lawnmower shed. They worked all day with only a brief stop for lunch, before flopping down on the lawn with me to watch the day turn into night.

"Lord, I am bone-tired." Simone stretched her entire body, head to toe.

"Don't say *Lord*," Stella said automatically.

"All right," Simone answered her. "Fuck, I'm tired—there, is that better?"

I giggled, enjoying the endless tug-of-war between my two oldest friends, the push and pull of them.

"So," Simone said, sitting up, "I've been offered the weekend news shift, if I want it."

"You didn't tell me that, Simone!" said Stella.

"I've only just been asked myself, and besides, there's a lot I don't tell you, Stella."

That was true, there were some things in Simone's world— her sex life, her occasional visits to the land of illegal substances, the fact that she was a card-carrying member of GALA, the Gay and Lesbian Atheists' Alliance—that she could not see any earthly good in sharing with Stella, and I had to agree.

Besides, Stella didn't necessarily share everything with Simone either, I thought, like the fact that she was pregnant again.

I always knew when Stella was expecting; her face became even more serene than it usually was.

The three of us headed up to our rooms early, completely knackered by the day, and I sat on Stella's bed and asked, "How many weeks, Stella?"

"Twelve and a half, don't tell Simone."

"I won't, but you shouldn't have worked so hard today."

"I didn't, you gave me all the easy jobs."

"So, are you all right? How do you feel about it?"

"Like I always do, grateful."

I smiled at her.

"I do, Lulu, I know, six kids seems like such a lot these days, and it is, but it doesn't faze me, you know, I just think, *Good, one more to love for all of us.*"

"You're lucky."

She nodded. "How did you know?"

"You've got that whole 'Lady Madonna' thing going on."

She propped herself up with the pillow. "I wish you'd have a baby, Lulu—you and Simone."

"Together? That's very liberal of you, Stella."

"Very funny—but I really would like you to have a baby one day, and Simone too, I think she'd be a fantastic mother."

"You do?"

She nodded.

"My mind's been open to a lot more things, Lulu, since Billy had sex with that girl from the agency—you know, 'Why do you look at the speck of sawdust in your brother's eye and pay no attention to the plank in your own?'"

"What?"

"Matthew—7:2," she answered, "although I always thought that if you were walking around with a great big plank of wood in your eye, you'd know about it, wouldn't you?"

Laughing, I handed her the glass of water on the bedside table.

"Drink this," I said. "It was pretty hot here today, I don't want you getting dehydrated, and you've got to promise me you'll take it easy tomorrow."

She nodded.

"Anyway, if it's a girl I'm thinking of calling her Simone."

"Stella," I said, "that's really nice of you."

And it really was, considering that every time Stella announced a pregnancy Simone would do that shuddering thing as if she'd just swallowed a porcupine, and mutter something about "the pope" and "sows" and "vasectomy" under her breath.

"Not really," said Stella. "If I name the baby after her, she'll have to come to the christening, and I want to see if her eyebrows burst into flame when she walks into a church."

"Oh, you're an evil woman, Stella McNamara!" I said.

"I know." She grinned happily and settled down into her pillows. Next, I knocked on Simone's door.

"Come in if you're Ellen DeGeneres," she called.

"That one's getting a bit tired, Simone," I told her, sitting on the chair in the corner of the room. "You've been saying it for years."

"I know," she sighed, "but there're just no interesting power lesbians around anymore."

"There's you," I said.

"Mmm, I suppose—and maybe Maxine Mathers."

"Maxine Mathers is not a lesbian, Simone."

"Are you sure? I thought I was getting some signals from her at Larry Hay's send-off last week from Channel Nine."

"Larry's retired?"

"Yes, and you would have been at his party if you were not too busy making your coconut cream pies here on Gilligan's Island."

I shook my head at her. "Anyway, Maxine Mathers is definitely not a lesbian."

"How do you know?"

I told her how Duncan, who *always* kissed and told—it had been one of his least admirable virtues—had confessed all to me about Maxine turning up to his hotel room the night of Frank's exhibition.

"No way!" said Simone, delighted to hear some tittle-tattle about her nemesis; and I, it must be said, remembering that awful, honeyed dissection of Annie, was equally delighted to give it to her.

"Mmm-mmm." I nodded. "They spent the whole night together."

"What did Duncan say?"

"He said her reputation exceeded her."

Simone laughed so hard the water she had been drinking came out of her nose.

⁓

Barney and I were walking along the back dunes, watching the ghost crabs emerge from their homes strewn like potholes along the sand, their eyes resting on stalks trained on the sea. Will had told me this early-evening dash to the ocean had a purpose.

"They go there to breathe," he said. "They need to let the water wash over their gills to get oxygen, and then they store it so that in winter they can retreat into their shells and hold their breath for six months."

Ever since he had told me that, I loved to watch them enter the water and catch their breath.

This was my favorite time and place on Willow, at dusk, on the beach that lay behind the dunes that met my back fence, in that quiet space between day and night.

Barney and I had given ourselves the afternoon off, stretched out on a couch, one apiece, in the lounge room, where I had read and Barney had dreamed whatever pictures he made in his head, making his black, rubbery lips curl.

Simone and Stella had left, but Harry, Rose, Mattie, and Sam would be arriving in a few days; there were lists pinned to the corkboard in the office with items to cross off, tradesmen to deal with and inventories to be made, and I had decided that Barney and I would do none of it. Instead, we had lain on the lounges until the air had cooled and the shadows had started to play on the shelves.

I reluctantly got up, unfurled my limbs, and said, "Come on, Barney boy, party's over."

He had slowly gotten to his feet, swaying a little as he took the weight of his great body, looking up at me with those lips, not pulled back, I was sure, but smiling.

We had walked the dunes for at least an hour when I whistled for Barney and turned back toward the house. He came lolloping up beside me, then his ears pricked up and a low growl came from the back of his throat as he pushed his body into mine.

"What is it Barney?" I said. "You all right, mate?"

His great chocolate eyes considered mine, staring directly into them for a sliver of a moment, then they slipped back into his head as he hit the ground.

"Barney!"

I fell to my knees beside him, put my face close to his mouth, nearly passing out from his fetid breath and relief that I could still feel it underneath my nostrils. But he was not moving and not responding to his name at all.

"Wait here, mate," I said, "just wait here."

I ran back to the house and saw Will leaning over the fence, nodding at my words, telling me to call Miranda Tate, a retired vet who lived on Willow, while he would go to Barney and wait with him.

"The number's on your fridge," he yelled, passing me as I ran into the house.

I rang Miranda's number and tried to stay calm as I answered her questions.

Was he breathing? Yes, I thought so. Did I think it was a fit? No, I told her, he just keeled over on the spot.

Keep him cool, she said, and try to get some water into him. She would come over as soon as possible; in the meantime, just get him some water and wait.

I filled an old milk carton with water and ran back to the dunes where Barney was sitting bolt upright, Will's arm flung over his back.

"You gave us a scare, mate," Will was saying, while Barney

stared, his eyes still and vacant. "Look, here's Lulu with some water for you."

Later, when we had got him home and into the nest of a bed I had made for him, Miranda arrived.

"I don't usually do house calls this late in the day"—she smiled at me—"but Barney's an exception."

He had fainted, Miranda said, maybe from the heat, maybe from exhaustion—"syncope," she had said, happened to a lot of dogs Barney's age and size, mot likely not serious, but it was probably a good idea to have a follow-up examination on the mainland, where they could run an MRI and check his blood pressure.

"You might want to check Lulu's too," Will said, looking at me.

Now we lay on either side of the luxury Snoozy Paws bed I'd bought him when we'd first arrived on Willow and which he had never, of course, slept in.

The room grew darker and quieter until Will said, "Are you going to stay here all night?"

I nodded across at him.

"I'll stay with you—in case anything happens."

I nodded again.

"It'll be like camping."

I smiled. "Sort of."

"With a great big bear between us."

I got us some pillows and sheets and we settled down for the night, our hands meeting across Barney's heaving chest.

It felt lovely, his fingers looped through mine, lovely and warm and safe.

But more than that, I thought, my eyes finally closing, as I heard Will's soft snores, echoed by Barney's thunderous ones, it felt right.

The day after Barney's collapse, I went to find Will in the boat shed—cleaned out, freshly painted canoes stacked on rails like layers of a cake, where he was sitting cross-legged on the floor, trying to untangle a roll of recalcitrant fishing line.

"Hello," I said. "That looks complicated."

"Not really." Will smiled. "You just have to have the patience of a saint—how's our boy?"

"He tried to eat the umbrella stand this morning, so I guess he's back to normal."

"He gave us quite the fright, didn't he?"

"He did," I said, remembering those chocolate eyes falling into nowhere. "Anyway, I wanted to thank you for helping out, Will, you were great."

"No problem."

"I didn't even ask you what you wanted when I came running through the gate like a madwoman. Was it about the B and B or just a social visit?"

"Both."

I waited.

"Lulu," he said, putting down the tangled knot, "I've been thinking about what you and Andrew want me to do here, and I'm pretty keen, but I don't reckon we should make it official until we sort out everything that's not going on between us."

I smiled at his choice of words.

"So," he said, "I wanted to let you know that if I come on board here, you know, become the water sports captain or whatever it is, I'm happy to leave it at that."

My heart fell just a whisker, taking my shoulders with it.

"I get it, Lulu, I do—you've got a lot to sort out in your head, getting this place up and running for one thing, so I wanted to tell you that I'm not about to go jumping out of the boat in the middle of the night and dripping water all over your doormat."

Tell him, I thought to myself, *tell him right now that's exactly*

what you do want him to do. Tell him you've been dreaming about
that exact scenario in glorious, dripping-wet Technicolor most
nights.

"Thank goodness for that," I managed. "I was so worried about you catching your death out there."

He laughed and came to stand beside me.

"It's okay, Lulu," he said. "We don't have to jump in either, we'll just tread water."

I nodded at him and turned to head back into the house.

"For now," his voice said behind me.

Barney was lying in his bed beneath the stairs, thoughtfully chewing on his own paw when I went back inside.

"How are you, Barney boy? How's my little Barnsterooni?" I said, burying my face in his, and holding his ridiculously floppy ears.

"Now that really is pathetic," Julia said from the doorway. "Hope you don't mind me barging in. I called out but you didn't answer, so I just followed the cooing noises."

She put down the tray she was carrying and got down on her knees beside Barney.

"Hello, how's my little soldier? How's my big, brave boy? Julia's brought you some biscuits, hasn't she? Biscuits for her big, brave soldier."

"Who's pathetic?" I said.

Julia smiled. "I'm allowed, because I'm his aunt."

"Want a cup of tea?"

"Yes, thank you, a cup of tea for me and some biscuits for you, Barney, your favorite, I made them especially, cinnamon apple snaps."

I rolled my eyes at her and went into the kitchen, where she followed a few moments later, her arms crossed.

"So, what's going on with you and Will Barton?"

"Excuse me?"

"Oh don't 'Excuse me,' Tallulah de Longland, you heard me," Julia said, and I noticed her long, gray hair escaping its tortoiseshell clip at the back.

"Nothing."

"Nothing? Doesn't feel like nothing in those meetings we've been having, feels more like watching one of those David Attenborough shows on mating."

"Julia!"

"Well, it does. I told Boris it's like watching two wild bobcats circling each other."

"We're not," I said. "We're not at all like that, anyway, we're not jumping into anything—we're treading water."

She shook her head and went out to give Barney his cinnamon snaps, so she did not hear me add "for now."

After Julia went home, leaving a bone for Barney from Lyle and Denise at the post office, the island tom-toms having carried news of Barney's collapse before he'd even hit the ground, the phone rang.

"Good morning, Barney's B and B, how may I help you?" I practiced, feeling slightly ridiculous. Andrew had said it would be a good idea for me to start answering the phone this way, and I was working on my proprietor's voice, aiming for professional and warm at the same time, somewhere between a newsreader and a talk show host.

"Tallulah, this is Linda Mayberry. Andrew Lyons gave me your number."

"Oh, hi, Linda, thanks for calling."

"No need to thank me," she said crisply. "There's not a lot I can do for your friend, I'm sorry to say—I'm a great admirer of Frank Andrews's work."

"I see," I stumbled, not expecting this. I had been, I realized, expecting her to call and say, "It's all sorted out," because Andrew had asked her to.

"When you say not a lot?"

"I mean not a lot. I've had a pretty good look at the council's position, I've been to the property and had a good look around, and checked the survey lines, I've even attempted to see if I could get the tree house itself exempted from six of the codes as a work of art, rather than a construction, but unfortunately because it's outside, it's subject to four clauses that preclude me from taking that line, so you're in for a bit of a long haul."

"I see."

"You probably don't, so I've written a full report for you to show Mr. Andrews—of course if he really wants to go the whole hog with this, I'd be delighted to represent him."

"No," I said, "I don't think he'll want all that fuss—he hates fuss—but leave it with me. I'm actually seeing him today, so we can talk about it then."

"Well, he has about two weeks left to lodge his objection."

"Right," I said, "two weeks—thank you."

"Tallulah," she added, "one thing I do know is that if you were to make your objection very long, and very hard to understand, and with lots of legal jargon, which I'm happy to provide free of charge, then we could buy ourselves a fair bit of time, during which I'm happy to keep squirreling around."

Andrew was right; Linda Mayberry was a good egg.

Two weeks; there wasn't much chance of Frank being ready in that time, but he was coming to Willow that afternoon with my family, so at least we could talk about it.

I wanted to save Frank's tree house; it was the least I could do for him, but there was something else I wanted to hold on to as well.

There, in those branches, where the wind whispered and the opossums scurried, two little girls played untouched by time and all that went with it.

Up there, beneath Frank's moon and stars, Annabelle and I

were safe, I thought, caught in time within Frank's American Oregon walls, where no one, least of all the future, could catch us.

I was so happy Frank had said yes to my invitation, and had spent most of the morning searching the island for the perfect stem of frangipanis not to burn off for him.

They arrived late in the afternoon. "We're here, Lulu," Harry's voice called, somewhere in the middle of Barney's barking.

"Hi, Louie-Pooey," my brothers chorused, bigger, if that were humanly possible, than the last time they were there.

"Oh, Lulu, you've done wonders." Rose, in Phoebe, smiling at the door.

"Lulu—it's delightful, a man could get used to this." Frank, in his Bonds singlet and baggy shorts I would swear were welded to his legs, was running his artist's eye over the corners of the WIASA.

Over the next few days, the house quivered again with the sounds of my family, and Frank meshed with the Willowers, Rose chatting to Julia, over like a shot when she'd heard them coming up the lane, Frank, Harry, and Boris, hands on their chins as they went through each room, Frank down on his knees running his hands over the slate, Harry up a ladder, checking the gutters, Will and my brothers in and out of the sheds, it seemed, all day long.

I wandered in and out of their conversations and watched them gathered around the enormous kitchen table, filling its spaces, just like Duncan had hoped.

Late one afternoon, I was upstairs rearranging some pictures in the hallway when I heard Rose and Julia chatting together in the third bedroom.

"What a lovely dress, Rose."

"Thank you, it's an oldie but a goody, as they say."

"Like us."

"That's right, Julia, exactly like us."

They were hanging the curtains Julia had brought over, Rose

admiring the way they fell, Julia confessing that Boris, in fact, had done most of the work.

"He doesn't like people to know," Julia said, "but he's an excellent seamstress."

"Really? Do you think he'd make me some new dresses? There's nothing I like in the shops, and I haven't got the patience anymore to sew myself."

"I can ask him, although I think the dresses you have are lovely, Rose, at least all the ones I've seen are."

"Well, you've probably seen them all; I've been wearing variations of the same frocks for years, Julia, and it's well and truly time for an overhaul, something completely different."

My ears pricked up. Was Rose really thinking about bringing some brand-new members into the chorus line?

If she was, it was truly astoundible.

"I'll ask him," Julia was saying. "I think he might be pleased. He had a shop once, you know, in Melbourne, before we met."

"A dress shop?"

"Mmm-hmm, just with his own designs."

"What happened?"

"He told me he never sold enough dresses to make any money, and his father hated him having it. In the end I think he just gave up."

"What was it called?"

"The House of Boris."

One of the things I loved most about my mother at that moment was that she didn't laugh.

~

"So," I said to Rose later, "I heard the House of Boris might be back in business."

"Heard or overheard?"

"All right, overheard."

Rose smiled.

"Well, now that I am going to be a businesswoman, I thought I'd better start dressing like one."

"I'll tell Boris to get out the shoulder pads."

We were setting the table for dinner, and I knew the next time so many faces would be gathered around it, I would not know any of them. Strangers—guests, I told myself firmly, guests who would come and love the WIASA's creaky old bones as much as I did.

Watching everyone at dinner that night, laughing at one of Sam's ridiculous impressions, Rose's face tinged to match her name, Will talking to Frank with a pen sticking out from behind one ear, Julia curled like a cat around Boris—I realized I was button-undone happy.

It had been one of Duncan's sayings, and I thought that of all the absent guests that night, of all the people who might once have been there but were not, it was Duncan's absent place at the table that seemed the emptiest.

Duncan had said button-undone happy was when for one moment everything was exactly as it should be. "You've gone to work and it's all gone smoothly, none of the bastards have been able to get to you, you go home and the traffic's not like a bloody blocked artery, and you have dinner and the person sitting across from you is the exact person you want sitting across from you, and the food is good and the wine is better, and you're having a cigar and you reach down to undo the first button of your jeans and let it all hang out.

"That," I heard Duncan say, "right there, that's it, that's button-undone happy."

That was how I felt that night, looking at the people gathered at my table.

It had been a long time.

Frank was throwing a ball to Barney in the garden early the next morning when I finally got the chance to tell him about Linda Mayberry's assessment of the tree house's chances of survival.

"Oh," he said, "that's bad news, should have gotten a wriggle on about it earlier."

"We've still got a couple of weeks. I need to stay here for a few days but I could come over after that and we could write the objection together, and I could drop it into council on my way back."

"Do you think it would do any good?"

"I think if we made it really, really long and really, really complicated, we could at least stall 'em," I answered, echoing Linda's words.

"That's my girl," he said, which I thought was very generous of him, considering his real girl was miles away, because of me.

"Lulu?"

"Yes."

"I'd like you to have Annie over to the island sometime."

"Oh, well, I don't know, Frank, I don't know if she would want to come. I'm sure I'm not her favorite person in the world."

"You're one of them," he answered.

"I don't think so, I don't really see how I could be," I said, remembering Annie that night on television staring out of the screen with her raccoon-ringed eyes, her mouth dripping crimson.

"You are, Lulu—the thing is, I think you've forgotten."

"Forgotten?"

"You've forgotten Annie—the best of her."

That afternoon, taking Barney for a walk on the beach, I thought about Annie and tried to remember. Annie, who seemed to come and go from that big house like some exotic tenant, filling it with her noise when she was there, shrouding it in silence when she wasn't; Annie who never remembered to help Annabelle with her homework, get her uniform ready; Annie whose signature both Annabelle and I had perfected so we could sign all the school forms she had forgotten so Annabelle could go on school excursions carrying the lunch box my mother had packed for her.

Annie who had left, just "upped and gone," the other mothers at school had whispered, half-shocked, wholly thrilled; Annie who had sent her daughter postcards that never said "Wish you were here," because she didn't.

But . . .

How many Doris days and nights had I slept under her roof, Annie dragging the camp bed out and putting it beside Annabelle's? How many times had I walked in with my school hat pulled down so low you could not see my eyes and Annie had tipped it back and said, "There, don't ever be afraid to show your face, Lulu"? How many times had Annie quietly been there for me, no questions asked, when my own mother wasn't?

With a shock, I realized that in her own way Annie Andrews had been as much of a mother to me as Rose had been to Annabelle, neither woman conventional but both filling the gaps the other left when they needed to.

chapter twenty-eight

W e all walked down to the boat together, Boris and Julia already waiting there to say good-bye, Boris handing my mother a folder—designs, I guessed, from the House of Boris—and I wondered if my mother would christen this new wardrobe. I decided that I would quite like her to have a Lily if she did.

Sam and Mattie raced into the water, yelping like overgrown puppies and ignoring Rose's futile instruction to two grown men not to get their clothes wet. Harry came and stood beside me, watching out for Will at the edge of the water.

"Well, love," he said, "thanks for a great few days, and call me if you need anything—that hot water system's a real bugger, but I think I've got it sorted. Rose will be over in a couple of weeks so I could come over with her then, if you like, check to see it's working properly."

"I assumed you would be coming with her anyway, Harry."

"No," he said, watching Rose giving up on the boys and hitching up her skirt to join them, Lauren's hem dragging through the water, "she says she'd quite like to come by herself."

"How do you feel about that?"

He looked at me, scratched at the stubble on his chin. "Like I did taking you to your first day of school."

"How was that?"

"Wanting to turn around and take you to work with me, where I could keep an eye on you."

I hooked my arm through his. "I'll look after her."

"I know, love. I thought I might take a few days off myself, go camping."

"Camping?"

"I used to do it quite a bit, on weekends, over the holidays, when I was a young fella."

I looked at him: Harry who used to camp a lot, who probably used to do a lot of things, before Rose came along and he raised a family with her and took the plumbing industry to new depths of excellence. Harry who, having taken care of his wife for so long, would not quite know what to do with himself when she no longer needed him to.

"Do you have a tent?"

"Somewhere in the shed, I think—just a one-man."

Harry went to join the others down on the beach, and I thought it had been a very, very long time since he had been that.

Just the one man.

Rose lingered for a moment and gave me a hug.

"We had a marvelous time, Lulu; I hope we weren't too much for you."

"No," I said, "you were a great help. I wish it had been longer."

"Well, I'll be back soon to set up the kitchen with you and to bring over some fabrics for Boris."

I giggled, thinking of Boris hunched over the Elna in his back room, furtively running up frocks for Rose and hoping that Deano and Mick from the bowls club wouldn't catch him.

A thought struck me.

"Rose," I said, "are you going to name them?"

"The dresses? Well, I thought I would; don't want them feeling left out."

"Any ideas?"

"I thought perhaps Romy and Charlotte, or I was thinking I should call one of them Julia. . . ."

"I thought Lily."

"Lily?"

I wanted my mother to have a lily—I liked the way they kept themselves inside, wrapping their petals around their throats and not unfolding their bell-shaped beauty until they were good and ready.

"I think it would suit you," I said.

"All right, darling," she said. "I promise I'll name one of them Lily."

chapter twenty-nine

I spent the next couple of days constantly on the phone to the Willow Island council, checking I had met every compliance order to open Barney's B and B, sorting out details like fire escapes and safety procedures, maximum number of tenants, procedural conditions for the "serving of food in a public place." I didn't tell them about Rose's biscuits—I wasn't about to fill out another two hundred forms for jam drops. No, I decided, Rose's biscuits would just have to be contraband, smuggled over from the mainland and doled out to darting-eyed guests under the cover of darkness.

I was exhausted as I lounged on the couch with Barney, too tired to even begin to try and move Barney's deadweight lying across my feet. I lay there, reading a book of Duncan's, watching the text bob up and down, when the phone rang.

"You answer it, Barney, go on, you lazy sod," I said, flexing my feet underneath him.

He grunted.

"You're right, we'll let it ring."

I heard my own high-pitched, too-hearty voice on the machine.

"Hello, you've called Barney's Bed and Breakfast," I squeaked—Andrew's idea, never too early to advertise, he'd said. "Please leave your name and number and we'll get back to you." Andrew had wanted me to say, "And one of our reservation staff will return your call," but I had balked, saying, "It's not the bloody Hilton."

My father's voice came through. "This is Harry de Longland, leaving a message for Lulu de Longland . . ."

"Harry"—I jumped up and snatched the phone—"what are you doing calling in the middle of *Parky*?"

Harry, Rose, and Michael Parkinson had a three-way date every Saturday night—Rose loved Parky, she said he had a face you could abseil off.

"Harry?"

He didn't answer.

Barney left the couch and pressed his body against me.

"Harry?"

He made a noise into the phone.

"On a scale of one to ten?"

My mother rustled past me.

"Harry, on a scale of one to ten?"

She put her floured hands up to her face.

"Harry," I said again, "on a scale of one to ten?"

She kissed me, butterfly wing against my ear.

"Ten, love."

She was slipping behind the kitchen door.

Disapanishing.

Rose.

She was outside my window then, in bare feet.

I saw the wind lifting Grace's skirt as she walked toward the dunes, and I started to run to her with Barney as my shadow.

She was walking straight toward the water, and she knew I was behind her, because she kept looking back at me over her shoulder when I shouted her name.

I ran all the way to her and the water was not cold at all, but warm as the eugaries began their dance.

They were tumbling back into the ocean, and Grace's skirt was getting wet as she followed them.

I shouted at them that she didn't know the steps, that she had only just begun to dance.

Then Rose turned and leaned in to me, and put her lips to mine.

"There is no such thing as afar," she whispered.

Grace and Alexis and Betty and Phoebe and Greta and Madeleine and Lauren and Kitty and Audrey and Constance put their arms around one another, smiled up at me, and bowed deep and low.

Rose.

My mother.

chapter thirty

There was something soft and warm around my neck, and someone's hand was moving up and down the small of my back quickly,
like they were trying to start a fire.

"Come on, Lulu"—Julia, in her dressing gown—"we need to
go inside now."

I nodded at her, wondering why she was outside. *She should
be home*, I thought, *with Boris, helping him with Rose's dresses.*

"It's the shock," someone said in a low voice, and I wanted to
tell them to go away but my own voice had slipped down deep
inside the sand, gathered itself there in a cool, dark place where,
I imagined, it would hold its breath for six months.

"We need to get her inside."

"Stop talking as if she can't hear you."

"Who found her?"

"Lyle Wilkins—he could hear Barney barking from his
house."

Will sat beside me.

"Lulu," he said, "I'm going to pick you up, all right? I'm just
going to put my arms around you and pick you up, like this."

I felt him lean down into me, take up my arms, and loop
them around his neck.

"You don't have to do anything," he said, "but hang on."

I nodded at him, still mute.

"Sweetheart," Simone said, at the boat ramp, standing beside Stella.

"Lulu," Stella said, and I saw she was crying.

"Stop it, Stella," I heard Simone hiss at her as they put my bags in the boot.

"I can't," Stella said, "I can't."

"It doesn't matter," I told them, looking out the window at the nothing, all the way home to Harry's.

Left onto Swan Terrace, right onto Plantation Street, past the bus stop and some ginger-haired girls sucking on ice blocks, looking at my face through the window. One of them poked her tongue out, stretching it out like a purple lizard in the sun, and I poked mine back halfheartedly at her. Past Mrs. Delaney's front blinds, closed like winks against the sun. Simone and Stella in the front, me in the back with Barney, his head in my lap, my hands around his collar.

I waited, looking for the sign.

DE LONGLAND PLUMBERS—PLUMBING THE DEPTHS OF EXCEL-LENCE.

"We'll walk you into the house," Simone said, pulling into the driveway.

"No, thank you."

"Lulu," she said, "I think you should let us come in with you."

"It's all right," I told her, getting out of the car. "I know the way."

I waited until I was sure they had gone before I walked up the path, and called out "Harry," and went out to the back garden, where I knew he would be.

"Hello, love," Harry said, looking at me with old and startled eyes from the garden swing. "Good trip over?"

I climbed all the way into him and we rocked back and forth, together.

It was an accident.

Nothing more than an accident, with no one to blame, no blood on anyone's hands, least of all Rose's, holding on to the wheel of her station wagon, on her way in Greta to the shops to get dinner. The other driver had been lost, distracted, Rose trying to get out of the way, too late, hitting the pole, all over that quickly.

"She wouldn't have felt anything," the policewoman told Harry, Mattie, Sam, and me, sitting across from us on the couch and eating Rose's biscuits. "When things like this happen so quickly, it's very comforting, I think, to know that the person involved didn't feel anything—it's so quick, you see," she continued.

Harry and I looked at each other and the woman who didn't see anything at all, because she didn't know Rose, did not know that Rose felt everything.

Later that night, I went to say good night to Mattie and Sam, Barney padding behind me like a shadow.

They were both stretched out in their childhood beds, much too small for them now, of course.

"I'm going to sleep," I said. "Do you need anything?"

"Can Barney stay with us?" Mattie asked.

"Of course—up, Barney," I told him, patting Mattie's bed.

I sat down at the end of Sam's, and he flung his feet over my lap.

We were tumbling back in time in this room, with its fading rocket wallpaper and glow-in-the-dark stickers still clinging to the ceiling.

I had sat at the end of these beds so many nights, the three of

us and Zac McCain and his very large brain. I would tell stories
until Mattie pulled his quilt up to his chin, and Sam drew his feet
up to his knees, then quietly reach over to switch off the lights,
and leave them to their dreaming.

Even though they were far closer to men than boys, I began
to tell stories again now, grown-up versions of Zac McCain. I told
them about the plans for the WIASA, how I'd like them to help
out Will during their uni holidays, repairing and repainting all
the water sports gear, and, if enough guests came, taking small
groups on guided tours down the river.

I talked into the night, until Mattie pulled his quilt to his
chin, his legs so long it left his feet exposed beneath it. I talked
until Sam drew his feet up to his knees, and I heard them both
relax in the darkness, Mattie's grunts eventually joined by Sam's
deep breaths.

I stood up to turn off their lamps, and Barney lifted his head.

"Stay," I told him, and he settled back down, Mattie's leg
thrown over the arch of his back.

Then I went downstairs to check on Harry.

"The boys are asleep."

"Thanks, Lulu."

"It's all right."

"I'm sorry, love, I just can't seem to help them at the moment."

Harry in his dressing gown, his reading glasses in his pocket.

"You'll lose those, you know," I said automatically, in my
mother's voice.

Rose was always trying to mend the holes in his gown's pockets, but Harry wouldn't let her, dangling his fingers out of the
bottom and saying, "Leave it, I like them the way they are."

Harry pushed his fingers through and waggled them at me.

"Hello, Rosey-girl," he said, and I knew my father was undone.

I waggled my fingers back at him anyway.

"Have you done anything," Father Duffy asked the next day, "about the arrangements?"

Harry looked out the window, and I answered for both of us.

"No, we've just been here at home, with Mattie and Sam."

Father Duffy nodded his head and looked at Harry.

"It isn't easy," he said. "It's never easy, that's why I've come, to help, if you need it."

Rose had always liked Joe Duffy, I remembered, said he liked a laugh and didn't mind if you sometimes didn't laugh with him.

"We need it," I told him, "we seem to have no idea what to do."

"I do," Father Duffy replied. "Rose told me."

Rose's ashes were scattered near the lake where she'd once dived naked and wonderful and had told Harry to do the same.

"It seems so far away," he had fretted. "It doesn't seem right she's not near us."

But Rose had left instructions about where she wanted to be, who she wanted to wear—Alexis, who would never go anywhere quietly—what she wanted to hear: "No ballads," she had written firmly, then in capitals: "NO ORGAN MUSIC WHATSO-EVER."

So we said our good-byes to Rose in the church in the town where she had grown up under the watchful eyes of the two sisters, Audrey and Constance.

"Why do you think your mum wanted the service here?" Simone asked me afterward, "instead of Saint Rita's?"

I wasn't entirely sure, but I told her what I thought, that Rose had wanted to leave the earth from the first place she'd felt safe on it.

~

We had a morning tea in the hall next to the church, everyone "bringing a plate," mostly, I noticed, of biscuits and slices made from Rose's recipes, but none of them tasting quite the same.

When the last person had left—Mrs. Delaney in bright yellow, "I loved your mother, you know, Lulu, so brave"—Harry and I walked slowly back to his truck, Harry's feet dragging, hating to leave Rose behind. We got into the cabin, and Harry started the engine, his eyes darting to the rearview mirror.

I leaned into him from across my seat.

"There's no such thing as afar," I told him.

~

I did not cry for Rose.

There was so much to do, calls to answer and letters to write, people to thank, dinners to cook, and words to find to tell people with the question half-open on their lips that no, it was just an accident.

I waited until about a fortnight after the funeral, until there were no more lasagnas left on our doorstep, or letters to answer, or calls to make, and then I went into my mother's kitchen.

"Righto, Rose," I said, "let's bake our way to goodness."

I found one of Rose's exercise books on the shelf and opened it on the bench in front of me. *Basic Butter Cake* in Rose's big childish writing—perfect. I wasn't about to attempt anything complicated.

Preheat oven to 180 degrees.

Cream 250 g butter, 1 cup caster sugar, 2 teaspoons vanilla essence in bowl.

Add three eggs—one at a time—with two and half cups SR flour and 1/2 cup milk, pour in slowly.

I began to add the ingredients in, hearing Rose's voice in my ear, and feeling her hand slide over mine holding the wooden spoon.

"Don't beat it to death, now," she said.

I remembered at the last minute to throw in some sultanas. "Don't skimp, Lulu," I heard her say, so I threw in another handful and poured the mixture into one of the battered old tins she had always refused to throw out. I laughed a little, remembering Harry trying to sell her on the idea of buying a new set of baking tins. "They've got Teflon ones now, Rosey-girl," he'd said. "Nothing sticks to them." Rose had looked up at him from the table where she had been rolling out piecrust pastry. "What's the point of that?" She'd smiled at him.

I put the cake in the oven, then sat down at my mother's table and waited for it to rise. Then, when it was done, when I had pushed the skewer in and it had come out clean, just as she had taught me, and the kitchen was filled with the sweet aroma of Rose's last cake, I took it out and turned it onto a cake rack, taking care not to break it.

I sat back and considered it.

Then I cried for my mother.

~

"Lulu."

I looked up to the kitchen doorway, startled to see Annie Andrews standing there.

"Lulu," she said again, Annie's voice so quiet, Annie herself so still that I had not heard her knock, not one jangled hint of her necklaces and bangles.

"I've brought you something," she said, walking over to place a book in my hands.

I stared at it, knowing it instantly, knowing the last time I had touched it I had placed it high in a tree house for her daughter's hands to find.

Annabelle had, Annie told me, kept it with her all those years, taking it with her wherever she and Josh traveled, wrapping it in plastic in places where the humidity could eat away at it, packing it in her carry-on luggage at airports, once, Annie said, having a stand-up screaming fight with an official in Thailand who'd said the made-up words were obviously some sort of code and tried to confiscate it.

Now she had sent it back to me.

"It arrived today, Lulu," Annie said. "I came to bring it to you. Annabelle says it's very important you have it."

She leaned down and kissed me, enveloping me in sandal-wood, and placed the book on my lap, where a striped bookmark held the page Annabelle meant for me to open.

"I'll let myself out," Annie was saying. "I'm staying at the old house—at Frank's—if you need me."

I heard the click of the front gate, and Annie's car start up on the street, taking her back to her own past as I stared at my own.

Opening the book at the page Annabelle had marked, I saw my own hand, big, flowery letters.

Emergensis: emergency/crisis—A situation so direbolical, either party must attend forthwith.

Beside it, Annabelle had written in her own loopy hand, *On my way.*

Annabelle.

On her way.

chapter thirty-one

I saw their shadows through the stained glass of the front door.

Josh and Annabelle.

I hadn't expected them both; Annabelle had written *On my way*, not *On our way*, but as I came down the stairs to open the door, I knew it was right the three of us should do this together.

Say good-bye.

To Rose, of course, but also to those initials engraved beneath her dining room table, entwined around each other for far too long.

"Tallulah," Annabelle said when I opened the door, "we're so sorry about Rose," and I half stepped, half fell into her arms.

Then Josh's arms circled around both of us, and as strange as it undoubtedly was, it didn't feel strange at all.

"Is it too early to say, 'Just like old times'?" he asked.

"*Josh*," Annabelle said, breaking away from his embrace. "I cannot believe you would say that right now—I'm really sorry, Tallulah, he's an idiot."

But I was laughing, probably more than a little hysterical at seeing them, at Josh saying the one thing that hovered in the air between us, at Rose dying, at Duncan dying, of moving all the way to an island to get away from my own reflection, at all the things that had happened to us since we spread our towels out under the same summer sky.

"I'm sorry," I said, biting my lip. "I don't know why I'm laughing, it's not funny."

Annabelle looked at me with her cat-green eyes.

"Well, maybe it's a little bit funny." She smiled. "You know, in an absopletely inappropriate way."

I smiled back at her and thought there was still no other person in the world who understood me like Annabelle Andrews did.

We went inside to sit and drink tea at Rose's dining table — Josh and Annabelle, I was pleased to see, holding hands across it.

We spoke for a long time about Rose, her cakes and her dresses, her Sunday roasts — "Legendary," Josh sighed — and how much, despite her unconventionality, or maybe because of it, we had all loved her.

"The best," said Josh, and in the silence that followed I thought about what my mother would want me to say, right at that moment.

Rip the Band-Aid off, Lulu.

"I'm sorry, Annabelle," I said, and the words I had practiced so many times came out naturally, as if it was the first time I had ever uttered them, maybe because I was finally saying them to the person they were meant for. "I am truly sorry for what I did to you on your wedding day. I have spent every day since hating myself for it, and I would do anything to take it back."

"So would I," Annabelle answered steadily, "but you're not the only one who should apologize. I did the exact same thing, and I could say that we were just kids and that it didn't matter as much, but it did." She met my eyes and held them. "I know it did, Tallulah."

I began to cry, her words releasing me, finally, from the girl by the river.

Josh stood up and put his hands on the back of his chair, rocking it back and forth.

"Well, obviously the person here who should really be doing

the apologizing is me," he began, "I'm a . . ." He stopped rocking, searching for the words.

"Dickhead?" offered Annabelle, as Josh plowed on.

"I'm a, well, I'm what you might call a crack slipper," he said finally, while I stared at him, incredulous. "There're some people," he continued, "who sort of go through life always looking for a place to park their bike and when they find it, they feel, well, amazed, really, that someone has let them park it, you see."

"Josh," Annabelle interrupted, "I have no idea what you're talking about."

But I did, the ghost of Duncan McAllister hovering in Rose's kitchen.

"It's all right, Josh," I said. "More tea, vicar?"

Later, when they had gone home to the River House, I lay in bed and thought about the three of us. "The bemusement triangle," Annabelle had said when the tea had been replaced by wine and the tears—mostly Josh's, still going on about his push-bike—by laughter.

People, I thought, would be bemused by us.

"How could she?" they would say of Annabelle, staying married to Josh; of me, the Juniper Bay Wedding Shagger; and of the three of us, somehow muddling through that night as the sky grew lighter to emerge as friends.

But some people, people who had a big first love, would understand—and I'd had two.

They had both been my first loves, and that night I let them go, finally realizing that your first love, no matter how big it may have been, wasn't necessarily your true one.

~

A week after Josh and Annabelle's visit, another silhouette appeared behind the stained glass of my front door, one that Barney and I nearly fell over each other on the way down the stairs trying to get to first.

I flung open the door to Will Barton, a bunch of island daisies in his hands.

"I told you I'd just turn up on your doorstep one day." He smiled, adding, "At least I'm not dripping wet."

Tell him, I said to myself, tell him now, Lulu.

A voice, not my own, but one belonging to some strange, high-pitched woman came out. "I wouldn't mind if you were," I squeaked, then immediately felt foolish.

Oh no, I thought, did that sound cheesy? What if he's just here to offer a shoulder to cry on? Should you even be thinking about stuff like that at a time like this? What is wrong with you, Tallulah?

But Will was laughing, reaching down to pat Barney's bullet-head, and simultaneously leaning in to kiss my mouth, his hand tucked beneath my chin.

We kissed for a long time, long enough for Barney to chomp all the way through the daisies, long enough for the whole street to whisper to each other that it looked like the de Longland girl had a new boyfriend, and long enough for me to know that I had traveled all the way to an island to find myself home.

I smiled at Will.

"You're very forward, Mr. Barton," I said, "for a business partner."

"Is that how you see me," Will murmured, his mouth close to my ear, "as your water sports director?"

I heard it, the quiver of doubt in his voice, and who could blame him? I had spent most of our time together on Willow ducking and weaving his every move.

"Something like that," I said, taking his hand and, leading him up to my room, diving in.

Later that afternoon, I lay with my head tucked under his arm, and he turned his head to smile at me.

"Thank goodness for that, Tallulah de Longland," he said. "I was sick of treading water."

"You have no idea," I told him.

epilogue

They were moving like mercury through the shadows, silvery silhouettes forming and reforming in clusters under the branches.

In the half-light, I began to make out their faces, the gang, as Duncan would say, all here six months after Rose's death, gathered beneath Frank's tree house.

Annie and Frank, Fergus, Christa, Josh and Annabelle, Simone, Stella and Billy, Mattie, Sam, even Ben, with Monica Golliana tucked under his arm.

"I hope it's all right that I am joining in," she said when she met me, and I liked her instantly, even if she did look unnecessarily pretty for this time of the morning.

The Willowers were there too, Julia and Boris, Will trying to keep control of Barney, who was giddy with the heady collision of old and new smells.

Annie had said we had to get there before the bulldozers did — "to take the bastards by surprise" — and so there we all were, wearing the shocked, wan expressions of the half-asleep.

"I may be a drunk old hippie," Annie had said at one of the meetings she had called at the River House, "but if it's one thing we drunk old hippies know how to do, it's how to stage a protest, so listen and learn, people, particularly you, Lulu, no wetting your pants when the policemen come."

I watched as Maxine Mathers picked her way with a camera crew down the path, and felt Simone bristle beside me.

"Remember"—I grinned at her in the semidarkness—"we're making love, not war."

Annie, of all people, had invited Maxine, given her this exclusive on the various warring branches of Frank Andrews's family banding together to save his tree house.

"We want maximum publicity," Annie had continued, "and that means, whether we like it or not, Maxine Mathers."

Annabelle had looked across at me and rolled her eyes, and she was twelve years old again, making faces at her mother for putting an unboiled egg in her lunch.

Annabelle and Josh were staying this time for a little while, to curate Frank's work, bits and pieces of art strewn throughout the River House, paintings and etchings and pastels stuffed in drawers and at the back of cupboards, and in the boot of his car.

Annie was helping too, she and Frank once more entwined together at the River House, Frank, I knew from personal experience, well acquainted with the art of forgiveness. It was during one of Annie's forays through the house for more pieces of Frank's work that she'd come across the council's final notice for the demolition of the tree house. Apparently she'd simply shaken her head and said, "No, I don't think so."

Then all of us had been caught up in Annie's kaleidoscope, a jumble of phone calls and meetings, with Annie at the center, not drinking at all now but barking out orders with a joint dangling from her dark-plum lips.

Somewhere in the middle of it, Ben rang to ask, "Can we come? I'd like to, Lulu," and Fergus strolled in saying, "So, what are we doing?" as if nothing had ever happened.

The Willowers arrived the day before the protest, Julia in a T-shirt and beach shorts, tanned legs and a bucket hat on her head, Boris in a button-up shirt and ironed trousers—"I don't know what to wear to a protest," he said.

The night before, I'd stayed at the River House, where Annie had called a last meeting, outlining what time to gather beneath the tree, what to wear, how to behave when the bull-dozers, then the cops, came: "Don't be rude," she'd said, "just stand your ground." She'd taught us to how to link our arms so they were hard to dislodge from one another. In the breaking dawn light, I heard a hum from the far end of the street and I knew it had begun.

"All right," said Annie, "link arms." I felt a little thrill rush through me.

Maxine Mathers straightened her shoulders and used a small compact to apply lipstick, and everyone was getting into position, except not everyone was there.

I looked around the tree and thought of Duncan, of how much he would have loved this, how he would have dug out a shirt that read *Bread Not Bombs* and pretended for the entire morning he had been a student radical in the seventies, when really he was hosting fondue parties in a full-length silk kaftan.

"Marvelous," I heard him boom at me from somewhere in the branches, "bloody marvelous, Lulu."

And Rose.

Rose should have been there, Rose who would have been so happy to see Annabelle and me together again with no prickles against our skin, who would have said to Josh, "You need some meat on those bones, come for roast this Sunday"; Rose who would have been handing out biscuits still warm in our palms.

But Rose was not there—and neither, I realized in a flash of panic, was Harry.

I unhooked my arm from Annabelle's.

"What is it?" she asked.

"Harry," I told her.

Annabelle stepped out of the circle, her eyes darting around it. She turned to me and held both of my hands in hers.

"It will be all right, Tallulah," she said. "He'll be here, and we won't start without him."

We both looked down the road to where the bulldozer's lights were bobbing up and down, and I started to worry, my breath little white puffs of anxiety in the air.

Where was Harry? Yesterday he'd said he would not miss this "for all the rice in China," and now he was not there, and I felt flutters of panic rising inside my chest.

I trained my eyes on the road, willing Harry to appear; then, as a bulldozer lumbered up the street, I saw a car with a smaller set of headlights overtaking it, and as it got closer I made out DE LONGLAND PLUMBERS emblazoned down its side, and underneath it, PLUMBING THE DEPTHS OF EXCELLENCE.

Harry swung the ute into the River House's long driveway and got out. "Sorry I'm late," he called walking toward the tree, slowing his pace as his eyes traveled to the exquisite flowers it bore.

From the mango tree's branches fluttered Grace, Audrey, Phoebe, Betty, Madeleine, Lauren, Constance, and Kitty, swaying like geishas in the breeze.

There was Greta's buttercup yellow, Betty's blue and white spots, Madeleine's reds and Kitty's lime greens, all of Rose's dresses there because she couldn't be.

"Oh, love," Harry said.

"Annabelle and I hung them last night," I told him. "Do you like it?'"

I had been worried it might be too much for him, so much of Rose to take in all at once.

"It's perfect, Lulu," he said. "Thank you."

Harry stood gazing at the dresses, his eyes taking in every one, until they came to rest on a new addition to the chorus line.

It had a sweetheart neckline, bell sleeves, a skirt that fell in folds like secrets from its waist, and Julia and I had spent weeks designing it for Boris to make with his gentle hands.

"I don't know that one, Lulu," Harry said, pointing to it, "I don't recognize it at all—who is it?"

I took my father's hand in mine and we considered the rose-pink dress together.

"That, Harry," I told him, "is Lily."

acknowledgments

Thank you very much to the team at Simon and Schuster for the infinite care they took with *Walking on Trampolines*. It has been a joy to work with Lauren McKenna and Elana Cohen, both of whom have welcomed me to the Simon and Schuster tribe with warmth, enthusiasm, and great editorial support. It is a fortunate writer who finds themself in their hands!

Thanks to Alison Clarke from Simon and Schuster, Canada.

As an Australian, it is a real thrill for me that my characters have made their way across the seas to be published in the United States and Canada, and I thank my wonderful agent Catherine Drayton for paving the way.

On the home front, thank you to my family and my friends, and to John, Max, and Tallulah, the collective garden in my pocket.

Author's note: I have always loved the name Tallulah, and when I was told I would not have any more children, I gave the name instead to another girl, the one in this book.

Then, much to our surprise and delight, we did indeed have another child, a little girl, who we called, of course, Tallulah. For a long time I thought about changing the character's name. But no other name seemed to fit, and I had by that time grown pretty attached to both of them! So now I have one Max and two Tallulahs in my life—the fictional one and the real one. How lucky can one woman get?

walking on trampolines

FRANCES WHITING

INTRODUCTION

Walking on Trampolines is a story about the thrill of first loves, the crushing pain of betrayal, and how to put the pieces back together after heartbreak.

In the small town of Juniper Bay, Tallulah "Lulu" de Longland and Annabelle Andrews are inseparable. Together they bond over their off-kilter mothers, titter about prudish Sister Scholastica, and spend hours devising an endless compendium of their very own language. When Tallulah meets the irresistible Joshua Keaton, a love triangle begins that will shape the rest of their lives, inextricably linking these three friends together even as their paths diverge and the years fly by. No matter how long the absence, no matter the distance, Lulu's first loves are bound to her forever.

QUESTIONS AND TOPICS FOR DISCUSSION

1. At the beginning of their friendship, Lulu and Annabelle tell each other everything. However, once Lulu falls for Josh, she begins to play her cards closer to her chest, admitting, "I could have told her that he tasted like almonds and smelt like lemons and that the softest place on his skin was everywhere. I didn't tell her those things, but in the end, it didn't matter— she found it all out herself" (pg. 38). Why do you think she begins to conceal her true feelings about Josh to her best friend?

2. *Walking on Trampolines* is populated with characters who play with words, using them to create special bonds or leave multitudes unspoken. Consider Annabelle and Lulu's mishmash neologisms, such as "glamorgeous" and "disapanish." How do these function in their relationship? Also consider the names for Rose's dresses. What does it mean when Harry remarks she's wearing "Doris," or when Lulu is relieved she's wearing "Betty"? How do these names fill in for tacit feelings and underlying understandings in this family?

3. As their time at school draws to an end, Lulu notes, "Annabelle had grown a different skin, shedding who she used to be when I wasn't looking. A new, brittle layer masked her softness. I saw less and less of her as the year wound down; we didn't always walk home together, and when we did she would walk slightly ahead of me, and I could never quite

catch up" (pg. 84). What marks this change in Annabelle? Might it precede her fling with Josh, or develop because of it?

4. On page 90, Annabelle and Lulu argue about Annie's affair: "And if people are too stupid, or don't care enough, to see what's going on right in front of them, Tallulah, then they get what they deserve." Though Annabelle is speaking of her parents' relationship, this statement causes Lulu to immediately realize what Annabelle and Josh have been doing behind her back. Why does Lulu finally reach this conclusion in this moment? Do you think the circumstances lend any sympathy to Annabelle's actions?

5. When Lulu first meets Ben, she notes, "Our lives blended neatly one into the other with no messy edges" (pg. 123). Is this a good or bad thing for Lulu? Ultimately, why is it not enough?

6. After Lulu discovers Josh and Annabelle's affair, Josh tries to apologize to her by saying, " 'It's complicated . . . it just kind of happened; I know it's really bad for you . . . But I love you, Tallulah-Lulu. I always will.' He leant in toward me. 'You're my girl,' he whispered' " (pg. 138). Why does Josh say this after committing himself to Annabelle? How does it meet or differ from Lulu's expectations of his apology?

7. While working on a new piece, artist Frank Andrews consults Harry de Longland: "I can't get the black right." Harry replies, "Black's black, isn't it?" Frank answers, "No, mate, there's all kinds of blackness" (pg. 144). There is a complicit understanding between the two as they think of their wives. Consider the many shades of both Annie and Rose's "blackness." How does it manifest for each woman? How does it affect their respective families; their respective daughters?

8. When Lulu receives the invitation to Annabelle and Josh's wedding, she despairs, "What had I been thinking? That Josh would leave Annabelle for me? That Annabelle would leave Josh for me? That they would take me with them wherever they traveled to next? That they would realize that out of all of us, I was the one worth hanging on to?" (pg. 189) What outcome do you think Lulu would prefer—that Josh would come back for her, proving her the more desirable of the two women? Or that Annabelle would leave Josh so they might rekindle their friendship? At the end of the novel, is either Josh or Annabelle the greatest love of Lulu's life?

9. Frank Andrews reveals the tree house in his backyard needs to be taken down, as ordered by the neighborhood council (pg. 285). What does the tree house symbolize for Lulu? Why is she determined to fight against its destruction?

10. When Lulu first senses the advances of the charming Will Barton, Duncan's friend on Willow, why does she seemingly try to avoid him at all cost, claiming she doesn't deserve him (pg. 289)? What ultimately allows her to give into her own feelings and give in to Will?

11. Discuss the role of guilt and forgiveness in *Walking on Trampolines*. How do the two intertwine and develop in the following relationships: a) Annabelle and Josh vs. Lulu, b) Lulu vs. Ben, c) Annie vs. Frank, etc. Most of all, think about how Lulu experiences guilt and forgiveness within herself.

12. Before Lulu sees Rose descend into the ocean, her mother whispers, "There is no such thing as afar" (pg. 320). After Rose's funeral, Lulu says the same to her father. What does the sentiment mean to Rose? Does it mean the same thing to Lulu?

ENHANCE YOUR BOOK CLUB

1. Read Frances Whiting's column for the *Courier-Mail* about her childhood and her appreciation for her mother: http://www.couriermail.com.au/news/opinion-thanks-for-always-being-there-for-me-mum/story-e6frerdf-1226437571360. How does Whiting's relationship with her mother compare to Lulu's? How does her childhood compare? How has time caused their respective relationships to grow or change?

2. Write a letter to your first love. Where do you think he, she, or it is now? How have they changed in your eyes? How do you think you've changed in theirs? Discuss your emotions and any new revelations that arise.

3. Imagine you're writing a column, much like Frances Whiting, and young, heartbroken Lulu de Longland has written in to ask for your advice: she's just discovered that the love of her life and her best friend have been having an affair behind her back—what would you say to her? Then, fast forward years later: Lulu has just received the invitation to Josh and Annabelle's wedding, and she's agonizing over what to do—what do you tell her? Discuss with the group; you may be surprised by the varying advice!

A CONVERSATION WITH FRANCES WHITING

You've written a weekly column for Australia's Sunday *Courier-Mail* for twenty years next August. How did your experience as a column writer prepare you for writing your first novel?

Probably the discipline of it. Because for nearly two decades I've had to write a Sunday column in Australia, I am accustomed to regular deadlines, so in terms of sitting down to write, I think I've had a lot of practice! Also, while they are two very different forms of writing, I would say the first-person style of the column, which has a warm intimacy about it, may have influenced the first-person style of the book, which I'm hoping also has a nice intimacy about it.

Walking on Trampolines took you seven years to write, while you were working part time and raising two children. What was it like to return to these characters as time passed in their lives as well as in yours, and what motivated you to continue writing?

Writing Walking was such a stop/start process for me, very much fitted in around my work and home life. There were times over the seven years that I did think, "I just can't finish this, it's too hard," but the thing that kept bringing me back to it was the characters themselves. Every time I did sit down to write again, and sometimes it could be after a space of some weeks or even months, it was like taking up again with old friends. Particularly with Tallulah and Annabelle; I would start writing them again and it was like having a conversation with an old friend who you know so well it doesn't matter how long between meetings, you just pick up right where you left off.

I found that enormously comforting and it gave me the motivation I needed to keep going. The other major motivation was a strong feeling that I needed to see all the characters through to their finish, that I couldn't abandon them halfway, and that I really wanted to tell their story.

What have you learned from your first novel-writing experience that might inform your second?

That I don't have to get it absolutely right the first time around, that there is much to be said about the rewrite! As a writer I have a strong tendency to want every sentence to be perfect the first time around and have had real difficulty in moving on from a paragraph if it is not just right. I have learnt that the rewrite is such a valuable tool, that you can get it almost right, not become fixated on it, and return to it later. I have found that very freeing as a writer, and I suspect there's a life lesson in there somewhere as well!

What was it like to tailor Walking on Trampolines to an American audience? Which parts are universal, and what, if anything, could be lost in "translation"?

I found it very exciting, actually, the process of thinking about American readers and wondering if they would "get" the story line, the characters, the quirkiness of the book, the humor of it, some of which is very Australian. But I came really quickly to the conclusion that its themes are universal, the agony and ecstasy of first love, the intensity of female friendships, the awkwardness of the teen years, the stigma of mental illness, the family ties that bind, the way laughter can dissipate our fears—I think everyone knows of these things and feelings, no matter what side of the globe we live on. At *least I hope so. No, I know so. The only things I thought might get lost in translation were some of the Australian products and brands, things like Tim Tams and Iced VoVo biscuits, which I guess would be called cookies in the States. Where possible, and working with my American editors, we tried to find ways to describe some of these things hopefully in a not-too-obvious manner! Tim Tams are delicious; by the way, everyone should try them at least once!*

Why do you think it is important to portray a character like Rose, a woman who has a mental illness but is not defined by it?

This was really important to me. In my work as a journalist I meet all sorts of families in all sorts of situations—single mothers, same-sex parents, homeless parents, homes where domestic violence sheds its ugly skin, very affluent households, multicultural households, and very so-called "normal" households, with nuclear families, mum, dad, two kids, and a dog. And also many families where a member had some sort of mental illness, be it depression, or bipolar, or anxiety, and what I found was that often they were living very successfully within that family.

That is to say they had found their place in it, and the family had found a place for them. They were both loved and loving, and I didn't see a lot of those sorts of stories or families in mainstream media. So I wanted very much to have a character with a mental illness who loved her family fiercely and was loved in return.

Not in a conventional manner or setting, but in a way that worked for them, which is what many families do every day.

What first sparked the idea for this novel, and how did the narrative shift as you wrote it, if at all?

Gosh, long story. I've been such a voracious reader since childhood, and I've realized I've always been attracted to stories where there is some sort of secret room or garden where the main character can go to find solace or escape. So originally the book was going to be about a girl who was given anonymously her own flat in the city and somehow that morphed into Lulu/the love triangle/the house on the island. So the narrative changed quite dramatically from my original idea, which was more about a woman leading a double life, and somehow became about a woman dealing with the life she had.

What made you decide to write *Walking on Trampolines* from Lulu de Longland's perspective?

Truthfully, my Australian publisher! Originally the book was written in both first and third person, but it was felt by my Australian editor that this was very much Lulu's story and it needed to be told from her perspective. Once I started writing it only in her voice, I realized this was the only way to tell the story, and I found it an easier process. Looking at what happened through her eyes made it a much more intimate process for me as the writer and I hope for the reader.

Which character was the most enjoyable to write? The most challenging?

Oh that's easy! Duncan McAllister was so much fun to write; in fact I would say he wrote himself. The funny thing is I had no plans for this character at all and it is fair to say that one night while I was writing he just kind of entered the room and demanded to be written. I loved writing him, he was so much fun, so irreverent, so appalling in so many ways but so lovable. I loved that he was very flawed, but was very aware of each and every one of those flaws. Writing Duncan was like spending some time with the naughtiest kid in the school!

The most challenging character was probably Annabelle, because on the surface, there was probably not a lot to like about her; she was not, I don't think, a character people would warm to, or empathize with. But I really didn't want her to be the villain to Tallulah's heroine—the Veronica to Lulu's Betty! I wanted her to be multilayered, and for people to see that she was basically a good person. I am not sure if I succeeded; readers often tell me that they don't like her, so perhaps I didn't! But I liked her very much; I liked her feistiness and her vulnerability beneath it.

Share with us what the title *Walking on Trampolines* means to you, and what it means to the characters in this novel.

Walking on Trampolines is a very nostalgic book, I think, a bit of a bouquet to my own childhood. It was a far more innocent time in many ways, and I really wanted to capture that. I also wanted it to be a visual snapshot of my childhood, and I remembered as a kid trying to walk on a trampoline with my friends. We would take these big, exaggerated steps and it would feel both exciting and unsteady. Which is how the teen years feel, the feeling of exhilaration and imbalance, of not quite knowing how to find your feet. So it's a metaphor for those years. It means the same to the characters, the setting out on a journey, not knowing where it will lead you, and feeling unsteady on your feet. But doing it anyway, as we all must.

Sometimes I feel like I'm still walking on trampolines!

Where do you think Tallulah de Longland is today? What about Annabelle Andrews and Joshua Keaton? Do you think you'd like to revisit these characters in another novel one day?

A lot of readers have asked if there will be a sequel, if we will see what becomes of Lulu on the island, if Annabelle and Josh remain together, and I would not rule that out, because I think I'd like to know myself!

Having said that, I am happy with the way the novel finished, with the loose ends it tied up and with a happy ending—of sorts. I am happy with where everyone ended up, and who they ended up with! I wrote the epilogue because I wanted that sense of full circle. I think Tallulah is still on the island, I think she is with Will, and I think she is supremely happy. I think she has found her niche and her true love. At least I hope so! I think Josh and Annabelle are together, because I think, as Tallulah comes to realize, they are made for each other. But their relationship will always be volatile, passionate, and full of twists and turns. I think that's who they are.

Tell us about your first love and your greatest love. Are they different?

Gosh! I'd say my first love was my high school sweetheart, who I can see—she says, blushing!—elements of in Josh. He was a surfer, he was cheeky, and we had the same sort of relationship Lulu and Josh did, kind of charming and innocent in many ways. My greatest love would be my husband, John, and I guess the difference is there's a maturity to it, a steadiness, maybe not that heady rush of first love, but that contentment of knowing someone's got your back, and is eternally in your corner.

Get email updates on

FRANCES WHITING,

exclusive offers,

and other great book recommendations

from Simon & Schuster.

Visit **newsletters.simonandschuster.com**

or

scan below to sign up: